Praise for
Saffire

"Captivating! Emotional and impeccably researched. *Saffire* is a sweeping, early twentieth century novel with a colorful supporting cast and a main character who is both steadfast and strong. Brouwer weaves historical fact and storytelling with an expert pen—leaving the reader satisfied and, at times, in awe of the mystery and intrigue reminiscent of the classic *Casablanca*. I didn't put it down until I turned the final page."

—Kristy Cambron, award-winning author of *The Ringmaster's Wife*

Praise for
The Christy Award "Book of the Year 2015" ***Thief of Glory***

"Emotionally riveting and exquisitely raw, *Thief of Glory* is an unforgettable tale about survival, not just of the body, but of the heart and soul, with an ending that will echo in your mind long after you've closed the book. Brouwer is a master storyteller."

—Susan Meissner, author of *Secrets of a Charmed Life* and *Stars over Sunset Boulevard*

"In *Thief of Glory* Sigmund Brouwer plunges readers into the mysterious embrace of the Dutch East Indies during the convulsions of the Second World War. Few authors have such an ability to immerse an audience in the sights, sounds, smells . . . and horrors! Brouwer makes you live it . . . sharing each moment of an exotic and terrifying time and place in a gripping, personal way."

—Bodie and Brock Thoene, authors of *Take This Cup*

"Sigmund Brouwer's *Thief of Glory* is a powerful story, richly told. Young Jeremiah Prins is a complex and fascinating hero, blessed with great gifts and challenged by choices to use them for good or evil. The details of life in a Japanese civilian prison camp are revealed in unflinching but compassionate realism, and the characters depict the human capacity for both great selfishness and great heroism. This is truly one of the best books I've read this year."

—SARAH SUNDIN, award-winning author of *On Distant Shores* and *In Perfect Time*

"I've been a fan of Sigmund Brower's books for ages, but *Thief of Glory* cocooned me in rich words, vivid descriptions, and true-to-life characters, making this book hard to put down. A fan of World War II, I've read countless tales, but World War II in the Dutch Indies was new to me, fresh and heart-wrenching at the same time. A true glimpse of light amongst darkness, made even more special due to the inspiration of his own parents' true story. *Thief of Glory* is going on my keeper shelf!"

—TRICIA GOYER, USA Today best-selling author of over forty books, including *Chasing Mona Lisa*

Saffire

Books by Sigmund Brouwer

Thief of Glory

Broken Angel

The Canary List

Flight of Shadows

Evening Star

Silver Moon

Sun Dance

Thunder Voice

Double Helix

Blood Ties

The Weeping Chamber

The Leper

Out of the Shadows

Crown of Thorns

Lies of Saints

The Last Disciple

The Last Sacrifice

The Last Temple

Fuse of Armageddon

Merlin's Immortals

The Orphan King

Fortress of Mist

Martyr's Fire

Blades of Valor

Saffire

A Novel

SIGMUND
BROUWER

WATERBROOK

SAFFIRE

This is a work of fiction. Apart from well-known people, events, and locales that figure into the narrative, all names, characters, places, and incidents are the products of the author's imagination or are used fictitiously.

The T. B. Miskimon letters are reprinted with permission from the Wichita State University Libraries, Special Collections and University Archives.

Trade Paperback ISBN 978-0-307-44651-0
eBook ISBN 978-0-307-72952-1

Cover design by Mark Ford
Cover photos by Per Breiehagen, Photographer's Choice; Horizons WWP / TRVL / Alamo

Published in the United States by WaterBrook, an imprint of the Crown Publishing Group, a division of Penguin Random House LLC, New York.

WATERBROOK® and its deer colophon are registered trademarks of Penguin Random House LLC.

Library of Congress Cataloging-in-Publication Data
Names: Brouwer, Sigmund, 1959-, author.
Title: Saffire / Sigmund Brouwer.
Description: First edition. | Colorado Springs, Colorado : WaterBrook Press, 2016. | Description based on print version record and CIP data provided by publisher; resource not viewed.
Identifiers: LCCN 2016022492 (print) | LCCN 2016016087 (ebook) | ISBN 9780307729521 (electronic) | ISBN 9780307446510 (paperback) | ISBN 9780307729521 (ebook)
Subjects: LCSH: Roosevelt, Theodore, 1858-1919—Fiction. | Presidents—United States—Fiction. | Panama—History—20th century—Fiction. | Canal Zone—History—Fiction. | BISAC: FICTION / Christian / Historical. | FICTION / Romance / Historical. | FICTION / Biographical. | GSAFD: Biographical fiction. | Historical fiction. | Love stories.
Classification: LCC PS3552.R6825 (print) | LCC PS3552.R6825 S24 2016 (ebook) | DDC 813/.54—dc23
LC record available at https://lccn.loc.gov/2016022492

Printed in the United States of America
2016—First Edition

10 9 8 7 6 5 4 3 2 1

Ivan: Here's to more journeys together along the road less traveled. Thanks for sending me to Panama for this one.

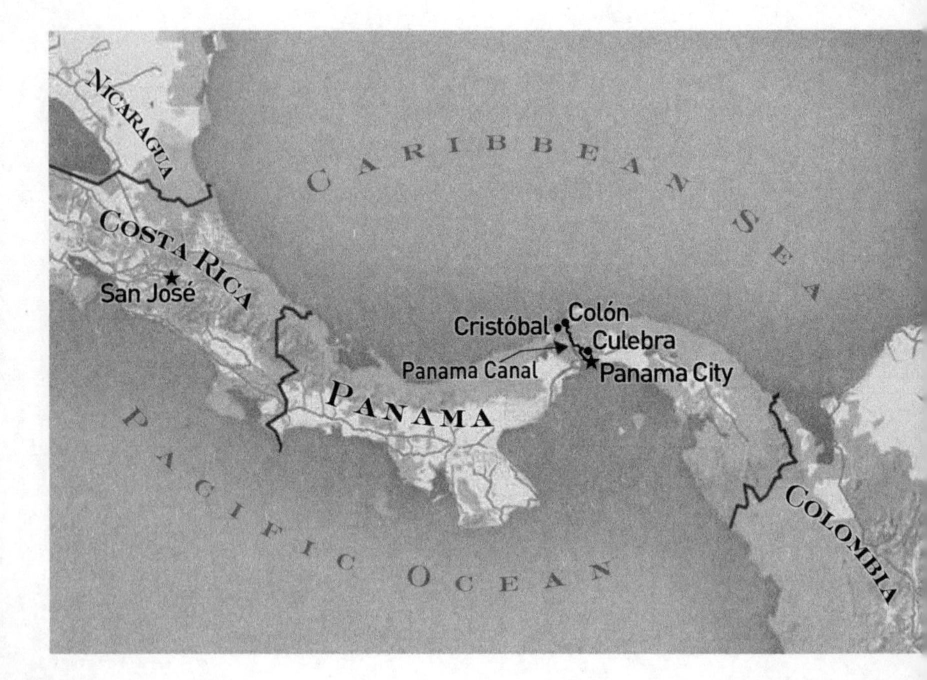
NICARAGUA
CARIBBEAN SEA
COSTA RICA
San José
Cristóbal
Colón
Culebra
Panama Canal
Panama City
PANAMA
PACIFIC OCEAN
COLOMBIA

Sunday

January 10, 1909

Col. Geo. W Goethals,

Chairman, I.C.C.

Culebra, Canal Zone

Sir:

I have the honor to report concerning the members of the Police Department smoking while in full uniform and on actual duty.

My attention is attracted every day by this breach of discipline. For instance, yesterday, the 22nd inst. 1st-class Sergeant Carter, in command at Empire, while in full uniform with badge on, was walking up and down in front of the railroad station at that place smoking a cigar. Today, at railroad station at Gorgona, 1st-class policeman No. 42, while on active duty, was leaning against building with one hand in pocket smoking first cigarette and then a cigar.

At same time and place, Policeman No. 77, also on active duty at time, walks up with a cigarette in his mouth.

These are only a few instances. Most every day at some of the depots a policeman can be seen lounging against something or even sitting down smoking.

It is certainly not a military position to assume and if there is no rule in regard to this matter, it would look like they could be instructed along this same line.

I also noted for the past month, the train-guard of train numbers 6 and 7, has worked up quite a flirtation with a Mrs. Wilbur of Bohio, wife of a former policeman. On last Saturday, he assisted her train at Bohio and on arriving at Colon, he immediately joined her after having reported to his station. On return trip, he sits with her the entire time on train entirely neglecting his duties. Today she again gets on train at that point and on arriving at Colon, takes a cab for Pier No. 11, Cristobal. He joins her there. On return trip he again sits with her and the conductor is obliged to hunt him to have an unruly passenger ejected.

These, while small matters, cause comment from bystanders and passengers, causing the police force, for lack of discipline in same, to be a subject for gossip.

Respectfully,

T. B. Miskimon

One

Reporters called it Hell's Gorge, the world-famous Culebra Cut of the canal dig, in the American Zone of the Republic of Panama.

My view was from an observation deck, with a dozen tourists alongside me at the rails. Like the solitary woman walking on a path below us, they had stepped off the train with me.

Stairs from the top of the hill led down to the observation deck where I stood. The deck perched on the side of the dig, and a footpath, like a goat track, led away from the base of the stairs. The woman had been picking her way along, lifting her skirt slightly to keep the edges from getting soiled.

But . . . why was she down there alone?

Instead of admiring the sight of Hell's Gorge or speculating on some woman's actions, I should have been in the town on the ridge above, across from the train station, at the main administration building. That's where I was to attend a meeting that had required weeks of travel, first on horseback from my ranch, through the Dakota Badlands, to the train stop in the closest town, Medora. Then nearly two thousand miles east by rail to New York, followed by a steamship a similar distance south to Colón, and finally rail again for a short journey south, across the isthmus to Culebra.

But this view of the dig would be my only sightseeing of the entire six-week journey, and only because I'd arrived early enough this Sunday morning for the indulgence.

If only my young daughter Winona could see what was in front of me. She would have been fascinated by the giant chasm filled with apparent chaos, at the shovel gangs and track gangs and surfacing gangs and dynamite gangs. Everywhere—on the floor of the man-made valley, on the sheer walls of cut rock, on the railroad tracks, and on the railroad cars—scrambled gangs of all nationalities, all dressed in the blue shirts and the khaki trousers that marked them as possessions of the Isthmus Canal Commission. Possessions of the man with absolute control over every aspect of it, an Army Corps engineer named Colonel George Washington Goethals.

If Winona were here, she would talk about it for days after. My daughter was nothing if not enthusiastic. I could have been like many of those on the observation deck with me, using a folding pocket Kodak or a Brownie to take photographs to show her, but I had neither. But then, Winona loved to read, so I would write a wonderful description in my journal and read it to her when I returned home. As usual, I would enjoy our conversation, for her quick mind would spur her to ask about details until she could see it as clearly as I did now.

Perhaps if her mother were alive, I wouldn't worry so about her. But it was just the two of us. And no job, no request awaiting me in the administration building, would keep me from her for one more day than necessary. I would do what I came here to do, refuse the offer, and immediately head back to Colón to board a steamer to begin my journey home—

I frowned. Something was wrong. No, not wrong . . .

Missing. The constant noise that had assaulted my ears was gone. Silence had fallen upon the gorge. Drills ceased thumping and workers scurried to a collection area. The observation deck had to be a safe place to witness why the workers had begun to scurry, otherwise it wouldn't be here. Was I the only one to understand the cessation of work and the movement of workers as something significant?

Apparently so, for those around me scarcely paused in their discourse.

I turned my attention back to the woman who had ventured onto the hillside below and to my right. "Ma'am," I called, "I'd suggest you hurry back up here."

She did not respond.

I set my valise on the floor of the deck and moved to the base of the stairs, raising my voice.

"Ma'am, can you hear me?"

On top of the hill, a strong constant breeze from the Pacific up to the Continental Divide whistled through the canopies of the palm trees. While the patterned bark trunks and notched broad leaves were new to me, wind was wind, something that seemed to have a life of its own. I had grown up with long grasses that rippled to the horizon, wind that rustled the leaves of cottonwoods, flashing the pale underparts of leaves like minnows scurrying from a heron.

No, the wind hadn't sent me from the top of the chasm down here into the Culebra Cut. Rather, it was the fact that down here I was away from the gaggles of tourists with the dangerous points of their careless parasols, nattering like geese out of range of a defeated coyote.

The tourists had come, even this early in the morning, because this, the acclaimed seventh wonder of the world, drew them from every point on the globe. They clogged hotels and restaurants at the anchor ports of

Panama City and Colón on each end of the Canal Zone, these tourists determined to send postcards as markers of pride. It was said that the only accomplishment that might ever be more wondrous than connecting the oceans would be a flight to the moon, and since that was impossible, the digging of the canal would be the pinnacle of human marvel.

But I had regretted my descent into the cut almost immediately. On the observation deck, it seemed like I'd dropped into Hades. Another hundred yards past the woman, the dig had exposed pyrite on the hillside. Tropical sun and moist atmosphere exacerbated the oxidation process, heating a narrow patch of ground the length of dozens of railcars. Blue smoke, rotten with the smell of sulfur dioxide, rose from fractures, adding to the haze of heavy clouds of soft coal dust that hung over all the machinery.

The woman, it seemed, wanted to get closer to the pyrite out of curiosity or idle boredom, both dangerous prospects.

"Ma'am!"

I did not like where I was. It had taken my exile years to appreciate that I preferred the solitude of canyons and mud flats where rivers cut through badlands. Horses were my choice, not machines. And yet here, stretched as far as I could see in both directions along the chasm, were the biggest machines in the world. Modern miracles. Steam shovels with buckets capable of filling a flatbed train with two scoops. Beginning at the top, these monstrosities had cut a widening gap, turning each of the opposing sides of the valley into sets of massive steps, with a series of parallel tracks on each level, the flatcars supplicant for their loads of dirt, ready to follow the belching locomotives.

I missed the soft haunting sounds of coyotes and owls and mourning doves, the snort of a startled deer. Before Sharps shooters had massacred the buffalo, the thunder of moving herds might have been an apt comparison to the deep rumble of the steam shovels below me, but now the screech of steel wheels against steel tracks was like bone grating against bone, and the hillside shrieked in protest as the steam shovels tore at its flesh. House-sized boulders tumbled into the shallow black water collecting at the lowest point of the cut.

Intense tropical heat induced the sweat that soaked my shirt and hatband. I missed my arid badlands.

A few hundred yards away, the woman kept picking her way toward the burning ground and the blue sulfurous smoke. What was she seeking? A souvenir?

I took a half step. Perhaps I should chase after her. Then, as my front foot touched down, it came.

A rock-heaving blast of epic proportions.

two

I clutched the rail of the steps to keep my balance and felt the steps shudder beneath me. The shuddering stopped moments later, and I saw that the woman was down.

Motionless.

I ran toward her, my boot heels clacking on the goat track. I prayed there would be no second blast.

When I reached her, she was struggling to sit.

I knelt and held out my right hand.

She took it with two small hands that nearly filled my single hand and pulled herself to her feet as I straightened.

She looked unharmed, this woman whose chin would have rested against the center of my chest during an embrace. A woman dressed in the finest spoils of current fashion. Dark hair spilled from her sunbonnet, and she wiped it away as she took in my unshaven face. I was wearing my cowboy hat, a plain shirt, and the riveted denims made by Strauss, well faded from use. Her gaze lingered on my nose.

That happened often.

"Oh my." This accompanied a slight widening of her eyes and a frank examination of me. "So this is how it feels when a woman is swept off her feet."

She had an accent I easily placed: New York. She had the New York awareness in her eyes too. During the travels of my exile years, I had learned to understand accents—and this kind of look from this kind of woman.

"Dynamite will do it every time," I said.

"Of course," she answered, unabashed. "Dynamite."

"They are building a canal here. Dynamite."

Nothing about her smile dimmed. "I'm glad you were here to help. Just wait until I tell my friends. A genuine cowboy." She paused a moment. "You *are* a genuine cowboy. I can safely conclude that, can't I?"

"Take an elbow, if you need it." I pointed back to the observation deck, turning so my right side was nearest to her. "There might be another blast."

I wasn't really worried anymore about a second blast. Already the workers were resuming their positions. I just wanted to get her back to the observation deck.

I turned my left wrist and glanced at my watch. The administration building would be opening at any moment.

"That's a wrist watch." Her words held a contrived touch of breathlessness. "Yes? A person doesn't often see one on a man. Although I understand they are becoming popular with soldiers. Are you a cowboy *and* a soldier?"

My watch was of Girard-Perregaux manufacture, the first watch commercially produced when ordered by Kaiser Wilhelm I for his German naval officers. It had become evident that modern warfare would be more efficient if officers could coordinate operations with precision. As a soldier, I had learned it mattered at San Juan too for land-based skirmishes.

The face of the watch was black, with thick orange numbers, protected by a grill of silver seamlessly soldered to the round rim of silver. The black patent-leather straps had lost some gloss, but the timepiece itself ran with precision. I remembered my father once saying that only women wore wristlet watches. I remembered my father once pulling out his pocket watch and saying he would sooner wear a skirt than a wristlet watch. That was long before San Juan. Long before the blizzards of 1887. When I was young enough to adore my father.

I also remembered the store in London on a crooked street off Trafalgar Square where this Swiss watch had been purchased and engraved. I remembered why it had been purchased and engraved. And who had purchased and engraved it for me. That had been at the height of my exile years. When it didn't feel like exile. It had been when I believed I craved crowds and noise and the adrenaline that came when a woman looked at me like this New York woman was looking at me now.

"Yes, it's a wrist watch."

She took my right elbow and drew closer as I walked her toward the safety of the observation deck.

"What's your name, cowboy?"

"James Holt."

"James, I'm Nancy Edwards."

"Nice to meet you," I said.

"So you are a cowboy and a soldier?"

"Just here to see the cut."

"As am I. Already I find there is very little to do. But the Zone hotel in Culebra has a wonderful band, and a Sunday night is upon us. While it's dreary that no alcohol of any kind is available in the Zone for us, I hope you don't think it's forward that I ask if you will be here long."

She was hugging my right arm to her ribs, with occasional indiscreet contact of her elbow to my body that had enough ambiguity to be construed as accidental. Or encouraging. Yes. A bold, wealthy New York woman, interested in a safe and discreet adventure with someone who didn't use pomade and cologne and didn't have soft hands with manicured fingernails.

"Not long at all, unfortunately," I said. "Steamship waiting in Colón."

"Such a shame that we can't get together."

"Shameful." I expected each of us meant something different.

Then I saw a man whom I'd noticed earlier when he had followed me from the steamship wharf onto the train.

He was my height, a thin man with tiny round spectacles. Some thin men appear wiry, others prissy. This man, despite his height, landed on the prissy side, perhaps because of the disapproving set of his mouth, wrinkles already established despite an age that I estimated to be midthirties. He wore a white shirt and dark pants. His sleeves were not rolled up despite the heat.

He stood almost at attention. Every hair ordered, in place. No creases in his clothing except where creases belonged. Quite an accomplishment in this humid heat. He adjusted his round eyeglasses with a practiced flick of his right index finger and alternated glances between me and the woman on my arm. Then that bespectacled gaze came to rest firmly on me.

"Mr. Holt," he said, "I believe your instructions upon arrival in Colón were to go immediately to the administration building."

Three

Cowboy hat in hand, I waited on a bench in the outer office of the administration building. The severe man had escorted me to the door and waited until I stepped inside. Then, because he didn't follow me any farther, I presumed he had walked away from the building. Or maybe he remained outside the door to ensure I stayed for my meeting.

I was here because I had received a letter at the ranch before Christmas, instructing me to meet with Colonel George Washington Goethals on the first Sunday morning after my arrival in Panama.

I did not know why the man who sent train and steamship tickets with the letter chose me. Nor did I know what the colonel wanted or expected of me for the substantial bank note I had been promised simply to meet with Goethals. Naturally, I expected the matter to be of importance, but I was here out of necessity, not adventure, and to be truthful, I had some resentment because of that necessity.

Still, with the funds I was about to receive, the bank would no longer be in a position to foreclose on my ranch. Which would free me to continue raising cattle among the brown and gray hues of the eroded hills, to savor being at our place, patched white with snow and brown grass in fall and winter, and patched green with new grass after spring and summer rains.

On the journey here, out on the Atlantic on the steamer, the only mystery that had engaged my curiosity was the requirement to wait until the first Sunday after my arrival. And that mattered to me only because if the ship was late and did not reach Panama until a Monday or Tuesday, I would have been forced to wait six or five days until the following Sunday. Six or five days of impatience before collecting the bank note and returning home. My greatest relief had been a landing at 6 a.m. on a Sunday morning, exactly as scheduled, allowing me to catch the day's first train to Culebra.

Now, on the bench waiting for Goethals, I understood.

A Sunday meeting ensured anonymity.

Sunday mornings, as I learned upon entering the administration building, were the mornings anybody in the Canal Zone could speak to the colonel. No appointment necessary.

Had I been there for a private appointment any other day of the week, a secretary would have made note. Colonel Goethals was one of the most recognizable figures in the United States media, and everything public in the colonel's life was recorded and scrutinized.

This told me that whatever the reason I'd been chosen, and whatever the reason the colonel wanted to see me, it had been determined I must be invisible among those who gathered and waited. There would be no record of our meeting.

This secrecy made sense, I supposed, given who had signed the letter sent to me, and given the scandal surrounding the sender's situation in regard to the Panama Canal.

I didn't speculate beyond this. The answers would arrive soon enough from Goethals himself, and after that I would be gone, carrying the promised bank note back home.

The administrative building in Culebra was an ugly barn-like structure. Rotating ceiling fans wobbled at the end of long hanging stems and stirred the humid air. I was grateful to get out of the sun. I had not expected this kind of heat here, different on land than at sea. Nor had I expected such a diverse crowd seated on the plain wood benches ringing the walls of the outer office, which was a huge shell of a room.

Upon my arrival, Goethals's secretary, a stooped, balding man named Billy May, whose task was to arrange the seating, took my name and directed me to a spot on the benches.

I was surrounded by a spectrum of those helping to build the canal. On a bench across from me was a coal-black laborer sitting with his wife, both with their heads bowed. There was a Spaniard, midtwenties perhaps, with a pencil-thin mustache and an eyebrow that seemed permanently arched, who glanced at me once and glanced away. He'd slicked his dark hair back over his skull and looked like a banker's assistant who wanted the world to believe he was a card shark. Around the room were men in suits and in khaki work clothes, women in linen dresses, and a man with a crutch and his pants leg pinned where he was missing his leg from the knee down. Dozens more. Engaged in quiet conversations.

They all knew the colonel's rules because Billy May had made it clear when he took their names. No appointments. First come, first served. On Sunday mornings, rank did not bestow privilege.

At my feet was my travel valise—a bag of worn tan leather with handles. Into it, I had placed my revolver and holster, which I'd rolled into my other pair of trousers. There was also a journal, with a pencil in the spring coiling of the spine and a photo of my daughter glued inside the front cover. I also had two spare shirts, my undergarments, and a toiletry kit with the newfangled safety razor Gillette had invented. Traveling light was easy for a single man. The remainder of the space in the valise was devoted to the reading materials I had chosen for my journey.

From the train stop in the town of Medora, where I'd been born when it was still the Territory of Dakota, I had set out with an even dozen novels. Upon arrival in New York, I had purchased two more, for a total of fourteen as original stock. I didn't collect books. I read them to absorb the contents, then jettisoned the weight, so when finished with one, I would give it away to a fellow traveler or leave it on a bench for someone else to take. The original fourteen were down to six, which was about right for the return trip to New York by steamship. I could restock in New York between steamship and train station for the cross-land journey back to the Dakotas.

When it did not appear I would get special treatment and an early meeting with Goethals, I leaned back and tilted my cowboy hat over my face and napped for the first part of my wait in the outer office, trying to avoid conversation with the middle-aged woman to my left. When I woke fifteen or twenty minutes later, I set my hat on the floor beneath the bench, opened my valise, and pulled out *The Virginian: A Horseman of the Plains.*

On the steamship, I had told myself I would not begin to read this book until I was headed home, for fear that Owen Wister's descriptions of Wyoming would be a painful reminder of what I was missing. But since my meeting with Colonel Goethals would be over soon, I rationalized that I was as good as headed home. Also, I wanted to lose myself in reading before the woman on my left began to complain again. She was a cigarette smoker, and I could only wonder how hideously high her voice must have been before the years of smoking had coarsened it.

I opened the cover, enjoying the anticipatory snap that came with first cracking a book's spine. That caught the attention of the girl on the bench to my right. I knew her name was Saffire, because that's how she'd spelled it out to Billy May as he took names of those waiting to see the colonel. She'd stressed her name had two *f*'s instead of a *p* and an *h.*

Saffire was mocha skinned, had cornrow braiding, wore a simple dress of red, and had bare feet. Her worn-out sandals sat tucked under the bench. No one would have called the girl cute or pretty. She had knobby elbows, thin arms, and feet that seemed big in proportion to her body. She seemed not much older than my own daughter, and I couldn't help but again think of Winona.

I smiled at the familiar ache of homesickness for my daughter. Until her birth, I'd never experienced homesickness or the fierce protective love behind that homesickness. It wasn't a homesickness I resented. It was one I cherished.

"Mister?"

I looked at Saffire. "Yes?"

"I love to read."

"Me too. It's one of my favorite things to do. If the reading is a story. Information, not so much."

She pointed at the novel in my hands. "What's the story about?"

"In general, how can a person know without reading it?" I closed the book and rested it on my thigh, giving the girl my full attention. "That's the point of starting. To see what the adventure is about."

"You must really love to read. You have more books than clothes. I'll bet most people don't travel like that."

Ah. She had been watching as I opened my valise and wasn't afraid to let me know she was a curious girl.

"So," she said, "if you're going to carry something as heavy as all those books, you must have had a reason to put them in there, even if you haven't read them. What's the reason?"

"In this case," I said, "I do happen to know the story, because I wanted to reread it. It came out a few years back, and I first read it then."

"Then it's good?" She seemed pleased that I was taking conversation with her seriously.

"Very good."

"Tell me what it's about." Nothing shy about this girl, unlike my daughter.

"It's about a place far away from here and a man who has to choose between love for a woman and his quest for justice."

She made a face. "Love story. Not something I'd want to read then."

I didn't add it had cowboys in it. I didn't need any conversation about cowboys, not with the way I had chosen to dress for the meeting with Colonel Goethals, and not with the fascination that people east of the Mississippi had with the notion of cowboys. I'd once made a living based on that fascination but had long ago tired of it.

"Some people like that kind of story," I told Saffire. "And a lot of people like this one in particular."

"What would you choose?" she asked me. "Love or justice?"

That was a much easier decision than one between the woman you loved and your unborn daughter.

"I'd choose the woman over justice each time," I said. "People spend a lot of time arguing over justice, so it's difficult to even know what it is sometimes. But when you realize that you love someone and that this someone loves you in return, I believe you should fight against anything that might keep you apart."

"Is that why you have a crooked nose?"

"From love or from fighting?" I couldn't restrain a smile at her boldness.

"Either."

"Both." Over the years, doctors had informed me that if I allowed them to break my nose again, they could set it straight.

The girl cocked her head. "I don't know much about love. But you are right about justice, that's certain. I want justice, but I can't get people to see it my way. Every week I sit here and every week when it's my turn, Colonel Goethals won't listen to me. But I'm going to keep coming back until I wear him out or he sends someone to look."

Before I could ask who or what needed to be looked at, the woman on the other side interjected.

"I wouldn't bother explaining much to the girl." This was Mrs. Penny. In her screechy voice, she had already complained to me four times about holes in her screens in her apartment and how the ICC—Isthmus Canal Commission—was trying to make her pay for new screens.

Mrs. Penny was skinny and middle-aged, in a Sunday church dress, wearing a scarf over bleached blond hair. She had her hands on her knees and stains of nicotine on her well-chewed fingernails. She was jittery, as if she needed her next cigarette.

Mrs. Penny continued. "It's plain to see the girl is a mulatto. Her mother cleans rooms, I bet. The girl might not even know her father. I'd say she just likes to put on airs in front of strangers, trying to tell people how to spell her name and then talking about books like she can actually read."

The girl gave the woman a silent stare. Saffire's eyes were almost emerald green, a startlingly beautiful genetic aberration in a face with skin color that showed the mix of two races. A face that held a promise of the woman this girl would become. I couldn't help but think about one of the fairy tales that Winona liked for me to read at bedtime, about the duckling that became a swan.

I raised an eyebrow in Saffire's direction, then nudged the book on my thigh toward her. I wanted to give her a chance, without putting her in a position of embarrassment, in case the shrew with the irritating voice was correct.

Saffire immediately caught on.

"I noticed you asleep for a while right here on the bench," Saffire said. "You probably still have tired eyes, Mister. Maybe I can help."

The girl had street smarts. She didn't want to dignify Mrs. Penny's insult by appearing to directly accept the challenge, but she wasn't going to let it go either.

She took the book from me and flipped past the title pages until she found her place. Then she began reading aloud at the beginning. "Some notable sight was drawing the passengers, both men and women, to the window; and therefore I rose and crossed the car to see what it was."

I'd traveled plenty and was unfamiliar with her type of accent. It had an echo of British formality, but with softened cadence. There was rhythm and poetry in her voice.

At her pause, I smiled. "I like how you read."

Saffire's disdain of Mrs. Penny was so honest she didn't even give the woman a look of triumph.

"And a good beginning, right?" I continued. "Makes you curious as to what was drawing them to the window of the train."

She didn't answer my question about whether the beginning was good, because she was already engrossed in the next paragraphs, silently absorbing the story.

I understood that kind of rapture. I leaned down and pulled out another novel, this edition used so there wouldn't be that satisfaction of a spine crack. *The Game.* Jack London. About a twenty-year-old boxer named Joe. I knew from reviews that it didn't end well for Joe. I preferred stories with happy endings but was a London fan and was prepared to make an exception. *The Call of the Wild* and *White Fang.* Great stories.

"A mulatto shouldn't try to reach above her class," Mrs. Penny said, probably in a huff at being ignored and in another huff because Saffire had proven her wrong. "Next thing you know, the silver-dollar people will start wanting to get paid in gold. Here she is taking up a turn when good folks need to see the colonel."

Mrs. Penny crossed her arms and set her jaw with self-righteous satisfaction and spat out one more word. "Mu*latto.*"

Saffire glanced at Mrs. Penny, then back at the book. I was in the middle, and I saw enough in that brief glance to understand that Mrs. Penny's poison dart had stung the girl.

Mulatto. Mule. Hybrid cross between horse and donkey. The girl beside me was not a mule. The girl was a girl. She had her own hopes and dreams, like Winona had hopes and dreams. Not long, I told myself, then I'd be able to begin the journey home, where I could again sit at my daughter's bedside every evening and read to her until she fell asleep.

Mulatto.

I couldn't get that word out of my head.

Mulatto.

Half-breed.

I reminded myself that once you start to defend someone, it's difficult to find a place to stop.

But I went ahead and took that first step anyway.

Four

"Ma'am," I said to Mrs. Penny, acting on a hunch. I pulled out a third novel and offered it to her. "I don't mind sharing all around. *A Room with a View.* Just out last year. Story takes place in Italy. You might like it, and with appointments here moving so slowly, looks like we'll be waiting awhile."

Mrs. Penny's lips tightened even more, and I restrained a smile. I was correct.

I pushed the book closer.

"Please don't trouble yourself," she said.

"No trouble at all." Yes, it was petty. I didn't care. "Try the first few pages. Let me know what you think."

The girl had stopped reading and was watching Mrs. Penny closely. Maybe she had the same hunch as I.

Given no choice, Mrs. Penny accepted the book.

"Lady," the girl said. "Want to read us the first page out loud? Maybe it's as good as the one I have."

Was that question posed innocently or as a challenge? If as a challenge, there was a nice devilish part to the girl that added to my immediate affection for her.

"It probably isn't a story suitable for children," Mrs. Penny said.

"Ma'am," I said, "go ahead. I'm sure if you find any offensive words, you would keep them to yourself as you read to us."

Mrs. Penny left the book unopened. "She obviously has her own book. I'd advise her to stay with it."

"Of course." I nodded to Mrs. Penny. "Just go ahead and enjoy it on your own to pass some time here." It gave me great satisfaction to observe Mrs. Penny's eyes as she pretended to scan the first few pages.

A minute later, Mrs. Penny handed the book back to me. "I find this to be boring."

I flipped to the opening words of the novel and read in silence.

"The Signora had no business to do it," said Miss Bartlett, "no business at all. She promised us south rooms with a view close together, instead of which here are north rooms, looking into a courtyard, and a long way apart. Oh, Lucy!"

"Strange"—I tapped the page—"when something begins like this, with a sword fight between two noblemen, I'm immediately drawn by the action."

"Not me," Mrs. Penny said. "I don't need cheap trash like that to hold my attention. That's exactly why I put it down."

"Of course." I set the book back onto my lap along with my copy of *The Game.*

"Sword fight?" Saffire said.

I winked as I handed her the book. For some reason, I wanted to see how she would react when she found out that Mrs. Penny was a pitiful illiterate woman lashing out at the world. I was ready to silence Saffire with a shake of the head if needed. One public humiliation didn't deserve another in return.

Saffire read the opening words and lifted her eyes to me, giving me a smile that made me feel like a knight in a King Arthur story.

"Sword fight." Saffire gave me a return wink. "I might like this too."

"Not me," Mrs. Penny repeated. "Trash."

"Stick with *The Virginian,*" I told Saffire. "Soon enough you might discover outlaws and shootouts."

Her eyes widened.

"In fact, how about you keep that book as a gift from me?"

"My *tito* would love that," Saffire said. "Perhaps you could inscribe the inside of the book for him and for me?"

"Tito?"

"*Grandfather* in Spanish. Well, actually, *abuelito.* But I like to call him Tito. Spanish is his first language, but not mine. He's the one who sent me to school and made sure I could read in both languages. He'll like a story with outlaws and shootouts. As for me, when I am around him, I sometimes stop worrying about what has happened to my mother."

I sensed that Saffire had again offered an opening, if I wanted to take it, to ask more about her, about why she was waiting for an audience with Colonel Goethals and why she expected to be sent away yet again when her name was called.

Sensing her trust, I toyed with the idea of taking the girl into my meeting with Colonel Goethals. Given that there was no higher American authority than the man who had sent me, I had the leverage to make Goethals listen to Saffire's story first—whatever the story was.

But the girl's story was not my business. Besides, Goethals probably knew the girl's story already. Therefore, either the story wasn't worth listening to or, if it was, Goethals didn't care or couldn't do anything about it.

Instead of asking questions about the girl's mother, I slid my journal from my valise and pulled the pencil out from the coils of the journal. It was here I recorded all the things I thought Winona would like to hear about on my return. On the steamship tonight, I'd write a description of Saffire and Mrs. Penny and how Saffire had shown a high degree of class by playing along. Winona would like the story. She would like Saffire.

I used the pencil to spell *Saffire* in the front pages of the book for her, two *f*'s, no *p* or *h*. I saw that my attention to the correct spelling gave her satisfaction.

"My mother gave me the name Safrana," she said. "But nobody remembers when I was called anything but Saffire. I decided to spell it the pretty way, not the way that the jewel is spelled. A *p* and an *h* is a silly way to spell the *f* sound. I think the people who invented the dictionary could have been more sensible about how to spell words. Like *colonel.* Do you see an *r* anywhere in that word in the dictionary?"

I touched my knee.

"Yup," Saffire said. "In my dictionary that part of your leg would be spelled *n-e-e.*"

We traded smiles.

"And your grandfather's name?"

"He's not my real grandfather, but he's just like a grandfather to me. Ezequiel Sandoval. He has always helped me and my mother."

She spelled out Ezequiel's first name and his surname.

During my exile years, show after show, I had signed thousands of souvenir leaflets for *Buffalo Bill's Wild West and Congress of Rough Riders of the World.* As I signed this novel, I forced myself not to use the automatic flourish in my signature that I once used with such misplaced pride.

James Holt.

I dated the inscription. *Sunday, January 10, 1909.*

I gave Saffire the book, and she accepted it gravely, as if the gift was a great honor. Then she opened it and immersed herself in the story again.

I doubted Mrs. Penny would bother us anymore.

So I began reading *The Game* and stayed inside the story until Billy

May told Saffire that Colonel Goethals would not see her and that since Mr. Holt was the next person in line, it was time for Mr. Holt to have an audience with the colonel.

She would not be dismissed that easily and asked, "Did the colonel read the note I left for him last week? He's the only person who can help me."

"I have no answer for you," Billy May said.

"Then tell him I am going to keep coming back until I hear his answer. And if I don't get an answer soon, tell him I meant what I put in the note."

Twenty minutes, I told myself as I stood to walk past Saffire, who said nothing to me.

Twenty minutes. At most, that was all it would take to turn down whatever Goethals asked me to do and for me to begin my journey home.

Five

Two men waited in the office. The man behind the desk I recognized immediately from newspaper photos and because I had expected him there—Colonel George Washington Goethals.

In the photos, he wore his military uniform, rounded collar fully buttoned up. Here, the uniform jacket was hanging on a hook on the wall, and he had on a white shirt already showing wrinkles from the heat and humidity, the sleeves rolled up. He had a squarish face with a thick, immaculately trimmed mustache as gray as his equally trimmed hair.

The other man I recognized too, but for different reasons. It was the prissy man whose face was set in permanent disapproval of life. He must have gone around the building to come in through the office's other door, at the back wall.

"Mr. Miskimon," Goethals said to him. "This will be a private audience."

A slight flinch crossed Miskimon's face. He probably had not expected to be dismissed, but that was the extent of his protest. Without a sound, he departed through the rear door of the office.

"Welcome to Panama." Goethals gestured at a straight-backed chair opposite his desk.

I remained standing. I wanted him to understand that while he might be the highest authority in the American Zone, I was not under his command.

"I've been fully briefed on what attitude to expect from you," Goethals said. "And it's not my intent to change it. But let's be gentlemen about this."

It was an admonishment I deserved. I sat across from him, putting my valise on the floor.

Goethals opened a desk drawer and pulled out a sealed envelope. "As promised, this is from the man who sent you here."

He handed it to me. I tucked it into the valise.

"You don't need to confirm the contents?"

"That would be an insult to the man who sent me. I wouldn't be here if I did not trust him."

Goethals nodded. "According to that man, you can be trusted too." He opened a file on his desk and scanned it. "James Holt. You were fourteen in the Dakotas when you and our mutual friend pursued a pair of horse thieves. That's where you first impressed yourself upon him. Before it became fashionable to want to impress him."

"He was deputy sheriff. He asked for help. Didn't take us long, and they didn't put up much of a fight. Most horse thieves are scared, desperate, and tired."

Those were the golden years of cattle. A darling industry to New York investors, the shipping of fattened cattle from our prime grazing lands to the markets in the east. One of those New Yorkers—devastated by the horrible irony of enduring a Valentine's Day when his mother and wife died within hours of the other, one from typhoid fever and the other from a kidney ailment—fled to the Dakotas, determined to build a new life. At first the working ranchers, including me, regarded him as a dandy, but his earnestness, while not exactly gaining him true respect, gave us an affection for him.

"The summer of '84 is what I have down here," Goethals said. "You left the area in '85, and he was gone in '87."

So much unspoken with that date, '87. Worst winter in a century, everyone said. Eighteen eighty-seven was less than a decade after our family had been among the first to run cattle in the Badlands, and just over a decade after Custer's ego had led him into defeat and death not far to the south and west of our homestead.

Eighty-seven. After that winter, the man who had sent me to Panama lost his cattle ranch and went back to New York to resurrect his political career.

Eighty-seven. It destroyed most of my father's ranch. Maybe it would have been different if I'd been there. But I'd left in '85, never to be forgiven for my treachery, and pronounced myself in exile

"Then '98"—Goethals kept his eyes on the file—"you and your father joined our mutual friend in Cuba."

"Again, he asked for help."

"Was San Juan everything he reported it to be?" Goethals looked up from the files.

"He tends to color his recollections with a romantic view. Some of us were a little less gung-ho about matters. But as you know, the press favored his recollections, and that was helpful to him."

"Again, in Cuba, you impressed him."

I stayed silent.

Goethals turned his attention to a second file on his desk. "Mr. Miskimon passed along a report from the ship stating that you played occasional illegal poker with reasonable success, did little drinking, showed politeness but nothing else to the married and unmarried women who showed interest in you, and mainly sat on the upper deck in the sun and read novels during the trip from New York to Colón. That reveals something about you, I suppose."

I let the colonel stew in what his report revealed about me.

He fixed his gaze on me. "It should be clear that I need to decide for myself if I can trust you."

"I don't know that your opinion will matter. My promise to the man who sent me was to listen. I'll listen to you for as long as you'd like to talk. That will fulfill my obligation to him. Then I'm on the next train to Colón, and I'll be off the isthmus by sunset."

Goethals frowned. "You've come a long way, and you've been paid for it. I expect you to listen to my request with an open mind."

I gave a half smile.

"I think you are working too hard at indifference. Along with revolver, holster, and books, your valise contains a mug, brush, and safety razor, yet here you are unshaven, as if to make a point."

He clearly wanted me to know that he had arranged for a search of my belongings during my time on the steamer. I wasn't going to give him the satisfaction of knowing that I understood that.

I shrugged one shoulder.

"You'll keep an open mind?" he asked.

"You have a canal to build. I have a ranch that needs tending. Cows generally begin to calve toward the end of February, and I'm looking at three weeks to make it home. Most of all, I miss my daughter. So, at the end of today, I intend to be on the evening sail out of Colón."

Goethals said, "I asked our mutual friend for someone tough and smart and someone outside of Washington circles with good moral character whom we could trust. So far, with the exception of your indulgence in poker, I happen to agree with his opinion of you. However, given your attitude, I now wonder if he sent you simply to appease me."

"Or maybe he knew that I needed the bank draft in this envelope to make all the delinquent payments on the mortgage to my ranch, and he was looking for an honorable way to get it to me because of how my father and I helped him on occasion."

"That you're okay with charity like that surprises me," Goethals said. "I had been starting to form an entirely different opinion of you."

"He knows me well enough to know it's a loan. The sooner I get back to my ranch, the sooner I can begin working in order to return him the money. With interest."

"Unless I decide otherwise." Goethals leaned forward. "With just a couple words, I could ensure you'd spend a year in the Zone penitentiary—located, conveniently enough, here in Culebra—for any one of a list of reasons. You would not be working your ranch."

Now it was I who fixed my gaze on him. "I recall you suggested we proceed with this meeting like gentlemen."

"The man who sent you also put me in charge of completing this canal at any cost. And he gave me complete and unquestioned authority. Putting you in the Zone penitentiary *is* the act of a gentleman, compared to the alternatives at my disposal."

We had now hit a stalemate. "I have discovered the hard way that one of my weaknesses is the unwillingness to be pushed around, no matter the cost. I'd suggest you either call in your assistants to arrange for my prison time or watch me walk out the door."

Goethals leaned back and smiled. "Does that weakness of character explain why your nose looks like it's been busted once or twice?"

"Just once. One punch. Not that I learned from it."

"What if my threat to send you to jail was a test and you just passed?"

"Do you have anything else you want me to listen to? If not, then I consider I have fulfilled my obligation to the man who sent me."

"Our conversation isn't quite finished, Mr. Holt. Someone else will join us. He's furious already that I did not allow him here immediately. I expect he'll be petulant as a result, so don't take it personally, especially because the petulance seems to suit his character and station in life. And, given his lack of stature, I find it adds an element of amusement when I am forced to deal with him."

"I am obligated to listen only to you."

"On the other hand, petulance diminishes you. I'm guessing you're aware of that and already regret it."

I sighed. Would I ever be successful at reining in my spitefulness? "My apologies."

"Accepted. Let's be clear on something before he joins us. Only you and I know who arranged for your trip to Panama. I think it would be wise to keep it that way."

"Of course."

"Thank you. Now let's bring in Cromwell."

I lifted my eyebrows. "William Nelson Cromwell?"

"Mr. Holt," Goethals said in his even tone, "by now you should have realized this is a high-stakes situation. Why else would you have been sent here by President Roosevelt?"

Six

I well knew of William Nelson Cromwell, as did anyone in America who followed headlines in regard to presidential politics and the Panama Canal, two of the most popular subjects in the media. After all, if one takes delight in observing vitriol, blatant lies, character assassination, cronyism, and corruption, then American presidential elections provide first-class entertainment—happily repeated by newspapers of all stripes. We read those headlines and tut-tut with the delicious sense of self-righteousness that it allows us; it would be hypocritical to suggest I had been any different during the campaign the previous fall. In the Dakotas, where I saw a newspaper only once a week, those headlines drew me into the pre-election battles as if I were watching our locals compete for a mayoralty. As a result, like most Americans, I had a thorough knowledge of the running battle between the Republican candidate,

William Howard Taft, and his Democratic opponent, William Jennings Bryan, who was making a third attempt to secure the presidency.

Theodore Roosevelt was the extremely popular incumbent, a man of honor who kept his promise not to run for a third term. He had persuaded his Republicans to nominate Taft, Roosevelt's close friend and his Secretary of War.

In contrast, Bryan's base consisted of the liberals and populists of the Democrats, and he ran a campaign designed to take advantage of the distaste and distrust of the nation's business elites.

One month before the election, Joseph Pulitzer's *New York World* handed Bryan a gift—one that should have sealed the election for him. Pulitzer ran a front-page story accusing Taft's brother and Theodore Roosevelt's brother-in-law of being members and beneficiaries of a secret syndicate. This syndicate had allegedly been set up to profit from France's forty-million-dollar sale of its Panama Canal Company to the United States at the turn of the century. This very sale allowed America to start building the canal on the heels of a convenient and successful Panamanian revolt for independence from Colombia. Headline after headline dragged Taft and Roosevelt through mud, to the point that an outraged Roosevelt initiated a libel suit against the *New York World*.

In short, given populist sentiments against the business elite and these unproven—yet widely believed—allegations, Bryan should have won. He overestimated that sentiment, however, and made a huge error in judgment by calling for the socialization of railroads. Bryan lost resoundingly, and at the upcoming inauguration in March, Taft would become Roosevelt's successor, the twenty-seventh president of the United States.

The relevance of all this for me was that William Nelson Cromwell had been at the heart of all those allegations of corruption, bribes, and cronyism. The *World* called him the Secretary of War in regard to the Panama Canal, and his law offices on Wall Street were commonly viewed as the real executive offices of Panama. The biggest unanswered question was about the disbursement of a now-vanished twenty-five million of the forty million dollars allocated for the United States to purchase—from Cromwell's client—the French rights to the railway cutting through the heart of the Canal Zone.

Twenty-five million dollars was a staggering number that I was unable to grasp. An average wage nowadays was twenty-two cents an hour. How was one to conceive of twenty-five million dollars?

Yet when William Nelson Cromwell strutted into the office from the doorway in the rear, his appearance gave me a better sense of the kind of man who would be involved in that kind of money.

He was a dandy, all right, enough to make Buffalo Bill Cody a jealous man. They shared the same loving attention to flowing locks of hair. The difference was that Cody preferred a goatee below an extravagant mustache, and Cromwell's chin beneath his equally extravagant mustache was clean shaven.

And Cody was taller.

Cromwell's dark tailored suit and vest gave him a sleekness he did not deserve, given his lack of stature. He had a high collar on an immaculate white shirt, a dazzling silk tie with a diamond tiepin, matching sleeve cuffs, a dainty kerchief in the left jacket pocket, a chain of solid gold draped across his belly to secure a hidden pocket watch—and the attitude to match the sartorial splendor that I guessed was worth two years of a working man's wages.

His strut included leaving his left hand in his pants pocket, while keeping his right arm loose, as if posing for a photo. He pulled out a massive pocket watch, flipped open the shiny gold lid, and stared at the watch face long enough to send a clear message that his valuable time had been wasted.

Goethals broke the silence. "Mr. Cromwell, here is the qualified man I have brought in as requested. You can trust him in the same manner that you trust me. Mr. Holt, meet Mr. Cromwell."

I had pushed myself up by the arms of the chair to stand and extend my right hand. Cromwell slid into the chair opposite me and turned his attention to the inside of his suit jacket, leaving me in a half crouch and an unanswered handshake, as if I was not in the room and he cared little for the introduction.

As I settled back into my chair, Cromwell pulled out a cigar. He found a cigar cutter from another pocket and snipped the end. When no one offered him a light, he pulled a matchbox from Goethals's desk and lit the cigar.

After a few puffs, Cromwell gave Goethals a bored glance. "What's his background?"

"As you know, when I trust a man enough to give him something to accomplish," Goethals said, "I also trust the men he hires. Without question."

"I'm not you. I don't trust anyone."

I'm not much of a cigar man, but I do like the smell. I wondered what each inch of ash had cost.

Cromwell studied the tip of his cigar. "He doesn't look like much."

"This will be one of the rare occasions that I agree with you," Goethals answered. "He doesn't look like much, but believe me when I say I have learned that he is stubborn and refuses to be pushed around. He also has traveled the world, and he's a lot more sophisticated than I suspect he wants you or me to know."

This was becoming absurd. I said, "His hearing is fine too."

"Is he intelligent?" Cromwell sent a frown at Goethals. "He doesn't appear intelligent."

"As you've made it clear you aren't going to trust my conclusions," Goethals said, "you'll have to decide for yourself."

Cromwell appraised me as if I were a horse in an auction.

"You can check my teeth." I lifted my gums to show him—and felt juvenile for it. Moreover, I was irritated at myself for giving a hint of how resentful his inspection made me feel.

Cromwell pursed his lips. "That is a distinctive nose. Complete this properly, and I can arrange for a premier New York surgeon to take care of it for you." He knocked cigar ash onto the floor.

"I'm a rancher. Cattle don't care what I look like."

"Looks matter to me. Two nights from now, I'm hosting a party for a dear friend. It will be important for your investigation that you attend, as that will show everyone who matters that you have an official stamp of approval for your questions. Undoubtedly your finest suit is sufficient only for roping cattle or shoveling manure, so make sure you arrive about a half hour early. I'll have my butler provide you decent attire. I do have a practiced eye for these sorts of things, and the suit waiting for you will fit perfectly. Keep it at the end of the evening. I can be a generous man. However, I do strongly insist you shave for the event."

I turned to Goethals. "Colonel, at the conclusion of our chat this morning, perhaps you will pass along my address to Mr. Cromwell so he can send the invitation to my own butler?" I inclined my head to Cromwell. "At my earliest convenience, I'll make sure my butler takes care of the RSVP."

Cromwell said, "No need for that kind of formality. I'll simply expect you there early."

"I insist," I said. "My butler is a man of propriety, and when I exhibit any kind of churlish behavior, he becomes an absolute beast and then it takes hours to soothe him."

I heard Goethals make a choking sound, which he quickly turned into a cough.

Cromwell flared. "You are mocking me. Colonel Goethals, I did not come to this meeting to be insulted."

Goethals steadied himself. "I promised to get you someone qualified to help you with your problem. I'd say sarcasm like that shows the intelligence you need to assure yourself he's that man."

"He's boorish."

"Not everyone can be as elegant as the French, Mr. Cromwell," Goethals said.

"Ah, the French"—I just couldn't help myself—"their elegance managed to dig, what, a couple hundred yards of canal?"

"Mosquitoes brought them down," Cromwell said. "Nothing else. Only a dim-witted boor would think otherwise."

"If that means I am no longer invited to your party, I won't spend much time wallowing in regrets."

Cromwell drew more on his cigar, evaluating me. Finally he spoke again. "Oh, the party is a necessity. Much as I don't like it, the colonel is correct about you. I will set aside my distaste and accept your employment for this situation."

I reached for my hat. It didn't need dusting, but I wiped away a few imaginary smudges and placed it on my head. I was about to stand and depart, when Goethals spoke.

"Please, Mr. Holt. I think you'll need to hear out Mr. Cromwell. I'm asking it as a favor."

I put my hat down.

Cromwell glared at me. I smiled in return.

"Just to be clear," Cromwell said to Goethals, "we have no one else but this cowboy?"

"Not within the parameters you demanded. I'd suggest you tell him what you need and why."

Cromwell sighed and gave me his attention again. "You are well aware of the media scrutiny given to this canal project and the allegations of last October made by the *World*."

"The allegations that you rigged the Panamanian revolt and helped arrange American military backing against Colombia?" I asked. "And allegations that you and your friends have benefited from some twenty-five million dollars in funds that can't be traced?"

Cromwell glared at Goethals.

Goethals shrugged. "You need him more than I do. I won't force you to use him."

Cromwell transferred his glare to me. "Allegations."

"Of course. Which is why Roosevelt has sued Pulitzer for libel."

Cromwell said, "What is not yet public record are the steps that Pulitzer himself is taking to prove the allegations true. He's sent investigative reporters to Washington, Paris, Bogotá in Colombia, and now one of them is here in Panama City."

"Allegations can be so pesky." Petty, I know, but it was fun to watch Cromwell struggle to contain his anger. That was also petty.

"Given those allegations, I cannot afford any hint of further scandal in the American media," Cromwell told me. "From my perspective, an official investigation into the situation at hand would involve an official investigator. You are here because I asked Colonel Goethals for someone with a simple list of qualifications. Whoever arrived should not be part of political circles, should be trusted, and should not know the reason ahead of time, as this would ensure as long as possible the secrecy of his presence here." Cromwell paused and puffed his cigar.

From the long silence, it was clear Cromwell expected me to say something. I gave no response.

Cromwell said, with irritation, "I would expect at this point, you would ask what needs to be investigated."

I angled a look at Goethals. "Colonel Goethals, given our earlier conversation, you are welcome to elaborate for Mr. Cromwell."

Namely that my lack of curiosity stemmed from the fact that I would be on the next train to Colón.

Instead, Goethals said, "I'm so glad you asked, Mr. Holt. As you probably know, Mr. Cromwell is considered the de facto governor of Panama. His circles are the Panamanian elite, the influential men who had the power in 1903 to trigger the revolution against Colombia and declare Panama an independent country. One of those men, Ezequiel Sandoval, is among Mr. Cromwell's closest friends."

"Ezequiel Sandoval." I felt a shrinking in my gut. I had just signed that name into a copy of *The Virginian*.

"I'll be the host for him at the party I mentioned," Cromwell said. "You should like the setting. It's a ranch down in the lowlands, in which he and I share ownership."

"Mr. Sandoval and Mr. Cromwell are in an awkward situation," Goethals continued. "At a similar party a few months earlier, one of Mr. Sandoval's employees ran away. Shortly thereafter, she fled to the United States with an engineer before anyone understood that she had betrayed Mr. Sandoval's trust in her by engaging in theft."

"Sandoval shouldn't have been surprised," Cromwell said. "These types of people are not reliable in any sense. The night she disappeared, not a small amount of jewelry was stolen from a collection. By her absence, there is no doubt she is the thief and, for good reason, has chosen not to be found. What makes it awkward is the child she left behind, who insists her mother never abandoned her."

He paused and drew on his cigar again.

I wanted to grab the cigar and snap it and feed it to him. We were talking about a child mourning the disappearance of her mother.

"My experience," I said, "is that a mother would not leave behind a child."

"You obviously don't know these types of people, then," Cromwell snapped. "The canal has brought the dregs of the world to lap at American expenditures on the canal. The silver-dollar people don't marry like decent Christians. The degree of their licentiousness is disgusting and they breed profligately. No birth registrations. No addresses to be responsible taxpaying citizens. They run from attempts to enumerate them as if we are trying to spread the plague. It wouldn't take much money to tempt them to leave behind a child."

His view made sense. Cromwell had no sense of morality when it came to accumulating wealth, so he naturally believed it was the same for anyone else.

"As you can plainly see, this is not a good time for me to be implicated in any kind of additional scandal," Cromwell said.

That left unspoken what might be scandalous about him being the victim of a woman who stole from his estate and disappeared. Goethals had said this was a high-stakes situation. Cromwell's wealth—ill gotten as alleged or not—was beyond imagining. I did not believe for a moment this was about missing jewelry. But since I had no intention of getting involved, I resisted the temptation to point that out to him.

Again, Cromwell waited for me to ask him something. Again, I did not.

"Ezequiel Sandoval has no interest in any media attention either," Cromwell said, obviously irritated again at my silence. Didn't he realize his irritation would just motivate me to more silence? "Sandoval has made this clear to the Panamanian police, and they had little interest in the matter anyway. As for involving our own Zone police, there is entirely too much chance that word of an investigation into the situation and our shared ownership of the ranch would reach the American reporter for the *World* newspaper. I simply can't and won't have that."

Cromwell waited.

He could afford to let the jewelry go, and nobody was looking into the situation. What, at this point, was high stakes about any of this?

Cromwell looked at Goethals. "If he had any degree of intelligence, he would be asking questions. It should have occurred to him I don't need to find the jewelry if the search risks triggering more scandal. He should be asking what scandal I don't need. And why there's a threat if neither the Panamanian police nor Zone police are going to look for the missing woman."

"Someone on the ship put together a report for us about Mr. Holt," Goethals answered. "Apparently he's a decent poker player. He reveals little about what he's thinking."

I liked Goethals. I didn't like Cromwell. Much as I wanted to tell Cromwell I wouldn't take the job, I wouldn't embarrass Goethals by saying so now. Goethals could find a way to tell Cromwell later, in a way that suited him.

"If he's not going to ask, someone has to spell it out for him and explain." Cromwell was positively peevish.

"If you ask me nicely," Goethals said.

This, I thought, was a fine response.

"Could you please explain to him?" Cromwell said, after another silence that showed Goethals was not bluffing.

Goethals turned to me. "In the waiting room was a mulatto girl who comes here every Sunday, and every Sunday I turn her away because I know why she's here. It's her mother who has gone missing. She believes I can order the Zone policemen to look into it or influence the Panamanians to investigate. But circumstances dictate I refuse to interfere. First, she is a child, and finding the truth will eventually show her that her mother was a thief who abandoned her. And second, I can't let it be perceived that I am taking an interest in matters that should be local. There is already enough resentment about American control of the Panamanian people. Third, there is a letter to the girl from her mother clearly explaining where she is going and why. Yet this is a persistent girl, and from what I understand, not without influence despite her station in life. Last Sunday, she sent me a note threatening to take her case to an American reporter if I don't help."

"Little blackmailer," Cromwell said. "It would be very convenient if she disappeared too. Easy enough to arrange, except for the risk that more embarrassing questions would be asked. And for some reason, Ezequiel Sandoval is fond of the urchin."

That's when I first glimpsed the absolute steel in Goethals, because he spoke with the quietness of supreme authority.

"If she disappears, embarrassing questions are not a risk"—Goethals skewered Cromwell with a hard look—"but a certainty. And I would be the one asking those questions. Anyone who harmed the child would pay full price. You may well have the borrowed power of the governor of Panama, but I have the full backing of the United States and complete authority in all matters within the Zone until the canal is complete."

Another inch of ash had grown on Cromwell's cigar, but he left it there, as if briefly paralyzed by the clear threat in Goethals's statement.

"If you want to help me," Goethals told me, "you'll be helping the girl. Three or four days, I would guess, is all it might take. Start a search for her mother and appease the child, without letting her know that her mother abandoned her."

I sighed. If only Mrs. Penny hadn't used the word *mulatto* and if only I hadn't seen the pain on the girl's face that she'd tried to hide upon hearing that word, I would be walking out the door right now, into the tropical heat, headed for Panama Railroad train No. 2 and the steamship ready to depart Colón at nightfall.

Yet calves could be born without my help, and as much as my daughter might need me or miss me, Winona would be deeply disappointed in me if she ever learned I had walked away from helping a girl close to her own age.

One more day here, then. Maybe two. At most. "What do you need me to do?"

"My secretary tells me you were already talking to the girl," Goethals said. "Help her as if you were doing it on your own accord. Don't let anyone know you are doing this at our request. You'll be provided with employment that will give you the freedom to travel the Zone. I'll pull whatever strings I can unseen. That way I won't be seen as interfering in local affairs."

"I'll do it."

"Don't forget you'll need to be at the ranch two nights from now to ask questions of all my guests," Cromwell said. "That way it will look like we are trying. All the girl needs to know is that someone is making an effort to find her mother. We don't actually expect or want results. Just for the girl to stop pestering us so all of this can go away."

I slowly turned my eyes to Cromwell. In my circles, fancy clothes and a bank account in the millions did not make a man. Theodore Roosevelt had learned that within days of becoming part of our community in the Dakotas.

I'm not sure what Cromwell saw in my eyes, but I guessed it reflected my utter scorn of him.

He recoiled slightly and tried to recover his bravado by hissing at Goethals, "You'd better be right about this man."

Cromwell stood, snapped his cigar to the floor, and spun away to make a dramatic exit, but on the custom heels he undoubtedly used to add height to his appearance, he twisted an ankle and almost lost his balance.

He slammed the door on his way out.

"I don't like him either," Goethals said a moment later. "But I need to dig a canal, and his influence on the isthmus is extraordinary. I'm a practical man, and he is much better to have as an ally than an enemy."

"Much as I respect the president and his office, that's not why I'll do this. I'll stay to help the girl. I don't intend to stay long, but while I'm here I won't be doing it just for appearance."

"Fair enough. Mr. Miskimon will arrange for your accommodations and whatever else you need."

I gathered my hat and valise and stood.

"One last thing," Goethals said. "Satisfy my curiosity. The man who broke your nose with a single punch. How did he fare in the fight?"

"She."

"She?"

"Not a he. A she. I should immediately have seen a doctor about it, but at the time I didn't think a woman's punch could do so much damage."

"A woman." Goethals paused. "I have to ask. Did you hit her back?"

I put on my hat. "Nope. That was another reason I didn't get around to seeing a doctor until it was too late. About two hours after she broke my nose, I married her."

I tipped my hat, lifted my valise, and walked out through the waiting room. I looked for the girl, but she was gone.

Seven

Richmond," I said. "Right? That's your accent."

I didn't walk much. That's what horses were for. Still, I wasn't yet forty, I had long enough legs, and after years of ranch work, I didn't carry fat, so it would have been reasonable to expect that I'd have no problem keeping up with a slightly shorter man close to my age.

But heat and humidity were working against me, and I found myself behind Miskimon's shoulder at a brisk pace through Culebra. I toted my valise, but he carried a briefcase, so the handicaps were nearly equal. Was he was trying to make a point, or did the man always walk this fast?

"Richmond then," I said.

With no answer coming from Miskimon, I just kept pace and kept my mouth shut. Normally, I was the taciturn one, but Miskimon was proving to be the master.

Culebra, on a plateau of the ridge, was laid in grids and dominated by

ICC houses, most of them newly built to keep up with the influx of workers.

"ICC hotel," Miskimon said as we walked past the square three-story structure boasting verandas on all sides. Its white paint was gleaming in the heat. "You'll eat there. Dinner is served from five thirty to seven thirty. As for evening pursuits, the sale of liquor is illegal in the Zone on Sunday. Nor will you find any women of ill repute."

"Poor memory?"

"I don't forget anything."

"Then don't pretend you didn't get a report from the steamship detective." I was still speaking to the man's shoulder. "I'm sure you already have a good idea of my habits."

"The only reports I trust are my own. I don't make mistakes." He didn't slow his pace.

A block farther, the houses were set on well-groomed lawns, with equally well-groomed hedges. All houses had squares of black screens on the windows. The next block, slightly smaller houses. And so it progressed until we reached bachelors' quarters—small and square.

Miskimon turned up the sidewalk to House 31.

"Four rooms to a house, and a shared bathroom," Miskimon announced. "You'll be in the northwest corner."

I would be gone in a day, maybe two. Three at the very most. It didn't matter to me.

"A room with a view?" I asked it mainly for my own amusement.

No answer, so I supplied it, again, mainly for my own amusement. "Wait, that would be the Forster house."

"We've arranged for the rest of the house to be empty," Miskimon said. "The colonel wants you to come and go as you please, with no one to ask questions."

"Seems like a quiet neighborhood."

"Not usually. It's mainly pick-and-shovel men at this end of town, and on a Saturday night and a Sunday, you can expect anyone not at the dig will be at the YMCA or outside the Zone." He paused on the outside porch. "You'll notice the window screens are in perfect condition. If you see a mosquito, inside the house or outside, please report it immediately."

"Of course." I matched the man's graveness, thinking he was trying to mock me in return for the room-with-a-view comment. If so, I needed to reevaluate the man, because I could admire that kind of subtle humor.

The door wasn't locked.

My room was as Spartan as I had expected. Thin mattress on a bed of cheap springs, and a sink, chair, and desk. Plastered walls, clear of holes and dents.

"No women allowed," Miskimon said. "This is bachelors' quarters."

"Thanks for the warning. That's why I spent three weeks of travel to reach Panama. So I could impress a woman with a place like this."

"Your sarcasm has little humor." Unmistakable disdain in Miskimon's voice. "In this case, it is also undeserved. It was only a few hours ago that one clung to you like a leech."

"It was horrible, and I hope the memory doesn't give me nightmares. Loose morals will lead to the decay of civilization. I'm sure you agree."

There was hypocrisy in my statement—the woman I loved and mourned had been pregnant when we married.

I set my valise on the bed.

"Please don't travel the Zone with the revolver," Miskimon said. "I had advised that it be confiscated, but the colonel thought otherwise."

Of course. The report from the steamship detective, listing all my possessions.

Miskimon set his briefcase on the desk. In the humid heat of the small room, his cologne was obvious. But thankfully, not overdone.

Miskimon opened the briefcase, pulled out a card, and handed it to me. "Read this for me."

"You're illiterate?"

That question was met with a stare that Miskimon probably believed was piercing.

I grinned and took the card and spoke the words on it: "'Instructions to Enumerators.'"

"Read it *for* me, not *to* me. I already know what's on the card. I need to know you've read it, and I expect that you will follow those instructions."

I scanned the card.

Instructions to Enumerators: When you have once signed on as an enumerator you cannot cease to exercise your functions as such without justifiable cause under penalty of $500 fine . . .

I looked to Miskimon. "Quitting costs five hundred?"

"Excellent. You *are* capable of understanding instructions."

. . . If you set down the name of a fictitious person you will be fined $2,000 or sentenced to five years' imprisonment, or both . . .

"Good thing you've managed to put penalties in place to scare those pernicious fictitious name writers away from inflicting their hideous crimes on the ICC. Do I sound like an insider, saying ICC instead of Isthmus Canal Commission?"

Another stare from Miskimon. I told myself to stop trying to provoke the man.

"Isthmian," Miskimon said. "Not Isthmus. Isthmian Canal Commission."

"Of course." I read the remainder of the card. . . . *You must use a medium soft black pencil (which will be furnished) . . . use no ditto marks and . . . take pains to write legibly!*

Nice touch, the exclamation point. Maybe Miskimon had written the instructions. This time, however, my impulse management was better, and I merely handed the card back to Miskimon without comment.

"Do we or do we not use ditto marks?" he asked.

I couldn't read Miskimon. Was his question a joke or serious?

"Definitely no ditto marks," I said, deciding on a straight face as a return volley. I'd traveled three weeks for this? Because if Miskimon was as serious about the ditto marks as he appeared, no wonder the thought of being a military person or part of a large organization gave me a rash.

"Now that we're clear on those instructions, I am authorized to give this to you, for which you'll sign a receipt." Miskimon reached into the briefcase, and one by one he placed items on the bed, speaking in an efficient monotone as he set each item down.

"One police badge. We want people to believe you are in Panama because you accepted employment. As a Zone policeman with enumeration duties, you'll have a lot of freedom to move throughout the canal without raising questions. You are Zone policeman number 28, replacing a man who died in an explosion near the Culebra dig. One hotel coupon book for your meals, good in any town in the Zone, consisting of fifteen breakfast coupons, fifteen lunch coupons, fifteen dinner coupons. Zone hotels don't take cash. It is illegal to sell coupons, since the coupon book is in your name. One laundry coupon book. One booklet with 120 trip tickets. These are blank passes between any stations on the PRR. You as the holder fill out embarking and arriving station. One freight train pass for the length of the PRR. One dirt train pass for the Pacific Division. Travel with caution; two Zone policemen died last week when a dirt sweeper knocked them off the flatbed. You are given one locomotive pass for the Central Division. One locomotive pass for the Atlantic Division. Passes to docks and steamers at ports on both ends of the Zone. Notebook. Enumeration tags. Yellow for unsuccessful. Red for completed. To be placed on the door of each domicile, removed under penalty of law. Don't worry. The silver-dollar people are terrified of breaking the law and getting sent home. Report cards for enumeration and envelopes for said report cards. Please insert one report card per envelope. Sign here."

I had stopped paying attention. I didn't realize that when he finished with "sign here," he meant that for me, to sign for the receipt. Which Miskimon was holding out, along with a pencil.

I signed. Miskimon put the receipt and pencil back in the briefcase.

"I hope that was a medium soft black." I said. "I forgot to look."

"After you swear the oath, you will be an enumerator as well as a badged policeman. Zone policemen in each division are completing the enumeration, and it is a natural way for you to go where you need to go and ask the requisite questions you need to ask—and any others. Make sure to fill out the cards as you visit occupants and tag each domicile that you've visited, red or yellow, to prevent duplicate efforts by other Zone policemen. There's a man at the Corozal police station. Policeman number 88. Harry Franck. He has instructions to assist you in any way."

"With what?"

"That, I expect, is between you and Colonel Goethals."

If I was reading Miskimon correctly, there had been the first trace of frustration in his voice. Maybe not. But then again, maybe.

I suddenly understood. Miskimon was a direct assistant to Goethals. A loyal soldier, he couldn't quite hide his frustration at that fact that Goethals had sent him out of the room to speak alone to me and then Cromwell. Miskimon, no doubt, trusted that Goethals had a reason for hiding the conversation but didn't have to like that it had occurred.

"Look in the drawer," Miskimon said. "There should be a Bible."

I did and pulled it out.

"Hold it in your left hand and place your right hand on top."

If he had no choice but to do as directed by Goethals, then between me and Miskimon, I was top dog for as long as Goethals needed me.

"Manners, Muskie. Try saying please." I said it in a jocular tone, hoping he'd find it funny, but I felt like a cad when I didn't earn a smile.

"Please hold it in your left hand, and please place your right hand on top," Miskimon said in a bland voice.

Once again, I did as directed.

"Repeat these words. 'I swear . . . ' "

"I swear . . ."

"Not merely to uphold and defend the constitution against all enemies, armed or armless—"

"Whoa." This disruption seemed to genuinely puzzle Miskimon, as if there was no other way ever to administer an oath but to repeat after the declarer.

Miskimon recovered quickly. "Manners, Mr. Holt. I know you're a cowboy, but I'm not a horse."

"How could I forget? Whoa, please."

Miskimon's mind clamped on to another detail. "Your right hand is still on top of the Bible. If you are reducing this to a frivolous conversation instead of a sworn oath, perhaps you could show reverence for the Holy Word."

I shrugged. I lifted my right hand off the Bible and gently set it on the desktop.

"What's the entire oath going to be?" I said. "Just in case I disagree with something halfway through. Probably something very wrong about a partial swear, wouldn't you agree, Muskie? I'd like to hear it ahead of any swearing, partial or full."

What I really wanted to know was how much I could push this man and how he reacted to being pushed.

Miskimon looked up and to the right. Already, I had figured that out as a tell. He was analyzing. His conclusion must have been that I had a valid point, not that I was mocking him.

"I swear not merely to uphold and defend the constitution against all enemies, armed or armless, but furthermore not to share with anyone any of the information I gather as an enumerator, or show a census card, or keep a copy of the same."

"First," I said, "you carry something like that in your head to use anytime?"

Miskimon fixed his unblinking gaze on me, as if the answer was self-evident, which, of course, it was. I was beginning to see there was steel in that gaze, despite the man's near comical fastidiousness.

"Second, even though the job is to take census, enumerators are appointed to uphold and defend the constitution? Against armed enemies? Against armless enemies? Who makes up these oaths?"

"Certainly not a poorly groomed cowboy in a sweat-stained shirt," Miskimon said, either deadpan or in utmost seriousness. I couldn't decide. Another point to him.

"And, third, the answer is no. I won't swear that oath. Good thing we didn't really get started or it would have been a partial swear and then what rules do we follow in that situation? Do I only do half the job with full effort or the full job with half the effort? You do have rules to cover that situation, don't you, Muskie?"

"My job is to do my utmost to help Colonel Goethals build the canal, so if you decline to swear that oath and still proceed as a sworn enumerator, let it be between you and your conscience."

Again, deadpan humor or utmost seriousness? I had the sense that despite my efforts to mock Miskimon, all I had succeeded in doing was to make a fool of myself.

"I shall bid you good-bye," Miskimon said. "Please bear something in mind. My name is T. B. Miskimon. If you insist on calling me something absurd, let that be on your conscience as well."

"What's T. B. stand for?"

"My name is T. B. Miskimon."

"Sure." I waited until he reached the door at the end of the room. "Aren't you forgetting something?"

Miskimon didn't turn back but stopped and spoke with his back to me. "I never forget anything. Whereas you've already forgotten that I made that statement less than ten minutes ago."

"Medium soft black pencil." I'd finish this conversation with a victory.

"Instruction card said it will be furnished for the enumerator. It's not here on the bed."

"In the desk drawer, where the Bible was." His voice came over his shoulder as he pushed open the door. "If you actually do some work, I'll need the pencil stub before I authorize replacement. Otherwise if it is missing and you have no stub to prove it was used, you'll be charged for a new one."

Eight

For my jaunt into Panama City, I decided to stay with cowboy hat and boots, regretting the need to leave behind my holster and the Colt .45.

Buffalo Bill had done a magnificent job, through the show that hundreds of thousands had seen as it crisscrossed North America and Europe over a couple of decades, of building a myth of the West. As well, in less than a decade since publication, Owen Wister's novel *The Virginian* had spawned enough imitators that it created a new genre in which cowboys engaged in unrealistic actions of walking toward each other in something called a showdown, where the man with the surest draw always triumphed. And the blockbuster movie *The Great Train Robbery* had built on the cowboy mythology. I had enjoyed watching the movie during a visit to Bismarck, the capital on the Missouri, marveling at a film that ran for an entire ten minutes. Rumor had it that the length had worked the theater's piano player into a lather. My favorite moment in the film was when the actor Justus D. Barnes, in his role as leader of the outlaws, had defiantly fired point blank at the camera and all of the audience yelped in delight. All told, I thought, the hundred and fifty dollars that had been announced as a production budget for the film had been a wise investment.

During my travel years, I played a small role in helping Buffalo Bill build the myth, and for that reason, I had no such illusions about myself. I had discovered the result of mythology was that people tend to overestimate a cowboy's athletic skills in the same proportion that they underestimate a cowboy's intelligence or education.

Both misconceptions were always helpful in barroom situations, so the cowboy hat and boots, I felt, were a good choice. After all, here on the isthmus, where else but such a place would I go to get local answers to local questions?

If the selling of liquor was illegal in the Zone on a Sunday, it was easy enough to realize why the pick-and-shovel men not at work were in Panama City. That's where I'd find them, and that's where I'd find them in the types of spirits—literally and metaphorically—most likely to engage in unguarded conversation.

I pulled my books out from the valise and set them on the desk. I unrolled my spare clothes and placed them under the mattress to flatten them and take out the wrinkles. I placed my shaving kit in the bathroom.

I then searched for a suitable hiding spot for the two things that mattered most to me: my revolver and the bank draft that would save my ranch from foreclosure.

My housing was too Spartan, however. And too well built. I couldn't pry any floorboards loose, nor could I find a way to access the ceiling. Any hiding spot that I found would be too easily found by anyone else.

I put my revolver and the envelope with the bank draft back into the valise, along with the coupon books.

I put my hat back on, took the valise, and stepped outside.

Hot. Very hot. Sunset was hours away. Panama wasn't very far north of the equator, and that meant sunset was around 6 p.m. almost every day of the year.

Nothing could be done about the heat. But something could be done about making sure my revolver and bank draft stayed safe while I visited Panama City.

I looked around for a place where I would choose to best observe House 31. It had to be close by and offer mobility. A house was close but wouldn't make it easy to leave unseen. Nor would a perch in a tree. I decided on the tall hedges across the street. I walked across the street, and no birds flew from the hedge. So, a good guess.

"Muskie." I spoke in a conversational tone to the dark green leaves of the hedge. "I need a favor. Well, actually not a favor. The way I figure it, you are under direct orders from Goethals to assist me. When you help me with this, it won't be a favor; you will be working for Goethals. That's important to establish because I don't want to owe you any favors. Is that understood?"

Except for the chatter of birds farther down the hedge, there was silence.

"Are we really going to do it this way? Do I have to walk around and embarrass you as you try to hide? If you weren't there, a flock of those fancy red birds would have scattered when I walked to the hedge. No birds. That means you already scared them away."

Miskimon's voice came from the other side of the hedge. "I'm merely waiting until I hear the word *please.*"

"Would you *please* come out and walk back to the train station with me? I'll tell you where I'm headed so that you don't have to skulk around and blend in with changing scenery as you try to keep up with me."

Miskimon stepped out from the hedge. He adjusted his glasses with that customary flick.

"Thanks," I said. "Here's my request." I passed the valise across to Miskimon. "There's a cashier's check in there, along with my revolver, so make sure it's in a place where no one can take either. Coupon books are there too, but I'm not as worried about them."

I'd torn out a few coupons for meals today, along with a couple of tickets for the train. "I'd like the revolver and cashier's check back when I'm finished dealing with the colonel's request. That will be in about twenty-four hours. Or less."

I knew the contents would be safe. Someone as fastidious and prudish and rule oriented as Miskimon would guarantee it. "As for where I'm headed, train station. You don't have to walk with me, but I think social graces demand it. And it's easier to have a conversation."

Miskimon fell in step with me, and we began the progression, block by block, from smaller houses to larger houses.

"Where do you intend to take a train, Mr. Holt, and when will you be back?"

"To Panama City. I don't know for how long. But if you like, when I get back, I'll report to you to set your mind at ease. It's silly for you to follow me when I don't care to hide from you what I'm doing. But I do want to be alone, so that excludes any kind of partnership."

Miskimon shuddered. "I'm not paid enough to partner with you."

"Nice to have an understanding then. Follow me if you feel the necessity. I'll even send you a drink across the room."

"I would prefer to believe you are not the type of man to tell lies," Miskimon said. "Consider this, then, an opportunity to prove yourself such a man."

"Trust me, my motivation is not to prove myself to you in any way. What's the best drinking establishment in Panama City?"

"You need to be more precise about what you consider best. I'm not sure yet of your particular bent for evening activities."

I sighed. "You always think the worst of people?"

"I've had considerable experience discovering it is an accurate place to start. I've also learned it leads to fewer disappointments in life. For the remainder of this afternoon, for example, since I'll be spared the wretched experience of following you, I get the equally wretched experience of attending to complaints about a broken screen made to the colonel this morning by a shrew whose voice makes me fear for shattered spectacles."

"Mrs. Penny."

He raised an eyebrow. Score one for me.

"What, then, suits you best for a drinking establishment?" he asked.

"Well, let me help you out when it comes to my particular bent. All I want is to get home as soon as possible because I have a young girl to raise."

"The report did say you were a widower."

"What would a report say about you?"

"Define *best* for me." Another twitch of his eyeglasses with his free hand. "Panama City is rife with drinking establishments."

"I first want a place where journalists gather like stupid gazelles at a water hole."

"Journalists? I don't think you yet appreciate how confidential all of this must be."

"Or maybe you don't appreciate that I want to ask, not answer, questions. How about helping me fill out one of these blank trip tickets and writing down directions to a few bars and then escorting me to a train to get me there."

"I'm not your servant."

"But you are the colonel's. Second, I want a working-class bar."

"It will be dangerous."

"Then definitely don't follow me this evening. I doubt you'd survive five minutes in a place like that."

"Strange," Miskimon said, "I was just thinking that I couldn't ever dislike you more than I do already. Yet here I am. Proven wrong. It's a novel sensation. Not my dislike for you. But being proven wrong."

"That's okay, Muskie. I'll be gone tomorrow. Keep that in mind. Confirm for me that you'll reimburse me for receipts for the booze I buy. Tonight is going to be nothing but work for the colonel."

"I would think nothing but."

"By the way, the bars in Panama City, they accept American dollars, right?"

"So do the con men and pickpockets and all the other riffraff." Miskimon sniffed. "If I'm lucky, you won't make it back here at all."

Nine

The Zone police had a station in Corozal, a few stops south of Culebra, and, conveniently enough, the second-to-last stop before Ancón, where I would disembark later to reach Panama City.

I stepped off the train and noticed immediately a man in a khaki uniform. He was a handsome, large man, skin ebony black, and when I asked for directions to the police station, he stretched a grin across his face. "Follow me, mon."

We didn't have far to go. It was on a knoll across the track, a pleasant-looking low building with a veranda and rocking chairs.

"What bizness you got here?" His voice was a rumble.

"I'm looking for Harry Franck."

"That man? I hope you not in no hurry. He talks and talks. Talks 'nuff to make a horse lose its hind leg."

We stepped onto the veranda, and he peered through the window.

"Yah, mon. Nuttin' different. Jess listen. He's a mon to tell stories. Good thing his stories are good."

He pushed the door open and motioned for me to remain quiet. We both snuck inside.

"I can tell you boys," Harry Franck was saying as I slipped past the open door to step into the station, "getting a transfer from Uncle Sam's quarters to bunk here with you is not something I mind in particular. Let me tell you about my roommate in House 81."

Harry had his back to me, and his audience consisted of two other men as ebony black as the policeman who had led me here. I would find out later from Harry that they were called First-Class Policemen and that the term was a euphemism for men of color in general, much needed for peaceful dealings with the laborers, who lived in segregated camps. Here, I would learn, their regular duties were to make sure the rocking chairs on the front veranda didn't get blown away by the occasional strong winds from the Pacific and to stroll the short distance from the police station to the train station seven times daily to see which passengers might disembark.

Those two First-Class Policemen on the other side of Harry looked as bored as teenage boys sitting on the wooden shelf in an open jail cell.

His audience cared so little about events around them that even my appearance didn't rouse them. They just let Harry enjoy telling the story.

"That fellow had one slight idiosyncrasy that might in time have grown annoying," Harry said. "On the night of our first acquaintance, after we had lain there, exchanging random experiences till the evening heat had begun a retreat and before the gentle night breeze arrived, I was awakened from the first doze by my companion sitting suddenly up in his cot across the room. 'Say, I hope you're not nervous,' he remarked. I told him, 'Not immoderately.' After all, boys, I have been around the world, and anytime you want, you can read the book about it."

"Hurts my head, mon," one of the First-Class Policemen said. I could not judge whether he meant reading or listening to Harry. Harry took it as encouragement, but I suspected already that Harry took any kind of movement from his audience as encouragement.

"Well," Harry said, "he answered by saying he suffers from a nightmare. What he said was that when he gets it, he generally imagines his roommate is a burglar trying to go through his junk. Boys, that's when he reached under his pillow and brought to light a Colt of .45-caliber and pointed it behind me. I turned my head and saw three large, irregular splintered holes in the wall some three or four inches above me. Those holes were the last three bullets he fired at his former roommate."

Against my will, I found myself wanting to know more and was glad when he continued. Some people know how to tell a story.

"'But I'm trying to break myself of them nightmares' is what he told me next," Harry said, "and then he slipped his revolver back under his pillow and turned off the light to go to sleep. For sure that's a story I'm putting in my book. What do you boys think of it?"

"We think you have a visitor," the boy said, pointing over Harry's shoulder. I'd find out later he was Trinidadian and did custodial work, for which he was provided sleeping quarters in the jail cell—when it was not occupied by prisoners.

Harry Franck turned, and I had my first full look at him. He was a man of my height but a decade younger and easily fifteen pounds lighter. He had short-cropped hair and a narrow handsome face.

"Visitor?" Harry asked.

"T. B. Miskimon said this would be the police station for my new employment tomorrow," I said. "I thought I'd look in today just to get a lay of the land."

"Miskimon? Walks like he has a broom pole going down his throat and coming out the other end?"

"I've learned not to talk badly of those who employ me."

"That's just a statement of fact." Harry wasn't put out at all at my implied criticism. "Unless you're blind, you have to agree with me." He didn't wait for me to agree with him. "You here about those men getting knocked out along the tracks?"

This was a man who, when he had a thought, would straightaway blurt it to the world. I liked him.

"It's like some invisible hand reaches down and strikes them upside the head," Harry said. "Miskimon is supposed to be looking into it for us. Even if no one figures out how that happens, I'll put that in my book."

All the men in his audience of three began to mutter and cross themselves.

"I'm here to introduce myself as your new enumerator," I said. "Badge 28."

Again, all the men in his audience muttered and crossed themselves.

"Don't mind them," Harry said. "Last man wore that badge died in a bad way, but I'm not superstitious. Are you?"

Regardless of what we were going to discuss, I wanted it more private than this, although my gut told me that Harry was such a storyteller that anything we spoke about wouldn't remain private for long.

"You hungry?" I asked Harry. "I need something to eat, and I have some coupons."

"Always hungry. Especially on someone else's coupons."

"You probably heard of my book," Harry said. "*A Vagabond Journey Around the World.* The subtitle says it all: *A Narrative of Personal Experience.* It's got my stowaway stories, how I survived crossing India during the famine, amazing stuff all through. Bet you're surprised to be sitting right here, with a real published author."

We sat just outside the YMCA building, in a screened-in room beneath a large overhang. At the YMCA commissary, I'd traded coupons for sandwiches of thick fresh bread, crisp lettuce, and ham so tender that chewing was a mere formality.

"It's been a day of surprises," I said.

"I'm only here to write another book, this one about my time at the canal. Back in the United States, people are crazy about the canal. But all they get is the official line. About how wonderful it is. I'm going to give them the inside view. I'm calling it *Zone Policeman 88: A Close Study of the Canal and Its Workers.* It's going to give readers an entirely different view of the canal, I promise. My view. What we've got here is a kind of socialism with a twist to it. People don't understand. You a socialist?"

"Catchy title. I'll look for the book when it's out."

"Book's nearly finished. So am I as a Zone policeman. Don't worry though; I'll show you the ropes just like I was making this my career. I'm the best, so you're in good hands. *¿Prefiere hablar en inglés o español?*"

"Little dusty in Spanish. Might need help with what you just asked."

He frowned. "We can get around that, I guess. Have you seen the dig? Thousands of men, hundreds of machines. Controlled chaos. They were in the wrong place, wrong time, as far as anyone can tell. Dynamite went off before the signal. Hill tumbled down."

"They?"

"Two policemen. Five workers."

"Seven all told?"

"Seven. Took awhile to find them. Only because the two of ours were gold men, not silver. Had all seven been silver they would have stayed part of the dig for eternity. Nobody wasting time to help the silvers more than necessary."

"Gold? Silver?" I remembered Cromwell making disdainful reference to silver-dollar people. And Mrs. Penny doing the same.

"Tell me," Harry said, "would you find it offensive if areas of the Zone stores and restaurants were clearly marked with 'white' for men like you and me and 'black' for men like the policemen back at the station?"

"Labels of any kind don't seem like a good idea," I said. "Anyway, I haven't seen any such signs since my arrival."

"Dexterously," Harry said. "Like that word? The colonel—and I'm sure you know who I mean—has very dexterously dodged the necessity of lining the Zone with those types of offensive signs that I've seen in the Deep South of the United States. This is supposed to be a place where men are equal."

I had my own agenda, but Harry would not be distracted by direct questions unless it suited him. So I sipped water. With ice in it. Amazing. In the tropics, yet ice was served at no charge. Americans changed the world to suit themselves.

"Let me tell you about a Jamaican woman and her trip to a Zone dentist."

I nodded, being patient.

"Inside, the first sign said, 'Crown work, gold and silver fillings.'"

Harry watched my face, as if trying to see if I could guess where this was headed. I had no idea.

"What she said when she saw the sign was"—he switched to a decent imitation of a Jamaican accent—"'Oh, doctah, does I *have* to have silver fillings?'"

"Uh-huh."

"You don't understand yet. She assumed she had to have silver, not gold, because she was a darker shade than you and me."

"Uh-huh."

"If you are a Zone employee, you get paid in gold or silver," Harry said. "White-skinned get paid in gold. Did you notice as we passed by the dining room below how it was sweltering and filled with laborers? They get paid in silver. You don't see signs for 'white' or 'black,' but gold and silver accomplish the same thing."

He scratched an ear. A waiter misinterpreted the signal and glided over, but Harry waved him away.

"Been to Cristóbal and Colón?" Harry asked.

"Through. On the way here."

"You get a chance, next time there stop at the Washington Hotel so you know I'm not lying. Look for the sign at the swimming pool. It says it's only for gold employees of the ICC or PRR and guests of the Washington Hotel. That makes the pool a whites-only pool. Then beyond the hotel are the great hospitals, where gold men stay in wards built out over the sea, and behind them the silvers have to be content with second-hand breezes. You'll notice it's white men in the wards built over the sea and not-so-white in the smaller, cramped wards."

He put up his hands to stop any comment I might make. "Just stating facts, not making judgment about how Goethals runs all fifty-thousand employees. In fact, the way he has set it is akin to socialism, and in a way, maybe there's nothing better. But it takes a man like him, a benevolent dictator, sitting in judgment on his subjects in his castle office on Sunday mornings to keep it benevolent."

This point I well understood.

"I think of the colonel as the three omnis," Harry said.

"Uh-huh." I added encouragement to my tone. I'd stopped at the office to learn anything I could about Goethals and Miskimon and Cromwell without looking like that was my intent, which limited any direct questions that might tip my hand.

"Omnipotent. Omniscient. Omnipresent. In the matter of omnipresence, it would be pretty hard to find a hole in the Canal Zone where you could pull off a stunt of any length or importance without the ICC having a weather eye on you. Omnipotent? You need to be careful around him. Those who cross him or his system have landed in the States a week later, much less joyous but far wiser. Omniscient? Goethals has spies everywhere. They have even Chinese secret-service men on the isthmus, and soldiers and marines not infrequently go out in civilian clothes, under sealed orders. There's not a reporter on the isthmus that works unobserved. Even women working for him. And that doesn't cover anything that might be said about the colonel's private gumshoe."

Ah, so that's where this was going. Thank goodness.

"Miskimon," I said. "I find him to be a curious man."

"Well, you're going to end up curious for a while. Nobody knows anything about him. Not even me, and that's saying something. When you going to report for work? Tomorrow, I suppose."

I nodded.

"And headed to Panama City tonight? Been there before?"

I shook my head. No point in wasting breath trying to talk around him.

"I was just describing that in my notebook yesterday, what it's like going from the Zone to Panama City. Our town, Ancón, is on one sidewalk of the Zone, with policemen like you and me in khaki on patrol, and across the other side of the street, their cops in dark blue and helmets marked the Republic of Panama, ruling their domain of Panama City. Not patrolling though, lounging. I mean, you step across the street you become a foreigner, and plenty try to take advantage of it. Your police badge is worthless tin in Panama, no protection at all. Want maybe that I go with you tonight? As a guide. Sunday nights in Panama City, they are crazy, what with no liquor sales in the Zone."

"I'll be good."

"You sure? Seems like you don't speak a lick of Spanish."

"If I get lost, I'll find someone who speaks English."

He gave me a doubtful look. "Well then, I hope I see you tomorrow."

ten

When I stepped back onto the southbound train from Corozal, the passenger car was half-full, with a wide range of passengers, from men and women in near formal attire sitting with anticipation of a Sunday night at fine restaurants, to young men with slicked hair and hopes of impressing a single woman in the city, to the shabbily dressed with slumped shoulders of exhaustion at the end of a workday.

The rail car was clean enough to seem like it just left the factory. It had gleaming varnished seats, painted windowsills with no nicks or gouges, and freshly swept floors.

The ticket man took my paper coupon with no comment, and I moved to the back to find a place to sit. Better to observe than be observed. Hat in my lap, I looked out the window at the slow-moving background of ridges and jungle foliage. I did my best to ignore the sweat that rolled down the skin along the side of my ribs. While I had walk-around cash in a money belt, a roll of bank notes along my lower leg, inside the upper of my left boot, gave reassuring pressure. As did the police badge in the same position inside my right boot.

Thus, I completed the trip across the isthmus that I'd begun at the north terminal of the American Zone, Colón, in the morning. Yes, north. The isthmus was a gooseneck. North was the Atlantic side, and south the Pacific.

From Colón, the train window had shown me the assembly of the giant locks at Gatún. Tracks went past the slow-rising lake created by the dam just west of the locks, surrounded by rich jungle hills, with alligators drifting in the waters on each side of the tracks. The train had stopped at a series of towns, and I had checked each against the folded map I'd taken from the steamer. Bohío, Buena Vista, Frijoles, Tabernilla, Gorgona, and Empire, all north of Culebra. Now, south of Culebra, I was seeing the remaining stops before Ancón: Paraíso, Pedro Miguel, Miraflores, Corozal. All the towns fit into the ten-mile wide by fifty-mile long American Zone. Taking the train was like strolling from neighborhood to neighborhood.

I reached the final American-controlled stop before Panamanian territory: Ancón. Here, the mountains formed a giant half bowl that held Panama City and gave a magnificent view of the Pacific that lapped against the bowl.

It was an hour before sunset, and the sky was of such a blue that it was difficult to see where the ocean met the horizon. With the train slowing, most of the passengers began to make restive movements to jockey for the door.

I was in no hurry.

During my Buffalo Bill years, each new city and each new country would give me enough excitement to blot away the doubts I could never quite escape about my decision to abandon the life that had been carved out for me in the Dakotas and, in so doing, abandon my father. Now homesickness suffocated any curiosity about visiting a foreign city in a foreign land.

I was the last to leave the rail car. Ten steps away, moving with the tail end of the crowd through a turnstile and down a series of steps, I discovered how correct Harry Franck had been about the international boundary from the Zone into Panama, for it involved only the formality of a few paces across a village street.

No flags or border guards marked the transition, yet the crossing was a clear divide. On the uphill side of the streets were the new Zone buildings of the Americans, each window screened against mosquitoes, each building set on luxurious green lawns with sidewalks trimmed of any straggling vegetation. On the downhill side of the street was a blur of old stone buildings with haphazard, low-profile architecture and not a blade of grass in sight.

On the streets in the Zone above me, rules and quiet and orderliness. Below me, a cacophony of chaotic movement. Above me, the dullness of arrogant Americans. Below me, the swarms of Panamanians determined to profit from that arrogance.

Even as I took those first steps out of the Zone, I was assailed. First by an elderly man bellowing an offer for carriage transit and then by a half-dozen children in rags tugging at my shirt. I slapped my pants pocket and barely managed to catch the wrist of a boy the height of my waist who had explored my pocket for valuables.

I raised an eyebrow, and the boy merely shrugged. Since his hand was empty, he hadn't actually committed theft.

I gave the boy a rueful shake of the head, and he gave me a broad smile. That's when I heard a familiar voice speaking Spanish at a rapid pace and with impressive volume.

The rest of the children, including the boy, turned to the voice, and Saffire marched to them.

"I did my best to get to you as soon as I saw you," Saffire said to me. "Have you lost any valuables? I will make them return anything stolen."

Experience in places like this kept me from patting my money belt to reassure myself that it was still around my waist. I'd been in cities where pickpockets put up signs to warn of pickpockets, just to watch tourists give that kind of indication. It was no different from the hawks of the Badlands, with their piercing screams from the skies meant to force small animals below to flinch and give away their hiding spots.

"Thanks for your concern. My valuables are safe."

"I have been waiting and watching for when you might arrive," she said.

"You knew I would visit the city?"

She shrugged. "Of course."

"Tonight?"

"That, not so much. But sooner or later."

Before I could comment, Saffire said, "Give me a moment, please."

She barked more rapid-fire Spanish at the children. They responded by looking at me, looking back at Saffire, then giving nods.

Saffire gave a wave of her hands, and the children scattered.

"They have been instructed," Saffire said. "And they will spread the word that the tall cowboy is a friend and must be protected anywhere in the city." She tugged at my right hand to lead me through the crowd. "You have no worries when you are with me."

"You are very kind to offer such protection." I hid my amusement at her earnestness. I'd spent enough time in London to understand that feral children formed their own invisible networks and allegiances. What impressed me was her apparent command of those children.

"I am but returning your kindness to me," Saffire said. "Remember the book that was a gift for me and my tito?"

"Of course." I gathered my thoughts and prepared for a slight deception. "I am curious. You mentioned that you want Colonel Goethals to help you with something and he refuses. Perhaps I can help instead."

"I knew it. I just knew it. You are like the knights in the stories I read. Noble and in pursuit of justice. That's why I was waiting and watching the arrival of each train."

This would have been the moment to make clear that Saffire's misconception would only disappoint her. I was no knight. I'd given myself forty-eight hours at a maximum to learn what I could to help before I left the isthmus.

But Saffire didn't give me the moment. "She must have been taken somewhere. My mother. Otherwise, she would find me. Wouldn't you say?"

"It would help if I knew more."

"She left a letter with my tito. In it she wrote that she was going to America with a man and that she would send for me."

"You don't believe the letter?"

"Of course not. She would never leave me."

"Is it her handwriting?"

"What does that matter?" Saffire said. "She would never leave me. Nor would she steal from anyone. That is how I know the letter is a lie."

"Steal?" It was dishonest to pretend I did not know. I felt small.

"There is a man that my tito knows, an American named Cromwell." Saffire spit. "That man. To hear his servants speak of him—"

"You have spoken to his servants?"

"Of course. To ask about my mother. It was at his ranch where she was last seen, at a gathering of my tito's friends. And this man, Cromwell, he accuses my mother of stealing from him before she fled the country."

"What do the servants say?"

"They have no answers. It is only the people of money who can tell me about that night. But look at me. Am I someone who can speak to them? Months now, and no one will look for her."

"What about your father? Does he have questions?"

"My father worked in the early years of the canal. He died of yellow fever when I was a baby."

Easy to assume that the color of his skin would have had a lot to do with that. Zone policeman number 88 Harry Franck had made that clear. White workers received the best medical attention. Darker workers did not.

"Your relatives?" I asked. "Can they help?"

She was silent.

"Saffire, where do you stay?"

"It is commonly known that I am under the protection of my tito. I stay where I please."

Although all around me was noise and chaos, in my mind was a horrible vacuum of silence as I had a moment of comprehension.

She caught my mood and stuck out her chin. "It is something I prefer."

I needed to treat her as an equal, or I would disappoint her. "I'm glad to hear that. I'm glad too that you were waiting for me. If you like, I can go with you to the police in Panama and ask about your mother."

Again, she spat. "They have been told about the letter. They choose to believe the letter against my word."

"Then how can I help? If the police won't do anything . . ."

"You are American. Talk to those who were at the party on the night she didn't return to me. The money people. I can give you their names, and you can ask questions on my behalf. Even tonight you could begin. I will take you to the National Hotel. There is no doubt that some will be there on a Sunday evening. Later in the evening, I can help you find any manner of things that you might want. When Americans leave the Zone, they are like men set free from prison. If you drink, I'll make sure you come to no harm."

In another hemisphere, my own daughter would fall asleep to the yelps of coyotes. In the morning, she would wake to songs of meadowlarks.

But Saffire . . . such lack of innocence. I wasn't sure if I wanted to hit something or weep. I hid my reaction from her.

"I am a man of solitude, but I would be glad to visit the National. I'm also told that's where I can find the reporter for the *Panama Star & Herald.* Miguel Vasquez."

"Oh," Saffire said dismissively. "Him."

"Him?"

She snorted. "When he gets drunk, he roams the alleys to look for this big woman who will dress him in baby's clothes and cradle him in her arms and sing lullabies to him until he falls asleep."

"Then it would be wise to spend time with him before he gets drunk."

Eleven

"Everyone takes a carriage in Panama." Saffire pointed me to a collection area with hackmen. "Anything more than a dime, and he is cheating you."

She left unspoken the assumption that a mulatto girl should not negotiate for someone like me.

"Let's walk," I said. "I've been far too long on the steamer, and I want to get my land legs back."

I moved past the clumps of horse droppings, and Saffire stayed at my side. Horse manure never bothered me. It was mainly digested grass and washed away with a single rain. Dog leavings, however, were another matter. The cobblestones of London had been stained with them. Smelly, clinging to a boot.

"Be my guide." I pointed at the round stone watchtowers of a building with curving parapets. "What's that?"

She looked at me and there was enough sunlight remaining in the day for me to admire again the deep green of her eyes and the beauty that would someday appear in her face.

"Chiriqui Prison."

It had that kind of institutional look, and uniformed guards with bayonets patrolled the parapets.

Because we were walking, each step took us down and closer to where the waters of the Pacific splashed onto stone ledges. The salt-spray smell mixed with the smell of open garbage that littered the streets.

"What was it you asked of the colonel?" she said. "What did you hope he would help you with? Everyone there on a Sunday has something to request."

"I was there to deliver a message to him, and because of it, I have general questions about Panama and the men who rule this country."

"Then I am glad that we both want you to speak to those same men. Are there questions that I can answer?"

"Yes, what is your mother's name?"

"Jade. She is Jade and I am Saffire."

"Of course. Jewels of great beauty."

"My mother is. I am not." She spoke matter-of-factly. It would have been condescending to contradict her or point out that someday she would be beautiful.

"Where was she employed?" I asked.

"In the home of my tito, here in Panama City. She worked in the kitchen. Tito was very fond of her cooking, so often he invited her to cook for him on his travels. He tells me often how particular his stomach is and that she soothed it all the time wherever she traveled with him."

"She was cooking, then, for him on the night that she—"

"My tito is very sad that she is no longer able to cook for him. Unfortunately, he believes the letter. I don't."

I walked along with her and did not force her to answer more questions.

I was grateful for the breeze and a chance to escape the humid heat that made me feel claustrophobic. The smells were cloying, so unlike the clean sharpness of sage along the Little Missouri, when the stems were freshly snapped by horse hooves.

We reached a market of sorts, with fish and slaughtered lambs in stalls across from vendors who looked to be in the business of selling rotten fruit. The buzz of flies seemed to growl at us as we continued toward the buildings of the town's core.

A tinny sound of music, straining for attention, came from ahead, nearer the city center.

Saffire noticed that this sound caught my attention. "That's the band concert at the Cathedral Plaza. Every Sunday evening. I could point you there, but it would be better if I stayed behind. I'm not allowed there. Only on Thursdays, when the concert for coloreds is at the Plaza Santa Ana."

"Then take me to the National. I am not interested in the concert."

Ten minutes later, we skirted the Cathedral Plaza, ringed by palm trees and packed with—as Saffire explained—the perfumed dandies of the aristocrats of Panama. From the cautious distance that I kept from the crowd, I saw the gaudily dressed women with elaborate hair and the men in white suits. Women and men of varying shades of skin, but none dark with pure African blood. I could easily identify the Americans in the crowd because their comparative height put their heads and shoulders in outline against the setting sun. As further contrast, their body language was unemotional and almost soldierly, while the Panamanians tended to sway in rhythm to the beat of the band. That lack of emotion of the engineers would no doubt change after enough nips at the flasks likely tucked in their suit jackets.

The plaza was surrounded by cathedrals and other magnificent stone buildings weathered over the centuries. These buildings had witnessed pirate attacks and revolutions. And on the hills that formed the bowl of the city, houses crowded on crooked streets that wound among the palm trees. This was not a city platted into recent existence, like the towns on the Northern Pacific, from one end of the Dakotas to the other. This city had seen centuries of gold miners and slaves and buccaneers and plantation owners and bankers and soldiers.

I pictured the straight, wide streets of the railroad town of Medora in the Dakotas, the wood buildings with false fronts, and the keening winds that swept my native grasslands—and again fought a stab of homesickness. One day, maybe two. Then I would be gone from Panama.

twelve

Saffire did not take me to the small cobblestone plaza that reached to the grand entrance of the National, or take me between the pillars on the broad front veranda, past the uniformed bellhops and through the magnificent front doors into the lobby with the frond-shaped fans making lazy circles above marble floors.

Instead, Saffire led me to the rear of the building, to the alley in deep shadow as twilight approached. Through a door that was propped open, letting aromas of spices and steamed food drift into the heat outside. An elderly black woman with a soiled white apron over an equally soiled white uniform leaned against the outer wall beside the door, sucking hard on a hand-twisted cigarette.

"It's early." The woman's croaked words, tinged in a Jamaican accent, were directed at Saffire, not me. "Nothing is ready for you."

"I'll be back again later," Saffire said. "Right now, my friend here needs an introduction from Stefan."

"As long as your friend is a generous man."

"He'd love to help," Saffire said. "He's a good man."

Saffire poked me in the ribs with a forefinger. "One dollar. American. That's generous enough."

While I could only guess at the reason for a bribe, going into my money belt in an open situation like this would be the height of stupidity. "On my way out. I'll donate then."

The elderly woman sucked again on her cigarette and exhaled as she scrutinized my face. "See that it happens." With that, she resumed an unseeing stare at the backside of the building on the other side of the alley.

Saffire led me into a kitchen crowded with fast-moving waiter staff—all black—and cooks who yelled at each other in Spanish.

Most were too busy to glance at Saffire or me, but those who did gave Saffire a quick smile and continued without much apparent curiosity about my presence with her.

"I wouldn't be allowed to walk through the hotel," Saffire explained. "This is the only way we can reach Stefan, and it's important that I'm the one who introduces you to Stefan. Otherwise, he has no reason to introduce you to those who can help with your questions."

Stefan was a huge Jamaican, a decade older than I. His tightly cropped hair was nearly fully gray, and he wore an immaculate, pressed waiter's suit. He was surveying the large dining room just outside the swinging doors that led from the kitchen into the dining room. The door on the right led out. The swinging door on the left led in.

Saffire pushed open the door on the right and hissed for his attention.

Stefan stepped backward with a smooth glide through the door on the left and joined us inside the kitchen.

"Stefan, this is my friend. His name is Mr. Holt. He has promised to help me look for my mother. Mr. Holt, meet Stefan. Stefan is a kind man and helps me a great deal with many things."

"A pleasure." Stefan offered a slight bow of his head. "Anyone who helps this young woman is a friend of mine."

"Miguel Vasquez," Saffire said. "Is he here?"

The slightest of grimaces crossed Stefan's face.

"It is business," Saffire said. "You can be sure of that. Mr. Holt is no friend of that man, but he wishes to speak to anyone who might be a friend of my tito."

"Mr. Vasquez is not here, but an American and a German are already waiting at his table. The American is a journalist who once worked at the *Star.* As for the German, he has been here frequently over the last few weeks, often with the young Panamanian crowd, from families who pretend to be rulers of the city. You know, of course, who I am talking about. The German claims to be a tourist, but I think he sides with Colombians."

Revolutions are never really over. Especially for the defeated.

"If you could arrange it," I said, "I would be interested in buying those gentlemen a round of drinks and joining them for a few minutes."

"Gin tonic for the American. Lemp's lager for the German, and he complains each time that it doesn't live up to the worst of German lagers. And for you?"

"Tonic." Assurances that the isthmus was malaria free didn't comfort me, so an extra dose of quinine never hurt. "Nothing added."

"Of course," Stefan said. He motioned for the nearest waiter, gave instructions, and sent him for drinks. He looked back at me. "Please wait here."

Stefan pushed open the swinging door on the right and moved into the dining room.

I used the opportunity to reach under my shirt and pull some dollar bills from my money belt. I handed three to Saffire, aware that it was a lot of money for a child who likely spent much of her time as a street urchin.

"One dollar for the contribution that you mentioned," I said. "I trust you'll take care of Stefan and the drinks with the remainder?"

There was something about Saffire's manner of dealing with Stefan that suggested she would be generous to him because of past and future favors.

Saffire folded her fingers over the money and it disappeared.

The waiter returned, carrying a tray with two glasses of tonic and a tall glass with the amber lager.

Stefan returned at the same time. "Please follow."

"I have to stay in the kitchen," Saffire said. "But don't worry, I'll wait for you, no matter how long you need me here."

I followed the waiter and Stefan into the dining room. Lights were already burning in sconces on the walls, and the dimness added the proper conspiratorial atmosphere to the muted conversations around the room.

Two men were seated at a table for six, with five place mats and settings. Easy guess that they were waiting for three more to make the total five.

"Mr. Holt," Stefan said, "these gentlemen would be pleased if you joined them."

Both stood. Stefan reached for the cowboy hat I held, probably to place it on a coatrack.

"If you don't mind, I'll set it on a chair, out of sight."

Stefan nodded, then spun on his heels and moved away in his gliding gait.

"Robert Waldschmidt," the man on the right said as introduction. Early thirties, I guessed. He had thinning hair combed over his head, an eye patch over his left eye, a bow tie, and a surprisingly wide chest for an otherwise skinny body.

"Earl Harding," the other man said. "Journalist. The *World*."

He, then, was the man who had been sent by Pulitzer in pursuit of anything to smear Cromwell, and by extension, Roosevelt's brother-in-law.

Harding was much taller than Waldschmidt. Pencil-thin mustache. Vertical stripes in a suit that had spent weeks between steam presses. This man was closer to my age. "Thanks for the drinks."

We moved through the formalities of handshakes, then sat and scraped chairs as each of us moved closer to the table. To fulfill my promise to Stefan, I put my hat on the chair beside me.

"I hope you don't mind," Harding said. "But when our expected guests arrive, we'll need privacy. Tonight I am combining business with pleasure."

"Understood," I said.

Harding was giving me a peculiar look. "I've seen you before."

"I don't live in New York."

"But I lived in Panama for years during my time at the local newspaper." Harding studied me. "Perhaps we met then."

"This is my first time in Panama."

"You can probably guess why I've been sent back here for a few weeks," Harding said. "Roosevelt has sued Pulitzer for libel, and Roosevelt needs to be reined in. He's bullied the country long enough. My former stint with the *Star & Herald* here puts me in a good situation to dig up the facts."

"I'm vaguely familiar with the situation, though not that interested." That was the truth, as my immediate interest was in regard to local politics. If Harding had once been at the paper in Panama City, I was at the right table.

"I know I've seen your face before," Harding said. "I remember faces. I pride myself on it. I'm in a profession where it's a valuable asset."

"We haven't met," I said.

"Then I've seen your photograph before. Newspaper?"

"Unlikely."

Harding kept examining me. "That answer implies your face *has* been in the newspaper before but you doubt I'd have seen it. But remember my profession." Harding snapped his fingers. "Train accident. Buffalo Bill's show."

Our three-car train, northbound with equipment and employees and livestock, had departed Charlotte, North Carolina, on the evening of October 28, 1901, for the last performance of the season in Danville, Virginia. Early the next morning, the engineer of a southbound freight had misread orders to wait on a side track as we passed, and the trains suffered a head-on collision on a straight stretch of track.

Harding nodded, enthusiastic at his own ability to recall. "North Carolina, right? Seven, maybe eight years ago. Collision with a freight train. Annie Oakley nearly killed, hair turned white as a result. No human lives lost, but one hundred and ten horses had to be put down. Those are the details, correct?"

That's how William Cody had played it for the press. *No human lives lost.* Easier to nod than to give any indication of how that accident had changed my life. Or that William Cody had been technically correct, but totally wrong. Months after Cody's statement, one person did die from injuries suffered, making me a widower.

"You were in a photo that made the *New York Times,*" Harding said. "I remember wishing the *World* had purchased the rights. Your nose was freshly broken, and the bruises were plain to see in the photo, which added to the drama. It happened in the train accident, I would guess."

I had never seen the photo. Never wanted to. I'd been told about it too many times. I'd been kneeling beside one of the horses, captured in a pose of grief. The photo had been deceptive. The accident hadn't broken my nose. And it wasn't a horse that I was grieving.

I gave no answer.

Waldschmidt filled the silence. "Buffalo Bill? That man that stopped the Indian Wars?"

Not so, but William Cody had done a superb job of building the myth around his minor role as a scout.

Harding nodded. "Officially, it was *Buffalo Bill's Wild West and Congress of Rough Riders of the World.* Did you see it when it toured Germany?"

"Yah!" Waldschmidt clapped and turned to me. "But so much noise with the buffalo and all the shooting and the Indians trying to take scalps. I confess I don't remember seeing you."

"There were many cowboys in the show. I'm not that memorable."

"Except for the photo," Harding said. "It probably sold a lot of papers."

"Still!" Waldschmidt took a drink. "A cowboy! Famous from a photo! Perhaps another evening we could buy you drinks. How gruesome, those scalpings. Such stories you could tell us. Yah? And this shooting of each other in showdowns. How exciting. We have nothing like that in Germany, I promise. All dreariness. Too much order and regulation. I so admire the freedom of the American West. Perhaps that will be my next stop on my journeys."

"Mr. Waldschmidt"—Harding watched me over his drink—"is a man with too much wealth and too much time on his hands. So he travels at his leisure, buying friends wherever he goes."

"Much better to buy friends." Waldschmidt's grin crinkled his rosy cheeks and nudged his eye patch. "If it's about money and gifts, you can trust that you understand their motives. Yah? You for example, Mr. Holt, perhaps I could cover the cost of a suite here at the hotel for a few weeks. Then you could tell me many stories, and we would be wonderful friends until I stopped paying for your suite."

"I don't expect to be here long."

"Well, you have me curious," Harding said. "And I make my living by my curiosity. You had a reason for wanting to join us, I assume."

"I thought, who better than a journalist to explain the local politics?"

"Which makes me curious why such knowledge would be important to a cowboy who won't be here long."

"I'm doing a favor for a friend."

"Does your friend have business interests in the canal?" Harding leaned back in his chair. "Or possible business interests?"

"Where I'm from, friends help each other without needing a reason except for the friendship. If this was a business trip, then it wouldn't be about a friend. It would be an employer."

Harding sipped at his gin and tonic. "Ask your questions. I'll probably learn as much from what you ask as you would tell me about yourself."

I wiped the condensation from my glass of tonic. "Tell me, if you can, about a man named Ezequiel Sandoval. I understand he is a close friend of William Nelson Cromwell."

Harding and Waldschmidt exchanged glances.

"First," Harding said, "let me point out that in some places in Panama, that could be a dangerous question for an Americano to ask. Are you sure you want to continue this conversation?"

"I'm here, aren't I?"

Harding gave a slow nod. "Very well. Panama truly is a small country. The fact that you ask so openly after my warning is either a reasonable coincidence or a remarkable bluff and you are involved at a level that I would be eager to know, considering my involvement in a very public fight against Roosevelt's libel suit and Cromwell's cronyism."

"Go with coincidence," I said. "I arrived in Colón this morning, and I hope to go back across the isthmus as soon as possible to catch a steamer back to New York. I'd like to know who Ezequiel Sandoval is."

"Ah," Harding said. "Here's why I could believe that your interest in Señor Sandoval is also coincidence. There are perhaps fifteen families who matter in Panama, and he is the patriarch of one of them. Mr. Waldschmidt and I are waiting for his daughter and her escort, so if your questioning is a coincidence, it's a one-in-fifteen happenstance. That doesn't stretch credence too far."

Harding turned to Waldschmidt. "What do you think, Mr. Waldschmidt? Coincidence? Or something deeper? After all, you do love this type of intrigue, don't you?"

"The wealthy get bored so easily," Waldschmidt said. "I live for intrigue."

Harding said, "I suggest, Mr. Holt, that you and I have lunch tomorrow. Just the two of us. Would that suit you? You can find me by asking at the *Star & Herald*."

"I hope to be gone by tomorrow."

"Unfortunate." Harding gave a nod to the front of the dining room, where Stefan was escorting two men and a woman. "Because it looks like our time here is over. Our guests have arrived. As promised, Miguel Vasquez from the *Star & Herald* is delivering Señor Sandoval's daughter, Raquel, and her fiancé, Raoul Amador."

"Amador," Waldschmidt whispered to me, a sense of awe in his voice. "Amador!"

"Of course, Amador." For my own amusement, I added the same sense of awe.

I was interested, however. Here were two who would know Saffire's mother.

Waldschmidt stayed in a theatrical whisper. "He is the son of Dr. Manuel Amador Guerrero, who headed the revolution that broke Panama from Colombia! And there are whispers of more intrigue, since many of the other families are so unhappy with the Americans."

"Fascinating," I said in a return whisper.

The German apparently didn't understand sarcasm, for he continued as if he believed I was hungry for more. "And Raquel, the only child in the

Sandoval family, is almost militant in her support of women's suffrage. She fully believes she can force Panama to give women the vote within a decade. It's the last subject you want her to start upon at a dinner. Yah?"

"Yah."

Then the guests arrived.

Thirteen

I rose with Harding and Waldschmidt to greet the newcomers, conscious that conversations had stopped around them.

Vasquez was a tiny man with a round face beaded with sweat, dressed in a crumpled white linen suit, who swayed as if he had already been drinking. I tried to shove aside an image of the man fully drunk, dressed as a baby, in the arms of a large woman singing lullabies. If Saffire knew about this proclivity, so did many others. So the drop in conversations was certainly not because of respect for Vasquez.

The other two who approached, however, seemed like royalty in both dress and posture.

Raoul Amador was tall in comparison to his countrymen. Midthirties, hawk-like face with all the proper edges of handsomeness. Long, flowing hair, perfectly barbered—a direct contrast to my hair, hacked by myself in front of a mirror. Amador's attire was impeccable, fitted across broad shoulders and a trim waistline.

As for Raquel Sandoval, who had her left arm linked in Raoul's right elbow, she looked to be in her late twenties or early thirties. My instant judgment was that in all the years traveling to countless cities and countries as a roughrider in the world's most famous Wild West show, I had not seen a woman of more stunning beauty.

Later that night, with clarity that would make it difficult for me to find sleep, I'd remember the sheen of the hair falling to her shoulders, the slight parting of her lips in a smile that showed a gleam of teeth, the curve of her nose, the lift of her eyebrows, the smoldering darkness of her eyes, the complexion of perfect skin. And I would remember the mischief in her eyes as she glanced at me, a dance of expression that suggested she did not take herself with the same seriousness that the world placed upon her because of her beauty.

"Ma'am." I'd played poker. I knew not to betray the surge of adrenalin that came with cards that would sweep a game.

"Mr. Holt is a cowboy," Waldschmidt said to the three new guests. "A real cowboy! Yah? From Buffalo Bill's show. A shooting of buffalos, scalping from Indians. That kind of cowboy! He should join us for dinner, yah?"

We all were standing.

Raquel's eyebrow lifted a fraction in the awkward moment that followed Waldschmidt's exuberance.

"Of course," Raoul Amador said. "He would be welcome to join us. We'll send Stefan to get him a jacket and a tie. I'd hate for him to be embarrassed by the stares at how he dressed for this establishment."

I smiled. I didn't know why Amador would immediately think I was enough of a threat to make such an open insult, but it was amusing. On the other hand, Amador seemed like a snake of a man who would fight with a knife.

"Please." Harding spoke quickly to break the extended silence of Amador smiling coldly back at me. "Let's all sit."

I complied only because it would have been rude to give my forthcoming refusal from a standing position. It left me at the portion of the table without a place setting. I'd pulled my hat from the nearby chair onto my lap beneath the table.

"Yes, please join us." Raquel's voice was as beautiful and melodic as I'd expected. "Now that you are seated, I don't see the need for a jacket or tie."

She placed a hand on my forearm. I caught the glance that Amador gave to her hand, then to my arm, and saw the man's brief flinch. I enjoyed seeing that. The man's challenge had been far from subtle, and my general response to a bully was to wade in closer, not back away.

"I was in London during the Jubilee to learn about the suffrage movement in Britain," Raquel said to me. Her accent betrayed the fact that English was not her first language, but she spoke it without flaw. "I was at the Buffalo Bill show when Queen Victoria sat in attendance. It was a magnificent show. I wish I could recall seeing you among the cowboys. Buffalo are such huge beasts; I believed all of you would be killed as you rode among them. I would like to hear more about it, if you don't mind."

Saffire was inside the swinging kitchen door, waiting. If I stayed at this table, she'd have to keep on waiting. For hours.

"Mr. Holt had a question about your father," Harding told Raquel. "Perhaps you could explain the situation for him?"

"My father?"

I caught some of her fragrance from the heat of her body.

"It would be best," Amador said, "if any discussion tonight did not involve Ezequiel Sandoval."

"And it would be best"—Raquel met Amador's gaze—"if I made decisions for myself."

It was crazy to take the satisfaction that I did at Raquel's not-so-subtle irritation. Even more so to read into it anything about her relationship with a man who exuded his arrogance like cologne.

I inclined my head to Raquel. "I met a girl today at the administration building in Culebra. She told me that her mother has gone missing. I understand that Mr. Sandoval takes a special interest in the girl and—"

"We have no interest in talking about personal affairs with a stranger from a far country." Amador made no effort to conceal his dismissive tone. "I suppose if you knew local matters better, you'd understand how disreputable this is for you, but since you are not of our country or our station, I suppose your ignorance can be overlooked."

Another snake smile from Amador.

It took a moment to control my tone. "I apologize, but much as I appreciate the dinner invitation, I'm not in a position to stay." I would not force Saffire to play the role of servant girl, out of sight and out of mind. I'd find out more about Ezequiel Sandoval at the next place, I was sure, and I didn't trust myself to stay long in Raquel's presence. Years and years and years had passed since a woman had had an impact on my emotions. If I reacted to those emotions, I would probably embarrass myself in front of a woman who would put me out of her mind as soon as I left her presence. "I hope you'll excuse me."

"Of course." Harding nodded to me.

I was standing now, my right hand on the back of my chair, my left hand holding my cowboy hat. I caught Amador's masked sneer, as if he believed I was a lesser man for rough clothing and lack of money, and believed that I believed it too and was making an escape. I thought of Raquel's irritation at Amador's attempt to command the conversation.

She might forget me, but I was going to make sure that Amador did not.

"By the way," I said to Raquel, still leaning on the chair. "I always enjoyed my time in London. Such a progressive city and such a progressive country and such a wonderful attitude toward the rights of women. My hope and guess is that because of suffrage there, the women will be able to vote within the decade. It makes me wonder how long it will take for the rest of the world to follow those footsteps of justice and bravery."

Waldschmidt made a sound like he was coughing a hairball. Amador turned a stony expression toward the far wall. And Raquel gave me a warm smile with those perfectly curving lips.

All told, three perfect reactions.

"Ma'am." I gave her a gentle salute as a metaphorical tip of my hat and walked away.

Fourteen

Later, in the dark of early morning, listening to the skittering of cockroaches as a captive in a squalid shack somewhere on the hillside above the Pacific, I would have hours to look back and try to understand the barroom brawl at the Coconut that put me in that place.

The blame rested on the shoulders of a diminutive man named Odalis Corillo, who had pushed a drunk off a barstool beside me and then climbed up to sit. Odalis pivoted toward me with his legs dangling above the dirt floor and introduced himself as a mayoral candidate beyond compare and declared that if he did not win the election, any hope of justice in the world would vanish.

Two hours earlier, Saffire had led me into Cacao Grove, a tumultuous ten square blocks of hotels, Chinese lottery shops, restaurants, dance halls, brothels, and saloons. Jammed with peddlers making way between carriages and horses, in this place, Saffire explained, the sound of gunshots would not disturb the serenity of bartenders polishing glasses. We went directly into the Coconut, one of dozens of drinking establishments. The dirt floor was no surprise to me, nor was the smell of stale beer and tobacco, nor the mixture of Panamanians and American laborers of all colors, singing bawdy songs in all pitches and notes. Had I been dressed for the National, I would have been sought out for a fight within minutes. But working men recognize other working men, and I blended in easily, even with Saffire staying close to my side and ensuring that the bartender delivered exactly what I ordered at the price that all the locals would be charged.

I spent the first two hours laughing at jokes delivered in broken English that I half understood, doing such a good job that soon enough the jokes were delivered to me in Spanish with much pantomime, and I'd laughed equally hard at those stories. I was impressed that the men respected Saffire's presence and ensured the jokes and stories were suitable for young ears.

After the displaced drunk had stumbled away, muttering curses, Odalis Corillo demanded that "Señor Vaquero Americano" buy him a beer for the privilege of listening to him answer any and all questions that Señor Vaquero Americano might have about Panama City in general, and about Ezequiel Sandoval in specific. I found it curious that Odalis mentioned Ezequiel Sandoval without prompting, for until the little man's arrival, not once had I mentioned the name or made inquiries about local politics. That's because upon first entering the Coconut, I decided it might serve my purposes better to be the jolly, large Americano happy to buy lager for anyone willing to sit with me in conversation. I wanted tongues to be well loosened by that beer before I began my questions.

The lager arrived for Odalis Corillo. Lemp's lager. Locally made, and warm. I had tasted worse.

As Odalis took his first gulps, lamplight threw shadows across his face, and his thick mustache threw shadows over his mouth. After tossing back far more than I guessed a little man could drink at one time without breath, Odalis used the end of his sleeve to dab at his mustache. For all the man's loose shirt revealed, I couldn't tell if he had a body of roped muscle or layers of fat.

"*Gracias,* Señor Vaquero Americano." Odalis's gruff voice seemed odd for such a small figure, as if he deliberately projected sounds from a harsh part of his throat to make up for his lack of size.

"He is calling you 'Mr. Cowboy American,'" Saffire explained. She had just returned to me.

Odalis frowned. "I did not assume the girl was part of our conversation."

"I am his guide," Saffire said. "Don't ask him to contribute money for your campaigning."

"This is so?" Odalis asked.

I shrugged. "With her in this city, I feel very safe."

"I will not speak freely in front of her."

Saffire wagged a finger at him. "Don't pretend you don't know me."

Odalis squinted a closer look. "Oh. It's you."

"And I will be very curious to hear what you intend to tell Mr. Holt about my tito," Saffire said.

"Some things should not be discussed in front of children," Odalis said. "Such as why Raquel Sandoval reached me with a note this evening and told me to search for the vaquero Americano."

Saffire shook her head. "You can't trust Odalis. He is not what he appears to be."

The man glared at Saffire. Her words hardly registered with me, though.

Raquel had sent someone to look for me?

I shrugged again, this time for Saffire's benefit. "A few minutes alone. I should be able to survive."

Saffire breathed hard through her nostrils, a small dragon filled with fire, glaring first at me, then at Odalis. But finally she moved away to a different corner of the bar. I followed her with my eyes, worried about leaving her alone in this rough crowd. She found a chair in the corner and sat, arms crossed and back rigid. Nearby a man in a shambles of an old raincoat nursed a beer beneath the brim of his hat, as though he hated the world.

"Mayor?" I said. "When is the election?"

Odalis snorted. "Election? Hah. You mean the stuffing of the ballot box. I told you, there is no hope of justice in this world. But if I can secure the bribes necessary, perhaps in a month I will be mayor. Then, let me tell you, Panama City will never be the same."

Odalis left the remainder of his beer untouched. I had been sipping at my one beer all evening, determined to keep a clear head. "Raquel sent you?"

"I am to answer your questions but to also find out the reason for your interest in her father." Odalis leaned forward. "But why the rush to discuss these matters? A much more enjoyable subject is the señorita. She is something to behold, wouldn't you agree?"

I merely gave Odalis a level gaze, choosing not to dignify his leer with any kind of answer.

"You already have a woman? An evening or two with Raquel would not interest you?"

I didn't dignify that either.

"But even if you did have a woman"—Odalis rubbed his chin—"why would it matter when you are here in Panama? Who is there to know what you do in our fine city with our fine women?" Odalis's leers were getting tedious.

I pinned him with a bland look. "Tomorrow, I'm traveling home to be with my daughter. I'm afraid your fine women will have to make do with someone else."

Odalis laughed. "I would be delighted to take your place. A man like me, I can make women weep with joy and—"

"The local politics. How about you tell me one beer's worth?"

"You are a serious man, it appears."

"One who can afford to buy you a beer."

"In that case, I will tell you it has been only a matter of years since Panama, once a province of Colombia, won independence by a revolution. I'm sure you're aware of that."

"Backed by American naval ships that refused to let Colombian soldiers into the harbor. And the hills and jungle to the south were impossible for Colombian troops to cross, so that was all that was needed to defeat the local police."

"It was a little more complicated than that," Odalis said. "But you only want one beer's worth, so let me say that the Panamanian joy at American help in cutting loose from Colombia has soured after discovering the price we must pay for our so-called independence. Some families have grown richer because of it, including Señor Sandoval. Yet there are rumblings of rebellion among the next generation, who are impatient to take on the mantle of power in this small country. There has been talk among the younger aristocrats that Panama now needs to rebel against the Americans. Señor Sandoval's opposition to such talk has made him unpopular with that generation."

"Including Amador?"

"Especially Amador, who sees himself as the next president of this republic. Why is it you have interest in Señor Sandoval?

"Easy enough to answer. It is the reason I stated at the hotel. I met Saffire in Culebra today. She asked me to help look for her mother."

"But she did not give you what you needed to know about Señor Sandoval?"

"Only her perspective. As you said, she is a child."

Odalis snorted. "That one? Give her ten years and she will run this city. She is everywhere and knows everybody."

"Somehow, I did get that impression."

When Winona was a toddler, I had an internal alarm that went off every thirty seconds if I did not know where she was. As she grew older, the internal alarm remained, but the interval lengthened. Now, at the ranch, I could go a decent time before reassuring myself of her location.

Though I could not explain it, I felt the same internal alarm about Saffire in the Coconut. Anyplace else, she would be old enough that I wouldn't have to worry about the equivalent of her falling in a water trough, something I'd constantly worried about when Winona was a toddler. But this wasn't anyplace else. I'd shuddered when letting Saffire step inside the Coconut with me.

I glanced at Saffire to confirm she was fine and, thus assured, turned my attention back to Odalis. "I have been told that her mother ran away with an American after stealing jewelry from Cromwell. Saffire insists that cannot be true, but the National Police won't help her look. Nor will the Zone police."

"It is true. Señor Sandoval is a man of much influence. He is embarrassed that one of his servants behaved in such a manner. Perhaps had he not found a letter from the girl's mother, he might have looked for an alternate explanation, if only to preserve his own honor. As it is, however, he wants this forgotten as soon as possible."

I turned my head again. The man with the shambles of a coat had disappeared, but Saffire had not moved from the chair. Nor had she relaxed her crossed arms or shifted her angry gaze from Odalis. I smiled inwardly. The man who one day married her would be a fool to ever upset her.

"Yet," I said, "Saffire appears weekly at the administration building in Culebra to ask for help from the Americans. Señor Sandoval doesn't appear to have much influence over the girl's attempts to find her mother."

"What is he to do, short of have her imprisoned or worse? His influence is money and power. Neither matters to Saffire. And it is well known that he has affection for the girl, as she was raised in his household from birth."

"It seems more than that. She calls him *tito.*"

"I'm sure you've noticed by now that the girl lays claim with impunity to anything she wants. Señor Sandoval is very kind to his employees. Saffire has benefited."

I didn't have a chance to comment because two men strode to Odalis and pushed him off the stool, taking his mug and dumping the remainder of his beer on his head.

Fifteen

Odalis sputtered beer as he stood. The liquid dripped from his short and thick dark hair. Oddly, he touched his mustache gingerly, as if concerned that the beer had somehow ruined its gloriousness.

"Ah." Reassured that his mustache still gave him a degree of panache, he smiled. "Critics of some of my campaign promises, perhaps?"

I slid off my barstool. The men were Panamanians. The one on the right had streaks of gray in his hair, and the other a thin mustache with twirls at each end. Both were much shorter than I, but bulky and wide, with the stench of the unwashed, and eyes and faces blank of any emotion.

Those blank expressions worried me. Usually men had to work up nerve to begin a fight. Men who didn't had too much experience hurting other people. Why were these two picking a fight if they weren't angry?

The bar had become quiet, so Odalis tried another lighthearted remark. "So let's replace my beer and have a discussion. I can easily make a different campaign promise."

The man on the right drove a fist into Odalis's stomach, sending him to his knees. Odalis reached out for my pants leg and tried to pull himself up. I brushed away the little man's hand. I had to keep my focus on the blank-faced twins.

I stepped in front of Odalis and spoke to them. "We're done with this. Understand?"

Saffire appeared and stepped in front of me. I grabbed her shoulders and pushed her to the side, still not taking my eyes off the men in front of me.

The younger man, on the left, spat out some Spanish. They probably hadn't understood any of the English Odalis had used to defuse the situation. Or maybe Odalis knew they spoke only Spanish and had just been putting on a brave front for my benefit.

"This man says," Saffire told me, "that you and the rest of the Americans can take your steam shovels and drop them in the ocean."

Odalis groaned, finally on his feet, moving to the other side of me. "That's not how I heard it. It would not be possible, however, for steam shovels to fit where he instructed Holt and all Americans to place them, one by one."

"Saffire"—I spoke as firmly and calmly as possible—"I can figure out where this is going without any translation. I need you to move aside to give me room. Lots of room. If you do that, everything should be fine."

Keeping my focus on my opponents, I leaned down to reach into my boot for my police badge.

Saffire spoke in Spanish to the two men, and finally their expressions shifted. The older man reached behind his back and pulled out a knife.

I froze, then straightened. Badge in hand.

Odalis groaned again. "Señor Vaquero Americano, you should ask instead that the girl keep her mouth shut. She just told them that you have two pistols and are the best shooter in all of the Wild West. So indeed, if this is true, I would dearly like to see either or both of those pistols."

"As would I." I held up my badge, hoping that would defuse the situation. One of the men laughed. The other spit to the side.

I slipped the badge into my pocket and said to Saffire, sternly this time, "Move away. I need room." I stepped back, grabbed the round top of the stool, and flipped the four legs out in front of me.

The two men focused on the stool legs, and Saffire took that opportunity to kick the younger man with the mustache squarely in the crotch. His eyes bulged and he clutched himself.

In turn, I used that distraction to charge forward with the stool, forcing the knife man backward in staggering steps until I had him pinned against the wall. The cross rungs at the bottom of the legs of the stool pinned the man's biceps, and the remainder of his knife arm from the elbow forward didn't come close to reaching the top of the stool, so the blade was well away from doing any damage.

"This would be a good time to ask the bartender for help." I spoke to Saffire without turning my head from the man I had pinned. "English. Spanish. I don't care."

I heard a thump and a short cry from Saffire. I maintained pressure with the stool and darted a look backward. She was on the ground, holding her ribs. The second man was now easily fending off Odalis. He'd planted his left hand on Odalis's forehead, so none of the short man's swings made contact.

I had to keep leaning against the stool to pin my opponent against the wall.

Would anyone else step up to help?

The mustached fighter kicked Odalis's legs out from under him, then pulled a revolver from his belt, under his shirt. He advanced on me—a steady hand aiming the dark hole of the barrel directly at my head—and spoke a quick barrage of Spanish.

No translation needed.

The man at the end of the stool legs was still waving the knife at me, and the mustached man with the revolver was two steps closer. So much adrenaline surged through me that I had no room for fear.

That would come later.

Then the man with the revolver simply collapsed. Onto his knees, then a topple sideways, the revolver spilling from his hand. His fall revealed someone standing behind him, someone with a full bottle of wine in his hand, holding the bottle by the neck.

It took me a moment to first comprehend that finally someone had stepped in to help, and a second moment to comprehend that this someone had used the bottle like a club. The someone was the man in a shambles of a coat who had been sitting near Saffire earlier.

It took me another moment to comprehend a third fact. The effort of clubbing the second twin thug had twisted the bottle man's hat, and his face was out of its shadows to reveal rounded spectacles and familiar features.

"Muskie?" I grunted, trying to keep my full weight pressed against the nearly horizontal barstool.

Miskimon walked around me, toward the first man, who was spewing Spanish from behind the legs of the stool.

"The skull is built to protect the brain from blows that come from the front or back." Miskimon spoke in the neutral tones of a teacher in front of a class. "So I find blows to the side take much less effort and are far more effective. But one must use precision because too easily one can kill a man. Hold him steady, please. I'll be aiming for the gray patch of hair near his temple."

He whacked at the knife man's right hand until he'd forced the knife loose. Then he held the man's wrist with one hand, and with the other hand used a sideways blow to smack the knife man's temple with the wine bottle. But it only dazed the man, who bellowed more Spanish.

"It's been a long day." Miskimon brushed an imaginary piece of lint from his coat. "Normally, I'm able to judge the first blow more precisely than that. On the other hand, considering what he just said about our mothers, I don't mind a second shot."

The man was spitting out more venom, and midbarrage, Miskimon smacked the man's temple again. This time I felt the knife man's full weight sag into the stool.

I dropped it and let the man fall at my feet.

Miskimon faced the onlookers. "Does anyone know either of these men?"

No answer.

"With this many people in the bar, someone should be able to identify them." Miskimon sounded mildly impatient.

"Not really my fight," I said, "now that it's over."

Miskimon sighed and spoke again to the crowd. *"¿Alguien sabe cualquiera de estos hombres?"*

He was answered by murmurs and shuffling as onlookers began to retreat.

I moved to Saffire and helped her to her feet. She wiped away a silent tear.

"Where did he kick you?" I steadied her. "In the ribs?"

Saffire nodded.

"We can get you to a doctor. There won't be a next time, but next time, no help, okay? And this time, thanks for trying. You are a brave girl."

"Next time is maybe now." Saffire pointed at the entrance. "Those men are National Police. But I am not stupid enough to try to fight them. Nor should you."

I looked for Miskimon, but the man was gone. Then the police were upon us. Two took Saffire and Odalis, and the rest took me. They separated us outside, putting Saffire in a wagon that started downhill.

Mine went the opposite direction.

Monday

January 11, 1909

Col. Geo. W Goethals,

Chairman, I.C.C.

Culebra, Canal Zone

Sir:

In a former report on this matter, I said "Mrs. Penny states she has no knowledge whatever of how the screen at her apartment was torn. She states, however, that she feels satisfied it was done by the workmen resting their hands, etc., against same. Contrary to this however, is a statement of Star Foreman Dixon and his men, that when they left at 11 a.m. there was not a hole in these panels of screening, and when they returned it was in the condition above stated."

You will note in Mr. Penny's letter he says, "The hole still remains where the last man crawled through after kicking down scaffolding." On the morning I made this investigation, accompanied by Acting Superintendent, Mr. Greer, there was no hole large enough for a man to crawl through. In fact these damaged pieces look more like tears. Even had these men damaged any of the old screening, while working on the house, it hardly looks like they would have neglected to repair same.

It is peculiar, indeed, that in using the same method in working on other houses, these same workmen do not leave screening which is damaged as a result of their work. It looks like the case resolves itself like this: Mrs. Penny denies damaging the screening, while the workmen insist that when they left there at 11 a.m. it was in good order, but when they returned at 1 p.m. the damage had been done.

You will note that Mrs. Holland, having apartments in the same building, admitted causing the damage in the screening at her apartment, and has so far made no objections to payment for same.

Respectfully,
Inspector T. B. Miskimon

Sixteen

Even though the felt of my cowboy hat wasn't the perfect material for the Panama heat, it bothered me greatly that I no longer had it. It took months to shape felt the way I wanted it, comfortable on the skull, enough of a brim to keep sun off the face and neck, a decent tilt so that rain ran onto the back and not down the collar.

I missed that hat.

In the chaos at the Coconut, someone had knocked it off my head, and I'd been too busy fighting arrest to retrieve it.

I believed now I was in a hut somewhere on the hill above the Coconut. Six armed men in National Police uniforms had sealed the exits from the bar, which made Miskimon's disappearance a mystery. A mystery, however, I gave no effort to solve in my current situation.

At the Coconut, one of the cops had engaged in a short conversation with the bartender, while the others kept me and Odalis at gunpoint and

Saffire's arm in a firm grip. The cops placed me and Odalis in handcuffs. I'd been forced onto one wagon outside with four cops, and Odalis and Saffire onto the other with the remaining two cops.

A cop threw a burlap bag over my head. It smelled like potatoes, and the rough fabric scratched my skin.

I could only guess by the lean of the wagon that it had turned uphill. After ten minutes of the steady *clip-clop* of a horse straining against the traces, I'd been bundled through a doorway, my shoulder banging into the side. Then I'd been guided a few steps inside, where the I had been briefly stripped of the handcuffs, only for my hands to be wrenched behind my back and around a pole with the handcuffs replaced.

Alone now, with the sounds of night insects my only company, I guessed I was inside a hut, handcuffed to the center pole. I'd deduced this from the three stumbling steps I'd taken into the hut. I pictured the pole supporting crossbeams of a tin-sheeted roof above me. As I slid down to sit, my boot heels scraped the loose dirt. Thank goodness I had enough slack in the handcuffs to shift my shoulders and find the most comfortable position. I listened for any conversation to alert me to my captors' presence.

All I heard was my own breathing inside the burlap and the cacophony of insects. During my time in Cuba, fighting under the command of Roosevelt, I'd been astounded at the variety and size of the beetles and butterflies and cockroaches and all the other flying swarms that I could not identify by species, let alone name.

Then, my fellow soldiers and I hadn't paid much attention to the mosquitoes, except to swat the irritants. In retrospect, we should have been terrified. Fewer than a thousand men had died in combat in Cuba, but over five thousand had died of yellow fever.

Not everyone who contracted yellow fever died from it. I had been one of the survivors. Yellow fever signaled itself with high fever and intense muscle and joint pain. The only cure was patience, and after a few days, the symptoms disappeared. But with the expected cessation and physical relief also came the dreaded wait and mental strain. Because it might only be a respite. For the unfortunate, the fever would attack again with a ferocity that led to projectile vomiting of black blood and the jaundiced skin that came with destruction of the man's liver. Then, slow and anguished death.

In Cuba, I had seen the death wagon too many times—a box on two wheels, with the single axle centered below an *X* on the side, and a single horse between the railings, pulling the box. I had stood at too many mass funerals, the coffins lined end to end, each draped in American flags, listening to the bugler with a combination of guilt and relief that my own body was not among the dead.

Then, with the brief Spanish-American War almost over, came the bleakest day of my life to that point—the hot July morning in Havana when James Holt Senior died in the sweaty canvas confines of an army tent, a victim of the same disease that had randomly allowed me to survive. My only grace had been the chance to reconcile and the deathbed promise I'd made to my father to take care of his ranch.

Because of my exposure to yellow fever and because of my father's death, I had followed the subsequent medical debate with interest as the search for yellow fever's source played across the newspapers. On one side were the traditionalists, who believed that bacteria in filthy conditions caused the disease and that strict hygiene could control outbreaks. On the other were advocates of a novel theory that mosquitoes carried both yellow fever and malaria and passed them along to humans.

Barely a decade had passed since my exposure to the disease. Since then, a military doctor had done the necessary experimentation to prove that the novel theory was accurate. Because of this, he was the man in charge of sanitation for the Canal Zone, and his near eradication of mosquitoes within the zone was probably the single biggest reason the Americans might succeed in connecting the Atlantic to the Pacific. Forty-thousand workers had died from yellow fever during the French attempt in the 1880s. In the five years since the United States had begun working on the canal, fewer than five hundred had died and the rate of deaths had trickled to less than one per month.

A man who survived yellow fever was immune to future attacks. Still, there was no cure for malaria, and while that disease probably wouldn't kill me were I to contract it, the recurring attacks would follow me back to my ranch in the Badlands and make me miserable for the rest of my life.

For that reason, with my back against the pole, I was in one sense grateful for the burlap sack that screened my face and neck from mosquito attacks. I was equally grateful for long sleeves and trousers, which gave me the necessary protection everywhere except for the skin exposed on my wrists and hands. When I felt a pinprick of a mosquito bite against the back of my right hand, I squashed the tiny attacker against the pole. I had to be vigilant. While years of travel had taught me that I could sleep anywhere, including with my back against a pole, I wouldn't allow myself that luxury in the darkness of the hut.

After waiting a sufficient time and not hearing sounds to tell me the police were in the hut watching me, I decided to experiment with an attempt at escape. I stood, squared my back against the pole, and pushed hard, my boot heels skidding against the dirt. The bottom of the pole barely moved, indicating that it had been buried a few feet into the hill. The top of the pole swayed a few inches however, and the roof creaked.

That immediately brought a shout from what must have been the doorway. At least it hadn't brought a bullet.

I slid my back down the pole and sat again. It was obvious that this had not been a typical arrest for a barroom fight. Any arrest after a brief fight like that would not have been typical. And to be taken not to jail but to a hut where the poor lived in squalid housing—hidden, anonymous—added to the curiousness of the events.

I wasn't afraid. Not only did the burlap sack protect me from mosquitoes, but it also served as a clue that whoever had ordered the sack over my head probably wanted to prevent me from seeing anything incriminating.

Odds were good that I'd not been brought to this place to be executed.

So the more important question was why had this happened? And the obvious answer was that my questions about Ezequiel Sandoval had triggered it. Except for those questions, to all appearances, I would've appeared a typical American loose outside the Zone, interested in what typical Americans pursued. Chasing liquor and women did not result in kidnappings by the Panamanian police. It would be bad for business, not to mention risky, to aggravate the US government as represented by Colonel Goethals, who needed his workers.

Even if asking questions about Sandoval was dangerous, I had other assumptions that set me at ease about the situation. Miskimon was working for Goethals. Therefore, he had to protect me so that I could report again to his boss.

Ah, Miskimon. I'd seriously underestimated the man. First, he had street smarts. He had played the role of a clownishly inept follower from the steamship in Colón to the stop at Culebra, lulling me into believing that he would always be that obvious. As a result, I had not spent much time looking for him in Panama City. Come to think of it, would I have been able to spot him even if I *had* been looking for him?

Second, during the fight in the Coconut, I had to admit the prissy man had showed physical toughness and an unhurried lack of fear. I might not like his fastidiousness and apparent worship of rules, but I had to respect the man.

Miskimon, I decided, had not run away from the Coconut out of fear of the National Police but, more than likely, because he'd assessed the situation and realized the best course of action was to escape arrest. Then he could, in an official capacity, extradite me later. So he would show up sooner or later.

Unless.

If Goethals, as explained, could not involve himself in the Panamanian squalls, would he order Miskimon not to intervene on my behalf?

No. Goethals still had to report to Roosevelt. And that meant Goethals had to send Miskimon.

With my fears thus allayed, I allowed myself to recall the earlier part of the evening—at the National, when I'd so enjoyed watching the curve of Raquel Sandoval's smile, smelling the fragrance of her skin.

It was a strange sensation, mooning like a schoolboy. I wasn't sure if I liked how much I liked it.

I slapped the back of my hand against the post to mash another attacking mosquito. As I allowed myself to pass time by picturing her eyes in that face and how her dark hair had outlined her cheekbones, I told myself that all this mooning was for the best. I needed to wear out the memory of our short meeting so I could forget about her as soon as possible.

Seventeen

The creaking and buzzing and whining of insects began to lessen, gradually replaced by the songs of birds. I began to sweat under the burlap sack over my head.

My bladder hurt.

I'd paced myself on beer at the Coconut, but since arriving here I'd been alternately sitting and standing for hours, sliding up and down the center pole to stay awake, growing more aware of the pressure of my bladder.

I called for the guard.

No response.

I pushed against the center pole and heard a warning shout as the roof above me clattered. Tin roof.

I pushed again and tracked the guard's entry by the rising volume of the volley of Spanish.

I tried body language to express what I needed.

The unseen guard must have understood, but all he said was, "Bah." Universal enough.

I bashed the pole to shake the roof again. Almost instantly, a blow struck me across the face, hard enough to daze me.

Universal enough.

I sat, and any chance of coherent thought was driven away by the willpower it took not to empty my bladder. Time began to move much slower than it had during my earlier cycle of thoughts about Raquel, then Winona, then what needed to be done at the ranch, then questions about my situation.

I was at the point of deciding I would simply void my bladder and soak my trousers when I heard the rustle of movement.

"Stand." English with a heavy Spanish accent. A deep voice, almost a growl.

"Only if someone takes off my handcuffs so that I can relieve myself."

"You do what we tell you and answer the questions that we ask."

"Not if I end up wetting my pants. I promise if that happens, you can cut off my arms before we have a conversation."

Whispers reached me.

A few seconds later, the deep voice said, "If you stand, the handcuffs will be unlocked. Then you will put your hands in front of you to be handcuffed again. At gunpoint, you will be led outside. After you have finished relieving yourself, you will be led back to this pole and handcuffed again with your hands behind you. The sack will be over your head. I advise you not to try anything heroic. The first bullet will be into your kneecap. The second, your other kneecap. Understood?"

Instead of a verbal answer, I stood. I heard the click of metal on metal. My wrists were released. I held them in front of my body. I was handcuffed again.

I did not feel powerless, however. My unseen captors had bent to my will, not the reverse.

Outside the hut, I heard a small snort of a horse. I wondered if it was attached to a carriage or wagon.

Behind the hut I eased the pressure of my bladder, aching with relief. When I'd finished buttoning my trousers, I was pushed roughly back through the doorway. The unseen man handcuffed me to the pole again with my wrists behind me. Ironically, with the pressure gone from expelled fluids, I became aware of my thirst. I doubted, however, that I would be granted water. I wasn't going to ask for something I wouldn't get. That would make me powerless again.

Behind me, someone slipped a cord over my head, lifted the burlap enough to slip the cord against my throat, and pulled so that my head was against the pole, with the cord cutting into my skin.

It was apparent I'd been deluding myself about having any degree of control over the situation.

"We are standing behind you," the deep voice said.

We. I guessed by rustles of movement that there were three or four men behind me.

The voice continued. "Your single hope of saving your life is to make sure you don't see our faces. I think you understand those implications. Please say yes if you understand."

I gritted my teeth to keep my mouth shut.

The cord tightened.

"Yes." I was stubborn, but I wasn't an idiot.

"Excellent."

The burlap was yanked off my head.

I blinked against the sudden light. When my eyes adjusted, I saw that my guesswork had been correct. Dirt floor, which I knew because I'd scraped my boot heels against it. Crossbeams above, tin roof. Shanty walls of odd-sized pieces of pressed tin. A hammock in the corner with mosquito netting. Improvised as it seemed, the hammock would have been an infinitely more comfortable place to spend the night.

One other object drew my attention. It had been placed on the floor a few feet in front of me. The base was a short and wide plank, unpainted. Screwed onto the center was a crank handle, attached to a generator shaft in front of it. I understood the concept. Move a magnet through a wire coil, and electric current would flow in one direction as the magnet was pushed through the center of the coil and in the opposite direction as it was pulled. An alternating current. The stronger the magnet, the bigger the coils, and the faster the magnet moved, the more current would be supplied.

I saw boot prints on the back of the plank. This generator was big enough that a man needed to stand on it to turn the crank, which was why the large generator had been screwed down to the center of the plank. It had probably taken two men to carry it into the hut. That would have been the reason for horse and carriage or wagon. Hauling a generator this big up the hill without horsepower would have been too much work.

The ends of the wires were attached to metal clips. This generator could power a lot more than a light bulb.

"Do you recognize that contraption?" There was no pleasure in the deep voice to indicate the questioner enjoyed trying to strike fear into me.

I didn't answer.

Again, I felt the bite of the cord into my neck.

"Speak!"

"I want my hat. It's a good hat. Don't know how I'm going to find one like it down here."

"Are you aware of what that is in front of you?"

I said nothing.

The next jerk of the cord was vicious.

"Yes," I grunted. "I'm aware of what it is."

What had I gotten into that unknown men were willing to torture me?

"Good. For your protection, you will be hooded again. Much as you might not want to see our faces, I've discovered that men will react violently to the current. The wrong turn of your head could be fatal for you. Nor do you want to see the man at the generator."

Someone slipped the burlap over my head again, and I breathed in the familiar smell of dirt and potatoes.

"We'll start with your ears," the voice said. "I like to start gentle. Otherwise I would have let you soak your trousers with your own urine. The current, as you might guess, travels well through damp saltiness, and those clips can be attached anywhere on the body, including portions far more sensitive than your ears."

Even though I had been warned, I still flinched when hands reached under the burlap sack. I felt the scrape of the metal clips against my cheek and then my neck as those hands felt around to clamp one clip to each of my ears.

The bite of the clamps made me gasp. How did women endure what it took to pierce their ears?

Despite the pain, I felt a sense of disbelief that allowed me that kind of inappropriate speculation in a situation like this. The concept of humans inflicting torture on other humans was an abstraction to me. Intellectually, I understood that some men stood behind me with the power of my life or death in their hands, and intellectually, I understood they had coldly trussed me and promised to inflict pain. But emotionally, it still did not seem possible that—

I screamed before I could bite off the noise and felt my heels drumming the ground and the arch of my back against the pole. A surge of sheer white kept stabbing through my body like I'd been dipped in molten steel.

Just as suddenly, it ceased. I panted, trying to recover.

Again, without warning, it hit. I managed to keep my jaws shut, and the only sound that escaped me was muffled groaning, low enough that I could hear the cranking of the generator. This time it seemed to last longer, so long that when it stopped, I wondered if the intense contraction of muscles had cracked some ribs.

I panted again. Hard.

"Imagine then," the voice said, "that after this, the clips are attached to other parts of your body. Usually, the chest area is next. And rarely, someone makes it to the third level, much lower on your body and much more sensitive. Shall we have a conversation? If so, we'll remove the clips."

"Strangely," I said as the heaves of my chest subsided, "at the moment, I find myself in a chatty mood."

I wanted to survive this. Just for the privilege of wrapping my fingers around Miskimon's skinny neck and squeezing until the man's eyes bulged. What had he kept hidden from me that resulted in *this*? And where was he? How difficult would it have been to follow me after my arrest?

Hands reached under the burlap and removed the clips.

A second voice reached me. It was barely more than a whisper, but I was paying very close attention and heard each word clearly.

"Why are you asking questions about Ezequiel Sandoval?"

I sucked air in through my nostrils. It felt great to fill my lungs. The electricity had seemed to shrink them into raisins. "I met a girl who asked me to help her search for her mother."

"We both know there is more to it than that. I have plenty of time. I can wait for the clips to be reattached. Why are you asking questions about Ezequiel Sandoval? Lie to me even once, and we go to the next level."

I remembered what Harding had said the evening before in the dining room of the National. *"Ask your questions. I'll probably learn as much from what you ask as you would tell me about yourself."*

"There's not much point in answering if you're not going to believe my answers. Trust me, I'm very motivated to tell you what you want. I am here because of the girl. There's nothing else I care about in this country to keep me here."

A long silence.

I flinched again as hands touched the front of my shirt. I made a hard twist with my upper body to shake the hands loose.

"Hold still," the first voice said. "We do have the cord at your neck to keep you obedient."

I felt a small jerk of the cord against my Adam's apple as a reminder. I stilled, and those unseen hands unbuttoned my shirt and left it on my upper body, the front open, my chest exposed.

"I think you understand where those clips go next," the voice said. "I suggest you make sure your conversation doesn't frustrate my friend here."

The whisper returned. "You sat beside the girl in Culebra as you waited to see Goethals yesterday. Nothing in your conversation with her indicated you had any interest in her situation. What happened during your meeting with Goethals to change that?"

"Ask your questions. I'll probably learn as much from what you ask as you would tell me about yourself."

So . . . there had been a spy in the waiting room. No point in speculating who it might have been. I didn't see how knowing that could help, but knowing there had been a spy reporting to this questioner told me that I needed to proceed with caution. The threat to reattach the clips was not a bluff.

"It was suggested that I find out more about the situation." I had no particular loyalty to Goethals, and they probably knew this anyway. "To keep embarrassment away from Cromwell."

"Suggested by Goethals?" came the whisper.

"Yes."

"Why did he choose you?"

"He probably thought I could keep my mouth shut. Bad judge of character. All you needed to do was light me up a few times and I'll tell you anything."

I *did* feel chatty. On the one-in-a-thousand chance that Miskimon would actually do something to intervene, the longer I dragged out this conversation without reaching the next stage of the clips and generator, the better it would be.

"Let me rephrase my question. You traveled a long distance and, from all sources, made it clear you had no intention of staying in this country more than a day or two. If so, why did Goethals choose you?"

From all sources . . .

The cord jerked at my neck. I'd been silent too long.

"Why did he choose you? Surely if you had no intention of helping, you wouldn't have made the trip. What was in the envelope he gave you and why were you sent?"

"The envelope had the coupons I needed to travel the Zone."

My turn to test him. Did his questioner know enough to know when I was lying?

"Answer the second question. Why were you sent?"

"To help Goethals."

"See, we are getting somewhere. Who sent you?"

This was a significant question. It was one thing to reveal that Goethals had an unofficial interest in Ezequiel Sandoval, because anyone with intelligence could make the deduction with or without my help. But to identify who had sent me could inflict severe political damage.

"You shouldn't be doing this," I said. "I'm a Zone policeman. The badge is in my pocket."

The deep voice hardened. "This is my country, not your—"

The whispering voice cut him off. "Let me handle this. We are making progress. He evades the answer. That tells me of its importance. I suggest we move to the next stage and give him a real taste of pain."

My brain scrambled for a lie they'd believe. "I know some land speculators. They sent me."

"Nothing in your background suggests you travel in those circles. With that lie, you have earned the next stage."

Hands pulled away the shirt as the cord bit against my neck to hold me in place.

I was afraid, not so much for the expected pain, but that I would discover how much of a coward I was. And that the cowardice would outweigh my loyalty to the president.

Then came the sound of singing children. A *throng* of singing children.

"What is this?" the whispering voice hissed.

"Was that question for me?" I asked. "Sounds like children."

The sting of a blow hit my head. Good. I'd frustrated my questioner. Maybe even angered him.

The singing grew louder until it was just outside the hut. I couldn't recognize the words. It was in Spanish.

"Cover your faces!" the whispered voice commanded. "Shirts over your heads! And flee as best you can. I will not hurt children."

Maybe a minute passed. With me in blessed solitude, with the approach of more singing and giggling. I tried to picture the situation. If the kidnappers were unwilling to hurt the children, they were gone, and the children were squeezing their way inside.

"Señor Holt," came a voice from earlier in the evening. "This is an odd situation. I have come to return the favor, have I not?"

Odalis.

I sagged against the pole. Who needed Miskimon?

As I slid down to a sitting position, the burlap was taken off my head. Odalis showed a face of concern. Around the little man with the big mustache, filling the hut, were dozens of children, giggling and pointing.

Behind them stood Raquel Sandoval, arms crossed. I could read no expression on her face.

Odalis nodded. "Saffire told us we would find you here."

Saffire.

Odalis had a soft touch as he examined my ears. "The bite of the alligator. As we feared. Raquel suggested it would be safer to bring children than soldiers. It took us awhile to gather them."

I glanced away from Odalis to the back of the hut, but Raquel was gone. "Where is Saffire?"

"She is . . ." Odalis looked around. Confusion played across his face. "I do not know. She was here. Now she is gone. But that girl is notorious for going her own way, and for her own reasons."

"I want to thank her."

I could not see her anywhere.

"Also, you should thank Señorita Sandoval," Odalis said. "It was her idea. She paid for all the candy it took to get the children together."

"Then please pass along my thanks to her."

"Oh no." Odalis smiled. "You must do that yourself. I think she likes the Señor Vaquero Americano. When I tease her about it, she gets angry with me."

Eighteen

I had a towel around my waist, lather on my face, and a razor in my hand when the three quick knocks came at my bathroom door. The bathroom door, not the hallway door. Which meant, of course, that someone had breached the hallway door to enter my room at the National Hotel.

I had booked a suite with a balcony overlooking the tops of palms trees, the stone buildings of the old city, and the blue of the Pacific beyond. I expected the type of privacy that came with a suite like this. A tray with breakfast had already been delivered, and I wasn't expecting a maid.

The massive bathroom was bigger than my entire bedroom back at the ranch, and I glanced around for anything that I could improvise as a weapon, not expecting much luck. I'd tossed my filthy clothes into a pile on the floor. My boots were at the foot of the claw-foot tub, and I had already filled it with water as hot as I'd been able to run from the tap, thinking I'd let it cool while I shaved and then enjoyed the coffee and toast and eggs.

Normally, I wouldn't feel paranoid about an unexpected room guest. That had happened often enough during my exile years, and for the most part, each occasion had been a pleasant surprise. But I was very conscious of how helpless I'd been with a burlap bag over my head and a clip attached to each of my ears. With that still fresh in my mind, I wasn't going to assume the person on the other side of the door meant well. For all I knew, that person was ready to fire a few shots through the door at the sound of my voice if I responded verbally to the knocks.

Best to err on the side of caution, which meant my only weapon was surprise. That wouldn't give me time to dress, although I was tempted to step into my boots. I missed having my hat.

I set my razor down on the edge of the sink, grabbed a second towel from the thick stack on a shelf at the far side of the bathroom, and tiptoed to the door.

I waited for the next knock, hoping for a repeat pattern of three. What I had in mind might work with only one person on the other side. More than that, I didn't have a chance anyway.

At the next knock, I flung the door open and tossed the towel where I guessed the person's face might be. The only reason I didn't open with a punch at stomach level was on the chance it might be a maid.

The towel spread open like a bullfighter's cape, and I charged through the doorway, trying to take advantage of the split second of confusion that the towel might have created, ready to throw the necessary punches.

What I saw, however, was Miskimon, neatly stepping aside to let the towel flap past him onto the hardwood floor.

"Oh my," Miskimon said, "let me recover from that intense moment of terror."

I drew a long breath of suppressed anger through my nostrils and held my covering towel at my waist with my left hand. Miskimon shifted his gaze to a scar that ran from my left shoulder diagonally downward until it disappeared on my chest, where hair covered the remainder of its length. Miskimon noticed my awareness of his gaze.

"Sioux warrior," I said.

"I didn't ask," Miskimon answered.

I kept a firm grip on my towel at my waist and returned to the bathroom, shutting the door and turning the lock on it, hoping the click was audible to Miskimon.

I returned to my shaving, then paused, razor in hand. I nearly opened the door again to warn Miskimon not to eat any of the breakfast or drink any of my coffee. That's what I would have done if the situation were reversed—helped myself to the food. But I realized Miskimon wouldn't stoop to that kind of juvenile pettiness.

When I finished shaving, I considered whether to try to ease myself into the hot water. It would give me pleasure to make the fastidious man outside wait for as long as I could endure the soak. I'd even make him listen to some bawdy songs while I lathered and splashed.

But a quick dip of my fingers into the bathwater told me I'd have to wait too long for it to cool enough to be bearable. If only I'd been smart enough to bring my breakfast tray into the bathroom. Now my choices were to step outside again or wait until the water cooled.

I looked into the mirror to wipe away all traces of lather, put on a bathrobe, cinched the waistband, and stepped outside.

Miskimon was standing in the center of the suite, hands behind his back, with a military squareness to his shoulders.

"I was afraid you'd still be here." I moved past Miskimon to the far edge of the suite, where the breakfast tray had been set on a small round dining table. The suite had more area than my ranch house. I'd have to make sure I put that description in my journal for Winona.

The events of the evening before? Definitely not.

I took the coffeepot and poured a cup. I almost offered a cup to Miskimon, but I was too angry at the man.

I walked to the window that overlooked the balcony and sipped my coffee as I stared at the Pacific, my back to my visitor.

He said, "Normally I find it distasteful to mix metaphors."

What? I turned. The day before, I'd felt tolerant of the prissy man. No longer. "I expect you find most things in this world distasteful."

Miskimon pointed at the bed and all the new clothes that had been laid out for me. "This makes it obvious that for someone who seems to prefer living like a lone wolf, after a rough night, you certainly know how to land on your feet like an alley cat. You really expect the ICC to pay for all this?"

"I'm in no mood to talk to you, let alone respond to some kind of implied scorn. I presume you have a reason for illegally entering a private room in a private hotel?"

"There is the fact that you have requested that the hotel bill the ICC for all charges, which makes it a room I have full rights to enter."

"If the ICC doesn't cover the bill, I know a newspaper person who'd find the backstory interesting."

"You're going to play it that way?"

"Already have. Thought that billing it to you and Goethals would get you here plenty fast. And look, it did."

"Where were you last night?" Miskimon said.

"More important, where were you?" I had no problem matching his scorn and anger. "The true alley cat here is the one who went slinking away when the real trouble arrived."

"Hardly. Real trouble is an unarmed man against another with a pistol and yet another with a knife. Let me try to recall if someone like that was there to rescue you last night in such a situation. Give me a moment. Ah. Yes. That would have been me. Keeping in the spirit of metaphors, let's examine if alley cats ever show much gratitude to those who help them."

"Gratitude? It doesn't take much effort to knock a man out from behind or to hit another man twice when his arms are pinned to the wall. Am I supposed to thank you for that? Or for spying on me?"

"Odalis at least did his best to protect the girl. Saffire. The one who worships you. Try to recall the girl. You simply disappeared and let the police arrest both of them."

I went back to the coffeepot because that would keep me from trying to strangle Miskimon. I spoke as I walked, making an effort to sound casual. "That just shows the extent of your commitment to any real fight. Had you stuck around, you would have learned a little more."

"Where were you throughout the night? Were you able to put the revolver to good use?"

I poured coffee. The roast of the beans was excellent. I should have expected that. I was surrounded by lush plantations. Whatever coffee made it to the desolation of the Dakotas certainly wasn't like this.

"The revolver," Miskimon said. "Is it in the bathroom?"

"You searched my suite. Then concluded I didn't have it in the bathroom. Not many gunfights where I'm from involve cowboys throwing towels at each other."

"Where did you leave it?"

"You know it's in Culebra, in the valise that I gave you for safekeeping." I paused. "The valise *is* safe? Tell me you didn't find a way to be incompetent about that too. It is safe, right?"

"In the Zone, at least away from the construction sites, safety is not an issue. I meant the revolver that was used to threaten you last night before—"

"—before you so boldly snuck up behind a man and dropped him with a mighty blow from a wine bottle? No, I don't have that revolver."

"It might have told us something about the person who sent those two."

I took a few steps toward him. "I had a lot of time last night to wonder about that. Time to wonder why you'd decided not to bother to watch my back after my arrest. I wondered why, right after the fight, you were so quick to ask if anyone knew those men."

"They first punched Odalis. Not you."

"So you're trying to get answers because you were there last night to protect him? Strange coincidence, then, that I was in the same place as Odalis."

Miskimon pulled out a handkerchief and removed his glasses and polished them.

As he put the glasses back on with his customary flick, I said, "If you want to know about my night, how about you tell me first how and why you disappeared. It would have been helpful for you to stick around after sending me out with questions about Ezequiel Sandoval. Questions that I'm guessing you expected would put my head into the jaws of a lion."

Miskimon gave me a long, long stare. Then he stepped closer and made no secret that he was examining my face. We were barely two feet apart. I lifted my coffee cup and slurped, guessing that it would irritate the man. His eyes moved to my ears. I resisted the urge to rub the small fresh scabs on my ear lobes.

Miskimon stepped back. "So. You met the lion."

"Not a lion, but *the* lion? I'm not in a mood to answer where I was last night. Whatever you know about all this is a lot more than I know. And you knew a lot more than I did when you put me on the train yesterday afternoon."

"What happened last night? This is important."

"I went for a long leisurely stroll. I composed poetry. Studied the stars. What did you do when the National Police arrived right after the fight?"

"Avoiding arrest took no effort, as you might guess. All it took to blend in was wearing that hideous coat. I threw it under a table. It was no sacrifice to lose it as I went out of the bathroom window."

"Difficult, isn't it, being a slave to fashion? Where I come from, other things are more important. Like sticking with a fight when your partner is in trouble. Not that you and I are, or ever will be, partners."

Miskimon seemed oddly subdued. "I didn't want to get arrested. It would have been politically embarrassing, and it would have led to questions that would have reflected badly on Colonel Goethals."

If Miskimon's anger toward me was lessening, the opposite was happening with mine toward him. I set my cup down on the table to keep from striking out at the man. "If only I could come up with an animal metaphor capable of conveying the scorn your excuse deserves. No wait. Give me a moment. Ah. Yes. I'll give you a hint. It has no legs and it slithers. Let's go with that animal metaphor."

I wanted Miskimon to lash back. I wanted a roaring shouting match. The night before, I'd humiliated myself with my fear.

I'd discovered I was a lesser man than I believed myself to be.

"I'm sorry," Miskimon said. "Sorry to you. Last night at the Coconut when the National Police arrived, as I weighed those factors, I also made the evaluation that if I was arrested with you, then I wouldn't be in a position to bail you out of the jail. I thought you would be safe in jail, like Odalis was with Saffire. While I was there within the half hour, I wasn't allowed to reach a judge until early morning to bail them out. The rest of the night, I spent looking for you. I apologize I wasn't there to prevent whatever happened to you."

So he accepted that I had a right to be angry. Normally, that would have appeased me. But I still wanted that shouting match. "Convenient that you couldn't find me then. Yet now, when the most danger you face is tripping on a carpet, you magically appear? Hang on, I have the answer. Because the ICC is concerned about a hotel bill."

"An hour ago, when the hotel called the administration office to confirm whether we would be responsible for the charges, I first assumed that your night had been much easier than mine. I was wrong."

If that was true, the man didn't deserve my continued anger.

"I'm tired of this," I said. "I'm just plain tired. I want to take a bath. Then sleep for a few hours. How about you go your way and I go mine? Later today, I'll find you in Culebra. We can have a civilized discussion then."

"If I can believe you accept my apology. Had I known or guessed the lion was ready to spring so quickly, I wouldn't have been complacent. You fought a man with a knife to defend Odalis, and I am forced to admire that. Believe me that I am sincere in my apology. Not that I intend any kind of partnership with you."

After a long silence of my own to evaluate Miskimon, I guessed that this admission and apology had not been easy for him.

"I was glad you were there when you were," I conceded. "Best way to handle a man with a revolver is to hit him in the side of his head from behind." I extended my hand.

Miskimon blinked.

I held out my hand for another few seconds, but Miskimon didn't take it to shake on the mutual apologies.

"We do come from different places." I couldn't rekindle any anger at the snub. I was just tired and wanted to be alone. "I'd be fine if you left now."

Miskimon blinked again and opened his mouth as if to say something, then closed it. He squared his shoulders once more. "I don't see that we'll need to meet again in Culebra. Colonel Goethals no longer requires anything of you. Stop at the administration office and ask for his secretary to give you your valise. I'll arrange a ticket for you on the steamer that leaves at noon tomorrow. Stay here tonight and check out in the morning."

"Suddenly not so curious about the two men in the bar and who sent them?"

"It would be best if we went our separate ways."

"Sure. Make sure the door doesn't hit you on the way out."

That gave Miskimon some of his previous attitude. "First, I'll need the police badge."

And his tone brought me back to a degree of irritation. "Let me guess. You couldn't find it in my room or my valise yesterday afternoon, after you put me on the train and searched all my items for yourself because you didn't trust the report of the detective on the steamer? And you didn't find it in here during your search while I was running water in the bathroom?"

"I am thorough. I have no choice."

"I trust you did not open my journal in the valise." I didn't want Miskimon to know anything of my personal life.

"I won't dignify that question with an answer. I'd like the police badge. I don't know why you'd take it out of the Zone. It's worthless metal here."

"I lost it last night." I was angry enough again to be petty. The badge was now in my boot beside the bathtub. "When you find the guys who started the fight in the bar, why don't you ask *them* if they know where it went?"

"I understand your irritation, but petulance doesn't become you."

"Anything else before you go, Mr. Miskimon?" I enunciated the *mister* and the *Miskimon* with exact formality and caught enough of a flicker on Miskimon's face to know he understood the full use of his name had been meant as an insult.

"No."

"Then I have hot water waiting for me. For some reason, I feel the need to be cleansed. Why don't you find your own way out."

I didn't wait for an answer and walked the length of the suite to go into the bathroom.

When I came out to dress after a half hour in the bathwater, I found my cowboy hat on the bed.

Nineteen

I had been promised I would find the *Panama Star & Herald* building only a few blocks away, between the hotel and the Pacific. And so I did. Easily. The walk from the hotel, directly into a sea breeze that cooled the sweat on my face, took a matter of minutes. The building looked squat, a square two-story with a second-floor balcony all the way around.

Even from the street, I heard the clatter of typewriters. *The Panama Star & Herald* was the only English newspaper in the city and did a wonderful business, I had been told.

Inside, it seemed as much a whirlwind of movement as I'd glimpsed of the dig at Culebra. I finally had to grab a man's elbow to stop him long enough to ask a question. The answer was to go to a street café, and it came with a point in the general direction.

I found Earl Harding there, at one of the three tables on the sidewalk, protected by an awning. He had a cup of coffee, an egg dish smeared with red spices, and a newspaper folded to keep it stiff enough to read with one hand.

"Cowboy," he said as I sat across from him without an invitation. "Rough night?"

Who in Panama City didn't know I had been rough-handled by the National Police? "I've had worse."

"You're buying breakfast." He raised a hand and made a little circle with his index finger.

A waiter immediately delivered coffee. I took a grateful sip.

"Read the rag?" He tapped the folded paper on the edge of the table before setting it down. "Big week for Teddy."

"The Great White Fleet," I said.

Roosevelt believed that America's naval power was crucial to its future. That was how he'd sold the United States on the Panama Canal. In '98, during the Spanish-American War, the US Pacific Fleet had to travel around South America to reach Cuba, barely arriving in time for crucial military action. Roosevelt argued that the canal was for the navy to protect American interests, that in a future crisis, a canal would make for speedy travel. He was correct, of course. The navy that controlled the canal essentially controlled the western Atlantic and the eastern Pacific, up and down all the Americas.

The Great White Fleet was another bold Roosevelt action. He'd dispatched sixteen of the US Navy battleships from the Atlantic Fleet to go on what he called a goodwill tour of the world. No one was fooled. It was an open exhibition of American might, and with hulls painted white, with red, white, and blue banners on the bows, the ships had earned their nickname. Just last week, the Suez Canal had been closed to all traffic except the fleet, generating headlines and editorial opinions.

"Roosevelt." Harding grimaced. "What a blow-hard. 'Speak softly and carry a big stick'? He hasn't spoken a soft word in his life."

He waited, probably to see if I would disagree with him. I just sipped my coffee.

"Anyway," Harding said, "that's old news. Don't know how we ran this business before the telegraph. First, on Saturday, Colombia finally voted to recognize Panama's independence. That should make Teddy happy. Except the day before, back in the States, the House of Representatives just voted to have him censured. Win some, lose some."

"Censured? I didn't read that in the paper today."

"*The Star & Herald* tends not to be critical. At least when it comes to Roosevelt. They wouldn't dream of publishing the story. Without the canal, this place is just another backwater town."

"Censured," I repeated. "Roosevelt?"

"I find that so ironic. Apparently the fine elected men of the House are a tiny bit upset that in his annual address to Congress last year, Roosevelt stated that there were criminals in the legislative branch."

Harding used the edge of his fork as a knife and cut into the egg. He took a bite that was delicate for a tall man, chewed slowly, swallowed, and chased it with coffee, then gave me a tight smile.

"It's what provides a living for me. All those elected criminals and their friends. As I explained last night, the *World* has sent me down here on an all-expense-paid vacation to dig into Cromwell's dealings on the isthmus. But I'm finding as little as I found in Paris. Cromwell's got too much influence. That's what you're buying me breakfast for, right? An angle on Cromwell?"

When I didn't respond, he pointed at my ears. "Odalis is a wonderful gossip. It's not a huge stretch to guess that when you indiscriminately asked about Ezequiel Sandoval, Cromwell would learn immediately and feel like you were asking about him. Last night's political lesson wasn't enough?"

"I'm leaving tomorrow."

"Yet here you are, asking questions of the one person in Panama whom

Cromwell is certain to be watching as closely as he watches every outgoing penny from his bank account."

"Haven't asked you any questions," I said.

"I expect them, though. Why else would you be here?"

"To poke a stick in the eye of whoever played with my ears last night."

Harding looked at me for long moments, as if reevaluating me. "I like surprises, and this is a nice surprise. We don't have to talk about a single thing of value, and you've already used me and squeezed me dry because we'll have been seen together talking, and it will be assumed you have given me information that I can use. Or that you asked indiscreet questions. I have to admire that kind of sneakiness."

"Buying you breakfast," I said. "Not enough as payment?"

He laughed. "Hardly. I'm in the business of trading information. Leave me with a little pride. There has to be some kind of story behind your questions. Promise that if you ever speak to a reporter, I'll be the only one."

"You have my word."

"Well, what do you want to know?"

"The lay of the land." I could ask that question of a dozen people and get a dozen subjective perspectives, all valuable to me.

"That's a general enough question to almost be worthless."

"You mean worthless to you."

He laughed again. "Then how about a general lecture? I've been working on it for an article on why the United States should settle with Colombia for stealing Panama, and I might as well give it a trial run with you as an audience."

"Mind if I get more coffee first?"

He made another lazy circle of his finger, as though the waiter were a trained monkey. It gave me a sense of how the Panamanians might view us.

I sipped the coffee as Harding began.

"First, since the day Teddy gave the command to let the dirt fly, this canal has been our one great national enthusiasm, aside from baseball. The great unwashed public is so engrossed in the building of the canal that, until Cromwell's involvement came to light, few gave any thought to how we secured the right to build it. Newspaper editors have learned that the public can't seem to understand the difference between attacking the corruption behind our acquisition and attacking the patriotic act of building it. The official diplomatic version of the secession of the province of Panama from the mother country of Colombia has been commonly accepted. So humor me—what's that version?"

"I'm part of the great unwashed then?"

"Without a doubt."

Fine. I would play along. "In 1903, we had a canal treaty in place with Colombia, where we would make a ten-million-dollar payment to extend the rights they gave to the French for the Canal Zone. They decided to blackmail us into paying more. So America helped Panama declare independence, and then Panama signed a treaty with us."

Harding inclined his head. "I've just spent a month in Bogotá, and I searched the record of diplomatic correspondence with the United States Senate, the Spanish version of the same records, the annals of Colombian congress, *and* the files of local newspapers, and I found no vestige of justification—official, semiofficial, or unofficial—to support an accusation that Colombia attempted to blackmail the United States. What's of enormous interest, however, is where this accusation originated. In Washington, the paid American lobbyist for the French owners of the Panama Canal Company pointed out in writing that he foresaw the Colombians demanding ten million dollars to extend the right-of-way concession belonging to the PCC. And then he turned around and made a public outcry that Colombia was attempting to blackmail Congress."

"Let me guess," I said. "This lobbyist was paid two million for convincing the United States to purchase the PCC from France for forty million."

Neither of us needed to state said lobbyist's name. *Cromwell.*

"If Teddy hadn't sued the *World,* I wouldn't have been sent to Paris to find out where that money went. In a sense, I've accomplished that. We were told that details were in a sealed vault. It took lawyers to get us access, as the French company was publicly held, yet the records inside the vault were nonexistent. Let me quote to you what our paper's British counsel said about this, since it's fresh on my mind. 'I have never known, in my lengthy experience in company matters, any public corporation, much less one of such vast importance, having so completely disappeared and removed all traces of its existence as the New Panama Canal Company.' Keep in mind, the United States needed to purchase the New Panama Canal Company to gain access rights to the canal."

Harding was on a roll now. "The mystery extends to this side of the ocean. In Panama, all I've really discovered is that vital cable evidence has been destroyed and that the original Panamanian revolutionaries are good at keeping political secrets. They won't even admit to meeting Cromwell. Yet here he is, on his estate, effectively running the country. And that would include his command—without any shred of evidence that could prove this in court—of the National Police."

He leaned forward. "You still okay with poking someone's eye with a stick? Great efforts have been taken to hide the money trail, and asking about Cromwell and Sandoval is like asking about the money. I'm safe because I work for the *World,* and with world attention on Roosevelt's lawsuit against my newspaper, they wouldn't dare risk anything happening to me. But you're a cowboy without friends."

His expression chilled me. As did his final words: "Keep in mind, Mr. Holt, that there's a lot of jungle between here and Colón, and you aren't leaving until tomorrow."

A few hours passed. Although I wasn't hungry, I wanted to pass time. I entered the restaurant through the lobby of the National, enjoying a faint scent of cinnamon wafting on a breeze sweeping through the dining room. The windows, though open, were screened for mosquitoes.

Stefan gave me a courtly nod. I removed my hat and allowed him to take it to the coatroom. This time I had no immediate plans after lunch and wouldn't mind waiting for the hat's return when the meal was finished.

Stefan led me to a table near the windows overlooking a wide veranda. The veranda reminded me of the one and only hotel in Medora—a hotel built when I was a boy, before the Dakotas had been granted statehood. Same type of overhang, same width of veranda. It was now called the Rough Riders, in honor of Teddy Roosevelt, who made a stop there as president in 1903, all those years after he'd played at being a deputy sheriff during his ranching days.

In Medora, the view from the Rough Riders was restricted to a stable across the street and a backdrop of the hills of the Badlands formed by the Little Missouri River. Depending on the time of year, those hills would be lush green, dusty brown, or mottled with snow.

Here, the view was dominated by the palm trees ringing the plaza, where the concert had played the night before. The squat stone buildings on the other side blocked a view of the Pacific. The plaza was empty during the heat of the day, and I remembered Saffire telling me that the coloreds had their own concerts on a different night of the week.

Stefan maintained his silent gravitas until I was seated and had placed a napkin across my lap. The first time I'd dined in a formal restaurant, I'd tucked the top of the napkin into the gap between my shirt and collar. The waiter had been aghast, and the older woman opposite me had giggled and then schooled me for the remainder of the meal and the evening.

Stefan opened the menu.

"Sir," he said, "it may appear as if I am discussing your lunch selection, but that is not so. I intend to have a conversation with you."

"I'm fine if you sit across the table from me."

"I am not." His accent was a rich, dignified mixture of West Indies and British. "Speaking in a direct manner like this to you would lead to my unemployment if you complained, but I would not have this conversation unless it was important."

"Please continue."

"Saffire is a remarkable girl. Even though she has a bodyguard, she— "

"Bodyguard?"

"A well-known secret that she is under the protection of Ezequiel Sandoval. Neither he, nor I, would like to see her come to any harm."

Bodyguard. I liked that. It let her move through the city as if she owned it.

"Neither would I," I said.

"You say that like a man who agrees merely so the conversation will end." Stefan lowered the menu slightly. "So let me tell you a story about her. This is a girl who saw children her age scavenging in the garbage each night behind the hotel, looking for the food scraped off the plates of those who dine in the hotel. She found a way to organize these children to each pay her a tiny amount from what they beg. This bounty she pools to pay our kitchen staff to put the waste food in separate bags so she can distribute it to the children so they no longer have to fight rats to eat."

I thought of the money I'd given Saffire the night before. I nodded. "A remarkable girl. Forgive me if I seemed insincere. I didn't sleep well last night."

"Of course you didn't. I can see that on your ears. We call it the bite of the alligator. Those clamps leave an unmistakable pattern. Sometimes we see it on the dead. You were lucky."

I took a deep breath. *"The bite of the alligator."*

"National Police. Ears first. Then downward."

I thought of the change in Miskimon's body language after he'd looked closely at my face.

"But I didn't need to see the bite to know you faced the National Police," Stefan said. "Saffire told me where Raquel found you. And the circumstances in which she found you. This is why I fear for Saffire."

I managed to smile. "I might point out that she's the one who rescued me."

"A remarkable girl, and it will do her no good to be involved with someone who felt the bite of the alligator. She will be here, within reach of the National Police, long after you are gone. Do you understand?"

I understood the depth of his affection for her.

"Tomorrow I will be on the noon sailing of a steamer bound from Colón to New York," I told Stefan. "There is nothing to fear from me."

My steak had been set in front of me, but before I could cut into it, Robert Waldschmidt swept through the restaurant and pulled out a chair to sit at my table.

"Tell me a Buffalo Bill story, yah?"

I sliced off a corner of the steak and popped it into my mouth and chewed. Very tender and flavorful. I swallowed and cut another piece.

"Just one story, yah?"

I assumed that sooner or later, as I enjoyed this steak, Waldschmidt would realize I would tell no stories.

He didn't appear to take it as an insult. "Very well, I have a story for you. About the first and only person to die in the first revolution for the country of Panama. It was a Chinaman. He was the unfortunate victim of a stray cannonball. Here, on the Pacific side. Other than that, no real fighting. Imagine, Panama the province leaves Colombia to become Panama the country and no fighting because the Americans have chosen to protect it."

I chewed slowly. Perhaps if I made my silence last long enough, he would leave.

"Of course, some might say the Americans made a choice to *steal* it, rather than protect it," Waldschmidt continued.

I cut yet another piece of steak and looked past him as I chewed.

Waldschmidt considered me. "If that doesn't interest you, perhaps if you tell me a Buffalo Bill story, I will tell you about my eye. People always ask."

I shifted my gaze as he pointed at his eye patch. "Yesterday, the patch was on the other eye, yes?"

Waldschmidt made a move to touch it and frowned.

I raised an eyebrow. All I'd been doing was testing him to see if the eye patch was necessary or for show.

"Very good then." Waldschmidt nodded. "You caught me in a small deception. But I am sure to always put it on the same eye."

I resumed my methodical attack on the fine piece of steak.

"We shall keep this our secret, yah? I am doing my best, after all, to pretend I am living a different kind of life here. I do hope you have heard the rumors that people think I am a spy. Such a rumor adds to the spice of life, and women find such imagined danger attractive."

"I imagine your money helps with the attraction," I said. "Your secret is safe with me. I have no one to tell and I'll be gone tomorrow."

"What if I am a spy pretending to be a man pretending to be a spy?"

"And what if I tell you that I truly don't care?" I cut another piece of steak.

"You Americans are a remarkable people. Although you are upstarts in the world, there is no longer any doubt that you will accomplish what the French failed. But have you considered that if the Americans left Panama today, another country could finish the project? A country, perhaps, like Germany?"

"Have you considered that I truly have no interest in a conversation like this?"

"When the province of Panama revolted against Colombia, the only value of this land was a treaty to allow the Americans a canal zone. But now that you Americans have proven the canal is a certainty, the entire world sees the value of a way to save weeks of travel by ship. Of more value is the fact that it establishes your country as a military power controlling this entire side of the Atlantic and the Pacific. Imagine if Colombia, with help from a naval power like Germany, could take possession of her former province. Or perhaps Panama could switch allegiance to Germany? Another revolution would accomplish that."

"That's between you and the kaiser," I said.

"I tell you all this because perhaps you should wonder more about the events of last evening."

What game was this man playing? "Or not. I'm just a cowboy headed out of town."

"A cowboy who greatly interests Raquel Sandoval, if I may be so bold as to pass this along. After our conversation here last night, she did send Odalis after you, did she not?"

I was down to a final piece of steak, which I cut with slow, precise movements.

"Would it surprise you to learn that Raquel is a major supporter of Odalis in his run for mayor?"

"I wish them both the best." I speared the piece of meat. "Please pass that along."

"Watch the mayoral candidate closely, and see if you can figure out his secret." Waldschmidt leaned his elbows on the table. "He is not much of a man. Some secrets are delicious, and it is all I can do to keep that one to myself."

"I wish them both the best," I repeated. "Please pass that along."

"Would it surprise you to learn that Raquel Sandoval is a widow of her own doing? That she shot her first husband dead?"

"As I have no intent of remaining long in Panama, I'm not that interested."

"How could a man not be interested in a woman of such beauty? By happy coincidence, she will be arriving soon for lunch with me, along with Odalis and the venerable T. B. Miskimon. If you stay, you can join us."

"I have an appointment."

"Does this appointment have anything to do with matters in regard to the building of the canal?"

"It surely has nothing to do with anything that is of your business."

Waldschmidt lost his jocularity and leaned close. "I would be remiss not to warn you that it might be very dangerous to your health if you continue to be involved in the types of questions you were asking last night. Much is at stake, yah?"

I departed before his guests arrived.

Twenty

My appointment was with a pillow in my suite several floors above the restaurant. The truth was that I did not have any plans except to avoid Miskimon and recuperate from the night before. My muscles ached from the violent contractions brought on by the electric shocks. I wanted to blame my malaise on the broken sleep rhythm, but I knew better.

In regard to my emotional state, seething was too strong a word. Irritated, not strong enough. Humiliation—I didn't want to think about it. I closed my eyes.

Stop. Thinking. About. It.

Better at this point not to feel. Or think.

I let myself into the room. Too bad I didn't have my valise. After a nap I could have added some journal entries to share with Winona. Or lost myself in one of the novels.

But as I stepped to the window to look down on palm trees, the thoughts of books led me back to thoughts of Saffire. And to the night before . . .

And to the helplessness and rage against the men who had tortured me.

Was I a coward? Would I have broken and divulged the name of the man who'd sent me if Saffire hadn't rescued me?

I wasn't sure I wanted to explore those questions too fully.

No books. No friends. And too much time on my hands.

I snorted. Here I was in a luxury suite that Roosevelt himself might have used during his visit to Panama, and yet there was no joy. Which led me back to thoughts of Roosevelt . . .

Would I have told them it was Roosevelt who sent me?

As I relived the torture, I couldn't accurately recall the jolts of electricity, only my emotional response. Pain like that couldn't be comprehended on an intellectual level. It was too abstract. Yet dread washed through me—the dread I'd felt waiting for the third jolt that did not arrive.

That's what was so insidious about the bite of the alligator. The first prolonged jolt came with no warning of how horrible it would be, and therefore, I'd been innocent to its arrival. I'd just begun to recover from the first jolt, exhausted with relief that it stopped, when the second jolt hit. Then, innocence replaced by the realization that at any moment a third jolt could arrive, I'd been weak with dread all through the conversation that followed. And when my captor removed the clips from my ears and exposed my chest for the clips to be applied where the electricity's venom would have exponential effect, I'd wanted to beg for mercy. That I'd managed to clamp my jaws shut instead gave me little solace, for I suspected I would have screamed for mercy after one more jolt.

That residue of shame left me . . . grimy.

Maybe that explained my rage at Miskimon this morning—a need to shove aside shame and find another emotion strong enough to mask it.

And now?

Here it was. I could not escape the truth that I'd been violated by other men.

With this realization came another, that I'd been pacing the length of the suite. I needed to be outside. Walking. That would do it. A couple of hours in the heat, with nothing to do but wander and leave my mind blank.

No.

I needed to admit to myself what I was trying to avoid.

I'd been ten the last time I'd felt this shame. My father had been down at the neighbor's corrals during a summer afternoon, in idle conversation with his fellow rancher. I wandered to a small, dry creek bed with no particular destination in mind, when two of the neighbor's dogs charged from a curve ahead.

Their silence unnerved me the most. It signaled a deadly intent, and I scrambled to a tree, barely getting to a safe height as they reached me, jumping and scratching at the tree base.

My father was within earshot, and I could have screamed for help. I did not. The shame of running from the dogs was compounded by the shame that I had wet my pants, leaving a visible large wet patch. I remained in the safety of the tree for another half hour, hoping my pants would dry in the heat.

But my father came looking for me before the stain had disappeared. I had no choice but to call out to him when he began to yell for me. That's when he marched up to the dogs at the base of the tree and kicked them aside.

When I climbed to the ground, he glanced at the stain down the inside of my pants legs.

"Know why those dogs ran from me?"

Shame turned into resentment. "You're bigger."

"From their perspective, they have to look up at you, same as they did to me." He spit to the side. "Size has nothing to do with it. Difference is, while they have to look up *at* me, I also made them look up *to* me. They ran because they knew I wasn't afraid of a fight and I'd keep kicking no matter what they did."

He looked at the stain on my pants again. "If you don't forget what they did to you, it's going to tear you up just as surely as if they got their teeth into you. And that kind of damage doesn't heal. We're coming back tomorrow, and you're going to walk around until either you find the dogs or you let the dogs find you. When they come running, if you end up climbing another tree, you're going to be there until you figure out a way down. I suggest you make them look up *to* you instead of up *at* you. And no, I'm not giving you a rifle."

This close to the ocean, the streets were set in grids, and finding the National Police headquarters had been as simple as asking for directions, then strolling beneath the palm leaves waving in the breeze.

I pushed through the main entrance, removing my hat as I stepped inside. There was a front counter, almost like a bank counter, but without a protective grill. The policeman behind the counter had a build that fit his sedentary role. Flecks of gray in his thick hair showed him to be well past his first years on the force. His wide face was remarkable only for the upside-down horseshoe mustache, ragged ends drooping well beneath his chin.

I walked up to the counter, hat in my hands. Cowboy hats were not usual in Panama, and I caught a flicker of comprehension in his face.

Señor Vaquero Americano.

He gave an involuntary glance at my ears. Then a few rapid blinks.

As I'd suspected, it was not a large police force. Rank-and-file cops, like soldiers, thrived on gossip. If Harding knew about the events of the previous night, it was no surprise that the man at the front desk knew.

"Is there something with which I can help you?" he asked.

His recognition of me had probably elicited the deference of heavily accented English instead of Spanish.

"Last night, away from here, I was having a conversation with someone who is probably now somewhere in this building," I said. "The conversation was interrupted. I'd like to continue it with that person."

The day my father forced me to face the dogs, I learned something. Fear can stoke rage. Cold rage.

"Such a conversation is, of course, a matter of privacy," he said. "Please forgive me, however, for suggesting that rumors have made it clear that the need for any more conversation has ended and there is no longer official interest in your activities. You might want to consider this a matter of good fortune."

"I have not finished with my end of the conversation."

There was a long hesitation. "For the record, señor, it is our policy not to allow weapons in our building."

Impressive. He had struck me as clerical, but to raise the issue, alone as he was behind the counter, he must have been prepared to enforce it. I half expected him to raise a pistol.

"I am unarmed," I said. "I am simply looking for a man-to-man conversation. There would be no honor in hiding behind a weapon."

Another long hesitation. Perhaps he was reevaluating me. Or sensing my buildup of rage.

"And the policeman's name?" he asked. "There are many of us here."

"I hope he might remember my name. I'll write it down if you want."

More thought from across the counter as he considered the options. He then folded a yellow piece of paper in half, in half again, and in half again. He tore a small square of paper where it had been folded and handed me a pencil and the piece of yellow paper.

After scratching my name on the paper, I slid it toward him. "I'd be grateful if you passed it along. I'll take a seat and wait right here. It was a rather intense conversation, so I suspect he'll remember me. Please let him know I'm anxious to meet him again to resolve it completely."

Much as I tried to be casual, I suspected the tightness in my tone betrayed me. He took the paper and studied my face.

I could feel it inside now and hoped it showed.

Deadly intent.

The day after the dogs forced me up a tree, my father delivered upon his promise and, despite my pleading, did not allow me a rifle. But he didn't expressly forbid any other weapon. I found a broken branch and held it like a club. The dogs found me near the tree of the day before and, as before, silently ran toward me. But this time I advanced on them, my club at the ready, and it had given me great satisfaction to watch them slow as if puzzled. Then I'd realized the club made them afraid, not me. So I threw it aside and let the murder inside me grow, suddenly glad they kept advancing on me—not at a run, but with calculation. The ends of my boots were weapon enough. I was prepared to take whatever their teeth might inflict. I would get my licks in . . .

"Do you have a cigarette?"

I looked at the policeman. "I do not."

"Pity. I'll have to use my own."

There was a gate in the counter. He lifted it and walked through. "Outside, señor. First, a cigarette, no?"

He was a head shorter than I, yet probably outweighed me as if he were a head taller. By the way he walked, I saw that his width was not necessarily the softness of indulgence. Would my fight begin with him?

I followed him to the shade. He offered me a cigarette. I was not a smoking man, but it would have been rude to turn down an offer of hospitality.

He lit my cigarette first, then his, both from the same match. He handed me my cigarette.

He inhaled deeply and then blew out a long stream of smoke.

I had not drawn from my cigarette.

He grimaced on my behalf. "Yes. A shame I cannot offer American cigarettes. So much better than ours. But too expensive."

"I am interested in continuing my conversation of last night, not in comparing the merits of tobacco."

The first dog had lunged at me, and my first kick was a matter of luck. As it leaped, I punted it fully in the chest with my foot. My knee, unintended, connected squarely with its jaw.

"I am a family man." The policeman drew another puff, then patted his belly with his other hand. "At the end of the day, I love to go home and sit at dinner with my wife and daughters. Some find the sound of children bickering annoying, but I listen and smile because someday I know I will be old and the girls I adore will no longer be in my home."

He looked down the street, then back at me again. "Are you impressed at my command of your language? I am educated and belong to an old family here. With ambition, I could be like some of the young ones, the hungry ones who get promotions and better pay. Sometimes I endure insults from those who think it means I am weak, but I know what matters to me, and that is my family. You, señor, do you have children?"

"A daughter."

"How old?"

"Nearly seven years old."

"I suspect we are much the same, you and I. At night, if someone broke into your house or mine to try violence against our children, would we lack courage to fight?"

I kept a level gaze. All those years ago, the first dog had scrambled backward at the guttural rage coming from my throat. The second dog curled its tail under its belly. I turned and saw my father, observing. He didn't smile. Only nodded. I'd realized then how angry I was at him too.

"You and I"—the policeman in front of me was halfway through his cigarette—"to defend our children, we would fight until we were dead, no matter the odds. The younger men at the station, who are not yet fathers, they don't understand that kind of love. But even as they insult me at how fat and soft I might appear, they know never to insult my family."

His conversational tone was languid. It didn't fool me.

"To survive the bite of the alligator is one thing, but to go back into the pit with a dozen alligators is another. Especially if you are risking death to prove you are more man than the one who inflicted the bite, a death almost so certain that some might call it suicide."

From his pocket, he took the small yellow piece of paper with my name. He held the embers of his cigarette to the paper and sucked air through the cigarette, heating it to a deeper glow until the paper began to burn. He dropped the curled, blackened paper and crushed it beneath his heel on the cobblestone.

"I would suggest, señor, that pride is worth far less than ensuring your daughter will be protected by your presence each night. Is it enough for your pride that I will be the only one in this world to know that walking away from this city with the bite of the alligator on your ears is a far braver act than facing the alligators again to prove you are a man?"

He drew a final puff of the cigarette and crushed it beneath his heel as he had done with the burned paper. He met my gaze. "Señor, already I admire you for putting your name on that paper. I will admire you more if you permit me to go back inside alone."

He walked up the steps without looking back.

I finally drew on the cigarette he gave me. I tasted acrid bitterness.

I did not follow.

Twenty-One

A half hour later, back in the hotel suite, I paced again. This time not from bottled frustration and anger but from a need to work the trembling out of my muscles. It was more than relief that made me weak. It was a feeling much like I'd had in Cuba during a hot afternoon when most of the other Rough Riders were doing their best to nap in the drowsy heat.

I had sat on one low stump, facing the camp cook, who sat on another stump. Between us was a third stump that held cards and some scattered matchsticks serving as gambling tokens. We weren't playing for big stakes, keeping the poker friendly.

I drew a four of clubs to fill a straight and grinned as I flipped the cards over. In fake exasperation, the cook tossed his own cards onto the dirt, so with exaggerated courtesy, I insisted that I help him clean up his mess.

The cook laughed as I leaned over to grab the scattered cards. His laughter became a choked cough. An instant later came the snap of rifle fire. I dove and rolled. Shouts told me that the other soldiers in the camp were reacting to the sound of the single shot.

Sniper.

When I found my feet, the cook was on his back, dead. When we opened his shirt, the entry wound looked innocent, clear of blood because the man's heart was shredded by the slug and had stopped pumping.

Cooks were not targets for the Spanish snipers; soldiers were. I'd been saved from the sniper bullet by a four of clubs.

I'd felt guilty that I didn't feel more guilt, because my overwhelming reaction had been trembly relief at how close I'd come to filling a casket.

Now I had the same reaction. What had I been thinking? That, to preserve my honor, I could walk into the headquarters of the police force of a foreign country and challenge someone to a boxing match?

My relief was tempered by my guilt. It shouldn't have taken a pudgy and friendly policeman to remind me that my greatest duty was to protect Winona.

I continued to pace until I could sit without feeling my legs twitch.

I made a call to the front desk, requesting a plate of fresh fruits and cheese. I'd settle my stomach and perhaps nap after that. All I had to do was find a way to pass time until the steamer sailed the next day. I could leave with a clear conscience. Goethals didn't need me, and I'd resolved the issue of my honor against my unknown torturers.

But as I waited for the fruit, I could not escape what else was nagging at me.

Saffire.

Much as I wanted to get home, I knew I would feel better if I'd first done my best to help her.

Despite the heat, I would have preferred to walk. Inactivity and laziness did not suit me.

However, I was unsure of how to reach my destination, and I suspected that once I arrived, appearances would matter. To knock on the door drenched in sweat and to appear that I couldn't afford a carriage ride would work against me.

Outside on the plaza, in the shade of the hotel, I spoke to a tiny doorman. "I don't have the address. Will you be able to direct a carriage to the residence of Ezequiel Sandoval?"

"Of course." He smoothed his mustache, as if he were charging into battle on my behalf, and blew a whistle at a line of carriages. The nearest hack flicked his cigarette butt to the cobblestones before swinging up onto the carriage to take the traces. With an expert flick of the reins, he sent the single horse forward, then stopped the carriage so that all I needed to do was grab the rail and hoist myself up the step to the rear-facing bench seat behind the hack.

I stepped forward, then looked at the doorman. "Could you request that the horse and carriage wait at the residence for me?"

The hack said, "I speak English. That will be no problem."

There was insolence in his voice. I knew I was tired and on edge, because of my instant flare of irritation. I met the man's eyes. Yes, I was overreacting. My assumption about his language skills had been an insult to him.

"Name your price and it's yours," I told the hack. "But you'll charge it to my hotel bill, understood?"

He nodded.

"One more thing." I fought a wave of exhaustion. "I don't need a tour guide. Directly there. Directly back. No conversation."

Another nod.

I was reading insolence into the man's every action, and I told myself that this, too, was a function of my general irritation.

It was just past the hottest part of the day, and the streets were nearly silent. The carriage took us higher into the hills and away from the crowded buildings in the commercial district to the landscape of the larger houses with verandas and rotating fans. Birds screeching and insects buzzing among the leaves made it seem like a ride through innocent countryside, and I enjoyed the fragrances of blossoms that I could not identify. Still, I ached for the scent of sage crushed beneath a horse's hoof and the squeaking of prairie dogs sending alarms as they dove into their burrows.

It took perhaps ten minutes for the hack to settle our carriage in front of a large villa with a cobblestone drive. Like all the other enclaves of wealth, the villa showed no activity. Just the pastel outer plaster; small, high windows with bars; and a large door at the entryway, all framed beneath red clay tiles.

When I reached the portico, I welcomed the shade, glad for my decision to take a carriage. In front of me, a bronze panther head served as the knocker for a door that was easily ten feet tall. A circular Judas window was chest high to me.

I lifted the panther head and let it fall. The sound of bronze against wood echoed in the portico. I removed my hat, preparing for a wait of a minute or two, based on my assumption of the size of the villa.

It took five.

Someone on the other side slid open the Judas window. There was brief light through the circle, then darkness again as the person peered through.

I bent so that my face was visible for inspection. "I apologize that I have no appointment. I'm an American. James Holt. If possible, I would like to speak to Señor Sandoval about the mother of a girl that I know named Saffire. The mother's name is Jade. She was, I believe, employed as a cook for Señor Sandoval."

I half expected to be told to leave, based on my sense that society here was much more formal than in the badlands of Medora. Instead, there was a sound of a bolt scraping against wood, and the door swung open. I caught a glimpse of tile floor, a wide hallway, and large paintings on the walls.

I waited to be invited inside, but instead, a magnificently tall black woman, old enough to have almost completely gray hair and dressed in a maid's uniform, stepped out into the courtyard and shut the door behind her.

Her face was tight. She spoke in a whisper that didn't disguise a West Indies accent. "Señor Holt, it is not my position to tell you what to do, but even if Señor Sandoval was in the city, this is not a household where people off the street are welcomed inside. I only speak to you now because of the kindness you have shown to Saffire. It wouldn't be proper for me to allow you inside the house."

"It was a risk I thought I would take." I put my hat back on and tipped it to the maid. "You have my apologies. If I wrote you a note with a place to meet, would you be willing to discuss this with me at another time?"

"Please, I have already spent too much time with you. Saffire roams the streets, but she is welcome in Señor Sandoval's home at any time, so there is no need to be concerned for her."

The woman retreated, shutting the door, and I stood there, staring at the expensive wood.

At the carriage, Saffire was leaning against the rear wheel, arms crossed, a package in plain brown paper pressed between her arms and her body. Bare feet, spindly legs, faded dress. I should have expected she would find me. I found myself grinning, lifted out of my malaise by the sight of her.

I picked up my pace.

The hack was farther down the road, smoking a cigarette. I wouldn't be surprised to learn that Saffire had sent him there.

"You followed me here?" I asked her.

"I was in the villa." Her voice seemed subdued, matching the droop of her shoulders. "I come and go as I please. Señor Vaquero Americano, this was not a good thing that you did, visiting like this."

"To look for your mother," I said. "I want a conversation with your tito. Tell me how I can meet with him."

"That will not be possible. He is not in the city, but at his ranch."

"Then I will take you there."

"No." She shook her head. "Please go back to your hotel and then back to your country. I do not wish for you to look for my mother."

I examined her face.

Arms still crossed, she lifted her chin.

I gentled my tone. "We are alone. No one will hear this conversation. Why have you changed your mind?"

"This is for you." She handed me the package. Before I could open it, she spun and ran back to the villa.

I watched until she was gone. What had caused her change in attitude? I studied the package—it was about the size and weight of a book. It was *The Virginian,* the copy that I had signed in pencil for her. All the pencil markings had been erased.

I looked back at the villa, as if there would be an explanation forthcoming from the shuttered windows.

Whatever the reason, she had effectively absolved me of any responsibility to her.

Well, that was that. I'd done all I could—for the man who'd sent me to Panama, for Goethals, for my pride after the torture, and for Saffire. In the morning, I could, in good conscience, begin my journey home armed with a bank draft to save my ranch from foreclosure and the intent to live a quiet life with my daughter.

twenty-two

A knock at the door woke me from restless sleep. I heard a rasping of paper—someone had slid a note under the door.

I ignored it.

From Goethals himself at the top, to Miskimon, Waldschmidt, and even Saffire, I was tired of webs of intrigue. Panama, either as a colony of Spain or a province of Colombia or as a newly independent country, had existed for those hundreds of years, with those pirates and gold runners and plantation owners all leaving ghosts of their interwoven desires and sins and ambitions across the land. I came from a dry and desolate land where men solved their disputes in barroom brawls.

I closed my eyes and tried to fall back to sleep.

I had no success.

With a sigh, I padded across the luxurious suite and found the note.

Back home, I would have had to light an oil lamp to read it. Here, with modern comforts, it would simply take the flick of a light switch.

Was someone outside the hotel, watching, waiting for a glow from the window to tell them I had read the note? My first impulse was to go ahead, not caring whether I was observed.

My second impulse was deception—an impulse that showed I had already fallen into the web. Still, caution might serve me better, so I moved into the windowless bathroom of the suite. Then, just before flicking on the light, I put a towel on the floor at the door to hide the light.

Such was the power of the memory of the electric shock that had been applied to my body by hooded men.

The note was simple: *Please come down to the sea wall, where the avenue Federico Boyo meets the waters.*

Avenue Federico Boyo was a main thoroughfare, easy enough to find. I checked my watch. Already an hour past midnight.

I should ignore the note. If someone wanted to talk to me, the daylight hours should suffice. At the least, the person should have the courtesy to sign the note.

Practicality told me to get back into bed. The core of Panama City was a haven for pickpockets, prostitutes, con artists, and all the other desperate creatures of the night. Besides, I had already been dragged down once by an undercurrent. Why risk it again? Perhaps the National Police had decided to ensure I was alone in a place where I could be snatched back into a hut high in the hills.

Yet one simple word I could not ignore: *please.*

I began a convolution of looped thoughts. While adding *please* was not what one would expect on a deceptive note from National Police thugs, perhaps it was an artful attempt to fool me. Yet anyone who would try that kind of manipulation was intelligent enough to find other ways to successfully ambush me, so ignoring this note might lead to another attempt.

I only had five hours left before checking out of the hotel. Safe in this suite, what harm could befall me? So why not remain in this haven?

On the other hand, did I want to be like the fearful elderly woman, locked behind a door, startled at any noise in the night? And did this fearfulness prove that my moments in front of a generator with a clip to each ear had diminished me more than I wanted to admit?

Should I respond to the note to show I was not afraid? Doing so would counter the advice from the pudgy policeman, putting my pride above the need to protect my daughter by ensuring she would have a father's presence as she grew to be a woman.

All the mental blathering made me weary. And irritated at myself.

I put on my clothes and my boots and my hat and stepped outside the door. I wished my revolver was not in my valise, but with me instead.

Warm, humid air and the scent of jasmine embraced me as I walked across the plaza. It was quiet, and when I reached the other side, I stayed in the center of the street. When I rounded the next corner, grateful for moonlight with enough intensity to throw shadows, a small figure stepped out of the alley.

"Señor Vaquero Americano!"

Odalis Corillo, the candidate for mayor. While I recognized him, I did not relax. Was anyone in Panama who they appeared to be?

I stopped and waited, maintaining my position in the center of the street.

Odalis hurried to me. "Come, come." He took me by the elbow, leading me back toward the alley. "I'd rather we were not seen together."

"I'm happy here." I removed his hand from my elbow. "How about telling me why our conversation can't wait until morning?"

"You leave in the morning. When would we have the opportunity?"

I could have pursued how he knew my travel plans, but webs are essentially strands of a connected labyrinth. Learning how he knew still might not get me to the center—discovering who really plucked at all the webs.

"Odalis, I'm tired and I need my sleep. Give me a reason why I shouldn't turn around instead of going to the sea wall."

"First, let me thank you for saving me from a beating. You are a wonderful man and will always have my gratitude."

An idle part of my brain recalled Waldschmidt's words: *"Watch the mayoral candidate closely and see if you can figure out his secret. He is not much of a man. Some secrets are delicious, and it is all I can do to keep that one to myself."*

"Odalis, if you truly are grateful, find Saffire and donate some money to her efforts to feed the street children."

"Yes! Yes!" He tried to pull me toward the alley again.

"I'm tired and I need my sleep. Why shouldn't I just go back to the hotel?"

"First—"

"You already said that."

"This first is in regard to the note," he said with some dignity. "The sea wall is not our destination. That was only for anyone else who might read it and try to spy on you."

"Or in case I wanted to send others to follow me?"

"Of course, of course. Now you are thinking like one of us."

I suspect it was intended as a compliment, but I didn't take it as such. "Odalis, I'll say this for the third time. I'm tired and need my sleep—"

"It's Raquel Sandoval. She wishes to meet with you."

twenty-three

I did not like it that Odalis had chosen to take me into the darkness of an alley.

"No," I said, one pace into the alley. It smelled of cat urine and rotting fruit.

"It's much shorter," he answered.

And a fine place to ambush someone. What, after all, did I know about Odalis? There were too many places for someone to step out, too easy to get trapped if someone guarded both entrances while we were halfway through.

"No point in arguing," I told Odalis.

"Excellent."

By then, he was already speaking to my back, for I had turned back onto the street, the lighted entrance of the hotel behind us a reassuring landmark. In that movement, I caught a flash of motion among shadows at a storefront halfway between me and the hotel, so discreet I wondered if I had imagined it.

Had someone been following? Was the promise of a meeting with Raquel just a way to lure me into danger?

A more cautious man would have simply made a determined stride back to the hotel. But I could not resist the temptation to see Raquel, even though I would be out of this country before the next day's sunset. So it was more than impulse that led me to the storefront—it was the need to know whether this was a trap or if I could believe Raquel actually wanted to spend time with me.

I tempered that lack of caution, however, for I was not armed. So I crossed the street. If someone was in a doorway, distance would protect me from a knife. As for a pistol, it took a good shot to hit a man at forty or fifty feet. And anyway, had a follower wanted to shoot me, I wouldn't be safe anywhere tonight.

"Señor Holt," Odalis called in a low voice, hurrying to stay with my long strides. "This way!"

I ignored him as I walked on the opposite sidewalk, and I was proven correct about the motion of shadow when I saw someone in the doorway.

Should I confront our follower? The decision was taken away from me as I heard a sprinkle against brick and realized whoever it was had decided to urinate, his back toward me. The sound carried clearly in the quiet of the night.

When it stopped, the person staggered out of the doorway and began singing in a low voice. Spanish.

By then, Odalis reached me.

"I thought he'd followed us," I said.

"Bum," Odalis sneered, even though the man was too far away to hear. "Drunk." He took my arm. "If you don't want the alley, we'll do it your way then. But I can protect you anywhere in the city. You have nothing to fear, Señor Holt."

Her chosen spot was not where Avenue Federico Boyo ended at the sea wall but farther south, at a small peninsula with a beach hidden by palm trees. Odalis withdrew to a discreet distance, leaving Raquel and me alone on the narrow strip of sand at the water's edge, but I was aware of his scrutiny.

I had my hat off and in my hand. I could smell her perfume in wisps that were like tendrils in the fresh salt tang around us.

"I was hoping we might chat," I said. "Thank you for sending the children into the hut."

"No, forgive me, instead. I was the one who sent Odalis to talk with you last night, and I fear that's what drew the National Police."

I gave that thought. "Will you explain why?"

"No."

"Let's talk then about Saffire's mother. I've met the girl, you know. It appears there is no one to help her."

"That would involve speaking about my father, which is not something I wish to do either. Indeed, I speak to you with some reluctance, Mr. Holt, and I don't wish to keep you long."

"It was somewhat unkind that you chose this time of night for it. It's not a convenient walk back to the hotel, which is a lot of effort for a short conversation."

I couldn't help myself. This was a feeble attempt at self-defense, for the same dizziness I'd felt upon meeting her was betraying me now.

"It is this very inconvenience that I hope might keep you from disappearing as you have done almost immediately each time we've met, Mr. Holt."

"How about just Holt? James was my father's name, and his father's name as well. James Junior never set well with him, nor with me. Somewhere along the way, people just got accustomed to calling me Holt. I would be fine if you dropped the mister."

Tiny birds—in the Dakotas, I thought of them as sandpipers—ran up and down the sand, flashes of white in the light of the moon. The tide had recently retreated, and the sand was wet and packed.

"Not curious about the reason for my reluctance?" She paused. "Holt?"

"I can give you an answer that would irritate you."

"Try me," she said.

"Your reluctance is based on the impropriety of an unescorted woman engaging in conversation with a man at this time of night."

"Yes, that answer does irritate me," she said. "How did you guess it would?

"I believe a woman who stands for suffrage is a woman who doesn't like being told what to do. Or being judged for her actions when men in the same situation are not."

"So this is an issue because I am of the gentler sex?"

At the tinge of anger in her words, I snorted. "It's my observation that women are much tougher than men. You are oversensitive. I believe few people of either gender like being told what to do."

I was rewarded with light laughter.

"Fair enough. Are you chauvinistic enough to believe in this day and age that a conversation between the two of us is improper under these circumstances?"

"For the sake of propriety, I assure you that I will fend off all but the most persistent of your advances."

"*My* advances?" She stepped back, her anger more than a tinge.

"Because you are clearly sensitive to assumptions about gender, I didn't want to offend you by suggesting we should expect the man in this situation to attempt something improper. After all, you're the one who lured me here to be alone with you this late at night."

"Lured? *Lured?* If I don't laugh, it's because I'm doing my best to not be angry right now."

This was fun. Better her off balance than me. And I think she was accustomed to keeping men off balance. "Then I apologize. I've been told you shot your first husband. I think I'll do my best not to offend you until I know whether it's true."

She remained silent. I moved closer to the grass. I didn't want my boots to get soaked with salt water.

She followed.

"Waldschmidt?" she asked. Then turned it into a statement. "Waldschmidt. He loves to gossip almost as much as Odalis."

"Yes. I learned this from Waldschmidt."

"My former husband threatened to whip me. He told me it was a man's right to be master over his wife. As if I were some kind of beast of burden. I grabbed a pistol and told him it was a woman's right to defend herself. The story is overblown, however. I was aiming at his foot and only hit his big toe. Not surprisingly, when I aimed higher and threatened to shoot again, he dropped the whip and didn't resist the idea of divorce."

"Waldschmidt told me you shot him dead."

"My husband was very much alive and astounded. Waldschmidt lies because Waldschmidt loves intrigue."

"I don't, but I will point out that this seems to be going rather well, given your stated reluctance to engage in conversation."

"The logical thing for you to do is ask me why I have that reluctance."

"And give you the satisfaction of making me the supplicant when you are the one who initiated this rendezvous?"

The breeze was capricious. One moment it would bring her perfume, and the next, snatch it away. Dizzy as she made me, I felt an impunity. Since we would never meet again, what did I have to lose?

"I had illusions that you were a gentleman of sorts, despite your cavalier attitude toward your appearance. Such a comment suggests otherwise."

I had no hesitation in my answer. "If you believe a gentleman's character is based on clothing, then congratulations on your engagement to Mr. Amador."

She giggled. "Did you just say that?"

"Petty, I agree. But it was a satisfying remark, at least from my perspective."

"Well, he *is* one of the reasons I'm here."

"Ah, so he suggested we meet me in the moonlight, on a beach, beneath palm trees? I'm surprised. He struck me as the possessive type."

She was silent again, waiting perhaps to see if I had anything to add to my statement. But when she spoke, I realized it was a silence to gather her thoughts. "I doubt he would approve of the time and location of this conversation, but I am my own woman."

My resulting silence was of the former, and I was rewarded as she continued.

"My fiancé is among those who suggested I should be the one to learn more about you. The group consensus was that you might not be guarded around a woman. No one wanted to say it, but you do have a chivalrous air. What I found interesting was that none of the men wanted to state the obvious, which was that there is something dangerous about you too. Except for Mr. Miskimon. At lunch today, Odalis managed to convince Mr. Miskimon to betray the fact that you have a knife scar on your shoulder from a Sioux warrior. Mr. Waldschmidt nearly brayed his delight and begged for more stories, but that was all that Mr. Miskimon revealed about you to us."

"I'm surprised he said that much. Mr. Miskimon, much as I might not like him, strikes me as a very discreet man."

Raquel laughed. "Poor Mr. Miskimon is like a cat on hot coals around Odalis. Odalis and I share a secret that I think you would find amusing."

"You have no reason to trust me with a secret, but I am curious."

"Does that make you a supplicant?"

"Not curious enough to ask."

More of her laughter. It was addicting.

"Let's trade secrets. You tell me the story about the Sioux warrior, and I'll tell you about Odalis. I promise it will be worth your while. What harm could there be in exchanging confidences?"

"How about instead you explain your reluctance to speak to me. You've already admitted that you've been sent by the group."

"It is based on the group assumption that I should use womanly wiles to learn about you, something I resented. So while I agreed that I would ask you our questions, I've decided, without group permission, not to try to hide behind coquettish conversation and instead be blunt and explain that I am asking it on behalf of the group. Why are you in Panama asking about my father?"

"Who is in the group and why does it matter to them?"

She took a small step along the beach, her body language inviting me to walk with her. I could not resist.

"If you can't make an accurate guess," she answered, "then you have less intelligence than I estimated. Impress me. Live up to my expectations, and tell me who is in the group."

"What if I'm not interested in impressing you?"

"I would be disappointed."

She slowed so that I closed the gap between us, and stepped toward me, tilting that beautiful face upward to look at me directly. Had there been no moonlight, she would have been only an outline. Instead, I clearly saw those delightfully curved lips.

There was tension. Of the delicious sort. And enough of a hint in her smile to show she knew it.

I said, "I can see why the group consensus was to make you ambassador."

"Who is in the group?" She smiled. "Tell me, Holt."

She was toying with me. Knowing that the soft way she said my name was a seduction of sorts.

"Not your father," I said.

"No?"

"From what little I know of him, I can't see him whispering little plans with your fiancé or Harding and Waldschmidt and Odalis. Does that cover the group?"

"Essentially."

"Your father is not in the group."

"No, my father is not in the group."

"Neither is Miskimon."

"Neither is Miskimon. Odalis, however, does have a soft spot for that man."

I waited for her to reveal the secret about Odalis, but it did not come. "This group has a purpose?"

"Some of us resent the American occupation of our young country. Some of us think we are no better off than when we were a province of Colombia. The United States has taken a lot from us and given us little. Other countries have more to offer."

"Ah, Waldschmidt and his games. Tempting you with Germany."

It made clear sense. With a canal between the two oceans, this small country was worth a great deal on the world stage. And the kaiser believed in aggression. Germany's military assets made it formidable, and few doubted the kaiser's will to use those assets. All that Germany needed was a way to negate the British naval powers. From a military point of view, all it would take was a base at each end of the canal to hold the entire isthmus.

"Perhaps. Why are you in Panama asking about my father?"

"Why I'm in Panama is my business. I don't mean that unkindly."

"When you wander about this city asking questions about my father and his business, I think that makes it my business. Especially when you visit my family home and try to speak to one of our maids."

She'd stepped back. Gone was the seductive pose. I felt real anger from her.

"Your mistake is assuming that one is related to the other. Why I'm in Panama is my business. Why I wandered the city with questions about your father is something entirely different. And the simple reason is because of Saffire."

This seemed to startle her. "Saffire?"

"Here's the truth, Señorita Sandoval."

"If it's to be Holt, then please, call me Raquel."

"Here's the truth. Somehow, in less than twenty-four hours, that girl managed to drag me into a situation that I didn't see coming."

"Yes," Raquel said. "She has that capacity. And I do know about your troubles in the night. The bite of the alligator. I'm not surprised that your questions led to that."

"You'll explain that to me?"

"My father is a powerful man and dangerous to many. Even his enemies would want to know why you appear with questions about him."

I scratched my head, wishing I could put my hat on again. But that would be ungentlemanly.

"You are welcome to tell your friends—and your father's enemies—that I have no more questions. Tomorrow, I'll be gone. In fact, I visited your home this afternoon to assure myself that all would be fine for Saffire, so I could leave the country in good conscience."

"Why should you care about a girl you barely know?"

"My only child is a daughter close to her age."

"You are married then. That surprises me. You don't seem tamed."

"I am a widower." I knew why I wanted her to know that. I was rewarded again with a smile.

"I doubt I can get my friends to believe that Saffire is the reason. In this world there are many girls the age of your daughter. You can't save them all."

"At one time, I cherished a cynicism that allowed me to believe that was a good enough reason not to try to make a difference."

"And then?"

"I held my newborn daughter and wept for the joy of it. It's one of the best memories of my life." And one of my worst.

Raquel put an arm through mine and led me down the beach in a slow stroll.

"Soon"—her subdued tone wrapped around me—"I will be married to a man who would believe that kind of admission is a contemptible weakness."

"I wish you the best."

"It will be a pragmatic marriage. I have no illusions about what is ahead. I am also a woman of honor, and a woman of honor does not disgrace herself by shirking a commitment such as the sacrament of marriage. Keep that in mind, and know that while the admission I'm about to make might seem of little matter to you, it is of great significance to me because it is something that I'm aware will be close to a betrayal of that upcoming marriage. Yet it is something I know I will regret not saying if I do not take this opportunity to say it."

She stopped and faced me, continuing so softly that I strained to hear her above the lapping of water on the sand. "I am grateful for a shared walk that I will remember for a long time, with a man to whom I feel drawn, when I'd begun to believe I would never feel like this again. So thank you for letting me discover my heart is not entirely dead. It will be bitter and sweet to speculate on what could have been, had we met under different circumstances and had you felt the same toward me."

"I—"

"Do not tell me whether you feel the same. Let me believe what I want to believe." She lifted my hand and kissed my knuckles. "I would have liked to hear about the Sioux warrior. I wish you safe travels as you return to your daughter. Good night, Mr. Holt. And good-bye."

She turned and walked back to Odalis, and I watched her outline grow smaller and smaller. My emotions were as roiled as the waters coming in from the Pacific.

I did not sleep that night. Instead, I walked until dawn, thinking through every word she had said, every nuance.

When I finally returned to the hotel suite, there was another note under the door.

As you take the train to Colón, don't stop at the administration office in Culebra for your valise and its contents, as I have taken it. If you want it back, meet me at the Gatún Locks at 11:00 a.m. T. B. Miskimon.

Tuesday

January 12, 1909

Col. Geo. W Goethals,

Chairman & Chief Engineer

Culebra, Canal Zone

Sir:

On Saturday evening, May 30th, the Commanding Officer of Culebra Police Station, and the Commanding Officer of Empire Police Station, both on horseback, rode their horses at a lope into the saloon of Jose Sandy at Empire. Riding up to the bar, they dismounted and each took a drink. While in the saloon one of the horses deposited dung upon the floor, which the Panamanian servant was obliged to clean up. These men were not in full uniform, but as Commanding Officers of Stations are always considered on duty, an act of this kind certainly looks like rowdyism and these men are guilty of "conduct unbecoming officers." According to police regulations, this is considered a serious discharge and justifies dismissal. This is especially a serious charge inasmuch as these men are Commanding Officers of their respective precincts.

The Sergeant, Carter, of Empire, I am informed, resigns from the force in a few days, if he has not already done so, but even if he could not be punished for same through the Police Department, I think this matter should be taken into consideration in the granting of a saloon license at Empire for which I understand he has applied.

I was able to obtain the following witnesses to the incident:

Mr. Rome, Proprietor, Pennsylvania Hotel, Empire

The proprietor of this saloon, his wife and servant.

Mr. F. Werzenberg, Inspector, Tax Collectors Office, Empire

Mr. Rome states that he considered the men intoxicated, but the statement is not borne out by the other witnesses, except that Mr. Werzenberg stated to me that he did not consider any man sober "who would ride in a man's place of business at a gallop."

Respectfully,
Inspector T. B. Miskimon

Twenty-Four

It was a selfish and childish impulse that compelled me to rise early enough to prowl the streets of Panama City. Raquel Sandoval had seized far too much of my emotional attention. Had I been a teenaged cowboy with a first crush, I could have rationalized it, but I was far beyond those years, and not just in age.

The sorrows over the deaths of those I loved grounded me long ago. I was at peace with my role as a widowed and doting father, happy to worry about my daughter's happiness instead of my own. Since Winona's birth, I had not mooned over any woman, nor had I felt that my life would be incomplete unless I found a companion.

Desire, I understood. Desire, however, could be disciplined, ignored.

How could I actually love Raquel? Didn't real love grow with an investment of time, of slowly learning who the other person was? Why, then, did the prospect of sitting on the front porch of my ranch house as an elderly man, simply holding hands with her as an elderly woman, seem like such a wonderful, perfect thing?

I did not want to be afflicted with this emotion. And I certainly did not want to take it back with me to the Dakotas, where it would be too easy to romanticize the brief time she and I had spent along the beach of the Pacific on a moonlit night.

So, how to scourge it? My mind muddled on it until a plan formed. I would look past the romance and try to see the reality. Raquel Sandoval was nothing more than a high-society woman with a fashionable veneer of charity. Remove the illusion, and I'd see her more clearly.

All it would take was a few questions.

I changed my course, moving with firm steps to the sanitarium.

It was shortly before 8 a.m. that I arrived at my destination, my shirt heavy with sweat.

The gate to the high wall was unlocked, and I pushed it open. The well-manicured courtyard had a path of stepping stones that took me to a door on the far side. This, too, was unlocked.

I stepped inside to an unattended open area. Children's laughter drifted to me, as did the crying of babies.

I walked a generously wide hallway. With no one to stop me, I walked farther inside. The door to the first room was open, and I glanced within.

A girl with heavy pockmarks on her face, looking barely older than a child herself, sat in a rocking chair, a baby cradled in her arms.

"Hello," I said.

She didn't seem frightened by my presence.

"May I enter?"

She nodded. The baby clutched one of her fingers and gurgled.

"She is beautiful." I moved nearer and squatted so that my height would not be intimidating. "What is her name?"

"Olivia," the girl said.

I felt unkind now that my first thought when I saw her was about the pockmarks. For when she spoke her daughter's name, she smiled—and that bestowed on her a dignified beauty.

This place was a haven for the women who worked the streets at night, and I feared any questions I might ask would sound demeaning.

"Yes," I said. "A beautiful girl. I wish both of you the best." I straightened out of my crouch to leave.

"Why are you here?"

I could give a truthful answer—something I had not planned. But it was one thing to hear about what happened behind these walls and another to see it and realize the desperation of becoming a mother and having no help.

"I would like to donate money to help with expenses here," I said. "I wanted to see if the money would be spent well."

The young mother nodded. "Then perhaps you should speak to Señorita Sandoval."

"She is here?"

"Of course. Every day just after dawn. Someone is always sick or afraid or sad. For me, it was a difficult birth, but she was with me all through the day and the night."

"Where will you go? After?"

"All of us have two choices. Some simply leave and return to the streets, and the child is raised here or at the farm. Some choose to work at the farm to be able to stay with their child. Me, I will work at the farm. From there, many have found ways to live a life off the streets."

Her daughter, as babies are wont to do, began to wail, and the girl bent her head down and kissed the infant's forehead.

"She is hungry," the girl said.

I nodded and backed away from the room to give her privacy. Well, I had my answer about Raquel, and I wasn't sure if I liked it.

It would have been much easier to learn she was just a facade.

It was almost criminal, my decision to allow myself to sleep on the train ride from Ancón back to the locks at Gatún. It would be my final look at Panama, and I should have soaked up the exotic scenery, even if I had viewed it already.

The lush hills; the slow waters of the rising lake; the large, colorful birds; the hum of activity of men and machine—all of it was so different from the lonely, open hills of the Badlands.

Yet after the events of the previous few days, it seemed as if my emotions were not capable of absorbing anything else, not even the wonders of the isthmus. I woke shortly before Gatún, the second-to-last stop before Cristóbal and Colón on the Atlantic. Even so, it was enough for me to see the approach to the locks, those monstrous walls that would have swallowed a hundred rail cars.

As I disembarked, I saw a hideous yellow rail car parked on a shuttle set of tracks. What kind of idiot would crave that kind of attention?

Then I began to look for Miskimon, but he found me first, slipping up behind me and coughing discreetly.

I turned. "Muskie."

He merely drew a deep breath as if he were steadying himself.

His hands were empty.

"You promised me my valise. Not much of a man of integrity, are you?"

"Let me repeat back to you the words of the note I left at your door. A note, I might add, that I had to leave behind because you weren't in the room."

"Maybe I didn't feel like answering the door."

"No, you weren't in the room. I checked. One last night out in the red-light district before heading home to pretend to be a humble cowboy?"

"My valise."

"'If you want it back, meet me at the Gatún Locks.' Those were the exact words on the note. Your choice to infer that I would have it with me."

"I'd like it back. My steamer leaves in a few hours."

"Follow me."

"That will lead me to my valise?"

"Yes."

"Take the lead then. The sooner I'm away from here, the better." I stayed beside him as he walked away from the station, although I'm sure he would have preferred if I had kept my distance and trailed him like a younger sibling.

As we walked, I lifted my hat to give a breeze across my scalp. A felt cowboy hat truly was a thing of vanity in this humidity. Good thing I wouldn't be here much longer. "Hey, how are things with Odalis?"

His shoulders stiffened, just enough for my satisfaction.

"I'd give him my vote for mayor," I said. "You?"

"My only interest in Panamanian politics is in how it might affect the canal project. I doubt civic matters will have an impact, so I give it little thought."

It would have been enjoyable to press him more, but we were passing along the hideous yellow rail car behind the train station.

"What kind of buffoon would be responsible for this?" I gestured at the rail car.

"Why don't you ask Colonel Goethals? He's down by the locks, waiting for you. With your valise."

"Last question," I said. "What do your initials stand for? You can tell me that at least."

Miskimon picked up his pace and refused to speak again until we met Goethals, who stepped away from a couple of men holding blueprints to join us.

"Thank you, Mr. Miskimon." Goethals was carrying my valise. The colonel did not appear to be suffering from the humidity. My own shirt felt drenched, and rivulets of sweat ran down my back. Goethals, on the other hand, didn't show a bead of moisture anywhere on his face, and his uniform appeared as crisply ironed as if a maid had just handed it to him. "I trust you resolved the cigar situation to our satisfaction on a visit this morning to our offender?"

"As you suggested, it was a good opportunity to test our relationship with the locals after what happened to Mr. Holt," Miskimon answered. "I am glad to report that despite, or perhaps because of your firm words with them, it appears we can still work in harmony with the police in Panama. I was pleased at their timely and prompt cooperation in the matter. Based on a previous visit, the arrest and subsequent fine of the cigar seller took less than an hour. This relieved me, because as you know, I felt it was important to make it back here before Mr. Holt's arrival. You'll have the report tomorrow."

Goethals nodded.

"A shame, then, that you were on an earlier train," I said to Miskimon, wondering about the arrest and Goethal's firm words, but too stubborn to ask. "It would have been such a pleasure to journey with you across the isthmus."

"Yes," Miskimon told me. "A shame."

"Before you go," Goethals said to Miskimon, "you should know that a few more men have been found unconscious along the tracks."

Miskimon's forehead creased. "Same stretch as before? I've checked those tracks thoroughly three times already."

"Same stretch, same story. That the hand of God struck them from the sky. Same lack of memory of events right before. It is troublesome. You know that many of the laborers are superstitious. I don't want them walking away from their jobs."

"I will continue to make inquiries," Miskimon answered.

"Thank you." There was a tone of dismissal in his voice.

"One last thing, Colonel," Miskimon said. "You might be able to help

Mr. Holt with a recent question. It's in regard to our railway stock. He wants to establish the identity of a buffoon. I'll take my leave now."

Miskimon saluted and turned on his heel. That left me alone with Colonel Goethals and my valise.

"Let's get to my railway car first," Goethals said. "Out in the open, I tend to draw construction questions from just about everyone. I want us to be alone, and I want this to be private. Then you can ask your question about the railway stock."

Goethals led me directly to the bright yellow eyesore behind the station.

Inside the railway car, with a table between us, Goethals spread blueprints on the table. "Ten thousand buckets of concrete a day."

My hat was on the bench beside me. He was across from me.

"Crushed gravel from an island off Colón," he continued. "Cement bags hauled from ships, thousands of gallons of water, miles of metal supports. The world has seen nothing like these locks. We made a cut into the hill on the other side for them. We pulled out five million cubic yards of dirt, and the locks will take two million cubic yards of concrete."

"Those are just numbers." Numbers that could never express the vastness of the concrete walls towering above us. This truly was America coming of age. Brash. Bold. Accomplishing what no other country had been able to accomplish in all of recorded history. A person had to be here to truly comprehend.

"Just numbers?"

"I hope you'll pardon a degree of loquaciousness. Normally I avoid it, but the last few days have had their impact."

He examined my face. "Pardoned."

"Life is messy. Numbers aren't. We can understand numbers but sometimes not comprehend them. Standing here, feeling tiny, that's the real impact this has had on me. So if there's a point to why I'm here and why you are spouting off facts like an encyclopedia, I won't be upset if you get to that point. I have a steamship sailing in less than three hours."

"I don't like messy," Goethals answered. "I do like numbers. There is precision in numbers."

"You aren't holding my valise hostage—and the bank draft inside it— to deliver that kind of unsurprising statement from an army man."

Goethals pointed out the window at the ladders that reached up the massive concrete walls to a height that spun my head, where it seemed the two parallel lines of the ladders formed a single point. "A month ago, a cable snapped. Four workers died. It wasn't an accident."

"I trust you have your police looking into the matter. Or Mr. Miskimon."

Goethals seemed to ignore my comment. "A week before that, a derailment at the Culebra Cut killed seven men—you might recall that your badge belonged to one of those policemen. That wasn't an accident. And ten days before that, at the Gatún Dam, dynamite triggered a landslide that killed four workers. Not an accident. What do you make of that?"

"Fifteen men died who should still be alive. If I were you, I would be angry."

"I *am* angry. And baffled. It's unlikely that individual workers were targeted. It's too difficult to time the accidents to kill someone specific. And even if that was possible, it's not probable that all those individuals were linked to someone who might have enough of a grudge to choose to murder them like that. What does that leave?"

"The obvious. That someone is trying to slow the construction of the canal by hurting workers at random. But if you think past the obvious, it doesn't make sense. You have tens of thousands of workers."

"Fifty thousand. It would take a war to stop the dig. Now think like a politician."

I didn't try to hide the sour tone in my voice. "Not sure that bank draft is worth that much to me."

He laughed. It bothered me that it felt good to have drawn laughter from him.

"When I arrived," he said, "I divided the work into three divisions. The lock. The lake. The canal. All three were attacked, but with little impact on stopping any of those projects. I have no doubt all three attacks were linked, and, I suspect, symbolic attacks. The questions I faced were simple. Who did it? And what was the motive? But an open investigation would be disastrous. I can't tell you how much time is wasted by pandering to congressmen and senators who want to sightsee and use the excuse that they are here to ensure there is nothing fraudulent or wasted in our expenditures. You'll remember, of course, the French."

I nodded. During their attempt to conquer the isthmus, they had squandered millions upon millions in a bribery scandal that rocked the financial world. Because of that, nothing seemed more important to the American project than accounting for every nail and hammer used. In the Senate and Congress, careers were made and destroyed on the progress of this project.

Goethals lowered his voice. "You are well aware of the extra political pressure because of Cromwell and the president's libel suit against the *World*. It's a frenzy."

I nodded.

"Given those allegations, any suggestion of sabotage would be sensational not only in the American media but all across the world." He waited, apparently for a comment from me.

"Thus the need for a tethered goat?"

His brows arched. "Pardon me?"

"Miskimon said he has me booked on the steamer leaving this afternoon, and I presume that is correct."

"He is a precise man. He will not tell you something unless it is so."

"But he is capable of withholding information as it suits him."

"What suits him is what suits me. He does not deserve your rancor. Direct it at me."

Despite the din of construction all around us, it seemed our conversation was taking place in a hushed office, such was the total focus of our sparring.

"Yesterday, he booked me on that steamer shortly after meeting me at the hotel," I said. "That's where he first observed that I'd been held by the National Police. I think that gave him, and you, an answer that you needed. My purpose had been fulfilled. Using a girl's missing mother as an excuse, you sent me into Panama City to bumble around with questions to see what might happen. At our first meeting, I would have appreciated the kind of information that you waited until this morning to deliver in regard to the sabotage that troubles you."

Goethals opened his mouth to speak. I didn't care if he was the dictator of this little American Zone in the middle of Central America—I shook my head to silence him.

"It speaks volumes, then, that you chose this morning to finally divulge confidential information that would have been more than helpful to me when you went through the charade of asking Miskimon to swear me to an oath as an enumerator. That tells me something has changed since Miskimon booked my passage. It tells me you need me again. The question is how badly do you need me?"

I reached down to my boot and pulled out the badge Miskimon had given me. I placed it on top of the blueprints between us. "I'm happy to return it before I cross the planks onto my steamer. I have no obligation to you."

Goethals grimaced as he took the badge from me. "I'd rather not take this. Yes, we need you again."

"Before I even consider staying, I want full disclosure. Was I a tethered goat?"

"No. I did not expect that you would draw the attention of the National Police. I am not a man of intrigue like that. Soon enough, I was going to tell you about the sabotage and then have it look like your questions about the sabotage were an extension of trying to learn about the girl's mother. As if you believed the issues were related. Miskimon had strict instructions that your investigation was to end if it looked like it might put you in danger."

I touched my left ear. It still hurt. "I would guess, nicely enough for your conscience, that once you realized my questions drew danger from the National Police, you had your place to start and you also didn't need me anymore."

"It wasn't the National Police. Not directly. Something else is happening, and I'm not quite sure what it is. All I know is that you are the thread to help me unravel it."

I thought of that night in the hut and of the man with the whispered voice. *Someone with influence who wanted the police to do the dirty work.*

"You'll tell me how you know this?"

"Not yet," he answered. "But I promise I will when I can. I can also promise you that you are no longer of interest to the National Police and you are safe to resume asking questions."

"How do you know that?" I asked, thinking of Miskimon's reference to "strong words."

"I will not give you that answer. Either you trust me or you don't."

"Fair enough." Goethals did strike me as a man who placed value on trust. "If I stay, tell me what you want me to do."

"As you discovered, workers from all areas of the canal come in on

Sunday mornings to have disputes heard. Everyone knows that I send Miskimon across the Zone, week in and week out, to investigate those disputes. It's a public role that has allowed him to be discreet in questions about the accidents. All I want is for you to take his original reports and go back to each site to make it look like you have follow-up questions. I'll take care of letting the rumor spread that it is related to your questions about the girl's mother."

"I am not an investigator. I baby-sit cattle for a livelihood."

"What you learn matters little." He paused, as though searching for words.

I supplied those words. "Whoever sent the National Police after me will know I'm doing this. I'll be a threat again, asking about accidents instead of a missing woman."

"But you won't be a tethered goat. Tethered goats are unaware of why they are staked to a rope. Think of yourself as a hunting wolf. No rope. Fully aware that you are in pursuit of someone stalking you. I don't believe that person wishes to see you dead."

"Not interested."

"Did the color of this train car strike you as odd?"

"Incongruous."

"It was a calculated choice. I want my presence to be known, and it motivates workers. And there are other times when my presence is not so obvious. I understand you visited the National Police yesterday after Mr. Miskimon released you from an obligation to me."

Harry Franck had been right: *"Goethals has spies everywhere."* "Care to tell me why?" he asked.

"Nope."

"You were looking for a fight."

"Why ask if you already know?" I said.

"It's important to me to know I am dealing with an honest man. I doubt I'll test you again. You did not fight. Why not?"

"I've got a daughter who depends on me. What she needs is more important than what I want."

"Tell me what you think she needs. Keep in mind I'm a father too and love my children as fiercely as I can see you love your daughter."

"She doesn't need a hero. She needs a father who can protect her until she can make her own way in the world."

"I like you. I don't say that to many people."

As with his laughter, it bothered me that I cared. "I want to begin my journey back to the Dakotas this afternoon, but I have something that might help. In Panama City, there's a man named Waldschmidt. He's playing loose and easy that he's working for the Germans. Maybe there's your link. Is that enough for you to give me my valise and send me on my way?"

I watched Goethals to see if this would be of interest to him. It told me something that he moved on without question. Trouble was, I had no idea exactly what it told me.

"The bank draft in your valise—I understand it covers all the delinquent payments outstanding on your land mortgage, but there will still be the remaining mortgage in place."

Could it be . . . ? Had the president made this kind of calculation, expecting that at some point I would need to be leveraged?

"What if the mortgage was completely paid?" Goethals watched me. "Would that secure your daughter's future?"

Yes. President Roosevelt was a consummate politician. He would have made that kind of calculation.

But I was a stubborn man. "She needs a father, not a ranch."

"From what I understand, you are on the razor's edge of holding on to your ranch, even after the delinquent payments are made. Can a couple extra days in Panama be any more dangerous than being forced to head out on horseback in a blizzard because if you lose some cattle you'll lose the ranch? Have the ranch paid off, and you wouldn't need to take those kinds of chances."

Paying off the ranch, for me, was a substantial amount of money. Compared to one day of funding for the building of the canal, it was a fly that a horse flicks from its haunches with a swipe of the tail. Of course, if that metaphor had any truth in it, it meant I was just another annoying fly, settling for anything that smelled of manure . . .

Still, manure had value to a fly. To sit on the porch overlooking the valley of the Little Missouri while reading a story to Winona, to ride through gullies of a homestead that would become an inheritance to my daughter—all without the crushing worry of debt?

That could well be worth it.

I suspected the colonel could see those thoughts on my face.

"By meeting with Harding yesterday, you already established yourself as the determined cowboy seeking revenge for assault," Goethals said. "Play the role a little longer. That's all. Pay attention as you ask your questions about the accidents and you shouldn't get hurt."

I didn't show surprise at his knowledge of my meeting with Harding because I wasn't surprised. "I imagine you have a few suggestions on what kind of questions I should ask and where I should ask them."

"For starters, you'll have to go to Cromwell's party tonight and ask questions about Saffire's mother. That will solidify your motivations among those who will soon hear that you are asking questions about the accidents."

"So you suspect the hunter of the tethered goat is among them."

"I make no assumptions. But it is a small circle of power in Panama. If the hunter is not among them, he knows them well."

"Do you have anything to help me with this new task?"

Goethals reached under the blueprints for a large envelope filled with papers. He handed me the envelope and gave me back the Zone police badge.

"Of course I do."

Twenty-Five

I should have felt small and invisible.

I stood on a bank that gave me an overlook of the middle of the three Gatún locks. Neither my approach by train before the meeting with Goethals nor anything I'd read in the newspapers had prepared me for the close-up sights and sounds of construction. I tried to comprehend the audacity of the engineering marvel in front of me.

One of the reasons the French failed was that they attempted to cut a sea-level canal directly through the isthmus, without locks at any place on the forty-eight-mile route. This was doomed to failure because of the volatile Chagres River, capable of rising thirty feet in an hour during the frequent rains of the wet season.

The Americans decided to conquer this problem by damming the Chagres and allowing it to follow its natural course to the Caribbean, just west of the locks. The dam formed a lake that would allow ships to traverse a full third of the route.

It was a brilliant solution. Not only did it tame the Chagres and create a lake that gave fifteen miles of surface water along the canal route, but the dam would store the water needed for the locks as well as supply electricity to run the locks and all the lights through the Zone.

To use this route, however, the locks needed to elevate ships by eighty-five feet from the Atlantic to reach Gatún Lake. The bay at Colón allowed the Caribbean to reach inland, and a canal extended the ocean waters almost to the lake. At the end of this canal was where the locks would raise the ships to the inland route.

I faced north, to the Atlantic, and by turning my head back I got a sense of the rise of the three locks. Each one thousand feet long, they were designed with a wall down the center of the chamber to allow each lock to accommodate two massive cargo ships at a time. When complete, they would each be deep enough to swallow millions of gallons of water, fed from the artificial lake by culverts wide enough to accommodate a steam locomotive, water held by steel gates seven feet thick and as tall as an eight-story building, each gate weighing four hundred tons or more.

In this state, unfinished and empty of water, the concrete of the locks was painfully white in the sunshine. Swarms of men on layers of scaffolding poured more concrete for the locks' walls and floors.

Despite this marvel, I didn't feel small or invisible.

In my back pocket was a letter from Winona. It had been in the valise, addressed to the administration office in my name. When she concentrated on her block lettering, she had a habit of sticking the tip of her tongue out of the side of her mouth, and I glowed inside to imagine how she had sat at my writing desk in the ranch house, perhaps in the evening, using the light of an oil lamp because in Medora in December, daylight didn't last long. I could picture her care in using the thick pencil that she favored over the blotchiness of a fountain pen, and I fought the stabbing homesickness so that instead I could enjoy the sweetness of that image.

December 29, 1908

Pappy, each morning Unk Hunk lets me scratch off another day on the calendar. Then I count how many days. So far, we are up to three days. Unk Hunk says that I should figure on January 31, so that means me and Teddy only have 33 more sleeps until you get home. Teddy hurt his paw, but Unk Hunk helped me put a bandage on it, and I kissed it better like you also kiss my hurts better. It is snowing hard. Unk Hunk wants me to tell you that the cattle are doing fine. Unk Hunk is helping me with my spelling, but all these words are the ones I want to write to you. I am so glad you waited until after Christmas to go because I would have cried all the time thinking how lonely you might be without me. In two more days, I get to write you another letter. I love you and I miss you.

I generally tried to avoid philosophical thoughts because my tendency to get carried away could make me look like a mule's hind end. But standing on the edge of the greatest construction project that humans had conceived, I had little hesitation in ruminating on why I didn't feel so small.

Love trumps concrete.

Despite the urgency of the letter that sent me to Panama, and despite the authority of the person who sent the letter, I refused to leave Medora before Christmas. The trip was going to take me away from Winona for about a month and a half, and no force on earth was going to prevent me from watching the joy in her eyes as she unwrapped the stuffed bear I'd purchased on a trip to Bismarck in early fall, before roundup. Roosevelt's bear, it was called. Or Teddy's bear. All because the president, on a hunting trip in Mississippi, had refused to shoot a bear hounded to exhaustion. I knew full well how much Roosevelt hated the diminutive Teddy, but the name had stuck and the craze had started. Everybody wanted Teddy bears with button eyes.

On Christmas Day, I'd fully realized the irony of seeing Winona whoop with joy over Teddy's bear, but when I had purchased it months earlier, I'd had no idea of the request that would arrive to send me to Panama.

Against almost any scale, a man could look around and feel tiny. Against mountains or sky or ocean. Against the mighty buildings in New York. Or the unending concrete and scaffolds and loads of dirt that the trains carried here at the building of the canal.

Yet all it took was love to sustain the soul, and with the letter in my pocket, which I intended to reread again and again, I knew that it was the reverse. Mountains and oceans and sky and concrete would all eventually disappear and could never endure in comparison to the invisible, eternal fabric that was love.

I couldn't help but grin, thinking of the tenderness that my young daughter showed to a stuffed bear and the imaginary wound on its paw. I couldn't help but be overwhelmed by love that Winona's worry had been for my loneliness, not hers.

Sure, the canal would be a monstrous triumph of man over nature. The audacity to connect one ocean to another would be a combination of the world's largest man-made lake, the world's largest locks, the world's largest canal. But well within a lifetime, the decades would pass, and as they did, few would give thought to the wonder of it. Yet in a lifetime, none would ever forget a first love or a sustaining love.

Two more days. I told myself. Two more careful days.

I began to climb down the bank toward the buzz of construction below me.

Railway tracks ran parallel to the locks, where flatbed cars carried buckets of fresh concrete from the mixing plant. Overhead, steel cables ran from the railway tracks to sets of massive towers on the opposite side of the locks, carrying those buckets to be dumped into the empty forms for the walls, fifty-feet wide at the bottom, tapering to eight-foot-wide tops.

As I moved from worker to worker to get directions to the foreman, I kept a nervous eye on the buckets passing overhead. Six tons of wet concrete in each bucket, enough to bury a small herd of cattle, hung from what looked like threads of steel.

I finally reached the foreman near the base of some scaffolding that clawed those eight stories upward to the top of the forms filled by those buckets of concrete.

The foreman was a block of a man. Closing in on fifty, he had pale skin and short hair that had probably once been red, judging by the man's thick freckled forearms, which extended from the rolled-up sleeves of a sweat-soaked denim shirt.

"Geoffrey Denham?" I asked at the man's suspicious glance.

"I only speak to construction men," he snapped. Irish accent. "And plainly, you aren't. So whatever you want, the answer is no."

He turned back to his inspection of some welds on the scaffolding.

"I'll pass that along to Colonel Goethals."

Denham straightened and gave me attention again. "That's a name you'll not be wanting to throw out lightly. And anyone can do it. So when you bring papers to show authorization, I'll give you my time. Until then, I have some locks to complete."

Once again, Denham turned to inspect the welds.

From the large envelope that Goethals had given me, I pulled out the sheets and flipped through the pages. Humidity made them soggy—there was no satisfying crisp sound to give my actions authority. I found what I needed a few pages down: a letter with the ICC letterhead, signed by Goethals.

I walked around to get a view of the welds myself, then held the letter below Denham's eyes.

After a few seconds, the man raised his head again. Drops of sweat were beading above the man's eyebrows. His glare remained in place.

I took the letter and slid it and the other papers back into the envelope.

"Get this over with then."

I wiped my brow. "I'd prefer a place with shade."

"We'll not be talking long enough to make the walk worthwhile. Any idea of the logistics involved here? When it's all said and done, we'll have gone through five million bags of cement. Goethals came up with the idea of forcing the men to shake out every sack after it was emptied. All that came out was dust, but with all the bags we go through, it's saved fifty thousand dollars a year."

Impressive. That amount of money could pay the combined yearly wage for a score of gold-dollar engineers.

"We're hauling in sand from twenty miles away," Denham said. "We have three rock quarries going twenty-four hours a day for the gravel. And Goethals wants this done in two years. So we'll stand in the sun, and I'll answer what you have with yes or no until you get the hint and leave me to my work."

I understood men like this one. I respected them for the bluntness. It gave me no pleasure to pull the papers out of the envelope again and find the letter from Goethals.

"Shove it," the man said. "I read it through the first time. I'll tell it to Goethals myself if I need to. Every minute counts, and if he wants the canal done in time, he shouldn't be wasting my time."

The diplomatic response would be to act as if Denham meant that I should shove the letter back into the envelope. So I did so before speaking. "I've been sent to ask some follow-up questions about the cable that snapped."

"And you would be?"

"The person sent to ask those questions."

"How much expertise is it you have with engineering?"

"How much does a person need to understand gravity?" I was not going to be intimidated.

"I'd like to give your gob a good smack," Denham answered. "But I doubt it would shut you up. What questions have you?"

"Much the same as the first time around. Send me down the line, and have someone else answer for you."

Denham gave a big grin, maybe deciding that I was trying to help him by leaving him alone. In truth, I decided the more people I questioned, the higher the likelihood of drawing attention, and the sooner I drew attention, the sooner I could get back on a steamer for the Dakotas. I was sweating under my cowboy hat, but the hat—not the sweat—did make me noticeable.

"Then talk to my head negro." Denham pointed at a crew at the base of the opposite wall. "Jimmy. He's the one that nearly got killed."

Denham put two fingers in his mouth and gave a whistle that turned the heads of the half-dozen black men across the concrete floor. Denham pointed at me and gave a thumbs-up. "You'll be set now. Mind you don't take too much of Jimmy's time."

As I moved across the base of the lock, I tried to imagine it filled with water, with a two-hundred-ton ship floating those eight stories above my head.

Incomprehensible. Some men had dreamed this, and others were making it happen.

As I neared the workers, the tallest one separated himself. He, like the other workers, had stripped to the waist, and sweat sluiced off his gleaming skin. He could have been carved from black granite.

"A few questions," I said. "On behalf of Colonel Goethals."

"Then I'll have a few answers." Jimmy's broad southern accent didn't have the harshness of the hills of Tennessee, but was more flattened. Atlanta, I guessed. "Take your time. I don't mind stepping away."

The man had a breezy confidence that came with youth, muscles, and a sense of belonging to the world's greatest construction project.

"Four weeks back, give or take," I said, "one of the steel cables snapped."

The big grin dimmed. "In my sleep, I still see it falling. One end tore a man in half."

I squinted.

"Six tons a bucket." Jimmy gestured with his chin to the strands of cables above. "It only looks like slack in the line because of how the weight pulls them downward. Any idea of the tension on those cables? It was a sound like I'd never heard before, cutting through the air as that tension released. Loose end whipped right through his belly. I didn't find that out till later though. The bottom of the bucket hit this concrete floor like thunder. Splattered twenty steps in all directions. Took forty men with wheelbarrows to haul it away while it was still wet."

I offered a handshake, and Jimmy took it, his brows drawn.

"That's all I needed," I said. "Would be a waste of your time to ask about the cable. One of the men on the towers would know more, I'd guess."

"You'll only hear what we heard down here. Cable was cut, not frayed."

"Who could have cut the cable?"

"Any one of twenty men."

Not a helpful comment. "A foreman up there, could he tell me?"

"Gerald Dawson is the man you'd want. But he's in a cage in Cristóbal."

"Cage."

"Isolation cage. He took sick, and he's stuck there until he's cleared by doctors."

I couldn't think of anything else to ask.

Jimmy leaned in. "The last week or so, rumors have started. That the Germans found a way to do it."

"Germans?" I did my best to sound surprised.

"Think about it. Whoever controls this canal controls the oceans. And whoever controls the oceans controls the world. You do know the kaiser is building his navy twice the size it used to be, right?"

Twenty-Six

It wasn't until late morning that I reached Empire, essentially retracing a good deal of the journey I had taken earlier in the morning. This time, however, I was not asleep, and I watched the countryside pass by.

After leaving the elevated tracks, where eventually the dammed Chagres would form a lake, the cut went through areas of cleared-out jungle, where hut villages were set up in scattered clumps.

Out of the river valley were the barren hills, where occasionally giant mechanical cranes betrayed the activities just beyond the crests. And then, from those heights with each mile away from Gatún and each mile closer to Corozal, a sweeping panoramic view of the Pacific.

I took the trip to Empire because that's where I would find Harry Franck, Zone policeman 88, as he had so named the book that he was writing. I didn't expect it to be a wasted trip, since at the train station in Gatún, I had called the police station in Corozal and learned that Harry would be enumerating in Empire and would not be difficult to find.

Not once did I use a telephone without remembering the day, time of day, and the spot where I had first spoken to someone over the wires. I hadn't yet reached ten years of age when the telephone was invented. In the Dakotas, there was no point for even a wealthy person to own one because who was there to call if there was only one telephone in a thousand square miles?

In 1885, shortly after my fifteenth birthday, I had fled the ranch to join Buffalo Bill's Wild West show. That took me to Chicago for the first time. Such extravagance and noise, the crowded streets. The same day in Chicago, skinny and hungry for life and cocky as only a young cowboy can be, I was humbled first by the laughter around me in a hotel when I openly marveled at a voice coming out of the telephone. Before the setting of the sun, I was humbled again as I beheld the Home Insurance Building, ten stories tall, still as marvelous to me in my memory as the world's tallest building, built just over twenty years later in New York at a staggering fifty stories, the Metropolitan Life Tower.

I was living in the prime of human advancement—born before skyscrapers and telephone, now an adult in the United States where, according to the trumpeting of a daily paper in Bismarck, some three million telephones were connected by manual switchboards, and skyscrapers were so common—with the exception of the tallest in the world—as to not be worth discussion. There had been Kitty Hawk only six years earlier, and the Model T. We could fly, we could drive, we could send our voices across wire, and we could build monuments to the heavens. And in this time of wonder, nothing was more wondrous than what was unfolding around me—the connecting of the oceans, proof that there was not much left for humans to achieve. I thought about future generations that would look back and see the pinnacle of human achievement behind them. I felt sorry for them. Who, after all, enjoys knowing the best is behind them?

Yet I knew I was a different person from who I had been in those first years of the Wild West show, wide-eyed at all those wonders. Because I wasn't interested in wonders anymore.

I just wanted to get home.

American canal construction had begun with a few hundred workers in 1903, men who were adventurers and unafraid of pioneer life in a faraway jungle. Eventually, some had been joined by families, though the women and children lived in appalling conditions. Then someone realized that men work best if they have happy families for moral support, and canal budget money poured into bringing civilization to the canal. As a result, most of the train-stop towns along the isthmus railway had been constructed in the previous few years.

Empire was not one of these modern towns. Shacks and inhabited boxes crowded the backyards, all the way to the jungle edges, where heaps of junked locomotives and dredges, most from the French era, had been slated for eventual removal.

The main street was not whitewashed or sanitized but had the vibrancy of Panama City. On Railroad Avenue, I passed restaurants run by the Chinese, outdoor laundry facilities operated by the Jamaicans, and sidewalk stands for shoemaking and barbering.

Navigation was simple. I'd pass a shoeshine stand and ask for Harry Franck. Each time I'd receive a smile and directions with an extended arm and pointed finger. Harry, it seemed, was not a stranger in this town and had few enemies.

Eventually I stood in front of a three-story boardinghouse with peeled paint and a few broken windows—obviously outside of inspections and maintenance by the ICC.

I stepped inside to be assailed by a medley of smells, from cooking food to exotic spices to human sweat. I heard laughter up the stairs. Harry's laughter.

I followed the sound to find him sitting in a small room with beds alongside the wall and a wooden barrel marked ICC in the center. That must have served as the dining table.

"Who dat handsome mon be?" the large-bosomed woman sitting on a cane-backed chair asked as I knocked and entered. She had a washtub in front of her. "And what on eart' be happening with the strange hat?"

I removed it.

Harry nodded. He was holding a clipboard.

"Want me out of here?" I asked.

"Are you supposed to be learning to enumerate?"

"Of course," I said.

"Well then, go ahead and enumerate."

"How about I observe? As a way to learn."

"I'm the type that teaches someone to swim by throwing them in a pool." Harry gave me a grin.

"Dat's all right, strange hat mon," the woman said. "You ask what you want."

I cleared my throat. I'd rather be roping a wild horse than this.

"Well, how many live in this room?"

She laughed, a wonderful rolling sound. "What you see?"

"Okay then. Harry, mark down one."

He said to her, "What's your man's name?"

"Rasmus Iggleston."

"Two then," I said to Harry.

He said to her, "What's his metal-check number?"

"Mister Harry, ah don't know."

"Let's see your commissary book then."

Another rolling laugh. "We finish that already before last week."

"He Jamaican?" Harry asked. "Your man?"

"No. Him a Mont-rat."

Harry spoke out of the side of his mouth to me. "From Montserrat. Island in the British West Indies."

He turned back to her. "What color is he?"

Rolling laughter. "What you ask dem questions for? Him just a pitch darker than me."

"How old?" Harry asked.

"Why would I care about that?"

"Older than you?"

"Him be a ripe man. Yes, my love, him a prime man."

"Older then," Harry said to me. "Holt, guess her age."

Not a chance. I asked her instead.

"Lost my age paper. I is plenty old enough."

"Is Rasmus Iggleston married?" Harry asked.

Her face turned grave. "Yes, indeed. I sure enough be his wife."

"Can he read?" Harry asked.

"He can scratch out some words, yes, he can."

"And what kind of work does he do?"

For the first time in the conversation, she became haughty, giving me a sense of how status was measured in her world. "Him employed by the ICC."

"A laborer?"

"No, sweetness, no. He shovels dirt away in front of them steam shovels."

"That will do for Rasmus," Harry said. "Your name?"

"Mistress Jane Iggleston."

"How long have you lived in the Canal Zone?"

"Not too long."

I admired Harry's patience with her.

"Since when have you lived in this house?"

"Not too long."

"Do you do any work besides your own housework?"

"No, not any." Her eyes widened a bit, I guessed because her washtub was in plain sight. "Maybe I washes some gentlemen's clothes sometimes."

"Children? How many?"

"Not a one."

"How did that happen?" Harry asked.

This time her laughter was almost loud enough to shake the house.

Harry laughed with her, and that was the end of the interview. He handed her a tag so she could prove she'd been enumerated, and I followed him down the stairs and outside into the midday heat.

"You need a lot of help enumerating," he said. "Or maybe Miskimon has you doing something else?"

"Funny you should ask. You and I, we need to go to the dig."

Harry was a cheerful tour guide as we took a passenger car from Empire back to Culebra.

He explained that the railroad history of the isthmus was a story in itself. It essentially began sixty years earlier, when Panama was a province of Colombia, and before rail crossed the continental United States. Investors in the newly formed Panama Railway Company, as it was called back then, hoped to take advantage of the potential for a much shorter travel route from New York to San Francisco. Passengers could disembark on the Atlantic side, cross Panama in a matter of hours, and on the other side, take a paddle ship north again. This would no longer require the arduous and much longer trip by boat around the tip of South America—forty days' transit compared to well over a hundred by curving around Cape Horn and then north again.

On the Atlantic side, the terminus was poorly chosen—a treacherous marshy island where Colón would eventually be built. While convenient for ships to shed passengers, it required a pile-driven causeway that led into a jungle of swamps and alligators. As a result, building the railway took the same toll of cholera, yellow fever, and malaria that defeated the French attempt to build a canal decades later.

Only eight miles of track made it inland, but this was enough for the original railroad, given the California gold rush. Thousands of desperate fortune seekers paid dearly for their supplies to go that short distance, where mules and canoes took over. This infusion of cash was enough to finally complete the near fifty miles to Panama, and the PRC became the most profitable railway company in the world.

The French bought it, in part for the tracks and stock and profits, but more for the right of way to dig a canal, and when that failed, the US government—more accurately, Theodore Roosevelt—purchased it for the same purposes.

Because the causal link between mosquitoes and malaria and mosquitoes and yellow fever had not been understood until recently, the French were doomed before they started. But that didn't stop them from profiting in the cadaver trade. Medical schools and teaching hospitals paid well for bodies pickled in barrels. The thousands of deaths during the building of the railway itself, and during the French attempt at the canal, provided an ample supply of bodies of anonymous workers. Ironically, during the French years, the income from cadavers was enough to support the Panama Railway hospital, where one doctor, it was said, had a habit of bleaching skeletons as he tried to compile a bone museum of all the different races who worked on the railroad.

When the Americans purchased the railroad, the original route through the Chagres valley had to be changed, and the new route was built with heavier gauge and double-tracked rails.

All told, the current rolling stock consisted of 115 of the most powerful locomotives that could be engineered, along with all the passenger cars.

More important—in terms of the building of the canal—there were 2,300 railroad cars built to carry dirt, and 102 railroad-mounted steam shovels.

Massive.

By the time Harry finished the story, we had arrived at the station in Culebra, where—was it only two days earlier?—I had looked out at the digging of the canal from the observation deck and helped a woman to her feet after the explosion.

An even more devastating explosion that, I now knew, had recently killed the policeman whose badge I carried, along with six others.

As requested, Harry Franck took me directly to the dig, to the rock drills that thundered loud enough to drown out the steam engines of the mighty locomotives and the crash of falling boulders. It was a madness of machinery—pneumatic power drills, steam-powered cranes, rock crushers, steam shovels, cement mixers, and dredges.

Harry was happy to explain what was in front of my eyes.

Despite my earlier musings that love lifted mankind above a sense of puniness in a world full of the monumental, I did fight the sensation of insignificance in the midst of the activity around me.

I have no hesitation in declaring it was American ingenuity at its finest.

First, rock and dirt were loosened by explosions, such as the one that had rocked me on the observation deck. Steam shovels, mounted on the rail cars, moved along one set of tracks, scooped buckets of dirt from the excavation, and dropped each load on the flatbed rail cars on a second set of parallel tracks. These flatbeds had only one side, and dirt was piled against that side.

Each car lurched forward after it was filled, in strings of up to twenty. Then a locomotive pulled the cars away to a dumping ground.

Here, I could only shake my head in admiration at the engineer who had designed the system. For an angled plow was in place on the car at the rear and attached by a steel cable to a winch on the locomotive at the front. This cable stretched the length of all twenty cars and pulled the plow forward. There was a steel apron between each car, so the plow was able to scrape the dirt to the side in a continuous motion from car to car until it finally reached the car closest to the locomotive and all the cars were scraped clean.

The dirt pushed from the rail cars to the side of the track was then moved by other steam shovels, and when the dumping ground grew too high, sets of tracks were relocated upward by cranes able to move a mile of track a day.

I was a simple cowboy. Truly. And wanted to be nothing more than that. My head hurt trying to comprehend what was happening around me.

One hundred and sixty loaded dirt trains went out daily and returned empty. Multiply that by twenty cars per train, and multiply that by the tons of dirt each flatbed car could carry, and it was possible to understand how American audaciousness could tear through the backbone of a continent in a matter of years.

Harry had to yell as he explained all this to me.

I wasn't in a mood to do the same.

I had a notebook in my back pocket. I pulled it out and wrote, *Where did the men get buried by the explosion?*

Harry gave me an incredulous look, as if I were a five-year-old asking how Santa managed to squeeze down a chimney.

He grabbed the notebook and scrawled back as if he wanted my idiocy on permanent record, *They move entire hills in a day.*

There was the proof that I was really that simple cowboy. I somehow believed that seeing a spot where men died would answer questions, and I still couldn't believe that each hour, enough dirt was removed to fill ten valleys of the meandering Badlands that I so craved to reach again.

Foreman? I wrote.

His answer was to walk away. I did the only thing I could.

I followed.

"You look like the kind of man who can handle himself in a fight," Harry said. "But it would have been pointless."

He'd taken me back to the top of the hill, to the passenger tracks, where we waited for a scheduled stop.

"I'm open to an explanation." I'd been a meek sheep, walking away from the dig behind him, more than happy to find a place where the noise didn't claw at my brain. Still, I couldn't understand why Harry had pulled me away so quickly, so I had asked.

"These crews measure the dirt. Week by week, they compete against all the other crews to set new records. There's not a foreman down there who would have taken a minute to answer anything you might ask. They wouldn't have been polite about refusing the second time you asked the same thing, and you seem to favor persistence."

"When's a good time to find the foreman? And where? He doesn't work twenty-four-hour shifts."

"You can ask me. I just didn't think there would be any sense in telling you that until you had a close-up look at the situation and saw how pointless it would be to talk to a foreman. I know just as much as anyone else. Two policemen died. You don't think we had our own questions the next day?"

"You told me that the explosion went off before the signal."

"That's what happened. Signal man was too slow."

"That unusual?"

"Yes."

"Anyone ask the signal man why he missed giving the signal in time?" I said.

"Don't know."

"Zone policemen show up the next day, and no one asks the signal man why he missed a countdown?" That didn't sound at all right.

"Couldn't. The man was dead. Killed in a barroom fight only hours after the explosion. Some friend of one of the dead workers wanted revenge for the signal man's stupidity." Harry gave a pitiful chuckle. "Dead end to that accident inquiry."

What else should I ask? "Man's name? Maybe his friends knew something."

"See, that proves my point. These are rough-and-tumbles. They'd have no patience with questions. I have to ask, what exactly are you doing for Goethals?"

"Miskimon. He's the one who hired me."

"You're not a good enough liar, Holt. And didn't I tell you already nothing happens on the isthmus that Goethals doesn't know? If Miskimon sent you, it's because Goethals is behind it. Except . . ."

Harry looked one way, then another, then one way, then another.

"Out with it," I said.

"Sunday, when you dropped by, you mentioned Miskimon sent you to replace Badge 28. I had a few questions of my own but didn't say anything to you. The kicker was *no hablo español*—no speak the Spanish. There's not an enumerator on the isthmus doesn't speak Spanish. It's why I got the job. I didn't have a lick of police work or soldiering in my background. They wanted a white guy who could speak Spanish. So naturally I told my boss this. No Spanish, and Miskimon sent you. We both decided maybe you're a spy to keep an eye on us for Goethals."

"If that's the case, why tell me now, guessing I'd go back to Goethals?"

Harry snorted. "Around here, everyone assumes everything gets back to Goethals and also to the National Police. You have those scabs on your ears. Looks like whatever I told my boss got to them quick enough, and they got to you. I'm half to blame, I suppose, but I didn't think I was throwing you to the wolves. Because Goethals's men, the National Police never touch 'em."

Harry gave me a long examining look. "So you're asking questions for Goethals, but you didn't get protection from Goethals. What exactly is going on?"

"Harry," I said, "I sure wish I knew."

Twenty-Seven

In midafternoon sun, I stared at a stretch of lonely train track near Pedro Miguel, parallel to the construction of a single set of locks on the Pacific side of the canal, not nearly as massive as those in Gatún. Here, much of the lock work had been completed, and I was alone except for two small Panamanian boys a hundred yards down the track whose job it was to throw the switch for the occasional locomotive.

I was here out of curiosity, alone in person but not alone in wondering what manifestation had come from the sky to knock down assorted laborers over the last few weeks. Twice already, I'd heard Goethals and Miskimon refer to the troubling matter of men who had been found unconscious here. I'd heard the same thing once from Harry Franck.

The stories from Miskimon and Harry matched in details and peculiarity. It was a spot along the line where men walking the track from a job site back to their camps—those paid in silver, because gold men were either given coupons or had extra money to spend on train fare—would be found in comatose states, needing a day or two in a hospital in Ancón or Colón before waking up with no memory of what had knocked them down.

The switch boys were the only possible witnesses to what was happening and could offer no guesses. They were the ones who would watch a laborer walk past them and, shortly after, see him in convulsions along the tracks.

I tilted my hat downward to shade my eyes as I looked up and down the straight tracks. Nothing out of the ordinary. As I stood there, staring at the tracks, other images overpowered my determination to ignore them. I saw a different set of straight tracks, equally ordinary, except for a train collision just after three in the morning on October 29, 1901. The site of the Buffalo Bill accident, where over a hundred horses had been killed or put down.

I'd been asleep, snuggled against my wife in a passenger compartment.

Fifteen hours before the head-on collision between two locomotives, in a restaurant in downtown Charlotte, she had interrupted my dining experience with a southern belle interested in transient cowboys and delivered the single punch that broke my nose.

Thirteen hours earlier, we'd stood in front of a justice of the peace and exchanged wedding vows in a civil ceremony.

Ten hours earlier, she'd shyly announced that she was three months pregnant with our child.

My life to that point had been such an ugly tangled web of youthful callousness that in the years since Winona was born, I had spent many hours of contemplation and regret, alone in the gullies of the Little Missouri, thinking about the woman who broke my nose. During our time over the years as employees of Buffalo Bill, she had loved me with a loyalty as beautiful and eternal as the open plains where she had been born. A loyalty that compelled her to purchase for one of my birthdays the

Girard-Perregaux watch on my wrist and engrave her name and mine on the back. And I had wasted those years by not loving her in return.

I had never been unfaithful to her, because I had never pledged faithfulness to her. Indeed, she was younger than I, and for the first years in the show, she was a teenager with minor roles in the arena. I found her adoration as amusing as it was irritating. She well knew that I led an adventurous life, in various cities and countries, with women who enjoyed the illusion of a romantic evening with a cowboy. But she held fast to the belief that one day I would come to my senses and understand that she and I were destined for each other.

Then came a single moment when the two of us were alone, watering horses to be led onto a train, when I realized she was no longer a child. In that moment of clarity, I understood the beauty of her love and devotion to me. Even then, however, I did not pledge faithfulness. However, in the weeks that followed, I reciprocated her fierce loyalty, content in a peacefulness I had never understood before, happy that temptations placed before me were not tempting in the slightest. Oh, if only I had told her that instead of guarding my feelings out of fear that if I uttered my love, I risked losing it.

The southern belle across the table from me in Charlotte was a newspaper reporter asking questions about the show. The occasion had been innocent, but she had a habit of reaching out and touching my arm as she laughed at my stories, and I understand why it might not have appeared innocent from the window at the street.

The woman I loved marched in with imperial fury. I stood with a smile, knowing how easy it would be to explain the misunderstanding, and midway through my smile, I received that single punch. Pain mixed with bewilderment at such a volcanic reaction from someone customarily patient with me. In the restaurant, as she walked away, and as I held my face in my hands, blood from my nose freely running through my fingers,

I realized that if I lost the woman who punched me, I would lose the one thing in life that mattered most to me. I reached her at the sidewalk, pleaded my case convincingly enough for her to understand I had not once been disloyal since we had begun to share nights together, and dropped to my knees to beg for marriage.

When she announced on the train that evening that she was pregnant, I finally understood her reaction at seeing me in the restaurant with the reporter, and we giggled as she fell asleep. I watched the ceiling of the passenger compartment, trying to ignore the throbbing of my nose.

I was still awake at the moment of collision, unable to comprehend the violence, how our world shifted, the horrendous noises, the spinning of the passenger car, and then the horrible screaming of injured horses.

Buffalo Bill Cody was correct in announcing that no human lives were lost in the accident, but the woman I loved would never recover from her injuries, and week by week, she slipped away from me as Winona grew inside her. The woman I loved fiercely fought against the end, knowing that the longer she lived, the better chance her child had of surviving.

All I truly had left to mark her loyalty and love was the watch on my wrist, a reflection in a mirror to show me the long-term damage to my nose, and our daughter, waiting for me to return to the Little Missouri.

I turned from the memories of that night, trying to shake off my melancholy by thinking of Winona and picking out fragments of time with her to watch in my mind with gratefulness to God for sparing our unborn child from the worst of the train accident.

As I came out of my reverie, I noticed that I had spent some of it walking in the direction of the boys at the train switch.

They had a bucket of water with a dipping handle.

As I neared them, I pointed at the water.

"Twenty-five cents," the taller boy said with a heavy Spanish accent. "Americano dollars."

An hour of paid labor for a drink of water. Highway robbery. But it was a capitalist system. I didn't have to pay if I didn't want to, and I wasn't that thirsty.

"Too much." I gave them a smile.

"Where else you get water?" the second one said. "Long walk."

"Not that thirsty."

I looked closer and saw that a thin wire was draped down from the dipping handle and was almost invisible on the ground as it continued away for a few feet to where it was attached to a broom handle.

"Last chance, señor," the first boy said. "Long walk to water otherwise."

I shrugged and walked beyond them to where the tracks joined the main line, and continued on to the train station at Pedro Miguel.

At the request of William Nelson Cromwell, I had a party to attend.

Ahead, outlined against the sun, was the figure of a man, as if he were waiting at the end of the track for me. I stumbled over an upraised rail as I squinted to see if I could recognize him, and that took my eyes away from the figure.

When I looked up again, he was gone.

An hour before sunset, I arrived by carriage at the ranch Cromwell had informed me was in joint ownership with Sandoval. It had taken roughly thirty minutes of travel from Ancón at the edge of Panama City, going north along the east side of the canal route, with the mountains on my right rising from the narrow and almost nonexistent lowlands, showing a beautiful glow of green in the long rays of light at that time of day.

Because I was early, I arrived in the last light of the day, and from a distance, I could see the large tile-roofed villa and a collection of buildings around it. The hack took me up a tree-lined drive to a circle at the front of the villa. After I disembarked, he took the carriage to the stables. All the hacks would remain until the party ended and then, with lanterns, begin a procession back to Panama City.

During my travels with the Wild West show, I'd been to castles in the mountains of Austria. The main doors to this mansion matched the finest European entrances in grandiosity and size. With both doors open wide, a carriage with a team of horses could have driven into the entranceway of the villa.

The butler—a Panamanian of medium size and medium mustache, wearing a tuxedo—opened only one door for me and gave me a shake of his head, but with a hint of a smile.

"Mr. Cromwell warned you about me?" I asked.

"He said you would need a polish."

I followed the butler down wide, cool hallways decorated with watercolor paintings. By the lack of pretentiousness, I guessed Cromwell had little to do with the decorating, and instead had let Sandoval make the choices. The butler opened a door for me, revealing a large bathroom suite with all the amenities of modern plumbing.

"Of particular note," the butler said, "is a shaving brush and razor. I have been requested to stress this convenience for you."

He stepped into the bathroom with me. It was cavernous, so I did not feel cramped by his presence, but I was curious.

"Privacy is not a Panamanian custom?"

"I have also been instructed to take your clothing and have it laundered and waiting for you at the end of the evening inside your carriage." He pointed at a suit hanging from the hook, with black polished shoes beneath. "Lastly, I've been requested to oversee the accessories. Bow ties can be delicate."

"I've worn tuxedoes before. I am able to tie it myself. You can take the clothes, but the boots and hat stay with me."

"You'll shave?"

I had been thinking about Raquel. "If the boots and hat stay."

"Excellent."

I unbuttoned my outer clothing. "Who is your employer? Sandoval or Cromwell?"

He blinked a few times. He seemed like a good-humored man, and I took this as a sign of disapproval of my question.

"*Señor* Sandoval is my employer. This evening, as I assist you, I am merely following instructions from Cromwell."

With just a few innocuous words, he made it clear. Señor Sandoval deserved his respect. Cromwell did not.

"You know Saffire then?"

A smile. "Who does not?"

"You were here the night her mother disappeared?"

His smile vanished. "You will find that Señor Sandoval's staff does not discuss this matter."

"Saffire is convinced her mother did not run away. Señor Sandoval's staff is not interested in helping the girl?"

"Señor Sandoval's staff does not discuss this matter."

"What was her mother like?"

"Señor Sandoval's staff does not discuss this matter."

I was down to my underwear. I folded my trousers and shirt and handed him the pile.

"You'll find socks and underwear with the suit," he said.

"Wonderful. I'll keep mine."

"As you wish. There is a veranda at the rear of the villa. Please find your way there when you are ready."

He locked his eyes on the scar across my upper body.

"The last butler who bothered me put up a good fight," I said. Deadpan.

He smiled. "Of course."

I took my time to shave as I bathed, and dusk arrived by the time I pulled myself from the cooling waters. I toweled, enjoying the refreshed sensation. There were hair lotions at the sink, and I did my best to tame the uneven strands, frowning in the mirror at my lack of success.

I turned to the minor complication of properly wearing a tuxedo. I began with the ruffled white shirt, and that's what gave me the first inkling of trouble. I could barely button it across my chest, the collar pinched my neck, and the sleeves were at least a couple inches short.

With luck, the bow tie could conceal if I left the top button undone.

Then came the trousers. The waistband was ridiculously loose, and the cuffs of the trousers slopped onto the floor. The shoes were equally oversized, and I felt like a clown.

The only reason I tried on the jacket was because I silently predicted it would be equally unfitted, and I was proven correct. The sleeves as short as the sleeves of my shirt.

I had no idea when my own clothes would be returned to me, so it appeared my choices were this tuxedo or wandering in underwear, cowboy boots, and hat or not leaving the bathroom.

The choice was easy.

I'm as willing as the next man to deny vanity, but the truth is, most of us do care how strangers judge us in social settings. Better to spend the evening locked in the bathroom than meet the highbrow guests of Cromwell and Sandoval in this kind of discomfort. Especially if Raquel Sandoval was among those guests.

Before I could remove the ill-fitting clothing, there came a knock on the door and a familiar voice. "Are you dressed?"

"Go away, Muskie. Send the butler back with my own clothes."

Of course Miskimon would be here to baby-sit me. Could the evening get any worse?

"Muskie?" a female voice said with a giggle. "He calls you Muskie?"

"Holt is predictably tedious," Miskimon answered. "Please don't encourage him in any way, as he finds himself far more humorous than the world does."

"Go away," I said. Good for me that I'd locked the door.

I heard slight clicking at the handle, and Miskimon pushed the door open a moment later. I glimpsed him putting a lock pick into his inner suit pocket. Interesting skill, but perhaps not that surprising.

He stepped inside, followed by the owner of the feminine giggle.

He wore an elegant tuxedo, perfectly fitted. She wore a hoop dress with plunging neckline and a triumphant smile. She was shoulder height to Miskimon, with a face that some might call plain, yet she sparkled with vivaciousness. Her short dark hair elegantly framed her face, and her glittering necklace was a perfect complement to her attire.

Miskimon flicked his glasses as he surveyed my fashion misery.

The woman held a large flat box. She pushed shut the bathroom door behind her with her foot, then curtsied with the box still in her hands. "I'm Odelia Cordet, a good friend of Raquel Sandoval."

There was something familiar about her, but my discomfort took precedence over puzzling that over. "I'm James Holt, a cranky cowboy who firmly believes in the concept of privacy."

She giggled and spoke to Miskimon. "He's adorable. I don't understand why you say the things about him that you do. We'll have a fun evening with him . . . Muskie."

"See what you have wrought?" Miskimon sent me a glare.

"Am I the only one who understands that this is a bathroom?" I said.

"Put him out of his misery," Miskimon told her. "I prefer to spend as little time with him as possible."

She handed me the box. "It will fit, I promise. I'm a good judge of a man's size."

So we *had* met before. But when?

I opened it to find dark clothing. The jacket was on top, loosely folded.

She giggled again as I took off my ill-fitting jacket to show the ridiculously small shirt beneath.

I tried the new jacket.

She clapped her hands. "Excellent."

I looked through the box. A shirt was the next layer. Beneath that, trousers. Beneath that, protected by a layer of wax paper, polished shoes and accessories.

I looked from her to Miskimon. "Thank you. I wouldn't be opposed to an explanation of all this."

"Later," she said. "You must get dressed. Carriages are arriving in droves."

"Of course." I waited for her to pull Miskimon back out of the bathroom. The pause grew awkward, at least from my perspective. "All I need is privacy. The privacy customary to a bathroom."

"We'll wait here," she said. "I must see that scar. I really must see it. Sioux warrior?"

The only person in Panama who had seen it, aside from the butler, was Muskie, back at the National Hotel. Now I glared at him.

He shrugged. "Stories about you are far more interesting than stories about me. And, I find, a decent revenge for your usual behavior to and around me. Some of the stories I spread are even true." He turned to her. "About that nose of his. Colonel Goethals tells me that—"

"Out." I ground the command through a clenched jaw. "Both of you. Out."

Twenty-Eight

The view from the veranda would be spectacular during daylight hours. It was on the eastern side of the villa, opening to a short stretch of lowlands to the foothills and the mountains behind. During my carriage ride here, I had seen cattle dotted on those foothills where jungle had been cleared away for grass.

This evening, though, the spectacular view was on the veranda itself. With lanterns providing soft light, ceiling fans providing an artificial breeze, and a quartet of string players providing a delicate touch of classical music, the sense of entitled privilege had been properly bestowed on the gathering.

And what a gathering it was. The expansive veranda would have been appropriate for a hotel ballroom. If my count was correct, and it usually was, there were fifty people milling about in clusters of two or three or four, and still there was room to spare for the dozen or so servants walking about, carrying trays of bite-sized food and glasses of various wines.

Those clusters only emphasized my role of pariah, as I was the only person in the room not engaged in conversation. I stood alone, at the far rail of the veranda, one question paramount in my mind.

How soon could I make my exit?

I had expected this ostracized solitude when it became clear that I was here to ask questions about Saffire's mother. I'd introduced myself to the first couple and been received cordially enough until the question. The curt response came that *of course* she had stolen the jewelry, and then the couple turned their backs to me.

It was as if their disdain for me was carried on the slight breeze the fans wafted through the veranda. Each subsequent time I introduced myself, the body language and facial expressions of those in the new cluster made me feel like my suit had been smeared in cow manure. I couldn't imagine the scorn that would have been heaped on me had I worn my rough-hewn clothing. Or the absurd tuxedo Cromwell had provided.

All of which only amplified my usual discomfort in crowds. The only thing that sustained me was allowing my mind to drift to my own ranch and imagining the peace I would feel on my own much smaller veranda knowing that the bank no longer had a hold on me through the mortgage. I was enduring this for my daughter.

Moreover, I was nearly finished. I had fulfilled Cromwell's request to establish myself as someone asking questions on behalf of Goethals. All that remained of my duties—after making the obligatory investigations at the site of the locks—was to go to the site of the Chagres dam for final questions about the accident there. Then I could go home.

The only reason I had not departed Cromwell's party already was because I wanted a conversation with Ezequiel Sandoval. This was not for Cromwell or Goethals but for Saffire, to see if I could learn anything that might give her hope for her mother's return. It was unlikely, but speaking to Sandoval would clear my conscience of any final obligation to the girl. Ezequiel was elusive, however, and had managed to stay a few clusters away from me during my first hour of this soiree.

I had been able to observe him, however. He was a bull of a man, with a full head of white hair and a strong face unmarred with the jowls seen on so many of the self-indulgent rich. While easily in his early sixties, he exuded the confidence of a man who controlled a country, which I had no difficulty believing was true. If, as I'd learned, there were only fifteen or so families that made up the Panamanian aristocrats, he was clearly a man among them with influence, and most of them were gathering around him on the veranda.

As for his daughter, Raquel, I had caught her eye as she spoke in one of those clusters, and surprise had crossed her face first, then coldness. This was even before I began my odious task of posing the useless question I'd been consigned to ask.

I wasn't fool enough to approach her after that.

Twice, I felt the hostile eyes of a waiter upon me as he circulated among the guests with a tray of hors d'oeuvres. A younger Spanish man with a thin face blunted by a mustache, he looked vaguely familiar, but, like my first impression of Odelia Cordet, I couldn't place him. I stopped wondering almost immediately. I had other things to worry about.

I spotted Miskimon returning to the veranda and was surprised at the wave of relief that struck me. He'd stepped away at some point with Odelia for what I presumed was a stroll.

Miskimon took a solitary point in the opposite corner of the room. It was a marker of my own misery that I decided he could provide me comfort.

I moved to his side, and he barely gave me any indication that he knew I was there, but I was content. I could pretend that he and I were together and let the conversations ebb and flow around us.

I broke the silence only because I did have some curiosity that he could satisfy. "About the clothing that you brought for me—"

"Don't believe it was my doing." His gaze remained on a far spot. "I rather enjoyed the thought of you in that ill-fitted suit. With one look everyone here would understand how much of a buffoon you can be."

I was miserable enough to give that a low chuckle. "It wasn't necessary to put me in an ill-fitting suit to accomplish that. I do believe I've helped Dante discover a tenth circle."

"Hmmph."

I took that as the nearest he could come to expressing a degree of sympathy. "The suit?"

He finally turned his head to me. "This is not the place for an explanation. Trust me on that. Let's just say for now it involves a lawyer named Raoul Amador, who was given the task of arranging the formal wear for you."

"Which leads to me wondering how you knew I'd need it and why you decided to help."

"How much more clear do I need to be that this is not the place for an explanation? And for the record, I did not help. It was at Odelia's insistence we arrived early with proper attire for you."

"Ah. Odelia."

"What are you implying with that tone?"

I noticed a smudge of lipstick on Miskimon's neck, just below his ear. The perfect opportunity to try to rattle him, but he was my life preserver in a miserable ocean of hostile waters, and I did not want him to walk away.

I shrugged. "If you asked twelve separate people the same question about their view of an event, what are the odds that all twelve will have identical answers?"

"You have been a busy beaver."

That lipstick was much too tempting a target. "As have you."

"I?"

"I would assume that you are only here with Odelia because of some sleuthing role at Goethal's request, so I am impressed at how far you will play the role of a smitten escort."

"At the risk of dignifying your inference with a question, why would you assume that?"

Instead of pointing out the lipstick, I decided that the target was too easy and shifted the conversation.

"T. B.," I said. "The initials stand for what two names?"

"Hmmph."

More silence. Until I tried to broker a peace of sorts.

"You don't strike me as a person who enjoys crowds," I said. "Don't take that as an insult, for neither do I. In fact, I'll confess you are a place of refuge for me right now. While you might not enjoy conversation with me, I am clinging to your presence so I can pretend that I am not a complete outcast at this event, wandering from couple to couple without a single friend."

The ensuing silence was long. Had I actually managed to offend him in some way?

Finally, he removed his spectacles and rubbed them with a handkerchief, then replaced them before squarely giving me his full gaze. "There's something I've been meaning to tell you."

I sensed a degree of seriousness and responded accordingly. "What's that?"

"Yesterday morning, when we had our discussion at your hotel suite and you offered me a handshake . . ."

He'd rebuffed me. Yes, I remembered. "I'm a big boy. You made your feelings clear. I suppose I deserved it."

"You did not. For as long as I can remember, I find myself wiping things clean, endlessly, often forgetting I am doing it. I'm compulsive about straightening picture frames on walls and pieces of paper on a desk. I've learned to live with it and only regret it on the occasions when I note that my behavior adds discomfort for someone else. And, for as long as I can remember, I've had an aversion to . . . contact. Much as I wanted to accept your handshake yesterday morning, I allowed my weakness to stop me."

From what little I knew of this man, this seemed a very difficult admission. "Apology accepted."

"It was most certainly not an apology. It was an explanation."

"*Explanation* accepted." I grinned. "How about we shake on it?"

"You do find yourself humorous, don't you?"

"If I didn't, who would?"

"Precisely." He cleared his throat, as if anxious to move on from any emotional connection we might have made by admitting respective weaknesses. "As for your question about identical answers from each of twelve witnesses, am I to understand it is about Saffire's mother?"

"Goethals has finally let you in on this? That's why you're here?"

"This isthmus is a small world. I'd have to be deaf, dumb, and blind not to know you are asking those questions. And yes, Colonel Goethals has taken me into his confidence on all aspects of this."

"Yes, it's about the girl's mother."

He polished his glasses again. "My conclusion would be that twelve identical answers suggest collusion to a point that collusion is the only possibility. Which leads to other questions, and, of course, other conclusions. Cromwell—"

"Approaches. Over your left shoulder."

He nodded. "Indeed."

I inclined my head to the colonel. "Mr. Cromwell."

Miskimon turned toward him.

Cromwell extended a hand to Miskimon. I stepped in front and grasped the colonel's hand. "It is good to see you again," I said, pumping his hand as I spoke. "I sure appreciate the tuxedo. Mr. Miskimon here was just commenting on it."

I stepped away, leaving Miskimon at my right shoulder, in a place where it would have been awkward for Cromwell to reach across me to try another handshake with Miskimon.

Happily, as I expected, Cromwell was easily distracted by flattery. "You do look far better than I anticipated, Mr. Holt. This confirms I have a good sense of tailoring."

"As I mentioned, I am grateful."

And curious about Raoul Amador's involvement. But I kept that to myself.

"Grateful enough to return the favor, I hope," Cromwell said. "In the entranceway, on a desk, there's a package wrapped in brown paper and string. I'm wondering if you would be kind enough to retrieve it for me and then join me with Mr. Miskimon at the front of the room? I would do it myself, but I do have guests to attend to."

"Of course," I said.

Cromwell walked away with the peculiar strut of a man wanting to seem larger than he was.

"Muskie . . ."

"Thank goodness you avoided my baptismal name." He shuddered. "I was fearing that our shared misery at this party had actually established some kind of rapport between us."

I laughed. "Muskie, if you are going to be at the front of any room, especially this room, I'd suggest you wipe that lipstick off your neck. Below your ear. Looks like the shade that Odelia wears."

He touched his neck in the exact spot, demonstrating he remembered well the occasion.

"Yes, you have my sympathy," I told him. "Given your aversion to physical contact, I'm sure she caught you unawares."

William Nelson Cromwell stood on a small platform behind a table so that he and I were at head height to each other. The cloths over the table in front of us hid from the guests the platform he had used to achieve his illusion of height. He had arranged it so I stood to his left, and Miskimon left of me. It was my first sense that this was an extension of the game he'd been playing by insisting I attend this party.

Cromwell motioned for the string quartet to stop and tinkled a silver fork against the side of a champagne glass, and within seconds, the hubbub of assorted conversations ended and he drew everyone's full attention.

"Welcome to all of you. While, of course, much of the evening is ahead of us, I hope you will indulge me with a small favor."

Cromwell pointed at the wrapped package on the table, about the size of the box that had held my tuxedo. I'd found it where he'd told me it would be. From the feel of the package when I carried it, the contents were as soft and malleable as clothing. And about the same weight.

"Mr. Holt here," Cromwell said, "as many of you know, has been asking questions, and now he has brought me a package that someone sent along without leaving a card or signature."

He paused, and I felt the hostile stares of the crowd upon me.

"I don't know what we would do without Colonel Goethals and his American efficiency." Cromwell tinged his words with sarcasm, which drew titters from a few of his guests.

"Mr. Holt," Cromwell said, "if you would be so kind . . ."

He motioned to the package, and I dutifully passed it over. He was enough of a showman to not open it immediately. "Since we are all together, it seemed more efficient to do this here."

Yes, I was being played. Too bad I didn't understand the game or the rules and saw no choice except to nod. He handed me back the package.

"If you and Mr. Miskimon could be kind enough to open it? I must admit, now that you've brought it to me, I do have a degree of curiosity."

Did he think me a trained monkey? I untied the string and began to unwrap the package. Miskimon gave me little help and held his shoulders square in a posture that I interpreted as discomfort.

We unfurled a bright, colorful piece of heavy cloth. It had a green rectangle in one corner, and a red rectangle in the opposite corner, and three yellow stars.

I held one side and Miskimon the other, so that it was fully displayed to Cromwell's audience.

Seeing it only added to my bewilderment.

There were a few gasps from the crowd. Not delight, but rather as if those gasping had witnessed a social faux pas on the level of passing gas in front of royalty.

Cromwell seemed unfazed. "It appears to be a flag. While I admit to a bit of a letdown, I suppose if any of you would like to help Mr. Holt find out who delivered it, I'm sure he would be grateful. Speak to him, of course, at your leisure during the evening."

If sounds could be translated into color, the room became black with heavy silence, all of it directed at me.

So this was how it felt to face a firing squad.

"Well then," Cromwell said, "now that I have presented you with a much smaller mystery than I anticipated, let's continue with our evening." He nodded at the string players, and the music resumed.

I fixed my attention on the colonel. "What was that about, Mr. Cromwell?"

"Nothing more than it appears. I was curious about the package and who might have delivered it."

"I don't believe you." I resisted the urge to grab his lapels and yank him closer. "I suggest you tell me the truth."

He smirked. “Servants don’t make demands of their masters. Please keep that in mind for the future, Mr. Holt.”

He walked away, and Miskimon pulled on my suit jacket to keep me from following and making a bigger fool of myself.

I had been correct in my first judgment of Raoul Amador when I met him in the dining room of the National Hotel. He *was* a knife man. And he *did* prefer to bring a knife to a fight when his opponent was unarmed.

I took no satisfaction in my prescience, as I only learned it outside the villa an hour later, alone near the carriage that was to take me back to the train station at the border outside Panama City.

I had just placed my hat and boots inside the carriage, where, waiting for me on the seat, was the clothing I’d worn to the villa. It had been indeed laundered, folded in a neat stack, and tied with string. I stepped out to find out where my driver was when Amador appeared, knife in his fist, blade pointing at the ground.

He knew what he was doing. A man inexperienced with a knife will hold it palm upward, as if ready to thrust from low to high. A good knife fighter knows his fist is also a weapon. He can punch in one motion or use that same motion to disguise a downward knife thrust.

That was deadly enough, but I couldn’t flee because in his other hand he carried a pistol, pointed directly at my belly.

Although it was inky black in the night air, I saw all of this clearly in the light from the lantern at the rear of the carriage, which was well away from the other carriages. Arranging for the carriage to be solitary. I realized, had been no accident.

I glanced around.

“Your driver has been sent away. It’s just you and me, Mr. Holt. Let’s go for that walk, as I have questions for you.”

"Given that you have weapons and I don't, that would seem like a stupid thing to do."

"Stupidity fits with who you are." He waved his pistol, motioning me to step away from the carriage. "Do as I say."

"No." I'd been told that someday my stubbornness would be the death of me. This could be the day. "You might as well shoot me here."

"I predict that when faced with the certainty of dying in the next few seconds, you'd rather walk, hoping somehow that you'll find a way to disarm me. Which, by the way, won't happen because, of course, I'm anticipating such an attempt. And surely you are curious. Let's move away from here where I'll have the leisure to ask the questions I want to ask. I'll even answer a few of your own. Wouldn't you rather die at least knowing why you are going to die?"

"No. Not that curious."

Where exactly was Miskimon? Wasn't it his job to have my back? Especially given the conversation we'd had after Cromwell unceremoniously turned his back on me? The conversation where we'd agreed something was in play and we needed to be cautious here, away from the safety of the American Zone?

"Goethals's man won't be showing up," Amador said. "You can trust me on that. I repeat. It's just you and me."

"And everyone else who will appear after they hear a gunshot. Otherwise, you wouldn't try to get me away from here where you can corner me with that knife."

"Not really a concern. After I've shot you dead, I'll just put the knife in your hand and call it self-defense."

"You'll have to shoot me in the back. Running from a knife seems smart anyway. And there goes your statement of defense."

"You *are* irritating. You really think your death would be important enough to warrant a trial?"

He raised the pistol and, before I could react, switched it to his right hand, dropping the knife so he could steady the pistol with both hands. I could see the intent in his eyes. He pointed the pistol at my chest. He was going to shoot.

I could not force myself to turn and flee. I would not give him the satisfaction.

"Coward," I said. I braced myself.

The shot did not come. Instead, there was a blur of motion behind him that I couldn't quite understand, given the flickering light of the lantern. I did hear a heavy clunk, and he fell forward, so completely and immediately unconscious that he made no attempt to break his fall with his arms.

I kicked the knife to the side and grabbed the pistol. I doubted he would wake soon, but no sense in taking a chance.

Only then did I look to the back of the carriage to seek the person who had intervened.

All I found was a shovel used to scoop horse manure. I took the lantern from the carriage. It showed a clump of hair on the shovel, stuck in horse manure. Amador's hair. I scraped it off with my shoe and tossed the shovel away.

I moved to a squatting position beside Amador and felt for the pulse in his neck as I weighed my options.

He was alive.

Given my status among these aristocrats, did I have a chance of convincing them that Amador had stepped outside with the intent to murder me? Not likely.

What about dragging him away and finding a way to wake him up and force him to answer questions. But would he answer? And would I have the coldness to back up my threats with the knife since a gunshot would draw attention?

No. Not a good plan.

Did I want the carriage driver to return and find Amador here?

Clearly not.

The best thing to do was the simplest thing to do.

Goethals had wanted me to be a tethered goat until we found out who the hunter was. I had the final answer for him. The predator was the man on the ground in front of me. Tomorrow, I would give Goethals the answer. I didn't even need to waste time going to the site of the Chagres dam. Goethals could decide what to do with the information. Tonight, I would sleep in the safety of the American Zone, and tomorrow, after meeting Goethals to tell him about Amador, I was finally headed home.

I grabbed Amador's heels and dragged him away from the carriage. He was chest down, and his face bumped on the dirt and gravel, his limp arms outstretched in front of him.

I suppose I could have taken more care, but in my fine leather shoes, I stepped in clumps of fresh horse droppings, which Amador smeared further with his chest and face as I continued dragging him away from the building, through my footsteps.

What a shame.

When I judged he was far enough away that the driver would not see him, I walked back to the carriage and called for his return so we could ride the half hour back to the lights of Panama City, where I would catch a train back to my bachelor quarters in Culebra.

In the morning, I supposed, during my meeting with Goethals, I'd need to thank Miskimon for his work with the shovel.

Wednesday

January 13, 1909

Col. Geo. W Goethals,

Chairman, I.C.C.

Culebra, Canal Zone

Memorandum to Col. Goethals:

Referring to the attached:

Early yesterday morning I caught Marian Octega at his room at #206 Central Avenue Panama, this building being a Spanish boarding house.

Representing myself to be a saloon keeper from the Zone, I told him I was in the market for Golofina and Panatella cigars at the reduced price he was offering them to his Spanish friends, closing stating I had been referred to him by some of these people. He had one box partly full of "Golfina" (not "Golofina") and six other full and sealed boxes of the same brand. The Panatella's, he claimed, to be out of at present.

The cigar manufactured in Jamaica and called "Golofina" is the one sold in the commissaries, not "Golfina" as stated by Major Wilson, on information given him by a representative of the accounting department.

This "Golfina" cigar is undoubtedly made to fool some of the buyers of the "Golofina" brand: the box, printing, lettering, etc. is identically the same with the exception that the letter "O" is omitted from the name in the fake brand. Up to this time, I had not noticed anything wrong in the spelling of the word, as I was depending on the way it was spelt in the attached complaint. However, I bargained with him for the six boxes at $2.20 a box, to be delivered. Then I noticed the difference in the spelling of the name of the brand. Owing to the fact of the name being spelled differently it made two separate and distinct brands and I doubted if we could do anything in the matter, especially when the price was much lower. Still owing to the fact that one could scarcely notice the difference in the pronunciation of the two words, and possibly be fooled, I thought he should be punished if possible and warned to stop selling that brand in the Zone. Accordingly, discovering through the wholesale dealers that the cigar he gave me was neither "Golofina" or "Golfina" and knowing this was the same as was in the partly filled box, I went to the Alcalde and asked to have him arrested for misrepresenting the brand of cigars or "fraud". He sent one of his men with me and in the presence of this representative, I purchased this party filled box as "Golfina" cigars (it was a Panamanian brand). We arrested him and took him before the Alcalde who fined him for the mires presentation and warned him to be more careful in the selling of same under penalty of imprisonment.

The Pantella brand, he claims, is also spelled differently but I was unable to find out anything along that line as he was out of the same, however, I expect is as he states.

Respectfully,
Inspector

Twenty-Nine

In the Dakotas, I'd become attuned to the positions of the sun as the seasons went through cycles, marking the gradual movement by where it seemed to leave different ridges of the Badlands at each new sunrise and touch down again on the opposite ridges at sunset. Summer solstice gave sixteen hours of daylight, and the winter solstice half of that.

Here, at the equator, there was no progression. As I woke in my spartan room with the sun at 6 a.m., I left my head on the pillow for a few moments, wondering about the monotony of an equatorial sun that gave twelve hours of sunlight every day of the year, dry season and wet.

Not that it mattered to me.

All I needed to do was dress, pack my valise, and give a final report to Goethals.

Before pushing off the thin mattress, I speculated briefly about Raoul Amador. The blow to the head might have caused him serious injury, and that would undoubtedly raise an outcry. I expected to be on a ship, however, and wasn't going to let the prospect of an inquiry give me much worry.

More than likely, however, he'd woken with a throbbing head and his fine clothing caked with horse manure, a prospect that childishly pleased me. I doubt he would seek vengeance, given that he'd have to cross an ocean and then a continent to find me.

More to the point, he'd have to deal with whatever investigation Goethals decided to apply once I delivered my report and his name.

I rolled my feet onto the floor. I'd draped the tuxedo jacket and trousers across the back of a chair and left my laundry package on the seat, with my boots below the chair and my hat atop the laundry.

I would take the tuxedo jacket and suit trousers back to my ranch with me. The clothing would roll up easily enough, and there would be at least one or two occasions in my life where I might have need of it.

I stretched, tossed my shirt and hat on the bed, and pulled on my denims and socks. I shook out my boots, a wise habit from living in places where any kind of critter might crawl inside during the night.

A folded piece of paper fluttered to the floor from the left boot.

Had someone been in my room while I slept?

No. I'd left my boots and hat unattended in the bathroom at the villa the night before. Easy enough to slip the paper into my boot there.

I sighed. I was tired of intrigue. But not so tired of it that I could ignore my curiosity. I opened it to see feminine handwriting: *Please join me at the bullring in Panama City this afternoon for the beginning of the fight. The time and location will be easy enough for you to find. I will be across from the Chinese restaurant.*

It was signed by Odelia Cordet.

Well, enough was enough. I had no intention of meeting her. I'd pass along regrets to Miskimon and ask him to inform her that I had departed the isthmus.

Sitting on the edge of my chair, I slipped on my boots. Boots go on as soon as possible—this was another habit from endless mornings waking out of doors, where it made no sense to give buttoning a shirt priority while I hopped around barefoot in mud or thistles or ice or snow. I had a great amount of affection for my boots. The leather was supple and the fit perfect.

It wasn't until the final stages of dressing, then, that I found what had been tucked into my folded shirt—a small stack of photographs in a large envelope, each about the size of a sheet of letter paper, wrapped in wax paper to protect them from the humidity.

The stack was upside down, and I looked at the backing of the top photograph. Had these, too, been placed there by Odelia Cordet? While it was possible, given that the laundry had been taken away from the bathroom, it wasn't a foregone conclusion.

My first impulse was renewed irritation. I was leaving. I didn't want any more bother. Curiosity, again, triumphed.

I flipped over the photographs.

It was the same letdown as when I unfurled the flag. The first was a photograph of a typewritten sheet of paper, as was the second, third, fourth, and fifth, with each photograph plainly showing a seal and sets of signatures.

I set the photographs in order and examined the first one more closely. While not quite as clear as reading the original, everything was legible.

> **Constitution of the New Republic of Panama**
>
> Preamble
>
> With the ultimate purpose to strengthen the Nation; to guarantee the freedom, ensure democracy and institutional stability, exalt human dignity, promote social justice, general welfare, regional integration and invoking the protection of God, we, the undersigned, decree the Political Constitution of the new Republic of Panama.

I set the photographs down, giving them as much room as I would an angry rattlesnake. What I was holding . . .

. . . was treason.

Punishable by execution.

"Can you tell me what you know about the events of November 1903?" I studied Earl Harding.

I'd found him again at the same sidewalk café, shortly after the first train from Culebra to Ancón had delivered me once again to Panama City.

"That would be the revolution of Panama against Colombia." He pursed his lips. "But you could just as easily go the *Star & Herald* and get the information yourself. Haven't I already done enough for you?"

I'd woken him at his hotel by telephone and asked for copies of some newspaper clippings and a chance to buy him another breakfast at his earliest convenience.

"Even if the *Star & Herald* presented those events in an unbiased manner," I said, "I've learned that rumors travel fast. I'm not sure I'd like anyone in this city to know what I'm looking for. I have an aversion to electricity applied to tender parts of my body."

Harding gave me a wolf smile. "I like the implications here. If you know something that is dangerous, it must be of value."

"I'm just looking for general information." And hoping that the National Police didn't learn what I was doing.

Harding tapped a manila envelope on the table. "General information. Along with newspaper clippings with photos of Cromwell, Sandoval, and Amador?"

"Still general information."

"That you did not want to retrieve yourself."

I held the lives of fifteen or so people in my hands. These weren't the types of conversations I was accustomed to navigating. I didn't want him to know how jumpy I was. I sighed. "You're enjoying this, aren't you?"

"It's how I make my living." He leaned forward. "And it's a living based on the fact that I've never betrayed a confidence. Because if I did, no one would ever trust me with a new confidence again. Why are you asking me these things? Does it have anything to do with the little uproar you caused at the Sandoval ranch last night? I've already heard that you and Miskimon were about as popular as men handing out lumps of horse manure."

"Will you tell me about 1903, or do I need to look for another way to learn what I need to learn?"

"Cowboy, your original promise still good?"

"If I ever speak to a reporter, you'll be the one and only."

"Fair enough. I get the sense that you're too stubborn to let me push you much more than that."

Harding needed to talk faster. The National Police might even now be looking for me— Ah. Of course. That's what was bothering me.

Across the street, at a similar sidewalk café . . . hadn't I seen that man before? I leaned back, hands locked behind my neck, as if surveying the neighborhood in the manner of a tourist.

Yes. Alone at a table was the Spaniard I'd seen in the administration office on my first morning in Panama. Then, he'd had slicked-back hair and a pencil-thin mustache. And last night . . . *he* was the waiter giving me the hostile glances. For all I knew, he was the man at the end of the tracks yesterday, monitoring my movements, or the man outside the alley on the night I'd walked the beach with Raquel.

"All right," Harding said, unaware, of course, of the surge of adrenalin I felt in noticing that I'd been followed. "Here's the short of it. In 1903, Manuel Amador Guerrero, who became Panama's first president, was chosen by a small separatist network to travel to the United States to garner support for a revolution against Colombia. It was a very small group. They wrote their own constitution and designed their own flag because they wanted everything to be ready once the Americans showed up with a warship to block the harbor. They—"

I stood. "Thanks."

"What?"

Cromwell had suckered me and Miskimon into unfurling that flag at his party. It wouldn't take long for Harding to figure out the significance of it, given my questions. "I'm aware that I should let you ramble a little while longer so it wouldn't be quite so clear what information I need. But sooner or later, you'd figure it out anyway. And I'm pressed for time."

I'd landed in the middle of a second revolution. This was a deadly type of politics. I was not safe in this country. I needed to reach the American Zone—Ancón—but that meant somehow making it through Panama City untouched. With a spy right across the street.

I said, "Do me a favor, would you—"

Harding arched a brow. "Nothing I do is a favor. It's all about payback."

"Then take a chance that I'll owe you for a long time. Find Waldschmidt and ask him to take a train to Culebra. I'll be waiting for him at the administration office at noon."

He gave me a cynical smile. "Sure. We'll see where it leads."

I grabbed my hat, threw down payment for breakfast, and started to stroll down the street—then spun and sprinted to the café on the other side of the street.

It didn't fool the Spaniard with the thin mustache. He pushed away from his table and toppled over some chairs to block my pursuit, then dashed into the café. By the time I made it inside, he'd disappeared. Probably through the kitchen, because a tall cook stood at the door, arms crossed and his face set in an imposing glare.

I turned back to the sidewalk, and Harding was there, waiting for me.

"What was that about?" he asked as I joined him.

"Chasing a ghost." I walked away slowly, as if it were a leisurely day, and doing my best to give no sign that I was fleeing to save my life.

Thirty

I stood on a massive man-made hill, photographs of revolutionary papers still with me, pretending to continue Goethals's investigation. It was a necessary deception if I was going to get the information about the papers I needed from the man in front of me. Oliver MacDonald, the foreman of this area of the dam construction. He was a roly-poly man whose face transformed into the Cheshire Cat with each grin, and MacDonald could rival Harry Franck for chattiness.

"Let me tell you about last month's congressional delegation," MacDonald said. "The colonel was here, right where you are standing, and looking that way."

He pointed almost due south, at jungle hills rising about five or six miles away. In that span of lowland, thousands of acres had been razed, leaving behind stumps of once-magnificent mahogany trees in the swamp formed by slowly rising water.

"Right here," I said to echo him. A half mile to the east were the Gatún Locks, and construction sounds carried clearly to us. The day before, my chat with the foreman there had been much less congenial than this.

MacDonald could afford the luxury, though. The dam was close to completion, and therefore he felt none of the urgency of his counterparts in the other two divisions.

"Yes, right here," MacDonald said. "And let me tell you, those congressmen thought they were the most important officials of the project. First I explained to them why we had chosen to dam the Chagres River. Behind us, the river channel is about six miles to the ocean, and in heavy rain, water might rise thirty feet. Thirty feet! Every bridge put in has washed out. The French were so arrogant after completing the Suez that they wouldn't budge from a plan to keep the canal at ocean level, thought they could come up the Chagres, but it was an enemy they couldn't beat. What we did was genius, I tell you. Genius. We're turning the Chagres into a lake, and that means nearly half the entire route from Atlantic to Pacific is on top of those waters. All we needed was an elevation of eighty-five feet to bring the ships to the lake. Mother Nature is doing most of the work for us, because we use the water from the dam to raise and lower the ships in the locks. In short, we've conquered the Chagres and turned it into a servant."

"Yes," I said. I already knew all of this. I needed to be patient, to get the questions I really wanted answered. "Brilliant."

"Right here, those five congressman looked at the same view that you are seeing and had the gall to doubt our fine engineering. And not only that, but voice those doubts to the colonel himself."

"Yes?"

"Understand," MacDonald continued, "this is not a conventional dam. Do you see concrete?"

It was a rhetorical question. Besides, who was I to knock him off his rhythm as an enthusiastic tour guide?

"Not a lick of concrete," MacDonald said. "The design of the dam was as brilliant as the reason for it. Below us, we began with two walls of big rocky fragments. Then with hydraulic dredges, we pumped silt from the river channel of the Chagres and filled those two walls. Silt! It doesn't wash away, not with the protective rock walls. And it fills every pore, and the pressures of weight above it turn it into something more solid than stone. Where we stand is well above the final water level, and all that remains is to finish turning this into a hill and planting vegetation. A year from now, it will look like part of the landscape and not a drop of water will percolate through all the silt beneath it guarded by those rock walls."

That dirt to cap the hill was also being hauled in by train on temporary tracks. MacDonald oversaw about a thousand men.

"So," I said, "there was an explosion on one of those trains, and that slowed things down?"

"Who is talking about a train?" MacDonald frowned. "Aren't you listening? With the colonel himself standing where you are, one of those spindly congressmen pipes up and says sure enough this might be the biggest dam in the world, but compared to the lake it's supposed to hold, how can something this small keep back such a tremendous amount of water? And the colonel—well, you probably know how he believes in letting a man be responsible for his own work—turns to me and says, 'Mr. MacDonald, why don't you explain?' So there I am, with the honor of slapping those doubting Thomases with the facts of engineering. I mean, really, what did they think, that the colonel didn't know what he was doing, choosing to make a lake that would do almost half of the canal's work? And I told them, clear as day, that the pressure of a body of water is determined by its height, not its volume. That's a hydrostatic law of engineering, not too difficult to understand, I would say."

"Of course." I hoped MacDonald would get around to answering my question about the explosion when he was ready, so I played the role of a good listener. "Don't tell me, then, that your answer wasn't good enough."

"Not even near good enough! That congressman flat out told me that if he had a big enough foot to kick the dam, the more he had behind that kick, the more pressure he'd put on the dam, and how was he going to explain his votes for maintaining the canal budget when he couldn't tell anyone back home he believed a dam this small could do the job? Right in front the colonel he said this. Right in front! But let me tell you, the colonel didn't get to where he was because he suffers fools, not at all."

"Of course. Not at all."

"So the colonel just gives the man a smile and says, 'Sir, if your theory is true, how could the dykes of Holland hold back the entire Atlantic Ocean?' And just like that, in one sentence, the colonel paints the prettiest picture of the hydrostatic law that a man could hear. Those congressmen walked away happy as could be, and the colonel winks at me and slaps my back and then follows. He's terrific, all right, the colonel is."

MacDonald paused. "You had a question about the explosion?"

Finally. "Just following up, on the colonel's behalf."

"Well, it knocked a car off the tracks, killed some silvers, is all. Nothing like that has happened since. What we decided was someone might have left a box of dynamite in the wrong place."

"Seen this man before?" I showed him a newspaper photo of Ezequiel Sandoval.

"No, sir."

"This man?" I showed the newspaper photo of Raoul Amador and was rewarded by a flinch.

"No, sir."

"That's all." I'd have to ask Miskimon a few questions about Mr. MacDonald. "Thank you. I can find my way back."

I walked past the work crews and the slow-moving cars filled with dirt. Colón was my next destination, but not, unfortunately, to finally take passage on a steamer.

Not quite yet.

Just after dawn, when I'd realized that the photographs showed a new constitution signed by a group of revolutionaries, I had been given the responsibility of all their lives. I couldn't be certain this was the only set of photographs. I *could* be certain that Cromwell had an inkling of its existence and that he'd made sure many of those who'd signed it saw me pull out their newly designed flag, as if I were the investigator who'd discovered that flag.

Given that Raoul Amador's name and signature was the first among all the others, it now made sense why he had confronted me with a pistol and knife.

But who had slipped those photographs into my laundered clothing, and why?

Had I been wiser, I would have simply delivered the evidence to Goethals. He'd wanted to know who was hunting me and who was behind the sabotage. Those photographs had the full answer.

Had I been wiser, I would not have continued with this charade of investigation, assuming that Goethals was keeping track of my movements in the way he kept track of every activity in the American Zone.

The trouble was, among those fifteen whose signatures were tantamount to treason against the republic, fifteen people who would face execution, was the signature of a woman with whom I was utterly smitten.

Raquel Sandoval.

Harry Franck had described it correctly. Here too, stepping from the American Zone at the train stop of Cristóbal and into Colón and the Panamanian republic was a simple matter of crossing the street.

Buildings behind me in Cristóbal were neatly framed, neatly painted, and well protected by mosquito screens at every window.

Ahead of me, in Colón, was the flatland of a former swamp. My first time through on the Sunday morning of my arrival had only given me a view from the train. On the street, I could see that, unlike the crooked streets of the hillside of Panama City, Colón was laid out in grids of square blocks. The buildings were shrouded by vines, and the whitewash tinged with the brown of mold.

Although I could have stayed in Cristóbal to be safe, I knew I hadn't been followed, and since my route was parallel to the invisible border, I decided to walk through Colón. I passed a merry-go-round of giant wooden horses, where silver-dollar men, obviously drunk, clung to the necks of the horses and rode with the giddiness of children.

Prostitutes wandered freely, as did beggars.

I had missed all of this on the Sunday of my arrival, going straight from steamship to train. It seemed a gloomy city, but maybe that was more a reflection of my state of heart.

I passed the boxcars that were used to house silver-dollar men, and after this sad detour, I turned back again to Cristóbal in the American Zone, where the new streets were wide and lined with mature palms, and the buildings were magnificent once more.

Because I was curious whether Franck had been exaggerating, I took a moment to meander through the Washington Hotel, where Theodore Roosevelt had stayed during his visit to the canal a few years earlier. Franck was right about the sign at the pool, restricting the area to gold employees. I glanced at the men and women lounging on beach chairs and saw only skin that would turn pink with too much sun.

That's why I wasn't surprised farther along at the cramped, breezeless wards in the hospital, where dark-skinned men groaned in rows of beds or sat in wheelchairs, showing amputations where once had been limbs.

Beyond that, at the wards built on stilts over the water to capture maximum wind, and after showing my letter from Goethals to the appropriate administrator, I was directed to the area of the hospital where isolation cages had been set up in a high-ceilinged room. There I was delivered to the man I sought, who lay on a bed in an isolation cage.

The cages were not much different from prison cells, with the exception that the support beams were designed to hold the stretches of fine meshed screens that would not permit any mosquitoes inside.

These cages held men who had contracted yellow fever. Most would recover, but some would die in agony. These patients were inside the mesh to prevent any adult mosquitoes from drawing their infected blood and passing it on to the general population.

The man I came to see would not be among the living beyond the next day or so. I had learned too well in Cuba the symptoms of the final stages. His name was Gerald Dawson, and he was the foreman able to answer my questions about the cut cable at the locks.

His mustache hung limp from sweat, and his narrow face was tight with the agony that came from the abdominal cramps caused by internal bleeding. His skin was the hideous yellow of a failed liver, and blood seeped from his nose and his eyes. He had curled his body in an attempt to fight off the shaking and chills that came from his fever.

A middle-aged nurse in starched white hovered behind me. I'd told her that I'd been sent by Colonel Goethals and needed to visit the man, and she'd accompanied me to ensure the cage door did not open.

I pulled a chair up to the side of the cage. The man turned his eyes toward me, dull with fever.

"I am James Holt."

He did not speak.

"I need to ask questions about the day at the locks when the cable sheared and dropped a bucket of concrete."

He groaned. I thought from pain, until he croaked out a plea.

"Pray for me."

I frowned. "Pray?"

"I have sinned, and God has punished me."

Each person travels his own journey to or away from God. My own belief came at a price that I was still not sure I would have paid if given a choice: the death of my wife, who in leaving this world had shown me the joy that comes with faith and how it strengthens us to endure all circumstances. Even then, I had never lost my disdain of the window dressings of religion—of public prayers and pious self-righteousness. Whatever had this man done to put himself in such spiritual anguish?

"Let me ask my questions first." That might have seemed like a cruel reply, but I would not use a balm on his desperation as a means to obligate him to answer me.

"I'm guilty. What more is there to tell? Because of me, men died."

"Was that your intent? To kill?"

He moaned. "No! Dear God, no. I accepted payment to hacksaw the cable. What was a day's worth of lost concrete in comparison to the entire dig?"

I pulled the newspaper photos from my shirt pocket and showed him Ezequiel Sandoval. "Was this the man who paid you?"

He shook his head.

I showed him a second photo. "This man then?"

"Yes," he groaned. "Yes."

I wasn't surprised.

Thirty-One

I reached Miskimon's office shortly before noon. It was located in a small separate building near the larger administrative building in Culebra.

I heard the clacking of a typewriter. The door was ajar, so I pushed it open.

The interior was as sparse as I had anticipated. Framed photos of various parts of the canal project hung on the walls. He had a shelf with a stack of paper, envelopes, typewriter ribbon, and dark blue carbon papers.

His desk was bare except for a small stack of papers on the right side, perfectly aligned with the near corner. No clutter anywhere.

What did surprise me was that he had positioned his desk so that he sat with his back to the door. He continued typing as I walked toward him.

He stopped typing and said without turning, "Mr. Holt."

Interesting. I gave the interior another look. There it was, a small mirror on the underside of his desk angled to give him a view of the door.

"Tricky." I met his eyes in the mirror. "Why not just face the door?"

"I'm always curious what people will do when they think no one is watching."

I stepped close enough to see letters on the top half of the sheet of paper in the typewriter.

January 13, 1909

Col. Geo. W Goethals,

Chairman, I.C.C.

Culebra, Canal Zone

Memorandum to Col. Goethals:

Referring to the attached:

Early yesterday morning I caught Marian Octega at his room at #206 Central Avenue Panama, this building being a Spanish boarding house.

Representing myself to be a saloon keeper from the Zone, I told him I was in the

"And generally," he said, "I prefer they mind their own business."

He stood and moved to his shelf to retrieve a canvas cover for the typewriter.

Naturally, to irritate him, I kept reading.

market for Golofina and Panatella cigars at the reduced price he was offering them to his Spanish friends, closing stating I had been referred to him by some of these people. He had one box partly full of "Golfina" (not "Golofina") and six other full and sealed boxes of the same brand. The Panatella's, he claimed, to be out of at present.

The cigar manufactured in Jamaica and called "Golofina" is the one sold in the

That was as far as I was able to read before Miskimon covered the typewriter.

"The cigar bandit that you and the colonel discussed yesterday?" I asked.

"You have many failings, Mr. Holt, but I never counted one of them the pettiness of being a busybody."

"Well, Muskie, normally you would be correct in that assessment. So forgive me for this, will you?" I slid into his chair and faced his typewriter, curious about more than the letter.

"As you might also guess," he said in a neutral tone, "I'm a proponent of personal boundaries. So I'll ask that you return that chair to its original position."

I glanced at the mirror. I did not see the door in it, but only because I was slightly taller than Miskimon.

I felt underneath the desk and my fingers brushed an object clipped beneath it. Given Miskimon's role for Goethals, it seemed a wise precaution. If someone opened the door with bad intentions, seeing Miskimon's back would create the illusion of an easy target. The mirror would reveal those intentions, and Miskimon could swivel in his chair, holding a weapon in his hands.

"Yes," he said in a tired tone, correctly guessing what I had searched for and found. "I find that a .38 caliber can be persuasive when necessary."

I slid away from the desk, leaned back in the chair, and looked up at Miskimon. "I prefer the Peacemaker." A six-shot, .45-caliber.

"A name I've always found ironic. Nobody should point a gun at anyone without the full intent to use it. State your business here so that I can return to my routine. Oh, and remove yourself from my chair."

I locked my fingers behind my head and leaned back. "I thought your routine was following me around the isthmus in case you needed to thump someone on the side of the head with a wine bottle."

"Not after the colonel sent you to ask follow-up questions to my investigations into the accidents. You've been on your own since then. Please remove yourself from my chair."

"Except for the various spies on my trail since my arrival. One of them I've asked to meet with us. Waldschmidt. At noon at the administration building."

That caught him. "Spies?"

"The woman at the dig on Sunday morning who wandered onto the slope, New York accent . . . she was one of Goethals's, right? Not a coincidence that she was on the same train and wandered down to the observation deck when I did?"

"It seemed prudent, and she was improvising. There was and is so little we know about you. We expected that given some time alone with you, she would be able to provide us with much information." Miskimon blinked a few times. "It would be embarrassing for both of us if I were forced to try to physically remove you from my chair. Even knowing I might not succeed, I will put in the effort."

Fun was fun, but I did like the man. I stood and moved away from his desk. However, I did move his stack of papers slightly out of alignment.

"There was a Chinese laborer," I said, "on the 10:37 train out of Empire yesterday morning, with suspiciously clean fingernails for a laborer. At different times, there was a Panamanian with enough of a limp that he should have been using a cane, and his shoes did not match his working clothes. Two women tourists, early forties is my guess, who seemed little interested in the steam shovels yet used their Kodaks with great frequency. A petulant man in his late teens who was poorly dressed, which was at odds with the careful grooming of his hair. And a nondescript Spanish guy who slicked his hair to give him a different look from when he pretended to be a waiter at Cromwell's soiree."

"You are more observant than I give you credit for."

He eyed the stack of papers on his desk and hopped ever so slightly from one foot to the other.

"Years of keeping a careful eye out for rattlesnakes in the Badlands," I said. "But I prefer rattlesnakes. They give warning and won't strike if you back away. I'm not sure I can say that about you and Colonel Goethals."

"Sticks and stones, Mr. Holt. This project will change the course of history. It's more important than your feelings. Or mine. Now, if you wouldn't mind, why exactly do you want Mr. Waldschmidt to meet you shortly at the administration building?"

"Curiosity," I said. "To see if he'll appear."

Miskimon seemed to barely hear me.

"Oh for heaven's sake," I said. "Go ahead."

He pounced on the stack of papers and realigned them with the corner of the desk. I doubted he realized he'd given a sign of relief.

"Tell me again why you want Waldschmidt to appear?" he asked.

"If he appears, I think that will be significant. And I have questions for him."

"He makes it obvious he is a German spy," Miskimon said. If Miskimon knew this, it explained the lack of reaction Goethals had shown at the lock the day before when I mentioned Waldschmidt. "I doubt he'd answer any direct questions."

"Will you?"

"Depends on the questions."

I stood. "How about we sit in the shade on the veranda of this fine little building and watch for Waldschmidt's arrival. Then you choose which of my questions you want to answer."

Neither of us spoke for about five minutes. Strangely, it was not an uncomfortable silence. Miskimon had his peculiarities, but I admired him for choosing not to hide them. Also, he had saved my life the night before.

Perhaps my body was getting accustomed to the humidity, but the heat was no longer uncomfortable. We sat in chairs a few feet apart, both watching the entrance to the administration building.

Noon passed with no sign of Waldschmidt.

Miskimon finally broke the silence. "What did you learn of interest at Gatún and Cristóbal?"

"Which you know about thanks to the petulant man in his late teens. I'm not sure you should keep him in that role. He was entirely too obvious as he followed me."

"Now you are simply showing off."

"As are you. Demonstrating your conclusion that I am here because of Gatún and Cristóbal."

"I could simply be assuming that you are following up on questions that Colonel Goethals assigned you to ask."

"Yet after visiting the lock and after visiting the dig," I said, "I did not stop by your office."

"Point made. What did you learn, then, at Gatún?"

"The amazing engineering that it took to tame the Chagres by building a dam site bigger than anything seen before."

Miskimon gave me a deadpan sweep of his eyes. "Vulgarities are never humorous, Mr. Holt."

It took me a second to think through what might have been a vulgarity. Of course. *A dam site bigger.* My pun had not been intentional, but not bad. I bit off a smile and stayed as deadpan as Miskimon.

"First thing a fish says when it smacks into a concrete wall?" I watched Miskimon. "Dam."

"Juvenile vulgarities exhibit even less class. Besides, unlike most, the Gatún Dam is not built with concrete. So that doesn't apply here."

"Still, wouldn't you agree that America is a dam nation? Blocking water everywhere Americans go."

"It's a poor comedian who abuses a captive audience."

"Do you understand the concept of fun? Did you ever play at anything when you were a boy?"

"I never was a boy. And this idle chitchat, I repeat, is a waste of time."

I thought of a new pun, but it was going to need a buildup. "When the valley is filled, it will be the largest man-made lake in the world. What happened to the villagers who lived along the river?"

"They've been compensated," Miskimon said.

"And they moved without protest?"

"They've been compensated."

"I see." I couldn't wait. "The relocation of the dammed."

Miskimon sighed. "You take advantage of my loyalty to Colonel Goethals. Had I any choice, I would be far, far away from you and your dam puns."

Miskimon winced when he realized what he just said, and put up a hand. "Please. Don't say anything."

I grinned. Could it be? Was that a slight upturn of Miskimon's mouth, as if the man was fighting a smile?

We resumed our observation of the comings and goings at the administration building. Robert Waldschmidt was nowhere in sight.

"Raoul Amador," I said, finally. "Colonel Goethals wanted to know who the hunter was. There is your answer."

"It's not much of an answer. We've known of his involvement since the night he had you tortured by the National Police. We want whoever it is that sent Amador after you. Whatever Amador is doing, he does not have enough influence to do it on his own."

"Last night—"

"Yes, I'm also aware he disappeared from the party shortly after you did last night. From what was reported to me, he—"

"Who reported it?"

"Odelia, naturally. The same person who knew Cromwell had given Amador the task of getting your tuxedo and had deliberately ordered your suit in the wrong size. She suggested we bring proper attire and would not listen to me when I insisted it wasn't necessary."

"How did she know?"

"Raquel is like a sister to Odelia. Raquel passed it along after Amador bragged about his little joke. Apparently Raquel has a soft spot for you."

"As does Odelia for you, Muskie. I offer the lipstick on your neck as proof."

Miskimon glared at me but chose to ignore the remark. "Amador refused to make a public appearance after you were through with him last night, probably because he looked much the worse for wear. The colonel and I expected to hear from the National Police this morning with a complaint about your abuse of the man. Naturally, we would not have handed you over to them, disappointed as we were at the rough handling you gave him."

"*My* abuse of *him*?"

"The Wild West days are over, Mr. Holt. Yes, he tried to humiliate you with improperly sized clothing, but to drag a man through horse manure is an overreaction from just about any perspective. Odelia said his nostrils were caked and he kept trying to blow his nose clean."

"That is ironic, given that you used a shovel as a Peacemaker. For which, by the way, I'm grateful."

"Mr. Holt?"

"Yes, Muskie."

"Time is one of the most crucial resources in the Zone. The money spent by our taxpayers every hour simply boggles the mind. My preference would be direct questions and direct statements. It would lessen the time I need to spend with you and increase the time that I can devote to the tasks given to me by the colonel. Your statement about a shovel and a Peacemaker is too obscure for me."

"Last night. Near the carriage that was to take me away from the party, Amador threatened me with a pistol in one hand and a knife in the other. You intervened by striking him across the back of the head with the flat of a shovel. You have my gratitude. Is that direct enough?"

"Repeat that, please. But with more detail."

I did.

Miskimon removed his glasses and polished them with his shirt. I waited as he composed his thoughts. When the glasses were back on his nose, he said, "That was not I. Had I been there, I would have chosen a different method to disarm him. Which leads to a couple of obvious questions. Who wielded the shovel, and why would Amador risk the wrath of the National Police by trying to kill you?"

My turn to show surprise. "Risk the wrath of the National Police?"

"Shall we trade information, Mr. Holt? It is a grudging admission that I believe you to be a man of honor, despite your casual regard of authority and rules and regulations. Tell me what you hoped to gain by inviting Waldschmidt here, and I'll tell you about the National Police."

"Hoped?"

"If he is indeed working for the Germans, he won't appear. This is the American Zone. The Republic of Panama is his refuge."

"That's really all I wanted to establish. Whether it still was."

Miskimon paused as he gave that some thought. "Well done. I would like to know why you think he could believe himself to be in danger in Panama."

I had two simple answers: the flag had been exposed, and someone gave me photographs with a treasonous constitution. Waldschmidt was the one person I knew who was linked to Amador and could be part of it.

Instead of giving that answer, I said, "You first."

"Me?"

"National Police." I wanted—no, needed—a reason to trust Miskimon.

"Very well. After you swear an oath of confidentiality."

"Muskie."

He sighed. "The colonel was as furious as I was at how the National Police dealt with you on Sunday night. After I saw the bite of the alligator on your ears, I realized we had put you at too much risk. The obvious solution was to send you home. Except when I reported the events to the colonel, he overruled me. He did something very unusual. He threatened war."

"War?"

"He met with the governor and the chief of the National Police. He promised them that, regardless of the consequences, if you were harmed in any manner, he would send in two hundred soldiers and commandeer the police station, thereby, in effect, taking control of Panama City. His reputation is such that they understood he was not bluffing. It did not take them long to agree. The Chinese laborer and the Panamanian with a limp, they weren't ours. I'm wondering if they were sent by the republic to learn what you were doing, or to make sure that you didn't get hurt under any circumstances, or both."

This, then, explained Miskimon's comment the day before about the colonel's firm words.

"Last night, then, Amador was knocked out by one of theirs? Protecting me to ensure the colonel stays happy?"

"That would be my presumption."

This was my decision point. Would I believe what I'd just been told, given that I'd been followed by spies everywhere since arriving and given all the information that had been withheld from me? I'd wondered all morning whether Goethals and Miskimon were involved in some way with the photographs placed in my clothing. After all, Goethals himself had informed me that while he did not like Cromwell, he needed the man to be able to complete the canal. It came down to this. Either Goethals was colluding in all this intrigue with Cromwell, or he was not. Because Cromwell *was* part of this. He'd established that by asking me and Miskimon to unfurl the flag.

Yet everything I knew about Goethals confirmed he was a man of honor. As was Miskimon.

"Nice to get that kind of protection," I said.

Miskimon shook his head. "You really do think highly of yourself, don't you? It was a slap of the face to the colonel for them to treat one of his men in that manner. If he didn't stand his ground, it would put him in a weak position. The colonel is not a weak man, and he will not let his authority be challenged. As for the republic, they dare not incur the colonel's wrath. Your safety was simply a matter of politics."

If so, my fear earlier in the morning that I would be whisked away after meeting Harding had been unfounded. "I trust, then, that in his discussion with the National Police, the colonel discovered who directed them to apply the alligator bite to my ears? The man who hid his identity as he questioned me?"

"They gave him the answer. Raoul Amador."

While that didn't surprise me, it did not explain his motive, so I asked the natural question. "What was Amador's reason?"

"We would like to know as much as you would. The colonel made it clear that they were to warn Amador that if you were harmed, Goethals would unleash his wrath. Why, then, would Amador again threaten you last night, and so openly?"

"I had the distinct impression he thought I would end up dead and be unable to report his actions."

"Still, a risk. And what would motivate him to want to question you on Sunday night in the first place, let alone attempt to kill you last night?"

I let out a breath. My decision about who to trust was made. "In regard to last night, I think it was the flag of the new republic that you and I put on display."

"New republic?" Miskimon started, his brows creasing.

"I think Amador is working for the Germans. Let me tell you what I learned this morning about the cable that broke at the locks."

First I described Oliver MacDonald's reaction, then suggested the man might not be as honest as he tried to appear. Next I described my time at the isolation cage and the information that Gerald Dawson had confessed. I told Miskimon that Dawson had pointed to the photo of Amador as the man who had paid him to saw the cable.

"My guess," I finished, "is that after each act of sabotage was committed, Amador found a way to make sure the man behind it died, thus ensuring he would not be linked to those acts. He couldn't find a way to reach Dawson, however, not with the security to keep a man with yellow fever out of the general population. Convenient for Amador that Dawson will soon be as dead as the others. As for my testimony, if I understand the law correctly, it would be considered hearsay."

"You are correct in that understanding," Miskimon said. "Furthermore, it's a big leap from learning that Amador hired out the sabotage to the argument that he is working for the Germans."

"Except for the flag. And this. Look for Amador's signature on the final page. He's a lawyer. It wouldn't surprise me if he drew up the entire document."

This morning, I'd returned the photographs to the protection of wax paper and placed them inside the envelope, which was damp from my sweat when I pulled it out from under my shirt. The wax paper, however, served its purpose, and the photographs of page after page of the new constitution were glossy and immaculate.

"Six years ago," I said, "Panama revolted from Colombia thanks to the backing of the United States. It's not a stretch to think that another revolt is being planned now with the backing of Germany."

Miskimon tapped the photographs. "Conceivable. Many Panamanians feel they signed away too much for too little and have regrets about the treaty. And given that completing the canal is simply a matter of a few more years' work at this point, setting up a naval base on each side of the canal would give Germany control of the oceans."

Miskimon picked up the photographs and glanced at the final sentence. "Mr. Holt, just above Amador's signature, I see this: 'We, the undersigned, pledge our loyalty to this new republic and loyalty to all who make this bold step.' "

"I saw that too. Makes sense. While the reward is great if the coup succeeds and this group forms the new government backed by Germany, but if it fails because someone loses nerve, they are all looking at execution for treason. They'd want to make sure everyone in the group is committed, and their signatures would ensure both that and their silence."

"Yet," Miskimon said, "that last page is missing. There is no 'we, the undersigned,' no group of conspirators. There is only one person who can be found guilty of treason, based on the signature to the constitution. That would be Raoul Amador."

"The final page is not missing. It's in here." I pulled one last photograph out of the envelope and handed it to him.

It only took him a quick glance to see that someone had razored out all the signatures, leaving the photographic sheet dotted with small open rectangles. "Strange."

"Yes," I said. "Strange."

It had taken me a half hour to cut out those rectangles. I had done it because Raquel's name and signature had been on that photograph, and the only way to keep her anonymous was to protect all the others too.

Saffire's question to me on Sunday morning at the administration building echoed in my mind . . .

Choosing between justice and the woman I wanted to love had not been difficult at all.

thirty-two

My invitation to the bullfight had been for 2 p.m., giving plenty of time for a diversion before a visit to Waldschmidt. So at my insistence, Miskimon and I disembarked at Pedro Miguel, the train stop down from Culebra, before Miraflores, then Corozal, until Ancón, the final stop at the edge of the republic.

At the sound of muted thunder, I scanned the sky. It was habit. In the Dakotas, you could see storms building miles away. I saw only pale blue, no anvils of dark rising clouds. This was the dry season. I'd been told there would be no storms until March. So the sound, though we were well south, had to be the machinery at the Culebra dig.

"You'll find the walk worthwhile," I told Miskimon, as I led him away from the train station.

"I have only your word for that," he said, reaching my side.

"Frightening, isn't it?"

He walked on the outside of one rail, and I walked on the outside of the other.

"Tobias Benjamin," I said. "Titus maybe? Theo? Bryce?"

"Tedius," he answered. "Boring. Instead of irrelevant questions, perhaps explain why we are on a trek to steal water?" he said. "I'll remind you again of the importance of efficiencies. If this is some wild goose—"

"What's ahead?" I pointed down the stretch of tracks.

"The construction of the Pacific locks and . . ."

I had no doubt that Miskimon was quick thinking and intelligent. He had just proven it again. "Yes. That's what's ahead."

He looked to me. "The spot where men claim to have been struck down from the sky. What have you found?"

"Tut-tut, you have your secrets, I have mine. The difference is that as soon as we get there, my secret will be yours, whereas your refusal to divulge the T and B of your names will haunt me forever."

"This manufactured mysteriousness is juvenile. But I suppose if the shoe fits—"

"Remind me again how much you haven't told me during my time on the isthmus? Like your affection for our cross-dressing candidate for mayor?"

Miskimon stopped. The expression on his face was a mixture of embarrassment and bemusement.

"I presume this ploy is part of Raquel Sandoval's efforts for women's suffrage?" I asked. "Getting a woman into office as mayor of Panama City by having the woman campaign dressed as a man?"

"You know then? Who told you?"

"Once I'd met both, it wasn't that difficult to decide for myself. Odalis Corillo, the self-proclaimed candidate of choice of Raquel Sandoval? Odelia Cordet, the close friend of Raquel Sandoval?"

He shook his head. "You have no idea how relieved I was myself to learn they were one and the same. Until then, I'd found myself with an unnatural attraction to Mr. Corillo during our lunches with Raquel Sandoval. It was . . ."

My only interaction with Odelia Cordet had been in the bathroom at the Sandoval ranch as she delivered my tuxedo, but in that brief period, I could tell she enjoyed a degree of impudence. I could imagine her, dressed as a man, flirting with someone uptight like Miskimon just for the chance to discomfort him.

He hesitated a beat longer, then continued. "Mr. Holt, you are a rogue of sorts. I have observed women are attracted to men like you. I am not that kind of man, and I will reluctantly admit that to worsen it, I am shy with the fairer sex. In short, I have little experience. Mr. Corillo seemed to delight in provoking me with sly comments about how attractive I was, and I found it so charming and alluring, I'd even begun to wonder about my own inclinations."

I couldn't help myself. I roared with laughter.

He gave me a miffed look. "It is of little humor. Really." Then, for the first time in my presence, he smiled. "Perhaps, yes, some humor."

I patted his shoulder.

He recoiled.

"Forgot," I said. "Not good with contact, are you?"

"You won't take it personally?"

"Nope. And contact with Odelia? Are you becoming accustomed to that?"

He sniffed. "I am a gentleman, and gentlemen do not share such details."

"How about generalities? Does a gentleman share generalities?"

He couldn't help but smile again. "I have discovered that romance is not near as ridiculous as I'd believed it when a mere observer of interactions between a man and a woman."

"I'm proud of you, Muskie. I'll send a wedding gift. A bottle of fine whiskey. If you're going to join the human species, you might as well experiment with all our weaknesses. After that, you could even break a rule and discover how wonderful it feels."

"Hmmph." He began walking.

I fell into step with him.

The two Panamanian boys were at the train switch, the same position as the day before.

As we approached, I said to Miskimon, "When I tell you to steal some water, lean forward as if you are reaching for the dipper. But do not, under any circumstances, touch the dipper. Will you trust me on this?"

"Reluctantly."

We closed the gap and reached the switch on the tracks. Side by side, we squared off against the boys, as if this were the choreography to a gunfight in a silly Western moving picture.

Like the day before, I pointed at the water.

The taller boy spoke up. "Same price as yesterday. Twenty-five cents. Americano dollars."

Clearly, my cowboy hat made me easy to remember.

"Twenty-five cents!" Miskimon exclaimed. "That's—"

"I know," I said. "Highway robbery."

"Robbery is theft," he said. "This is extortion."

"There's a difference?"

The two boys swung their heads back and forth as they watched our bickering.

"Regardless," Miskimon said, "I refuse to pay twenty-five cents to drink water from a bucket that is undoubtedly as filthy as—"

"I think they speak okay English," I told him. "We all understand you are outraged."

The two boys crossed their arms, and the taller one spoke again. "Twenty-five cents."

"What if I just take it from you?" I asked. "How are you going to stop me?"

"Twenty-five cents."

But the second boy had reached for his stick.

"You'll hit me with that?"

"Twenty-five cents," he said.

I turned to Miskimon. "Imagine you've worked hard with a shovel all day. You take a shortcut down these tracks because you don't want to pay train fare. You're thirsty. You're outraged at the price they ask, and it's only you and two boys. Would you feel justified in pushing them aside and taking that dipper hanging on the side of the bucket?"

"I do not give in to emotions, Mr. Holt."

"I'll ask Odelia about that. Just to prove you are not always correct."

"Don't make me regret my trust in sharing a confidence with you. Too late. I already do."

"I apologize. Let me rephrase my question. Could you imagine an indignant laborer pushing these boys aside and grabbing a dipper full of water?"

"Not everyone lives up to my standards." He paused. "Actually, very few."

"I'll take that as a yes?"

"Yes."

"Then tell them you're not going to pay and go ahead and steal some water."

Miskimon glared at me. "I am not that kind of man."

"Trust me. Remember?"

He turned to the boys. "Fair warning. I think it is wrong to take advantage of someone in need of water. I'll give you five cents. That's my final offer."

"Muskie." Had he forgotten my instructions? "Keep your nickel. Just reach for the dipper."

"Twenty-five cents," the tall boy said.

Miskimon leaned forward to reach for the dipper. I was watching the younger boy with the broom handle. Instead of using it to strike Miskimon, he touched the other end of it to the center rail.

Miskimon straightened.

"I did it. Followed your ridiculous instructions. What have we accomplished?"

I motioned for the smaller boy to give me his broom handle. He glanced at his partner, who nodded.

The smaller boy dropped the broom handle and fled, with the taller boy directly behind him. A hundred yards down the track, they turned their heads to see if we were in pursuit.

We were not.

They slowed to a jog. Just as well. Miskimon would have wanted their names for his next typed report to Colonel Goethals.

It was safe to lift the dipper from the bucket, so I did, letting Miskimon come to his own conclusion about the setup.

He saw the wire from the dipper, leading to the broomstick. He saw a groove along the broom stick and where the wire was embedded the entire length to the end, sticking out a few inches like an antenna. He let his eyes rove, then stop at the center rail, the one that supplied electricity to the locomotives on this stretch of track. He looked at me and raised an eyebrow.

"Yes. When you made a move for the dipper, the boy with the broomstick reached out and touched the wire to the center rail. The wooden broom handle would insulate him from any shock, and the current would go straight to the dipper."

"A jolt like that," Miskimon said with a tone of awe, "would come close to killing a man."

"At the very least, it would knock him on his back like a hand from the sky. You are welcome to keep my name out of your report."

In Panama City, at the National Hotel, Robert Waldschmidt did not respond to a call from the lobby telephone.

Nor was he in the restaurant.

Back in the lobby, I said, "We need to talk to him."

Miskimon shrugged. "This is the republic. We have no jurisdictional say. He can move around the country as he pleases."

"Not if the current government believes he is involved in inciting a revolution."

"We have no proof of that. Only strong speculation. I cannot in good conscience take speculation to any authorities in the republic. It would be signing his death warrant."

"Suggestions? Give the Panamanians the photos with Amador's signature on a new constitution."

"That will be for Colonel Goethals to decide."

I finally asked the question that mattered most to me. "So I am finished here in Panama?"

Miskimon gave it consideration. "I usually report to the colonel at the end of the day. I'll confirm it with him and let you know immediately after. The next steamer to New York doesn't leave until tomorrow anyway."

"Until then?"

"I won't be out of Panama City for a few hours. I'd feel better if you stayed with me instead of wandering these streets on your own."

"I appreciate your concern over my well-being, Muskie, but that won't be necessary. I have plans of my own."

"It has nothing to do with you. I'm just trying to protect Colonel Goethals from any and all of your irresponsibilities."

"Tell you what, Muskie, I promise to be good."

I tipped my hat and walked out of the lobby.

Thirty-Three

Odelia found me easily enough at the time written on the note I had found in my cowboy boot in the morning. I had positioned myself to the side of the bottleneck of spectators at a gate, on the northeast side of the arena. Her note had stated to meet her across from a Chinese restaurant, which was accurate. But it also showed a difference in perspectives. She marked her geography by buildings; I marked mine by the compass.

She stepped toward me and touched my arm with her left hand. She wore a dress similar in style to the one she had worn the previous evening—but far less formal—with brightly colored flowers on a light blue pastel background. It contrasted well with her jet black hair and equally dark eyes. She was—as Miskimon had pointed out—very alluring.

"James Holt." She gave me her impetuous smile. "I'm delighted you decided to meet me here. After last night, I feared you might not trust any Panamanians."

That was an accurate assumption. I was here out of curiosity, not because I trusted her. "It seemed like a fine afternoon. I was delighted for the invitation."

"Then let's find our places, shall we?" She lightly held my elbow and guided me away from the stream of spectators into the shade of the outer arena. The arena was about three stories high—a large circle, much like a coliseum. Given the purpose of the arena, it was fitting that the name came from the Latin word for *sand,* which the ancient Romans used to soak up the rivers of blood generated by their infamous spectator sports.

Odelia spoke quietly as we walked away from the line of those at the gate. "As you know, Raquel Sandoval is a dear, dear friend. We've been like sisters since childhood."

"You also have her political support. Always wise to stay close to a benefactor."

She laughed. "I suspect my run for mayor will be over before the election. Already rumors fly. It is too difficult to keep the secret, and I have been careful to ensure that most believe it was my idea, not hers. But I think she knew I would be unmasked, so to speak, and simply wanted to make a point. I have nothing to lose, you see, which is why I was happy to help her make that point. She, on the other hand . . ."

"Yes?"

"Has always believed that marrying Raoul Amador would make for an alliance to put her in a position where she can help the poor much better than if she were known as a woman who tried to ridicule the political system."

"Yes. Raoul Amador. A wonderful specimen of a human being."

She caught the tone in my voice and giggled. "He was spitting angry with humiliation last night. What did you do to him before dragging him through horse manure?"

"Made it clear I wasn't interested in a discussion with him."

"There was more to it than that."

"Yes."

"And?"

"I'd rather not discuss it."

"You're no fun."

I grinned.

"He was in a foul mood all night," she said. "Part of it, I believe, is because you were not wearing the suit he had chosen for you. He is a petty man, and I dislike him greatly, which is why I insisted that you had proper attire. He and Raquel had harsh, harsh words last evening as the party ended."

"I'm sorry to hear that. What matters is that Raquel is happy."

"Happiness?" She snorted. "Who marries for happiness?"

I smiled sadly, thinking of the woman I had loved and now mourned. Or maybe the sadness came because for the first time since her death, there was a woman that I wanted to love. I could not escape a sense that love for someone else might lead to the death of my memory of the woman I mourned.

"You, Señor Vaquero Americano," Odelia said, "have given my friend Raquel a reason to be unhappy. She is drawn to you but is bound to Panama by a sense of duty and practicality."

"I'm not sure why you would tell me that. Last night, it was distinctly chilly when she glanced my way. Which was only once. And that was before Cromwell added to my unpopularity by asking me to open the package. Are you able to tell me why it seemed to cast such a pall over the crowd?"

Odelia didn't answer my question directly. "Don't you understand? Raquel feels she made a fool of herself during her walk with you along the beach. That night, she confided to you her interest in you only because she believed she would never see you again. Had you left as we expected,

Raquel could have kept that memory and clung to a romantic illusion for the rest of her life. So to see you again, knowing that she had shown weakness and vulnerability? Well, I understand her aloofness. It did not help that Amador was watching her at the party. He would be an idiot not to sense she is intrigued by the cowboy with the broken nose, and while Amador is many things that I do not like, he is most definitely not an idiot."

"I leave tomorrow. He has nothing to fear."

"I suppose, yet there remains much to be discussed before this afternoon is over."

That was certain. I was aware of the envelope of photos still inside my shirt. Odelia's name and signature had been among those that I excised from the document.

We had reached the north end of the arena, and she pointed to a small door and led me to it. "Special privileges."

I understood this from my own days of performing for the Wild West show. In each city, the rich found ways to separate themselves from the unwashed—in seating and in mingling with performers behind the stages.

She knocked, and a finely dressed man opened the door. Seeing her, he smiled and made an elaborate sweeping gesture with his arm to allow us inside.

The tunnel was dark and filled with the smell of livestock. I could not ignore the homesickness that had lurked beneath the surface of my senses since arriving in Panama.

Each side of the tunnel held separate rooms, which I guessed had been set aside for the matadors. At the end of the tunnel, a door was propped open to the arena, letting in sunlight that helped our navigation. When ready, the matador, I assumed, would step out of this door to greet the crowd, and the door would be shut firmly behind him, with a crossbar in place on this side to prevent a rambunctious bull from knocking it down.

At that door, we turned to our left, away from the trampled sand, to a set of stairs that brought us up to the base of bleachers, already nearly full of spectators.

This did not seem like an area set aside for the affluent. It was crowded and smelled of wood wet with spilled beer—a scent that competed with the smoke of roasting meat and baked flat breads sold by aproned men screaming for attention.

"You will be discreet, Mr. Holt?" Here, she had to raise her voice to be heard.

I was thinking of the constitution with signatures. "I am nothing but."

"Excellent. As you probably know, the best place to hide is in a crowd."

She took me to the highest set of bleachers, what I presumed were the cheapest seats. Two steps away, I saw Miskimon, already seated. Then a woman beside him, dressed in the rough clothing of a peasant, an inexpensive bonnet giving shade from the sun and almost concealing her face.

But I knew who it was.

Raquel.

The circle of sand was empty, but the stands were crowded, and the excitement of collective anticipation combined with an equally collective festivity surrounded us.

The seating arrangements were not subtle. Odelia sat on Miskimon's left. I sat on Miskimon's right. And to my right was Raquel. Because of how she was dressed and because of the bonnet, unless someone was standing within one or two rows, a casual observation would show Odelia and Miskimon and me, and Raquel would be invisible among the other spectators.

While I was highly conscious of Raquel's proximity to me, she and I only said polite hellos as the extent of our conversation for the first few minutes after I took a spot on the unpainted bleachers.

"Mr. Holt," Miskimon said in greeting as I settled and tried to get comfortable. I was happy to have my cowboy hat to give me shade.

"Muskie. Full day for you. I suppose you knew I'd be joining you here when you suggested I spend the afternoon with you?"

"Shocking that some things escape my encyclopedic knowledge, but I had no idea. I now see that this was a well-planned and well-executed maneuver by two women. In private conversation, Odelia has speculated to me on your interest in Raquel, but I assure you, I give it little attention."

"Hmmph." I tried to imitate his manner in saying it.

On the other side of him, I saw Odelia pat his knee. He didn't recoil, as he did when I had done the same to his shoulder. He was in an official position to help her if she needed it, and because of the photographs, I knew she might desperately need it soon. I hoped, for him, that her motives were a genuine affection for the man.

As for Raquel, a discreet meeting in a rowdy public place was exactly the best way for the two of us to have a conversation, and I ached with the desire to believe her true intention was motivated by interest in me, not by interest in finding a way to protect herself from a man she feared knew of her signature on a treasonous document. For even if neither woman knew that I possessed the incriminating photographs, both had watched me unfurl the flag the evening before. Both no doubt knew the significance of that flag. Both women—obviously intelligent—would assume, then, that I had investigated more of the nascent rebellion and would wonder how much more I knew.

It was going to be difficult to keep my suspicions from tainting this time with Raquel. I decided, however, to ignore my suspicions and proceed as if I could trust the inclinations of my heart.

I looked out at the arena. "I know little about bullfights."

She took her eyes off the sand inside the empty circular walls below. The smile she bestowed upon me felt sincere—

Stop it, I told myself. Stop evaluating her intent and simply enjoy the smile.

"I'm astounded at that," she said. "You are a cowboy."

"One who makes a living by trying to keep his cattle alive in the badlands. The more cattle I put on train cars at the end of the season, the more successful I am."

"I cannot help but wonder what it looks like where you live in the Dakotas. I imagine towns with wide dirt streets and men in masks riding horses up to a bank and robbing it at gunpoint."

"It's not the way that moving pictures portray it."

"I wish to know more about where you live. Paint a picture for me, please, Mr. James Holt."

Her voice caressed. Her accent gave a lyrical sound to my first and last name, imbuing it with intimacy that accelerated the beat of my heart. The chance to describe my home made me feel like I had been asked to slay a dragon.

I told her about the blizzards and the temperatures so cold that a man's spit would turn to ice before hitting the snow. I told her about the gray-water floods that tore at the hills of the Badlands in spring, bowing the resilient bankside willows almost horizontal, and how when the waters subsided, dead grass would tuft the tips of the willows and remain a crown all through the summer. I told her about arid winds and the tinkling of a meadowlark's call and the melody of coyotes that seemed so in harmony with huge silver moonrises over the ancient hilltops—hilltops worn to strata that sometimes exposed the fossilized bones of creatures that could only live in the illustrations of the fantastic. And all the while, I watched her face and soaked in a sensation that I had never expected would course through my heart again.

She sighed. "It sounds like a place of poetry. Sometimes this heat and humidity and mountains are cloying, suffocating."

"I marvel at Panama. Life springs everywhere, hungry for every inch. Every creature possible finds a way to swim, crawl, fly. It is astounding."

Yet I could not live here, not without far horizon and limitless sky and freedom that some mistook for desolation. I did not voice this.

"You haven't spoken of your daughter," Raquel said.

"Winona. You only asked about the land."

"So now I am asking about her. Are you not afraid for her life while you are here and unable to protect her?"

"Afraid?"

"Savages. Raiding your homestead."

She seemed serious. Of course. She saw the Wild West show in London. Buffalo Bill had sold the image she expressed to the entire world.

"There was a time," I said, "when the Sioux rightfully defended their land." I chuckled. "In fact, the United States lost a war to a great Sioux warrior named Red Cloud. But the treaties have since been signed, and it's been decades since anything like that happened."

"So your daughter is not in danger from savages?"

"Winona is with one right now."

Those beautiful eyes widened. "I beg your pardon?"

"Cetanwakuwa."

"I don't understand."

"He's Sioux. Roughly translated into our language, his name is Attacking Falcon. I call him Hawk. Winona calls him Unk Hunk. Started when she was too little to say Uncle Hawk properly."

Unk Hunk had been in the Wild West Show with his sister. He was the Sioux warrior responsible for the long scar on my ribs. An accident when a stray buffalo had knocked him off his horse, and he'd flailed for balance with his feather-notched spear extended.

"A savage?" Raquel said.

"A Sioux."

"And you trust her with him?"

"Of course I do," I said. "As I mentioned, he is Winona's uncle."

It took her a few moments. "She is . . . your wife was . . . your brother-in-law is . . ."

"Cetanwakuwa is full-blooded Sioux. I married his sister, Ojinjintka, who was also full-blooded Sioux. They were both part of Buffalo Bill's show for years. As for Winona, she carries the blood of two peoples. Those who are cruel call my daughter a half-breed."

Not for the first time it occurred to me that Roosevelt would have passed this knowledge along to Goethals and that the colonel guessed that seating me beside a girl like my own daughter would have predisposed me to sympathy for the girl.

"Those here who are cruel use the term *mulatto,*" Raquel said. "Saffire . . ."

Raquel seemed to be letting me fill her silences, but it didn't matter. My regret was that, regardless of whether she enjoyed my company as much as I enjoyed hers, this afternoon would end. She would return to her life and I to mine. She to the fecund green vibrancy and color of Panama, a place swelling with the noise of insects and birds and machinery and people. Me to the whites and browns of a Dakota landscape, remarkable at hiding the life it supported.

"Saffire," I said. "She is an amazing girl."

"I love her like a sister," Raquel said. "But I wish she wouldn't come and go with such impunity. I haven't seen her since yesterday afternoon. Have you seen her today?"

"No. Not since Monday afternoon."

The girl had lived up to her promise to put me out of her life, and I was surprised at how sad it made me, given the short time I had spent with her.

"I won't worry. She always reappears. And such a fierce and smart girl.

If women could vote and run for office, she would become president of the republic someday."

"Her mother," I said. "Do you believe she ran away? Do you believe the letter she gave to your father was the truth?"

Raquel looked away for a long pause, and then back at me. "I came here to sit with a cowboy who intrigues me and makes me smile. Not for an interrogation by an investigator. Please, let us enjoy this time together. Will that be acceptable to you, Mr. James Holt?"

"Of course," I said.

She touched the back of my hand with the tip of a finger. "And Mr. Holt?"

"Yes?"

"Perhaps we could correspond by letters after you depart Panama?"

Before I could answer, the moment was burst by a roar of the crowd. The matador had just entered the ring, resplendent in his clothing, bowing to the spectators. And on the other side, from a cattle chute, a massive black bull had stepped onto the sand, bellowing its blind rage at the sticks with nails used to prod it forward to its eventual death.

"We have arrived at the *tercio de muerte.*" Raquel leaned toward me. "This is the final third, the third of death. I am glad we approach the end and I will no longer have to endure the spectacle. If we could have met anywhere else but here, I would have chosen to do so."

She pointed at the matador, who carried a small cape of red. "There is the reason that I do not like to ever wear a dress of red. People say the color of the cape is to enrage the bull, but that is not so. The animals are color blind. Instead, it is meant to hide the stains of the bull's blood."

In the first third of the bullfight—the *tercio de varas*—the matador, distinguished by a suit of gold, had orchestrated his three silver-suited banderilleros in a series of passes with the bull to test the animal's skills and quirks. At the end of that stage, a picador, a man on horseback armed with a lance—*vara*—had stabbed the mound of muscle on the bull's neck, drawing the first blood to weaken it. More important, this injury forced the beast to lower its head during subsequent charges.

All this, Raquel had explained with scorn as it unfolded.

Then had come the *tercio de banderillas,* the middle of the bullfight, where the banderilleros tired the bull further, and with formalized moves, each of the three banderilleros planted two sharp barbed sticks—banderillas—into the bull's shoulders. All this was done to prepare for the final third, when the matador, armed with cape and sword, would engage the bleeding animal in a series of passes designed to weaken the animal more and more.

This, too, Raquel had explained, pointing out with derision that for most of the passes in the tercio de muerte, the matador used a fake sword made of wood, much lighter than steel. Thus, the matador could save energy in the heat of the ring, while the bull continued to exhaust itself.

Given that I raised cattle to ship to the great slaughterhouses of Chicago, I knew my shared revulsion of the event playing out below me was hypocritical, but that didn't lessen my distaste of the slow torture and killing of a magnificent beast.

The hundreds of spectators roared approval as the matador swirled his cape, narrowly dodging each thrust of the enraged bull. That mass approval, however, was tinged by the collective unspoken thrill at the possibility of witnessing a man's violent injury or death.

I had heard the same roars in my exile years in the great arenas of Europe and the large cities of the United States while I rode a nimble pony among thundering bison. As one of the Buffalo Bill riders, I was aware that—with the spear accident an exception—the danger was more illusion than reality. While it was possible to die beneath the hooves of a bison, there was more danger at my ranch in trying to rope a calf away from a mother cow. I guessed it happened the same way below, that spectators were sold on the illusion of danger. Because of the lance wound on the bull's neck and the six banderillas still sticking from the bull's shoulders, and the bull's weakness from loss of blood and the dozens of unsuccessful, enraged charges, the matador's greatest feat was likely not in avoiding the horns but in making it look like each sweep was a close miss.

"As you can see, Mr. Holt," Raquel said, "it is clearly not a fair fight. That is what angers me. Not the animal's death. Death is part of living, is it not? The bull's fate is as certain as the fate of each of us. No, it is the injustice of the fight itself. The bull faces, in turn, the matador, the picador with lance, the three banderilleros, and finally, the matador again. It is a system designed to give the matador all the advantages, a system meant to slowly bleed the animal and exhaust it. Such a system is what the people of Panama face, especially the women. Those at the top have all the advantages, and they are ruthless. The estate owners use their bankers and lawyers and police as swords and lances and banderillas against the people, never deeply enough to kill in one blow, but the end result is the same. It is the poor who suffer, and I am among the wealthy. This country needs to be changed."

Here it was. Raquel was about to present the reason she had wanted to meet with me—a plea for her band of rebels that she believed I had threatened in a public display of their captured flag.

Earlier, before the bullfight started, when I asked about Saffire's mother, Raquel had looked away for a long pause, then back at me. I found myself doing the same to her.

"Until last night," Raquel said when our eyes met again, "I believed I was marrying a solid man. I didn't need to love Raoul, but I thought I could live comfortably with him. I thought that becoming his wife would allow me to accomplish some things in this country, to help those poor. I thought that the satisfaction of raising my own children would fill my heart. And then last night—"

She stopped as if I had interrupted her. But I had not. It was the roar from the crowd, a roar with a life of its own, unlike any of the previous roars.

We both turned to the circle of sand, already dotted with brandy stains of blood.

The matador and bull were no longer alone.

A man had staggered from the door that led to the matador's tunnel. I saw the door close, as if he had been pushed into the arena.

By this man's gait, it was clear that he was drunk.

More clear to me, however, was his identity, his distinctive eye patch a marker of confirmation.

Robert Waldschmidt.

He was bedraggled in his suit, and his hands flipped helplessly as he twirled and tried to comprehend the noise and the sand.

Miskimon stood. As did I.

For a moment, it appeared the matador was unaware of Waldschmidt's presence on the sand. But when the bull rushed past the matador, well beyond the swirl of his cape, the matador turned with the bull and froze at the sight of another man with him in the ring.

Waldschmidt staggered, barely keeping his balance.

The bull moved toward him in a great rush of rage.

Waldschmidt staggered again, and the bull brushed past him.

The animal roar of the crowd changed in tone again, from shock to a mixture of jeering and cheering, as if half believed the man to be drunk and deserved death for sullying the ritual of the tercio de muerte and half believed this was some kind of vaudeville act—a skilled athlete pretending to be drunk and teasing the bull.

"Unless we stop the bull, he's a dead man!" Miskimon reached inside his jacket and pulled out a revolver from a hidden shoulder holster. "Clear the way and I'll follow."

The steps from top to bottom were crowded with spectators who had moved from their seats to where there was more room. I started pushing them aside.

But it was too late.

The bull had whirled. Rushed again, with monstrous head lowered. Wicked, sharpened horns aimed like lances.

Time seemed to slow at the moment of impact, and Waldschmidt flew into the air as if he had been struck by a locomotive.

The matador valiantly tried to divert the bull, darting in close and waving the cape. But the bull's rage was beyond any distraction as it continued to gore the fallen man.

I turned away. Watching the spectacle seemed like an act of voyeurism.

Raquel's arms were outstretched. I moved to her and she clung to my chest and pressed her face against my shoulder. I held her, eyes closed, as aware of how much I wanted to keep holding her as I was of the vivid and horrible death that had put her into my arms.

When I opened my eyes, Raoul Amador was a few feet away, pushing his way up the steps, his eyes focused on mine.

He glared, then walked away.

Thirty-Four

In the Dakotas, given the distances we traveled to visit our nearest neighbors—whether by horseback or by carriage—it seemed pointless to make the effort unless the visit lasted long enough for dinner with coffee afterward. This meant upon arrival, the horses needed to be unsaddled or unharnessed, and before leaving, it was necessary to spend time to saddle or harness our animals again. All told, then, a social call was a minimum of four hours. Except when urgent, daylight governed our travel because travel in the dark was at best worrisome and at worst hazardous. Thus, in the summer, anything past five o'clock in the afternoon was pushing it as a decent hour to arrive for a formal or semiformal social call. In the winter, of course, when the sun set much earlier, few social calls began after two o'clock, and only if the weather was good.

Over the telephone, the night of the bullfight, Raquel assured me that, in her culture, this was not the situation at all. Nine o'clock in the city, she said, was a perfectly normal hour for friends to gather, and soirees often went into the early hours of the morning.

I took the phone call in the lobby of the hotel in Culebra. A bellhop had been sent up the street to my bachelor quarters with a note, asking me to accompany him back to the hotel for the conversation. Had the note come from anyone but Raquel, I would have declined. The bellhop woke me from an early night's sleep, as Miskimon had promised he would arrive at sunrise to escort me by train to my waiting steamer and to tell me all he knew about the circumstances of Waldschmidt's death.

But this was to be my last night in Panama, and I would regret choosing a good night's rest over the chance to hear what Raquel might have to say to me, especially given Amador's reaction to witnessing the embrace that she and I shared at the bullfight. The man had simply turned away and walked down the steps again. Afterward, his silence and lack of reaction had weighed upon Raquel and me during our carriage ride to the train station at Ancón, and her good-bye to me held little emotion.

At the hotel, the switchboard operator put me through to the number on the note, and Raquel answered immediately, asking me to take a train back to Ancón and a carriage through the hills of Panama City to her fine villa. I did not point out that when I went to the villa Monday afternoon, I'd been turned away. She said her father would like to speak to me, and, moreover, she would like to have a private conversation with me, properly escorted, of course, by her dear friend Odelia.

She had her world and I had mine. Did it really matter if I spent a few more hours with her before a permanent good-bye? I could have rationalized that it would have been an embarrassment to her if I declined the invitation and that it was strictly from propriety that I accepted her request and embarked on the next available passenger train of the PRR.

But I knew better. I was a smitten fool. I would have waded across a swamp just for the chance to have her hold my hand and wish me safe travels as we gazed into each other's eyes.

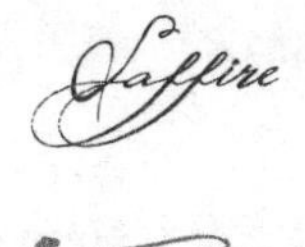

At the villa, with carriage wheels clattering on cobblestone as the hack drove away, I lifted and dropped the panther-head knocker on the door and was answered almost immediately with a sliding of the circular Judas window. The elderly woman who had greeted me before opened the door and nodded for me to step inside.

She led me down a wide hallway lit by candles. Two right-hand turns eventually brought us to the back of the villa, at a double door. This she opened to a large drawing room, pointing me inside. After I stepped forward, she closed the door behind me.

Had I not spent my younger years in travel, I would have felt like a rube in the subtle but immense display of wealth evident in the soft glow of light, provided here not from candles but from the bulbs in floor lamps supplied by electricity. The wall trim was dark, lustrous mahogany. The walls were dominated by large oil paintings. The rugs were luxurious, and the furniture, to my eyes, Chippendale.

All of this was simply something I gave only a glance because Ezequiel Sandoval was in one of those chairs across the room. He wore a dinner jacket, whereas my only sartorial splendor was the cowboy hat in my hand.

Raquel sat in the chair to his left, wearing a ruby-colored full-length dress. Her hair was pinned behind her head, showing the elegance of the line of her neck.

A few feet to her left was another chair, empty, and a fourth had been placed across from them at a distance that suggested formality. A side table to the left of the chair held a decanter of wine and a full glass and something that in the soft light looked like stacked bracelets resting on a sheet of paper.

Neither Raquel nor her father said anything at my entrance, or even seemed to turn their eyes toward me, as if I were invisible. I hesitated . . .

how should I proceed? I wanted to be respectful of her father, so because he didn't rise to greet me, I remained where I was.

I looked closer at the stacked bracelets, and it struck me that what I was seeing were two sets of handcuffs.

As I puzzled about this, from behind me and to my right came the unmistakable sound of the hammer cocking on a revolver.

"Drop your hat."

No mistaking the voice. Raoul Amador. There was a set of heavy drapes along the wall where he had hidden himself.

"Go sit in the empty chair near the wine. Move slowly. This pistol is not aimed at you but at Raquel, and if you try anything heroic, the first bullet is hers."

I dropped my hat. I didn't turn my head. I estimated by his voice that he had been careful enough to keep more than a few steps between us. Enough to shoot twice. Once at her, once at me.

I slowly stepped forward.

"Excellent," he said. "Before you sit, I want you to handcuff your left ankle to the right leg of the chair. After you sit, the next set is for your right wrist to the left arm of the chair."

Had I been alone, I would have risked death by attempting to tackle Amador, even with the distance between us. A tiny chance was better than no chance. Once I was handcuffed to the chair, I would be in his control.

But I wasn't alone.

At the chair, I scooped up the first set of handcuffs. I knelt, and the ratcheting of one bracelet to my left ankle was loud to me. I glanced at Ezequiel and Raquel. They showed no expression.

I continued with the other bracelet, securing my ankle to the right leg of the chair. All I would have to do was tilt the chair, and that handcuff would drop free of the chair leg, but it would take a second or two, and against a man armed with a pistol, that was an eternity too long.

After I bound my right wrist to the left arm of the chair, Amador said, "Lift and jerk against the handcuff hard. I want to see that it's secure."

I did so.

A moment later he entered my vision, near Raquel, both hands gloved with a delicate kid leather, finely stitched. He held my cowboy hat in one hand and a pistol in his other.

Like mine, it was a Peacemaker. Single action, six-shooter. A bullet for each of the three of us, if Amador wanted, and three to spare.

He dropped my hat and stepped on it, crushing the crown.

He slid the fourth chair a little behind Raquel, where she would have to turn her head to look over her shoulder to watch him. Her eyes remained straight ahead though. I tried to discern something from those eyes. Pupils that should have been luminous because of the low light were constricted needle tight.

I saw the same in Ezequiel's eyes.

"Pick up the certificate from the side table." Amador kept the pistol pointed at Raquel. "Read it."

I picked it up. I saw the words. I kept my face blank, even as my gut tightened. If he wanted a reaction from me, he wasn't going to get it. It was about all I was in a position to muster as defiance.

"In this light," I said, "I can't seem to see the lettering."

"Set the paper down."

I put it back on the side table. It was a small triumph, far too small considering the situation.

He leaned forward and with the butt of his pistol thumped the back of Raquel's head. Her soft grunt of helplessness was more horrible than the sound of a gunshot. That was her only reaction. The muscles on her face remained slack, giving her expression a vacuousness that chilled me.

"Did you enjoy thinking you had fooled me? Now tell me what that paper is."

"A marriage certificate."

"Go on. Who is the husband and the wife? Not by pronoun."

He knew it would hurt me to say the names.

"Raoul Amador," I said. "Raquel Sandoval."

I'd seen enough to know the date and time on the certificate was 5 p.m., Wednesday, January 13, 1909. They had married in a civil ceremony this afternoon, after the bullfight, about an hour after Raquel had said good-bye to me at the train station in Ancón.

"I'm glad you understand," Amador said. "She is my wife. Tomorrow, I will be distraught that she has disappeared. I will remain distraught for months. Perhaps her remains will someday be found in the swamps. Perhaps not. But after a suitable period of mourning, I will collect her inheritance. She was a good wife, wouldn't you agree?"

I looked to Raquel to see her response. Nothing.

"I only tell you this so that, until the noose drops over your neck, you can regret that you are responsible for her death. I didn't need her love. Only her loyalty, and you robbed me of that when she broke our engagement last night. Now drink the wine."

Sudden comprehension. If I did, my own pupils would shrink to dots, and I would become as catatonic as Ezequiel and Raquel. Yet I had no doubt he would hit Raquel across her skull with his pistol if I refused, so I took the wine glass with my free left hand and brought it to my mouth. I stopped with the rim well short of my lips. Each second that passed would bring all of us nearer to rescue. The arrangement with Miskimon had been that if I did not appear outside on the cobblestone drive within five minutes, cowboy hat in hand, he would assume that I was in danger. Or that if I stepped outside wearing my hat, it would also be a signal that something was wrong in the house and I needed his help.

I met Amador's gaze. "I have the photos of your new constitution.

This country's politics mean nothing to me. I am open to negotiation here."

Amador casually leaned back in his chair, raised his pistol, pointed it right, and pulled the trigger.

The roar of exploding grains of gunpowder and the resulting burst of massive sound waves felt like a sudden sledgehammer against the side of my head. For a moment, as tendrils of smoke wafted from Amador's shooting hand, I thought he'd simply done this for effect. Raquel was unharmed.

But Ezequiel gurgled once. He slid sideways, his head limp on his shoulders, his handsome face still remarkable and dignified—until a cough sent blood down his chin. He shuddered once. But that was all. The entry wound was somewhere at the back of his body—on this side, the appearance of his magnificence was preserved.

Amador turned the barrel of the pistol toward Raquel's face. The kid leather gloves were speckled with soot.

"Drink the wine," he said. "All of it. If the glass is not empty by the count of ten, you'll hang for her murder too. One . . ."

I drank it as if it were water, unaware of any taste.

He lowered the pistol. Had enough time passed for Miskimon to find his way inside the villa? Would any servants investigate the sound of a gunshot?

Amador rose from the chair and took a few steps to close the distance between us. He placed the pistol in my right hand and returned to his chair.

A Peacemaker weighs about two and a half pounds. There was enough play in the handcuffs for me to twist my wrist and aim it at his belly. Already, however, the weapon was beginning to feel much heavier than the weight to which I was accustomed. Whatever had been in the wine was acting upon me.

"Will you shoot an unarmed man?" he asked.

The answer was yes, to save a woman's life. I doubted there was another bullet in the pistol, but I would wait as long as possible before confirming it. I had to consume as much time as I could.

"Toss me keys to the handcuffs," I said. "I won't hesitate to pull the trigger if you don't."

"The National Police detained your friend Miskimon the moment he stepped into our republic," Amador replied. "The servant who brought you here is already on the way to the police station to report that you accosted Señor Sandoval with an American pistol. The new science of fingerprinting is a fascination to me. If finding you here with a dead man isn't enough to hang you, I'm sure that police procedure in regard to your grip on the weapon will be enough, wouldn't you agree? As for your kind offer to return the photos, it appears that Cromwell has already betrayed you. The revolution is over."

"Cromwell?" My tongue was thick and my voice strange in my ears. I felt an incredible thirst—and the sensation that my brain had turned into a liquid that was seeping down into my body.

"Since I can't understand what you said," Amador told me, "I think I can safely set you free."

Amador rose again. With fogginess shrinking my vision to a small circle, I realized that he had pulled out a key. I felt a click at my wrist and then at my ankle. He scooped up both handcuffs and placed them in his trouser pockets.

He helped me to my feet.

The world swayed. I lurched one way, then the other.

I tried to lift the useless pistol in my hand, but it felt chained to the floor.

I collapsed and sat in the chair again.

Amador stepped to me and pulled the pistol from my hand.

I was in the vice grip of paralysis, my vision fading almost to nothing.

Once, years earlier, I had been helpless, watching the woman I loved die. I would *not* let it happen again.

I tilted forward on the chair. I didn't have a hope of stopping him, but an irrational satisfaction of fighting to the end filled me. As the chair continued to tilt, I let myself fall forward, trying to knock him over.

He stepped aside and laughed, as I fell forward onto my face. He kicked my ribs, then knelt and held the barrel of the gun to my forehead.

"Beg," he said.

Rage cut through the drugged fogginess and sustained me. I did not. Nor did I turn my head aside.

He pulled the trigger. The hammer clicked on an empty chamber, dissipating not a burst of hot gas to propel a bullet but more mocking laughter from him.

He dropped the pistol near my hand—

Glass shattered, followed by a *thunk* and a groan. I heard Amador speak in disbelief.

"This?"

He fell to his knees, and I saw the knife handle in the center of his chest.

In the dimming fog, I saw Saffire's face first. Then the face of the Spaniard with the thin mustache who had followed me from my first days in Panama.

The knife man.

As I closed my eyes and gave in to the fog, I heard Saffire begin to weep as she called out to Ezequiel.

"Tito!"

Thirty-Five

I woke to a face that was far from beautiful.

"Muskie." I groaned. "Go away."

He stopped slapping my cheek, and I closed my eyes and tried to sink into oblivion again. Memories returned, however, so I tried to sit.

The effort hurt and I fell back. I could see that I was in a hotel suite. In a bed. Not in a room with a murdered man.

"Water," I croaked.

"I am not your maid."

I allowed my eyes to roll back in my head and made gagging sounds as my arms and legs went rigid and my back arched, throwing my chest off the bed.

"Oh mercy!" Miskimon rushed away from the bed.

I stopped shuddering. When Miskimon returned with a glass of water, I grinned as I sat up on the bed.

"Thanks, Muskie." I sipped on the water. "Any chance you can fluff my pillows for me?"

"Your antics well prove that you have suffered no harm," Miskimon said. He half turned.

"As I assured you, young woman, all it would take was a little time."

That's when I realized Saffire was in the room with us.

Miskimon leaned in and whispered to me, "And the amount of time you took was inconsiderate, I'll add. Poor girl was frightened."

Saffire sat on a chair at the foot of the bed. Her eyes were swollen from crying. I had questions, but her tito was dead. This was not the time. I put out a hand and she took it and squeezed. I could not think of any words of comfort that might help her. I met her eyes. "I'm so sorry for you."

"Everything is my fault." The words escaped on a sob.

"Miss Saffire," Muskie said. "If you hadn't been there, things would have been far worse. It was your bodyguard who saved Mr. Holt's life. And Raquel's life as well."

Bodyguard? I would try to make sense of that later.

"Raquel—" Words stuck in my raspy throat, so I tried again. "She . . . ?"

"Is recovering in another room. With Odelia. We decided it would be better for her to wake in the hotel."

Saffire's gaze had shifted to the far wall. Tears still rolled down her face.

"Saffire." I softened my tone. "You can't be responsible for the bad things that other people choose to do. If you don't agree with me on that, I'm going to get grumpy. You've never seen me grumpy. You don't want to see it."

She sniffed and gave me a half smile that lasted so briefly it might have been my imagination, because her face immediately contorted in renewed grief.

"Mr. Holt does talk sense," Miskimon told her.

Her shoulders shook with silent sobs, and I felt shame that it had taken me this long to understand how unthinking it was for Miskimon and me to offer her sense. That was not what she needed.

I rolled out of bed, ignoring the cannons of pain that detonated in my head. I moved to her chair and knelt in front of her. I held out my arms and after only a moment of hesitation, she threw herself against my chest and clung to my neck and wept with abandon.

Over her shoulders, I could see Miskimon's face. He gave me a smile that was beautiful in its gentleness, and then I closed my eyes and tried to absorb her grief.

It's what a father would do.

January 14, 1909

Col. Geo. W Goethals,

Chairman, I.C.C.

Culebra, Canal Zone

Sir:

I have the honor to report back to you concerning the identity of an American who died yesterday afternoon in the bullring in Panama City.

Last evening, during an unrelated visit to Panama City, I was met by representatives of the National Police who insisted that I immediately accompany them to their headquarters. Because I have no jurisdiction within the republic, I had no choice but to accept this request.

At the police station, I was given a brief report, which I have attached with this letter. My early speculation that the man who stepped into the bullring was drunk was proven incorrect, as a brief exam of the body had not given any indication of the smell of alcohol.

While a search for witnesses to how the man entered the bullring has proven fruitless, I was told that it was more than likely that the man had ingested a powder that is known locally as "The Devil's Breath". It is derived from the Borrachero, a common tree native to Colombia. The pollen alone from this tree is said to conjure up strange dreams and native children are warned not to play beneath the branches when it blossoms. In greater portions, it renders those who intake it to a large degree of docility and memory loss.

Indeed, the Spanish word Borrachero is roughly translated in English to "get-you-drunk".

I suggest that we send out bulletins to each Zone station and alert our own police to the dangers of this powder and warn workers to beware when entering the rougher districts of Colon or Panama City.

It is also my duty to pass along information in regards to the identity papers belonging to the dead man, which were found only after a thorough search of his hotel suite. While he had been posing as a German tourist named Robert Waldschmidt, his real identity was Neale Braden, with an address listed in central New York. As near as I can ascertain via a series of telegrams to the N.Y.P.D., until the last few months, he was an unemployed actor, forced to vacate his apartment and depart New York because of unpaid rent.

If requested, I will look further into the circumstances of his situation in Panama City, as to all appearances, under the name of Robert Waldschmidt, he lived an indulgent lifestyle far beyond his means.

Also, in regards to Zone Policeman Badge No. 28, the man has resigned from his position, and accordingly, I escorted him to Colon for the noon sailing of a steamer bound for New York, and confirmed that he has indeed departed from Panama.

Respectfully,
Inspector Miskimon

Epilogue

I am going to speak frankly, Jim." Theodore Roosevelt didn't bother to get up from behind a massive desk. He was the only person who ever called me Jim. I did not, however, call him Teddy.

Although I'd seen him up close many times, his physical appearance still had a mesmerizing affect. His head seemed huge, made larger in appearance by small ears and eyes set wide apart. His teeth were perfect for political cartoonists—the less kind called them hang-and-rattle teeth—and all it took on paper to suggest his face were bold pencil strokes for a set of spectacles and those white, white teeth. These were the teeth of a man who never let go once he bitten down for a good grip on whatever task he pursued.

He and I were alone in his office. Somehow, I'd expected more of the office and of the White House. Aside from the flag and an array of photos, not much suggested the pomp of the office. Stacks of files were in disarray on the floor, along with the stuffed heads of a lion, a gazelle, and a bear.

Roosevelt continued, "I resent the manner in which you forced me to set aside time for you. Today of all days."

Except for a file and the handwritten note I'd given to the Secret Service men in the foyer of the White House, the desk was clear. It hadn't been easy, convincing one of the Secret Service to bring my note up here to the Oval Office. But a photo of me, my father, and Theodore Roosevelt standing at ease at a camp during the Spanish-American War had turned out to add enough credibility for me. That, and the phrase "national security."

"It was a long wait to hear back from you," I said. "Then I decided maybe you hadn't seen the letters I sent, so I went ahead and just showed up. Would have been here a day or two earlier, but it was a long way to travel, and you know how weather can get in the way of horses and trains. As it turns out, I did cut it close."

Tomorrow, he would no longer be president. Or have the power to do what I needed him to do.

"Have you any idea of the chaos I'm facing today?" Roosevelt leaned against his massive desk, softening his earlier reprimand by appealing for me to share his exasperation. "Same kind of mess that ends up keeping me from getting all my letters, I suppose."

The mention of unanswered letters had probably embarrassed him, as I had intended it to. He knew well the code of ethics that he had proudly chosen to wear during his time in Medora, before any hints he'd become president. I was reminding him that he'd at one time—when he lived at the confluence of Beaver Creek and the Little Missouri—that he wanted to be one of us, and that held certain obligations.

"Bad day for snow," I said. "Back home, cattle would be looking for the low spots."

It was not a subtle reminder at all of our days together. If I had to, I'd remind him of how I was at his side as we chased down horse thieves, him a lot more scared than I was as a teenager.

"Much more snow falls, and we'll have to move the inauguration ceremony into the Senate Chamber." Roosevelt settled into the role of a man sitting on the front porch with a friend, staring at the Little Missouri, having a casual conversation. "Everyone is screaming at me to cancel the parade."

A glance out the window showed the reason for his concern. A springtime blizzard had Washington in its jaws.

"You're building a canal by hauling away millions of tons of dirt every month," I said. "Imagine how much fun reporters would have if you didn't find a way to round up workers and wagons and keep the roads clear."

Roosevelt stood abruptly. He walked past where I was sitting in a cane-backed chair and opened the door to a smaller office outside, where I'd had to wait for half an hour.

"Send a message down the chain," he barked to the male secretary who had studiously ignored me during my entire wait. Maybe it was the cowboy hat and boots. "I don't care how many workers and how many shovels and how many wagons we need. Get them started on the parade route to haul away snow and keep those roads clear."

Roosevelt marched past me again and took his position behind the desk.

"Big Lub's okay," Roosevelt said. "But Helen is enough to send me into the jungles of the Amazon for a month. First time in inauguration history a president's wife has insisted on leading the parade with her husband. And she's turning this place into a shambles. Ordered new sets of everything. Dishes, furniture, bedding, stationery. Made it clear that no dead animals were allowed to hang on the wall. No sense of propriety. None at all."

Given that I knew the new First Lady's name was Helen, I guessed "Big Lub" meant William Howard Taft. All three hundred pounds of the man, along with a pound or two of waxed and upturned mustache.

I didn't have a response for the president. Silence was never a bad thing, so I didn't fill it, aware that it would send him a message.

"I was sorry to hear about your wife," he said. "Takes awhile to get past, doesn't it?"

I nodded. He was referring to the circumstances of his first wife's death, and that he'd lost his mother on the same day. I'd watched my wife choose her own death so that her baby could live.

I let the silence build. Soon enough, he'd get to the note I'd sent ahead. Aside from my name and signature and the date—Wednesday, March 3, 1909—it had only three words: *William Nelson Cromwell.*

"We've got ten minutes." He tapped the file on the desk. "I've read the colonel's report about your time in Panama. I'm not sure there is much to discuss."

"I'm wondering if a girl's name showed up on that report. First name is Safrana. No last name."

He had the decency to open the file and scan through it. "No, it's not here."

"She saved my life. Safrana is her Christian name. Prefers to be called Saffire."

After insisting I stay away from her, Saffire ordered her bodyguard—the one who'd been watching her in the administration building on my first day in Panama—to protect me as he followed me around the isthmus. He'd been the drunk in the doorway. He'd been the one with the shovel to knock out Amador, and he'd been the one, with Saffire along, to follow me to the villa.

I found out later, after I was conscious and coherent, that he and Saffire had been standing outside the window at the villa, watching what was unfolding.

Had the man been armed with a pistol, he would have shot Amador through the glass, but he was a knife man, afraid to make a move against a pistol that could shoot me or Raquel. The moment Amador showed that the pistol was empty, Knife Man had used the butt of his knife to break out the window, and he'd charged into the room, making quick work of Amador.

"This Saffire sounds like a remarkable girl," Teddy said.

"She is."

He made a point of pulling out his pocket watch.

"Don't," I said.

"Don't?"

"We'll take as much time as needed," I said. "I won't be long, but I won't leave until our business is finished."

"One does not speak to the president in that manner."

"I'm not speaking to the president." So I did need the reminder. "I'm speaking to a man who spent two days on horseback with me, each of us wondering if we'd get shot out of our saddles."

"And you're speaking to a man who repaid that by ensuring you can keep your ranch." His voice rumbled with power. "Am I clear?"

"As long as I was equally clear in the note I passed along to you this morning. Wasn't it you who said speak softly and carry a big stick?"

If he was going to play this game, I was all in. But I already knew that those three words—William Nelson Cromwell—were a big enough stick. Otherwise he wouldn't have sent for me during the chaos of his final day in office.

"What do you want?" Roosevelt grinned at me with those brilliantly white hang-and-rattles. A difficult man to dislike.

"The girl's mother was a Jamaican servant."

What I didn't say was that the girl's father was Ezequiel Sandoval. Saffire and I were probably the only two people in Panama who hadn't been able to figure it out. No wonder he doted on her.

"The girl's mother was murdered," I continued. "If you go through that file, you'll see the name of the man responsible. Raoul Amador."

Saffire's mother, Jade, had been in the wrong place at the wrong time, caught overhearing the plans of the revolution. Amador, much to Ezequiel's anguish, had taken the woman's body to the swamps, just as he'd intended to do with Raquel.

"Raoul Amador," Roosevelt said. "He's dead. I understand that from the report? Shot a man in your presence and was posthumously found guilty of murder because of gunpowder speckles on his gloves and his fingerprints on a decanter with drugged wine?"

That was, indeed, in the report. What wasn't there was that the evening before the bullfight, an hour before Amador confronted me at my carriage, Raquel broke off their engagement. Or that after the bullfight, Amador forced her into a civil ceremony by promising to have me executed if she did not marry him. Or that she had intended to file for divorce as soon as I was clear of the republic.

I nodded. "Raoul Amador is also the one who tried to organize a revolution to form a government that would sell the rights to the canal to Germany."

"That's in the report too," Roosevelt said. "Messy situation. The kaiser is rattling sabers louder and louder. I've warned Taft that we can expect some kind of confrontation in the next few years. This country is riddled with German spies. Just proves how important it is to have the canal."

"Raoul Amador," I said, "was a man who fully believed that the German navy would back up his revolution. There were coded telegrams from officials in high office in Germany to assure him of this."

Roosevelt gave me the look of a man good enough at poker to hide whether the cards were a disaster or jackpot winners. "Interesting. That wasn't in the report from the colonel. Proving the existence of such telegrams could lead to some interesting world politics."

"Destroyed, I was told."

"Shame," Roosevelt said.

"There's another piece of conjecture that I suspect Goethals avoided. That's why I'm here today. To ask you a question. Did you know?"

"Did I know what?" He almost glanced at his pocket watch, but caught himself and held my gaze.

I said, "In all likelihood, Cromwell had hired an unemployed actor to pretend to be a German spy."

There was not a prominent politician who wasn't also a brilliant actor. Roosevelt was no different. He'd chosen to play the role of a gruff, hardy outdoorsman, a man of the people. There was enough truth in the role that it resonated with the voters. His popularity had spilled over onto his chosen successor, who would be at the head of the parade tomorrow instead of a Democrat.

Roosevelt stilled. "Repeat that."

"I believe Cromwell hired an unemployed actor to pretend to be a German spy."

It appeared as if he were making the calculations himself and coming to a conclusion that Miskimon and I had shared as he had taken me to the ship for my departure from Panama, a conclusion that would not, and could not, appear on any piece of paper.

Cromwell had been in danger of being exposed for all his machinations in the first revolution. All Earl Harding needed as a journalist for the *World* was one or two reliable witnesses among the Panamanian aristocrats involved in the revolution in 1903. To keep those witnesses silent, Cromwell needed leverage. His leverage? A German "spy" to recruit someone like Raoul Amador to engage in acts of sabotage to make the plot believable. After Cromwell's spy found a way to tempt the sons and daughters of the aristocrats into a new revolution, Cromwell was armed with signatures that proved treason. With this as blackmail, he could hold them all hostage and ensure their silence. This was my theory.

"It's just conjecture," I said. "There is no way to prove Cromwell used Amador to stage a fake revolution unless somebody can link a man named Neale Braden to payments from William Nelson Cromwell, which we both know would be impossible if Cromwell wanted to keep it hidden."

"Neale Braden?" he asked.

"Unemployed New York actor, pretending to be the German spy."

Cromwell needed more than Panamanians suckered into committing to a fake revolution, Miskimon and I decided during our conversation on my last day in Panama.

To get his leverage, Cromwell had needed someone to conveniently expose the fake plot—enter a rancher from Medora. I'd never know if Cromwell would have gone as far as ordering his unemployed actor killed, but he probably knew Amador well enough to guess that would be the end result.

"This conjecture," Roosevelt said. "I trust it will never be speculated upon again outside of this office?"

So. Roosevelt had either come to my same conclusions about Cromwell, or he had known it all along.

"I'm not interested in politics," I said. "I only want one thing, and I've already asked for it."

He leaned forward. I was speaking a language he understood—negotiations. I would save my own moral recriminations for later.

"The girl named Safrana," I said, "is an orphan because of the events during my time in Panama. I would like her to be granted American citizenship."

There was no point in mentioning that Raquel had no intention of ever abandoning Saffire, her half sister. Or that Saffire was not an orphan in any dire sense whatsoever. Her tito, in death, as during his life, had taken care of her, and his will ensured she would never be destitute. I'd learned all of this through letters sent to and from Panama—the correspondence that Raquel had requested of me during the bullfight.

Teddy studied me. "That's it? Citizenship granted to a girl?"

On the surface, yes. I'd needed an excuse to confront Roosevelt about Cromwell. The negotiation for Saffire's citizenship had provided me with that opportunity. But more than telling Roosevelt about Cromwell, what I'd needed was to see the president's reaction.

Because that was what would tell me if the information I gave him was something he'd already known. And if he'd possibly even been involved in some way.

The stillness of concentration he'd shown convinced me. Roosevelt was absorbing new information, considering if what I was saying was possible and, if so, how it might serve as political leverage for him.

My gut told me that Roosevelt had not been involved. While he and Cromwell had worked together behind the scenes for the 1903 revolution, sitting across from Teddy now, I believed he had not known of Cromwell's machinations for a pretended second revolution, and like Goethals, had sent me to Panama simply to have someone discretely investigate what seemed like sabotage at the dig.

I was glad for this. I liked the man and wanted to believe that he was honorable. Had I sensed otherwise, I would have paid him in full the amount I'd received to remove the mortgage from my ranch. While I now felt I'd earned the second portion of it by working on Goethals's behalf, my land would not be purchased with blood money.

"Yes, citizenship," I said. "Your last day of office. I was running out of time."

"You'll have it by tonight." He looked as relieved as I felt. "Is there anything else?"

"How about two tickets to the inaugural ball? I brought my daughter, Winona, with me, and she would be thrilled to attend."

"As long as you don't wear a cowboy hat." He offered that wonderful grin of his. "Seems like a long way to bring a child, so I hope it's worth it for her."

"This is just a stop on the way. We're headed to Panama to deliver those citizenship papers in person."

"Someone saves your life," he said. "It feels good to pay them back."

He'd meant something double in that, and I was okay with it. With that bank draft, he'd paid me back in full for backing him in the Dakotas and at San Juan. He didn't know I'd eventually get the first portion of the money back to him as a matter of honor.

But delivering papers to Saffire as gratitude for her protection of me wasn't the only reason Winona and I were bound by steamer for Panama. With modern travel, a rancher from the Dakotas could spend a substantial part of the year in the dry season of the tropics, the same way that a woman from Panama could spend the other part of the year—spring through fall roundup—in the Dakotas.

Because of this, the second and more compelling reason for my return to Panama was nestled in my back pocket.

A one-word telegram answer. From Raquel.

YES.

Author's Note

What *Was* T. B. Miskimon's Full Name?

Barely a hundred years have passed since the Panama Canal opened; time and progress have blurred how much of a wonder it was that Teddy Roosevelt and the brash Americans were able to overcome all the obstacles it took to join the oceans. I hope that *Saffire* re-created some of that wonder for you.

While I did my best to ensure as much of the backdrop of the story is as accurate as possible, I did take liberty with the building of the locks, as concrete did not begin to pour until later in 1909, months after I portrayed it in the novel.

Also, not until February 4, 1917, did the *New York Times* run an article with this headline: German Spies Active Here for Months, with the subhead "Hostile agents reported to number 10,000—Espionage Extended to Panama Canal." Based on this, it is reasonable to speculate, I'd suggest, that in 1909, those living in Panama could legitimately believe German spies to already be at work in Panama.

As for whether Germany would encourage a foreign country to revolt against the United States, there is the matter of the Zimmermann Telegram, where British cryptographers deciphered a January 1917 message from German Foreign Minister Arthur Zimmermann, offering US territory to Mexico in exchange for joining the German cause. (Historians cite this as one reason the United States entered World War I by declaring war on Germany on April 6, 1917.)

The backdrop to *Saffire,* of course, is based on the history of that time and place, including the 1903 Panamanian revolution against Colombia and a subsequent scandal that involved William Nelson Cromwell, and Theodore Roosevelt's libel lawsuit against Randolph Hearst. You can find a fascinating look at this in two books: *How Wall Street Created a Nation: J. P. Morgan, Teddy Roosevelt, and the Panama Canal,* by Ovidio Diaz-Espino, and *The Untold Story of Panama,* by Earl Harding.

The historical figures in the novel include Colonel George Washington Goethals, Randolph Hearst and reporter Earl Harding as noted above, and Buffalo Bill Cody and his Wild West Show.

I hope it surprises you to learn that Harry A. Franck, Zone Policeman 88, and T. B. Miskimon are also historical figures I met during my research.

First, Harry Alverson Franck. He was a travel writer of the first half of the twentieth century. Unlike the overwrought and romantic prose by most travel writers, Franck presented the everyman's view with a delightful sense of sarcasm. For the material he gave us in his book *Zone Policeman 88,* Franck worked as an enumerator in the Zone. Because his book is in public domain, it was a lot of fun to use some of his own descriptions in the conversations he shares with Holt, as well as the story about the men mysteriously knocked out along the train tracks. At my website, I give a complete listing of the material used from Harry's book. Many thanks to Brenda Huettner at www.harryafranck.com for help with this.

T. B. Miskimon?

He was indeed an inspector for Colonel Goethals, and indeed Goethals held a King Solomon–type court every Sunday morning, open to any and all, where rank did not matter. That Goethals listened to complaints each Sunday is not entirely new to anyone who has learned about the building of the canal. However, after checking dozens of sources, it wasn't until I read Julie Greene's book *The Canal Builders: Making America's Empire at the Panama Canal* that I found one of the few references to T. B. Miskimon.

As Julie Greene notes, "Records maintained by T. B. Miskimon, Goethals's inspector, provide a world of insight into the Zone's daily affairs. ICC employees and their wives complained about everything from drunken or adulterous neighbors to fraudulent commissary managers, insulting foremen, cruel policemen, blackmailing supervisors, women of ill repute, gamblers, abusive spouses, salesmen bearing indecent photographs, and a judge who engaged in sexual harassment. Miskimon dutifully investigated each case and recommended a solution to his boss. In one case where Miskimon found fraud involving commissary books, Goethals suspended the men responsible without pay for fifteen days. When a yardmaster of the Panama Railroad was accused by a colleague of working while intoxicated, Miskimon's detailed investigation resulted in a six-page report for Goethals, in which the inspector concluded that while the yardmaster certainly imbibed, the charge of intoxication on the job may well have been the creation of his jealous and hostile colleague."

I learned this before I'd begun to write *Saffire,* and I was immediately intrigued at the story of a right-hand man sent out by the colonel to investigate complaints. I discovered that one of the only ways to learn more about T. B. Miskimon was through the reports he typed up for Goethals, available for viewing at Wichita State University.

As a result, I spent hours there, in a quiet room, lost in those letters, letting my mind rove through another time when it did matter if men in uniform smoked on duty, and when a woman's complaint about holes in window screens was a complaint worthy of investigation.

A follow-up trip to another collection of T. B. Miskimon letters at Georgetown University gave me more of a look into life in the Zone, as well as a sense of T. B. Miskimon as a person.

With gratitude for help from Dr. Lorraine Madway, the content of the first four of T. B. Miskimon's letters in the novel is directly from the Special Collections and University Archives at Wichita State University, with the dates changed to reflect the novel's timeline. As you might guess, the fifth letter, which refers to Holt, is entirely fictitious.

Nothing in those letters, however, helped me learn Miskimon's first or middle name on Holt's behalf. That involved more research, and I'm happy to share the answer—as well as a complete listing of research sources and a timeline—at www.sigmundbrouwer.com/saffire.

An excerpt from Sigmund Brouwer's

THIEF OF GLORY

Christy Award for Book of the Year
Alberta Readers' Choice Award
Lime Award for Historical Fiction
www.thiefofglory.com

ONE

Journal 1—Dutch East Indies

A banyan tree begins when its seeds germinate in the crevices of a host tree. It sends to the ground tendrils that become prop roots with enough room for children to crawl beneath, prop roots that grow into thick, woody trunks and make it look like the tree is standing above the ground. The roots, given time, look no different than the tree it has begun to strangle. Eventually, when the original support tree dies and rots, the banyan develops a hollow central core.

In a kampong—village—on the island of Java, in the then-called Dutch East Indies, stood such a banyan tree almost two hundred years old. On foggy evenings, even adults avoided passing by its ghostly silhouette, but on the morning of my tenth birthday, sunlight filtered through a sticky haze after a monsoon, giving everything a glow of tranquil beauty. There, a marble game beneath the branches was an event as seemingly inconsequential as a banyan seed taking root in the bark of an unsuspecting tree, but the tendrils of the consequences became a journey that has taken me some three score and ten years to complete.

It was market day, and as a special privilege to me, Mother had left my younger brother and twin sisters in the care of our servants. In the early morning, before the tropical heat could slow our progress, she and I journeyed on back of the white horse she was so proud of, past the manicured grounds of our handsome home and along the tributary where my siblings and I often played. Farther down, the small river emptied into the busy port of Semarang. While it was not a school day, my father—the headmaster—and my older half brothers were supervising the maintenance of the building where all the blond-haired children experienced the exclusive Dutch education system.

As we passed, Indonesian peasants bowed and smiled at us. Ahead, shimmers of heat rose from the uneven cobblestones that formed the village square. Vibrant hues of Javanese batik fabrics, with their localized patterns of flowers and animals and folklore as familiar to me as my marbles, peeked from market stalls. I breathed in the smell of cinnamon and cardamom and curry powders mixed with the scents of fried foods and ripe mangoes and lychees.

I was a tiny king that morning, continuously shaking off my mother's attempts to grasp my hand. She had already purchased spices from the old man at one of the Chinese stalls. He had risen beyond his status as a *singkeh,* an impoverished immigrant laborer from the southern provinces of China, this elevation signaled by his right thumbnail, which was at least two inches long and fit in a curving, encasing sheath with elaborate painted decorations. He kept it prominently displayed with his hands resting in his lap, a clear message that he held a privileged position and did not need to work with his hands. I'd long stopped being fascinated by this and was impatient to be moving, just as I'd long stopped being fascinated by his plump wife in a colorful long dress as she flicked the beads on her abacus to calculate prices with infallible accuracy.

I pulled away to help an older Dutch woman who was bartering with an Indonesian baker. She had not noticed that bank notes had fallen from her purse. I retrieved them for her but was in no mood for effusive thanks, partly because I thought it ridiculous to thank me for not stealing, but mainly because I knew what the other boys my age were doing at that moment. I needed to be on my way. With a quick *"Dag, mevrouw"*— Good day, madam — I bolted toward the banyan, giving no heed to my mother's command to return.

For there, with potential loot placed in a wide chalked circle, were fresh victims. I might not have been allowed to keep the marbles I won from my younger siblings, but these Dutch boys were fair game. I slowed to an amble of pretended casualness as I neared, whistling and looking properly sharp in white shorts and a white linen shirt that had been hand pressed by Indonesian servants. I put on a show of indifference that I'd perfected and that served me well my whole life. Then I stopped when I saw her, all my apparent apathy instantly vanquished.

Laura.

As an old man, I can attest to the power of love at first sight. I can attest that the memory of a moment can endure — and haunt — for a lifetime. There are so many other moments slipping away from me, but this one remains.

Laura.

What is rarely, if ever, mentioned by poets is that hatred can have the same power, for that was the same moment that I first saw him. The impact of that memory has never waned either. This, too, remains as layers of my life slip away like peeling skin.

Georgie.

I had no foreshadowing, of course, that the last few steps toward the shade beneath those glossy leaves would eventually send me into the holding cell of a Washington, DC police station where, at age eighty-one, I faced the lawyer—also my daughter and only child—who refused to secure my release until I promised to tell her the events of my journey there.

All these years later, across from her in that holding cell, I knew my daughter demanded this because she craved to make sense of a lifetime in the cold shade of my hollowness, for the span of decades since that marble game had withered me, the tendrils of my vanities and deceptions and self-deceptions long grown into strangling prop roots. Even so, as I agreed to my daughter's terms, I maintained my emotional distance and made no mention that I intended to have this story delivered to her after my death.

Such, too, is the power of shame.

Two

Laura.

Beneath the banyan, a heart-stopping longing overwhelmed me at the glimpse of her face and shy smile. It was romantic love in the purest sense, uncluttered by any notion of physical desire, for I was ten, much too young to know how lust complicates the matters of the human race.

The sensation was utterly new to me. But it was not without context. At night, by oil lamps screened to keep moths from the flame, I had three times read *Ivanhoe* by Sir Walter Scott, the Dutch translation by Gerard Keller. As soon as the last page was finished, I would turn to page one of chapter one. I had just started it for the fourth time. Thus I'd been immersed in chivalry at its finest, and here, finally, was proof that the love I'd read about in the story also existed in real life.

I was lost, first, in her eyes—unlike many of the Dutch, a hazel brown—which regarded me with a calmness that pulled stronger than gravity. She looked away, then back again. I felt like I could only breathe from the top of my lungs in shallow gasps. Her hair, thick and blond and curled, rested upon her shoulders. She wore a light-blue dress, tied at the waist with a wide bow, with a yellow butterfly brooch on her right shoulder. She stole away from me any sense of sound except for a universal harmony that I hadn't known existed. So as the nine-year-old Laura Jansen bequeathed upon me a radiant gaze, I became Ivanhoe, and she the beautiful Lady Rowena. Standing at the edge of the chalked circle, I was instantly and irrevocably determined that nothing would stop me from becoming champion of the day, earning the right to bestow upon her the honor of Queen of the Tournament.

As I was to discover, it was Laura's third day in-country and her first visit to the village. This meant I was as much a stranger to her as any boy could be, but the emotions that overwhelmed her, which she recounted to me years later, were as much a mystery to her young soul as my emotions were to mine.

I would shortly discover that Laura had accompanied her *oma*—grandmother—on the voyage from the Netherlands. Her *oom* Gert—uncle Gert—worked for the Dutch Shell Oil Company as a refinery engineer, and his wife had recently died from pneumonia. Laura and her oma had come to help Gert and his large family through the difficult situation.

That morning I surveyed my opponents gathered around her, a motley bunch of boys I'd vanquished one way or another at events where Dutch families gathered to celebrate a holiday or other special occasion. From marble games to subsequent fistfights that resulted from marble games, the fathers monitored our battles but wisely kept them as hidden from the matriarchs as we did. I knew all of these boys. Except one.

As the other boys took involuntary steps backward in deference to my established reign, I felt goose bumps run up my spine. The parting of this group had revealed a boy at the center whom I'd never seen before. He was kneeling, with a marble held in shooting position on top of the thumbnail of his left hand, edge of the thumb curled beneath index finger, ready to flick. Left hand.

The marble I noticed too. For good reason. It was an onionskin, purple and white, with a transparent core. The swirls were twisted counterclockwise and that made it even more of a rarity. Inside the chalked circle was an *X* formed by two lines of twelve marbles. At a glance I could tell none were worth the risk of losing the onionskin. Without doubt, stupidity was not part of this boy's nature, so either he was very good or he came from wealth that allowed him to not care about the worth of the onionskin.

When he stood, it was obvious that he had two inches on me, and a lot of extra bulk. His arched eyebrow matched my own. Dark hair to my blond. Khaki pants and tousled shirt to my pressed-linen shorts and shirt. Wealth, most likely, against the limited salary of my father's headmaster position.

I would learn his name was Georgie Smith. He was the son of the American sent to oversee the refinery where Laura's uncle worked as an engineer. He'd arrived by the same ship that had carried Laura and her oma.

I doubt Georgie's conscious brain registered the deferential movements of the other boys, but his animal instinct would not have failed to miss it. Or the reasons for it. Like an electrical current generated by rising tension, hatred crackled between us. I believe that had we each been armed with clubs, we would have charged forward without hesitation at the slightest of provocations.

This unspoken hatred was established in the time it took to lock eyes. With effort, I pretended not to see him as I moved to the edge of the chalked circle and squatted. I could feel the burn of his gaze on my right shoulder, as I imagined the caressing smile of Laura warming my left shoulder. It was no accident I had chosen a position that placed me between them.

"Who is next?" I asked, keeping my eyes on the marbles.

"We've been saving a place for you," Timothy said. He was eight years old, and a snot-nosed, obsequious toad, but his answer established that I was leader.

Still watching and waiting for the onionskin to enter the circle, I fumbled with my belt. I always carried two small pouches of marbles tied to my belt and tucked inside my shorts.

"He's not playing," Georgie said.

This earned a respectful gasp from the other boys.

I turned my head to give him a direct stare.

"He wasn't here when the game started so he can't be part of it," Georgie continued, speaking of me in the third person as if I were not there in front of him. "He should run back to his mother and she can inspect his pretty clothes so she can make sure he hasn't smudged himself or wet his pants."

He smirked and waited for my response.